The Powder, Their Paper and Pools of Blood

The Powder, Their Paper and Pools of Blood

Mark Hunter

Writer's Showcase
San Jose New York Lincoln Shanghai

The Powder, Their Paper and Pools of Blood

All Rights Reserved © 2001 by Mark Hunter

Writer's Showcase
an imprint of iUniverse.com, Inc.

For information address:
iUniverse.com, Inc.
5220 S 16th, Ste. 200
Lincoln, NE 68512
www.iuniverse.com

Readers seeking to identify a familiar person should reconsider this as fictional literature.

ISBN: 0-595-17134-6

Printed in the United States of America

Almost for me.

"The extraordinary thing about personal integrity is that it can never be stolen, subdued or revoked. The only way to lose it is to give it away."

DEA Academy Instructor
Quantico Marine Corps Base

I

I remember the first time I stole money.

Our enforcement group had been on the Far North Side of Chicago conducting a relatively simple two kilo deal, an exchange of money for cocaine which we commonly referred to as a "buy-bust." The phrase was misleading in that we intended to bust someone but certainly retained no interest in providing cash for anything. Desmond Brokenborough was the primary undercover agent, a role he was accustomed to playing. Brokenborough was an intelligent and street-smart DEA Agent who was also tall, handsome and black, persuasive features which added to his credibility as a street dealer. He was one of two black agents in our enforcement group and as such he was often requested to perform in an undercover capacity. Brokenborough enjoyed the responsibility and even though he balked at times, he preferred the peremptory significance of the undercover role to the secondary tasks of the mundane surveillance agent.

We had arrested two suspects who had attempted to trade their dope for our cash. Narcotics deals were usually simple affairs and on this occasion, the two kilo buy-bust had proved to be again. The accomplice was like the main suspect, a native of Mexico. One man sat patiently waiting in the passenger's seat of a 1982 maroon Oldsmobile Cutlass while the driver, a pock-marked and disheveled middle-aged Mexican approached Desmond's car and conducted the negotiations. Desmond Brokenborough had been directed to let the driver see the money, in this case $45,000 in U.S. Government furnished funds, only one time. Brokenborough had accomplished the dangerous undertaking when he escorted the driver, later identified as Roberto Orestes-Sanchez, to the rear of his undercover vehicle, a shiny black BMW325I with cream colored leather seats and a polished set of post-factory installed street rims. Brokenborough had flashed the money when he had lifted the trunk. There, Orestes-Sanchez was permitted to examine and finger the cash which had been strategically tossed into a tan, plastic grocery bag in a seemingly haphazard and indifferent manner. The arrangement of the money was done to impress upon the suspect the large amount of money was virtually insignificant and its delivery should be considered routine. $45,000 to kilogram dealers is not considered an abundant sum of money and is often carried around in the same regard a mother might transport a worn pair of galoshes. An inexperienced drug dealer is often induced by an individual who nonchalantly handles money and the novice Orestes-Sanchez smiled when he saw the manner in which Brokenborough transported his cash. Orestes-Sanchez believed the initial deal was just the beginning of a lucrative and rewarding relationship with his new, moneyed customer. Orestes-Sanchez was satisfied and he walked with an invigorated and confident kick in his step as he proceeded back to the rusted eyesore he had arrived in. It was apparent Orestes-Sanchez was intent on upholding his end of the negotiation, the delivery of the two keys of cocaine.

Admittedly, neither of these two unemployed Mexicans were truly high profile cocaine traffickers. They were middlemen which, in reality, was little more than a kind term for jail fodder. By remitting the dope, they had simply provided a craved service. The driver, Orestes-Sanchez, had negotiated a delivery between consumer and wholesaler, and in doing so, functioned as little more than a salesman linking an interested consumer with an easily obtained product. Unbeknownst to Sanchez, this time he had been negotiating with a federal agent who convincingly posed as an eager cocaine customer with the financial wherewithal to complete a $50,000 deal. Though he was delivering two kilograms of cocaine, Orestes-Sanchez was not truly a kilogram dealer. He had worked out a transaction where he had obtained the coke on consignment. Orestes-Sanchez would receive no more than he could add to the cost of each kilo which his supplier demanded. He probably tacked on a standard $1,000 to the price of each kilo and likely paid his collaborator, the vigilant passenger who was, no doubt, more like a drinking buddy than a narcotics trafficking accomplice, no more than fifty to one hundred dollars to provide his crude form of security. The individual who made the real money during all this was the source and, luckily, on this occasion, we had been able to identify him.

Pre-buy surveillance had been watching Orestes-Sanchez before any undercover calls had been placed to his residence. He lived alone on the first floor of a brick two-flat on Artesian Avenue, an anonymous apartment in a "lunch-pail" community of second generation Chicagoans who were mostly Mexican and Puerto Rican immigrants seeking the opportunity for a better life. Three cars had been dispatched to his apartment where they waited for two and a half hours. Each was occupied by a DEA Agent and I had been one of them. Brokenborough, via our car-to-car radios, had notified us he had placed a second undercover call to Sanchez and Sanchez had agreed to consummate the deal in the parking lot of a large grocery store later that afternoon. Shortly after Desmond notified us of the information, we watched Sanchez shuffle out of his modest home. He had been noticed by an alert agent and surveillance followed Sanchez as he drove calmly through his neighborhood. There were no evasive driving tactics like those frequently demonstrated on television programs about wily crooks and their keen abilities to avoid police surveillance. No, in this instance, Sanchez drove routinely to a neighborhood pharmacy where he only stayed long enough to purchase a pack of cigarettes. Sanchez unwrapped the package and indulged himself in a few puffs before driving to a crowded street off of Chicago's culturally diverse Milwaukee Avenue. He could not find a place to park his laboring Cutlass, so he impatiently drove around the block, finally electing to leave the car in front of a fire hydrant. There was a spot open with a regulated meter but he passed it by electing to risk the attention of the parking authority rather than deposit a dime and pay to park his vehicle. I suppose he surmised he would be more likely to get a ticket at an expired meter rather than in front of a hydrant. Satisfied, Sanchez exited his car and meandered into a northwest side bar called Los Darios.

Sanchez remained in the bar for about an hour. Only four customers had entered the tavern during the period Sanchez was inside and we noted none of them or anyone else had exited. The patrons we watched enter looked similar to Sanchez in ethnicity and demeanor with the exception of one, a curly, dark-haired male. Apparently he was also of Mexican descent but was slightly better dressed than the other customers. A thin gold chain and a modestly expensive wristwatch drew experienced attention to him. No one on surveillance had noticed where he came from before he approached the paint-chipped entrance of Los Darios. However, we quickly speculated the gentleman was not coming to Los Darios to solely enjoy a beer. Our presumptions were well founded since only a few moments elapsed before the unnamed individual popped out with Sanchez in tow. The two engaged in conversation while walking straight up the street towards me.

I had been parked in front of a burrito place monitoring Los Darios from a ½ block's distance. It had required great constitutional fortitude not to indulge in one of the restaurant's products. I was hungry and had not eaten since the evening before but, I knew, every time I ordered food on surveillance, I would return to my car, open the gastronomic delight and the person we were assigned to watch, the "Bad Guy" would move. Bad Guy was the slang term we used to identify the suspect. If there was more than one, we used Bad Guy

Number One, Bad Guy Number Two and so on. I suppose we were the "good guys" though I rarely heard any agents refer to themselves as such. Nevertheless, every time I ordered and set out to eat any food, the Bad Guy, seemingly on cue, would decide to move and consequently, most of the sandwich and it's condiments would end up spattered on my shirt and lap. Of course, I would rant and curse, to no avail, and eat what I could leaving the remainder precariously lying on the passenger seat, a situation which inevitably led it to be thrown to the floor at my first sudden stop. In the rare instances when I was able to eat my food, the pace at which I had to consume it usually left me suffering an uncomfortable case of indigestion which was often more irritating than a growling, empty belly.

I was happy I had not succumbed to the inviting enticement of the flashing neon burrito. I was eager to see what Sanchez and his confederate, referred to as Bad Guy #2, were going to do. Together, they walked past my car without so much as a glance in my direction. They continued until they arrived at a dark colored Thunderbird parked just three automobiles behind mine. Both stood in the street at the passenger's side of the vehicle occasionally leaning in to avoid passing traffic. They talked for several minutes. I kept surveillance apprised since I maintained the best view even though it was through my rear and side view mirrors. Each of them entered the T-bird, with Number Two walking around the rear and entering from the driver's side. The car pulled out and we followed suit, cautiously. The dark T-bird, which a license check revealed was registered to a Francisco Calderon of Chicago, drove past the bar with Brenda Xavier, one of our veteran agents, following loosely behind. The car drove two blocks down, one block west, three blocks north, one block east and back down the street from which it came until it arrived back on the same street as Los Darios. The route took no more than three minutes to navigate. This time, I returned to my original spot on surveillance but, was not in position to see Sanchez leave the vehicle. However, Xavier, who some fellow agents complained often followed suspects to closely, was in good position to monitor the activity. She watched the T-bird depart with the unknown driver as Sanchez walked, empty-handed towards the Cutlass. She reported Sanchez went to the trunk of his automobile, opened it a quarter of the way then quickly closed it, having placed nothing inside. I informed her I could clearly see Orestes-Sanchez and I observed him walk to his right, open the passenger door and simultaneously place his hand inside his light fall jacket. He removed a wrinkled, beige paper bag which he struggled to get out of his waistband. He gently placed the bag in the rear seat and I immediately suspected the package was the cocaine. It was apparent Number One had the coke and Number Two, a man who actually turned out to be Francisco Calderon, was the source. Xavier attempted to follow Calderon while myself and my partner, Chad Jennings, remained with Orestes-Sanchez, following him in separate cars. He traveled directly to the grocery store after briefly returning to Los Darios to recruit the volunteer to accompany him to the deal site.

Our assumptions about the dope deal proved to be correct. These buy-busts were not complicated and most experienced agents could complete them without much consternation. Though the transactions were dangerous, the essence of the deal was still an exchange of one bag for another. At the store's parking lot we watched as Desmond Brokenborough followed Sanchez to his Cutlass. Desmond walked around the car to the passenger side. He leaned in and confidently examined the product which he negotiated to purchase. Desmond stayed briefly then walked back toward the BMW, presumably to retrieve the money. As the undercover agent did so, he ran his hand across the crown of his head, the pre-arranged arrest signal indicating he had seen the cocaine. We converged on the suspects to make the arrests. Somebody slammed their brakes and skidded sideways into a shopping cart. The metal cage spun and flipped onto its side causing one of its black rubber wheels to break off and bounce across several aisles until it smacked against an abandoned kiosk. Otherwise, the arrest went smoothly. There was barely any time for a crowd to gather before we left with Sanchez and his unlucky passenger, both of whom forfeited the next several years of their lives to the federal prison system for their participation in the delivery. Possession or delivery of just 500 grams, a half kilo of cocaine and just a fraction more than a pound, is punishable by a mandatory minimum five years in prison and no federal judge in the judicial system of the United States Federal Court, regardless of tenure, experience or enlightened wisdom, is entrusted with the authority to modify the sentence. Two kilos would put Orestes-Sanchez and his friend away for at least a half decade and, depending on the length of their criminal record, perhaps considerably longer. Five years or more traded for a little more than what amounted to four pounds of powdered leaves.

Having safely arrested the two, our focus changed. It was time to find Calderon.

We returned to Los Darios. Our boss had assigned three agents to transport the hapless defendants to our downtown Chicago office for fingerprints and photographs. I had managed to avoid that duty and was placed on the team to identify and apprehend Calderon. Unfortunately but, understandably, Brenda Xavier, who had been attempting a difficult solitary surveillance while we arrested his two flunkies, had lost Calderon.

We assembled outside Los Darios, the most likely place we might find Mr. Calderon, waiting to collect his money. There were five other agents and me and we could hear the reverberations of a juke box cranking out music from native contemporary Mexican pop stars like Lucia Mendez and Juan Gabriel. We entered hoping to find an unexpectant Calderon enjoying a cold beer. The place was remarkably dark, with only a few dim lights. There was a dated, stained-glass chandelier flickering over a red, cigarette-singed billiards table occupied by two young Spanish men. The musky, faint bar looked to be half-filled with Hispanic males with the exception of one middle-aged Latino woman. She stood unimpressed and unfazed behind the bar. No one seemed disturbed by our entrance though none of the patrons made any favorable overtures to make us feel welcome. I was expected to identify Calderon since I had obtained the best look at him. I looked for the curly black hair and thin gold chain but did not see him. He wasn't inside. Though a reason for our intrusion was not requested, we played our entrance into the bar off by requesting identification from the patrons, a typical ploy to conceal the real reason we were inside the place. It was routine for Immigration and Naturalization Service Agents to enter bars in this section of Chicago looking for illegal aliens and our solicitation for identification, though irritating, was not considered entirely unreasonable. The inquiry produced an assorted degree of identifying information including two green cards, two driver's licenses and several easily-obtained state-issued ID's. Some of the fifteen customers had no identification at all and pretended they didn't understand what was happening. Those that did acted as if they didn't care. We were in the bar under pretentious circumstances so we ignored the contempt. We had introduced ourselves through the bar as police though none of us wore clothing that identified us as DEA agents. No badges were shown. No guns drawn. It was orderly. We had done this before and these customers had been subject to this routine on prior occasions in this tavern if not some other one. We called it "tossing the bar." It was calm and towards its conclusion, even friendly. Especially when each customer realized we were not there for him. We customarily checked as many patrons as we could for wants or warrants. One middle-aged flannel clad gentleman, who adopted the name of Pedro or Tino or something, had an outstanding traffic warrant out of Will County, Illinois. We deliberately overlooked it. Someone, I think Phil Vreeswyck, chastised the tipsy individual and warned him to report for his next court date. The man raised his beer bottle in a sign of concurrence though his carefree demeanor indicated it would have been no difference to him to go to jail or continue getting drunk.

I had checked four ID's myself. I had gathered up three wallets and a small pile of cards and papers casually wrapped with a rubber band. The pile I had inspected included a small black telephone book, assorted pieces of paper and some multi-colored business cards, most of which bore addresses to check-cashing agencies and automotive repair garages. The items had been placed onto the bar with other ID's and wallets. I waited as Vreeswyck verified the names of the patrons with our base operator to establish their status as either upstanding citizens or wanted fugitives. When Vreeswyck was finished I handed the ID's back to him. While I had been waiting I deposited the accumulated ID's and wallets into my coat pocket so my hands were free. Bored, I had thumbed through one of the wallets looking for anything interesting, like a nude, seductive photo of one of their girlfriends or something else reasonably entertaining. Two customers had returned to their game of pool and paid no attention to us while most of the others resumed their drinking. The cooperative woman behind the bar offered us a complimentary round of tequila. We all declined though I might have used one. I looked around the bar, examining its paneled walls and smoke-stained ceiling. There were old and yellowed posters touting beers whose manufacturers had since come and gone. One tattered poster featured the Chicago Bears from their Super Bowl year of 1985. The team's coach, Mike Ditka, looked much younger, I remarked.

Vreeswyck informed me our base had advised none of our other patrons were wanted on outstanding warrants. I walked over to a table and laid the ID's and wallets on the small glazed surface for their retrieval. I announced, "Grab your ID's. I don't know who is who or where they came from but, Uncle Sam says you're all good hombres, at least tonight. President Bush thanks you for your cooperation." Those who understood grunted and snickered. I wiped my hands with a dish towel and left with my co-workers.

*

Three days later, cooler weather had returned to Chicagoland and I was wearing the same coat I had worn the evening of the two kilo buy-bust. While driving to work I reached into my pocket and felt something unfamiliar. I extricated it and found it to be the rubber-banded telephone book I had collected the night we searched for Calderon, who eventually was found and arrested by a persistent Brenda Xavier. She was still needlessly embarrassed she had lost him and spent two days tirelessly patrolling his neighborhood until she developed a lead on his whereabouts. I had evidently forgotten to place the telephone book back on the table at the bar. I held it in my hand until I reached a stoplight where curiosity and the humdrum ride beckoned me to open it instead of throwing it out the window. I pulled the deteriorated brown elastic band off the collection and it seemed to surrender and fall apart as I removed it. There were several phone numbers which I recognized to be pager numbers followed by notes which looked like codes:

LALO 910/0427 #33

Leo's Car Wash 777-2839 Quilvio at 10 a.m.

SANTANA #18 1/8 on Sat. (Still owes)

Mariellena ** 5100424 **

I cynically considered the notes to be most likely the telephone book of a dope dealer consistent with entries containing dollar amounts, fractions and figures I had seen so many times before.

I flipped through some of the business cards stuffed into the back. Another auto detailing shop, a hair salon and a disc jockey advertising himself as "DJ Disc Spinks spins the discs," I chuckled and attempted to repeat the tongue-twisting slogan quickly, three consecutive times. I couldn't. As I thumbed the remaining pages I found a neatly folded and crisp fifty dollar bill resting in the final section marked "XYZ." Its discovery surprised me. I put it all back in my pocket and continued driving to work.

*

I spent the uninteresting parts of the day thinking about the creased fifty which I had let remain unacknowledged in my coat pocket. There was no option to return the money to its rightful owner because I had no clue who the owner was. The telephone book only contained a catalogue of contacts and acquaintances but, did not bear its holder's name. The money belonged to an unknown and anonymous person.

It had been four days since the two kilogram deal and no one had come forward to make mention of the money lost or taken at the bar. We had been out on another arrest since the shakedown at Los Darios and my fellow agents were preoccupied with other interests and activities.

I considered giving the fifty dollar bill to a pitiable man who begged outside the Dirksen Federal Building. His deformities had left him burdened with two grossly undersized arms. On the end of the right appendage was a single thumb-sized digit which he adroitly utilized to grasp a Styrofoam coffee cup. The container was used to collect offerings of passerby. He had no legs and laid facing frontward with his chest pressed against an imitation leather support which leaned forward in a thirty five degree angle from the base of his customized wheelchair. He looked uncomfortable but his eyes always seemed to twinkle and uncannily made contact with mine every time I thought I could peek at his condition and remain unnoticed. He always proffered a genuine "Hello" whether it was a ninety degree day saturated with concentrated humidity or a typical Chicago winter morning featuring blustery and bone-chilling wind. He had a small, fastidiously preserved American flag taped to an extended metal antenna mounted on the left side of his wheelchair. The flag was replaced every time it began to show evidence of wear and its condition was notably more defended than the frayed wheels of the conveyance in which he was anchored.

I had on occasion tossed a few quarters into his cup. The fifty bucks would have been very welcome, I'm sure. So much he would undoubtedly remember me and I convinced myself a gift of that magnitude would draw suspicion by him and by chance any co-workers who had witnessed me giving it to him. I opted not to place the note in his cup.

I took the bill home with me that night, figuring I would hold onto it for a day or two and then decide what to do with it. I discarded the phone book into my kitchen trash bucket and threw the folded fifty on the top of my dresser along with my pager, gun and badge.

*

A week later, I spent it. I just wanted to get rid of the money and the longer it sat on my dresser, the more I realized it was not missed by its rightful owner or anyone else for that matter. In retrospect, I knew it was mine the day I found it in my pocket, so there was nothing left but to spent it. After all, it was only fifty bucks. During the week it sat idle on my dresser, I had worked cases involving two separate cocaine deals. These two cases involved the seizure of six and a half kilos of cocaine which would have been sold for close to $150,000 on the street. Those figures only represented wholesale dollars too. The receipts would be considerably higher as the cocaine was diluted and sold in fractions like ounces, eight balls and grams. In addition to the seizure that week, we paid a cooperating individual, or a CI as known by police terms or a snitch on the street, a sum of $5,000 for the work he had done setting up a delivery which concluded with the seizure of four kilograms of cocaine. It was two and a half days worth of work for the informant, a twice convicted felon, and I was quite certain he had no intention of paying a nickel's worth of taxes on the five grand he received.

In addition, I had spent $245 for a new set of relatively inexpensive tires for my government vehicle or, G-ride, as we called it. Desmond Brokenborough had decided his car needed smoked windows and a new detailing job. The upgrade cost the taxpayers $375 more. Brokenborough believed he was safer sitting in a sanitized and unsoiled automobile behind tinted windows. It was an indulgence he could have lived and worked without. However, Brokenborough benefited from the commodious relationships he established with the Group Supervisor and the Administrative Officer who authorized such expenditures. If the Administrative Officer liked you and you bought him a beer once in a while, you could get authorization for such luxuries.

My wages like all federal agents were based on a Government Schedule. My salary at that time as a GS-11 step one including supplemental income provided by the living cost of the locality of my post, Chicago, was $39,811.00 a year. I was twenty-five years old and clearing $500 per week. This, after depositing 10% of my pay into a government sponsored retirement plan which also included a 5% agency match. I wasn't wealthy but, certainly comfortable and with the expectation of remaining so I would never have risked my secure position with the government to steal fifty bucks. It would have been utterly ridiculous and any agent who did so should first have been kicked very hard in the ass and then fully prosecuted. However, I reasoned, I had not stolen the money. It had simply ended up with me.

The $50 note was eventually tendered to buy junk. I left the office one morning and walked to a Carson Pirie Scott Department store on State Street with the intention of buying myself an item I normally would not purchase. A sort of little present to myself.

I walked in the store and the first section I encountered was perfumes and colognes. Overmade women with bogus, neon tans hawking a variety of fragrances in front of inviting glass counters. The store's associates often made me very uncomfortable with their aggressive sales pitches. I avoided making eye contact with them, just as I did the beggar. I walked past a middle-aged lady who didn't feel the least inhibited wearing sable hip boots and tawdry fishnet nylons. The woman didn't solicit me and I felt somewhat insulted. Why, I wondered? Didn't I look like someone who could afford her product. Worse, did she assess me as someone who did not even buy cologne. My considerations were brief. I was a government agent making $40,000 a year and I could afford their colognes besides, I had $50 worth of someone else's money to blow.

I bought a novel cologne the store advertised as the new wave in men's fragrances. I forget what it was called but, it smelled fashionable. It was expensive and I reasoned it had to be stylish since I could not pronounce its vowel-laden name. It sounded like something that came with its own propeller so I invested in a four ounce bottle for $48. The fifty was accepted and of course, tendered without question. I placed the change back in my pocket and later used it to buy a container of caramel flavored popcorn. I applied the cologne sparingly and after being told by a date it smelled "too fruity" I stopped wearing it altogether. I had three-quarters of a bottle left when I had stolen again.

2

My oldest brother Joe had encouraged me to enroll in a computer engineering program when I applied for college. He was the oldest of three boys with me having been the youngest. He was seven years older than me and had been in the work force for three and a half years when I prepared to enroll at a university. His experiences and difficulty in finding well paid and interesting work with a business management degree motivated him to attempt to persuade me from making the same mistakes he did in college. Specifically, he advised me taking a general course of study, like business management or physical education, combined with a moderately light curriculum of electives, gave him plenty of time to party with friends. It did not however, prepare him for the sophisticated demand of the working world.

"Computer software! People smart enough to get degrees in computer technology are going to be able to set their price."

At nineteen years of age, I was sapped by the drudgery of twelve years of regimented Catholic school. The last thing I wanted to do was surrender four more years of my life to the monotonous realm of zeroes and ones. I was entering college, land of frat parties and sexual adventure and I had my own wild oats to sew. I shunned his advice and sought to select a program which principally fit my social goals as well as appeased my own personal interests.

I had always been fascinated with real crime documentaries about the lives of swindlers, thieves, burglars and murderers. I was particularly interested in stories about psychopathic murderers such as the Son of Sam, Charles Manson, the Hillside Stranglers and John Wayne Gacy. Their depraved annals and the terror they inflicted sickened me but, I could never satisfy my enjoyment reading about the macabre behavior each demonstrated. I was especially intrigued by the manner in which their crimes of unspeakable violence were solved. I was impressed with the dedication, fortitude and the intellect of detectives who unraveled the cases. I aspired to become one of those detectives or ultimately, an Agent of the FBI, working in the Behavioral Science Unit profiling homicidal maniacs and cracking serial murder cases. When I finally confided in my brother I planned to enroll in a Criminal Justice program with that goal in mind, he derogatorily warned:

"With a CJ degree you won't be doing much other than relieving all the football players as a second-shift security guard at K-Mart."

I ignored his disparaging remarks and pursued my goals. Admittedly, the courses were not difficult for me but, I attributed a portion of the ease to my zest for the curriculum. I was absorbed in criminal law and procedure, crime and punishment and issues in modern law enforcement. Studying and preparing papers was something I did not loathe. I could not say the same for a Fortran course I studied in my sophomore year. My brother had urged me to at least sample it which I begrudgingly did for five weeks before dropping the course to avoid flunking it. More importantly for me at the time, the scarcity of arduous classwork did not prevent me from working, which was a financial necessity for me to remain in school.

My parents had been divorced when I was six years old. Primarily, my mother raised the three boys but, my father did play an important role in my life. Mom and Dad never seemed to get along and, maturity has granted me the vision to see that they were complete opposites. My Mother was contemplative, sensitive and tranquil. She preferred to stay at home and raise the children. My father was a story-teller who loved to have friends over to watch football and baseball games. He was friendly and boisterous especially when he was drinking Ortliebs or Piels, the low budget beers of the mid-Atlantic region where I grew up. I know his drinking contributed to the failure of the marriage but, it was not the sole reason. I reckoned in later years my parents never would have resolved their differences, drunk or sober but, what they lacked in compatibility did not translate to their individual work ethic. Both were dedicated, loyal employees of their respective companies. My Mom worked at a hospital, working fifteen years in an emergency room performing precise electrocardiograms on critical heart attack patients. When the work became too depressing, she transferred to the Admissions Unit. My father labored 39 years for a utility company working on the street with customers who were uncooperative and delinquent bill payers. He complained about company policies, the steady decline of the city and the temperament of his customers for most of those four decades but, he went to work every day for forty nine weeks a year until his back gave out and with great resistance, finally acceded to retirement. Both supported me through college, helping with tuition, books and a never-ending parade of automobile expenses for what I jokingly referred to as my custom-rusted '72 Ford Comet. Though their financial efforts were imperative to my education, their moral support and insistence on my pursuit of a college degree, which neither had, played a greater part in my development. My respect for both my parents was immeasurable however, I had a profound desire to find a vocation which would not require me to work as dutifully as they had for the next forty years of my life. Like most 19 year-olds, it was difficult for me to realistically envision the future. I felt that a Criminal Justice degree would put me on the path to fortune and if it only lead to a position as a security guard at K-Mart, as my brother had cautioned then, I would be the best they had and would be paid accordingly.

Consequently, my years at college were like most other students from medium income families. I lived at home and commuted to school, driving to classes in my beater car when it ran and finding other means like public transportation when it did not. I worked evenings and week-ends at a variety of easily acquired and skilless jobs, the longest of which lasted 2 years as a stock person at an appliance store. Though I worked close to forty hours a week and remained a full-time student, I still had the energy to socialize. I drank quite a bit of beer, wine, vodka, gin and whiskey. Sometimes all in the same evening. I ran with my friends, chasing girls, a majority of whom I never caught. Most of my close friends at the time did not pursue higher education and had more time to goof off. Despite my hectic schedule, I persisted in trying desperately to keep their pace.

Alcohol was a huge part of our lives but, drugs were not, at least for me. I had tried marijuana on a few occasions but, never having been a cigarette smoker, found the effects more irritating than relaxing. The smell of it made me nauseous, the smoke burned my throat and made it dry. Additionally, I seemed to always scorch my lip or my fingers on the poorly wrapped joints. I tried to enjoy smoking it but, never could. I always returned to liquor, an intoxicant with which I was comfortable with the results and effects. I suppose in choosing booze, I resolved hel-lacious hangovers were more tolerable to me than burned skin.

Stronger drugs such as speed, LSD, hallucinogenic mushrooms and cocaine were evident within my circle of friends but, not prevalent. I know my friends experimented with these drugs because I witnessed its use in basement parties and nightclub restrooms on many instances. Occasionally, one of my friends would act unpredictably wild after ingesting one of these substances but, their behavior was generally no more obscene than mine when I had been inebriated. It was the decade of self-indulgence, the eighties. The recreational use of drugs was accepted among my crowd and those who used them intermingled freely with those who did not. In retrospect, I recalled every one in our crowd abused something but, for most of us, the substance of choice was alcohol.

Though lack of peer pressure to use drugs contributed to my abstinence, I believe I never would have engaged in more than experimentation anyway. I was simply afraid of drugs and the source of that fear was my middle brother, Michael. Mike was only five years older than me but used that half decade to experiment with and abuse drugs and alcohol as much as he could. I assumed he tried everything including fiddling with dangerous combinations of substances. From the age of eight well through my teenage years and even on into college, I made countless trips to hospitals, police stations and narcotics counselors with my Mom in support of my middle brother. Along the way, Michael got himself involved in every petty criminal activity associated with substance and alcohol abuse like shoplifting, assault, disorderly conduct, driving under the influence, vandalism and theft. His behavior worried the entire family, especially my mother who must have prayed the plastic rosary beads down to the metal chain for his rehabilitation.

His recovery never occurred and it wasn't because God failed. Michael happily rejected everything about sobriety. His life was spent in search of the next high. I remember once the whole family was asked to attend a counseling session in advocacy of Mike's so-called rehabilitative efforts. My father, who always attempted to consummate his paternal duties even though he was out of the house, devotedly attended. Michael was the last to arrive and when he eventually walked into the office, he was a wavering, intoxicated mess. Drunk, high, the whole enchilada. Ridiculously, the counselor wanted to continue the session, a suggestion everyone but my Mother, ever hopeful, rejected. My father picked up my brother, who had fallen asleep shortly after arriving and drove him to a detoxification unit where he stayed approximately twelve hours before hitch-hiking home.

Perhaps the most influential moment regarding his drug use for me occurred when I saw my brother overdose on Phencyclidine or PCP, affectionately known as Angel Dust on the streets of Philadelphia at the time. PCP is a nasty, synthetically made drug which was sporadically used in the 1950's as an intravenous anesthetic and a pain killer. Its unpleasant and uncontrollable post-operative side effects prompted the medical profession to discontinue using the controversial drug. In very small doses, PCP causes sedation. In street doses, where the illicit manufacture of PCP is not regulated leading to the inability to govern the concentration levels of the drug in a single dosage unit, PCP can cause hallucinations, writhing convulsions and insensitivity to severe pain. PCP has been known to make people so disoriented they plunge through windows, dive into raging flames or leap in front of thundering city trains. An encounter with someone who has ingested too much PCP is a frightening experience and it's a phenomena to which I could attest, well before joining the DEA.

I recalled hearing a ferocious commotion in the basement of our modest three bedroom row-house where Michael and his friends often congregated while my mother was away at work. I was still in high school at the time, probably around my sophomore year. They drank and smoked reefer among other things and often tried in vain to disguise the odor and smoke of marijuana by spraying the room with flower scented aerosol cans. They probably huffed the contents of the cans while doing so. I remember one afternoon hearing furniture crashing against a wall. My initial reaction was to ignore it and hope it was another fistfight between my brother and a friend which would quickly subside. The commotion escalated and I began hearing wild screaming which sounded more like painful wails from a wounded animal. The cries were infused with random profanities and as I made my way to the basement to investigate, I began to hear the words more clearer. It was my brother invoking the name of God and Satan and screaming things about wolves fornicating with the Blessed Virgin Mary. The words and the depravity with which he spoke terrified me.

I ventured far enough down the steps to catch a glimpse of him. His face was a strained shade of violet and infused with rage. His shirt had been ripped from his body. He was on his haunches, thrashing his arms and threatening one of his friends who he had cornered between a hot water heater and an old coat rack. The friend, a neighbor, was horrified and cowered with an old walking crutch for defense, poking it almost helplessly toward Mike in a crude effort to keep him away. The fear across his face reminded me of an overwhelmed lion trainer I had seen on television moments before he was mauled by his rebellious ward. Seeking refuge anyway he could find it, his friend spotted me and begged for assistance.

Michael turned to see me and upon doing so, retreated, springing prodigally toward the washing machine. He crouched again and began gnawing at his jeans. His face became pale with dread. His friend seized the moment to flee and frantically ran for the basement door to escape. I went up the stairs in the same hurried fashion and called police.

By this time in my life, the local police were familiar with our family and had already responded to several domestic incidents at our household involving Mike and my Mom, me, his friends and our neighbors. I had warned responding officers about the unique situation and particularly Mike's condition. When they arrived, it was en masse and prepared. Seven officers entered the house and after assuring them we had no guns, I informed them the only item he was armed with was an old wooden crutch. Under normal circumstances, a teenager with a walking stick was no match for seven, armed men. Under the unpredictable influence of PCP, my brother was a formidable opponent. The police entered from two directions, the basement steps and through the first floor door. I watched as the small squad attempted to corral Mike, who fought wildly while continuing to spew venomous words about Bible figures and sports stars.

"Joe Frazier is going to kill God and then fuck your worthless bodies through your eye sockets!"

He kicked and punched and landed several blows on one particular officer who showed great restraint in not smashing his skull with a nightstick.

"Let me go, you mother fucking Judas's. You are all going to burn with the Pittsburgh Pirates."

The policeman concern seemed to be subduing my brother while preventing him from getting a hold of one of their firearms. I wanted to move forward and help but, I wasn't sure who I should help, the expedient police who were performing a duty I requested them to do or my brother, who was being twisted and mangled by imperiled officers who sought an end to the unpredictable situation. I remember them finally getting him under control, restraining his legs and arms with ankle bracelets and dragging him out of the basement door, much to the interest and delight of some of our neighbors who had gathered outside the rear of the house to witness the ferocious disturbance. I was grateful my Mother had been at work during the entire episode and only heard about the matter from "concerned" neighbors. For the sake of my mother's dignity, I downplayed the severity of it. However, the recollection of the incident stayed with me forever and contributed to my resistance of drugs, especially those of the hallucinogenic variety.

*

During my last year of college, I began to seriously consider my employment prospects. Much to my chagrin, I noticed they appeared as bleak as my oldest brother had warned. I had nonchalantly dismissed my grim outlook on a mere lack of interest in attempting to explore the employment opportunities awaiting one with a degree in criminal justice. I had spent the first three years of college working, testing and studying while trying to cram as much fun into my free hours as possible. As a senior, I had to confront the undeniable fact I had not been adequately researching any occupational opportunities. I visited the career resource center at the University and found there were tens of dozens of potential jobs for accountants, software programmers and engineers. Unfortunately, there were only about six positions offered in the folder entitled "Criminal Justice." Of these positions, four involved security guard work. A fifth brochure advertised opportunities with the Dallas, Texas Police Department, as if I was interested in moving to Dallas, home of the Cowboys, a team which me and my fellow Philadelphians truly despised. The 6th and final advertisement suggested exploring a position with the United States Border Patrol. The work, which I assumed had to be awful, actually made the job sound intriguing. The solicitation enticed me with words that drew my immediate attention, "Investigate," "Surveillance," and "Arrest."

I had already explored the Federal Bureau of Investigation. I had been well into my junior year's course curriculum when I discovered the FBI was not interested in individuals who possessed criminal justice degrees. Instead they sought people with business backgrounds, specifically experienced analysts and CPA's. I was quite discouraged when this information was disseminated to me from a field representative at one of the career seminars the university promoted. I was told after inquiring that most of the FBI's work involved white collar crime which required investigators with categorical and deciphering minds. Accountants and lawyers were considered exceptional candidates. I was a CJ major who had withdrawn from Calculus, twice. My core curriculum was somewhat difficult but, even I could not claim that I had spent considerable energy enhancing the deftness of my mind with electives like Bowling 101 and Urban Studies. Consequently, by the time senior year had rolled around, I was beginning to believe I had made a serious mistake.

Instead of complaining about my prospects like most of my classmates had chosen to do, I found time to fill out any application that was available. I completed a resume, with the help of my Mom who somehow managed to make my lack of experience seem like it was a benefit to a potential employer. I submitted an application to the Border Patrol and my research led to the discovery of a host of federal agencies who might be interested in a criminal justice major. I began soliciting those agencies and requesting employment information and applications from the Naval Investigative Service, The Bureau of Alcohol, Tobacco and Firearms, The U.S. Marshals Service, The Secret Service, both their Uniformed and Investigative and Protective Division and the U.S. Customs Service. Somewhere among the litany of agencies was the Drug Enforcement Administration.

I had not thought seriously about the DEA. I was probably one of the few people my age who truly was unimpressed by the television show, Miami Vice. It had been a popular hit on network television during my high school and college years and many of my friends faithfully watched the program. The actors who portrayed the main characters, Don Johnson and Philip Michael Thomas, had their faces plastered onto everything from interstate billboards to children's lunchboxes. The male gender took to wearing their pastel colored, cotton sportcoats, a style which I never adopted and couldn't imagine evoking respect when donned by a law enforcement officer. The plots featured heroic narcotics cops, grimy informants and provocative drug dealers parading through the glamorous nightspots and affluent marinas of Miami Beach, transporting themselves in high performance vehicles and customized yachts. Gorgeous and seductive bikini clad women were thrown into the mix along with brief cases stuffed with organized rows of large denominations of cash, all synthesized to make for an exciting hour of prime time television. The stories revolved around the Herculean efforts of Crockett and Tubbs and even though they were Miami Narcotics Detectives, as the name of the show implied, I associated their activities with the Drug Enforcement Administration and its agents.

I didn't view myself as the type of person who could comfortably fit into that world. I made that honest assessment based on my personality which was more introverted, like my mother. I didn't tan very well either so, ignorantly, I didn't think I would be an ideal fit for the DEA. Furthermore, though I did not use drugs, I wasn't a great proponent against them. During my college years, many people I knew experimented with dope and they were people I generally liked. The ones who didn't indulge, even though I really was one myself, were people I didn't really make much of an effort to associate with. Not because they didn't use drugs but, they weren't partiers and in my convoluted thinking of those immature days, I regarded them as straight people who were "no fun." They went bowling and attended church socials while my friends went to concerts, boozed all night and raised hell, usually getting away with it. The people who didn't at least drink were people I probably never even had a chance of knowing in those days.

Either way, the DEA is one of the federal agencies to which I submitted an official federal application, a standard form known as the SF 171. The SF 171 is an ominous document consisting of several pages requiring all types of general identifying information as well as specific information about relatives, references and associates working for the U.S. Government. Each Agency was a separate entity which required the submission of a new and individually completed application even though the forms were entirely identical. Through repetition, I started to become quite familiar with the damned SF 171 and by the time I had filled three or four out, I could complete the form without even reviewing the questions. Typically, I would sit, methodically filling out the papers while simultaneously watching a baseball game or listening to a double album on the stereo. I must have submitted over twenty applications, some to agencies whose purpose and function I was not even remotely acquainted.

By the time the second semester of my senior year arrived, I was seriously worrying about obtaining full time employment. There were no prospects. I had explored various opportunities with local police departments but, none were hiring. In an oblique way, I was relieved because I didn't want to invest four years at college only to become a suburban cop. It would have been a waste of tuition. I didn't feel the position as an officer was below me but, it was a position which did not require a college degree and I could have been accepted and hired without having to spend four years paying exorbitant prices to attend a university. Besides, most of the local law enforcement positions did not pay very well and I felt confident when I eventually did secure an offer, the starting salary would be substantially better than the compensation of a Philadelphia area policeman. Nevertheless, my senior year continued and before I had secured any full-time position, I had graduated from Temple University cum laude but, without a job. I began scrambling, looking for any type of work, even positions that had nothing to do with criminal justice. I applied for a job with the postal service. I signed up to take the Fireman's exam. I applied at UPS as a truck driver because I had heard it paid decently and included, as part of its benefits package, a comprehensive health insurance and a generous dental plan.

My father approached me about an opportunity with his utility company. It seemed they needed two persons to work as security shift assistants at one of their two nuclear facilities. He brought the announcement home to me which I read. The main responsibility consisted of "supervising" the on-site contract security force. I was disappointed the work revolved around security guard-type work but, at least I wouldn't be one of the watchman. The utility had plenty of those. Instead, they were looking for someone to oversee the guards. The employer preferred previous security experience, which I did not posses, and little else. A college degree was recommended but, again not required. Salary would be commensurate with experience and employees and their families would receive first consideration. It sounded like they would take anyone but, would they take me?

*

I learned several lessons at the initial interview for the utility company's security position. First, as a potential candidate, one was expected to attend the interview and exhibit knowledge, experience and charismatic presence. I realized the position for which I was interviewing was more than a job, it was a career. I had worked my way through college with shiftless jobs like stock person, audio salesman and delivery driver. They were positions most anyone could fill. They required little ability and once the routine was established, little thought. However, the utility company, in selecting an individual, was investing their time and money to train the two best people the human resource department could find. There would be competition for this job and through the interview process I was expected to demonstrate I was a superior candidate. Reality blind-sided me as I distressingly learned personnel directors do read and scrutinize all the information submitted on resumes. In order to appear more venerable I had foolishly listed my height as 6'2" believing I could get away with a contention which might make me seem more impressive. Besides, I surmised the people reviewing my resume wouldn't be the ones interviewing me. Where I garnered such a ridiculous hypothesis I can't say, other than to mention it was completely wrong. My first impression, judging by the style in which the human resources director examined me, was he recognized I had exaggerated my height. He looked at me and then the resume and repeated the process, raising a skeptical eyebrow as he considered me a second time. Finally, he extended his callused hand to greet me. It was a clumsy delay which made me feel awkward. In a calculated defense, I attempted to note characteristics which brought him to a level in which I could audit his shortcomings. I visually probed him looking for an ill-fitted suit or a dandruff sprinkled collar. I found nothing while his eyes continued their assessment of me, a review which had me unnerved. Ignorantly, I reconciled the notion I was the college graduate and it should have been me interviewing him. I learned after the interview he too, was a graduate of the same university I attended and so were four of the thirty-two other applicants who had applied for the two vacant positions. Over the course of the interview, he surveyed me with the typical questions I had expected:

"What can you bring to the company?"

"What are your best qualities?"

"What is your biggest weakness?"

I wanted to say I'm a tardy, disrespectful drunk who urinates in my boss' coffee and defaces bathroom stalls with filthy limericks but, instead, I told him I was impatient.

The generic questions continued and I gave him all the same standard answers he had probably received from all the other applicants. I assumed the interview wasn't going particularly well or poorly but, just going. I wanted to impress upon him I was a remarkable young man. I searched for the opportunity but, it never came. Instead, he proposed a demoralizing question which exposed the fraud I had attempted to perpetrate about my height. He asked, "Are you really 6'2"?"

I admitted I was under the figure by about a half inch. His forehead crinkled above his brow and my psyche squirmed as his facial expression indicated considerable skepticism about my rationale. Then he smiled faintly, out of the side of his mouth. Only a second or two elapsed but, it was more than enough time to allow both of us to know who was in control.

"I've known your father close to fifteen years," he announced. "I consider him a friend."

"So do I," I blurted from my mouth. I smiled hoping for relief but, he did not riposte.

"Can you handle the position, Mark?"

"Yes, I think I can." I responded.

I was contacted several weeks later by the company who unanticipatedly extended an offer. I realized my interview had not established me to be an exceptional or extraordinary candidate but, I was chosen because of my father's tenure with the company. Though I secured an offer from the company and accepted a position, the most significant lesson gleaned from the interview was I learned about the fundamentals of manipulation and intimidation and most importantly, the power of authority.

My starting salary was modest at $24,000 per year. It wasn't what I had expected to earn with a college education but, having been introduced to the real world and having been sucker-punched by it, I was happy to at least be embarking on a career. I worked the graveyard shift, with my main function being to oversee the contract security force the company had hired to protect the site between 11 p.m. and 7 a.m., when the labor force maintained just enough of a crew to keep the facility on line and generating electric. My title was a Shift Security Assistant but, what I really was could be termed more understandably, R-A-T. The armed and unarmed guards, whom I was expected to monitor, were hired to protect the plant and ensure its safe operation through surveillance, dedicated posts and foot and automobile patrols. However, I quickly learned it was the guards themselves who posed the most severe problems. The dubious security force was notorious for finding unique and unnoticed nooks and crannies within the nuke plant to sleep, drink and even get high. They were known to climb steel girders so they could conceal themselves unnoticed and consequently, unavailable in rafters forty feet off the ground. They would smuggle contraband like drugs or liquor bottles dunked in thermoses to avoid detection. They would find dark concrete crevasses in the reactor building where they would secrete themselves for up to an hour, avoiding work and altering their minds to the drone of creaking gears, growling turbines, and whistling valves. Incessantly bored, with nothing but inert and lifeless machines to guard, their favorite activity, other than ingesting chemical substances, had become engaging in sex. Many of the their hiding places were physically to small or unsafe to be occupied by two people but, the guards tried anyway. A few of them derived more pleasure from having sex right in the open, in the middle of spacious concrete floors where they could be easily monitored via closed circuit cameras by fellow guards in the central and secondary alarm stations. It became a game amongst many of them. It had gotten to the point where two veteran female guards were conducting titillating performances every Tuesday evening on the third floor of a generator building. A select few were supposed to have known and I didn't believe it myself until I saw one of the confiscated videos of their activity. As one of two recently hired shift assistants, it was my unenviable job to investigate and curtail all this activity, the only exciting thing happening in the middle of the night on a desolate flat prairie in the midst of Southern Pennsylvania farmland.

Of course, all of these entertaining pursuits were rigorously prohibited anywhere on the property of an atomic facility by the Nuclear Regulatory Agency. The NRC, which strictly policed nuke facilities was not the least hesitant to heavily fine a licensee for abusive infractions even if it was the utility's contractors and not its own employees who were in violation. The utility, as the entity holding the nuclear operator's license, was responsible for any and all blunders and indiscretions. In turn, my boss made me and the other young man hired, also the son of a current employee, an electrical engineer, liable for any continued episodes of misconduct amongst the contract security force.

In addition to the guards, the company placed the bureau of fire safety under our department's supervision. The fire safety group consisted of approximately sixty firewatches whose sole responsibility was to check floors, equipment and machinery for sparks, smoke or any sign of fire. They had assigned routes and scheduled rounds which they were expected and paid to maintain for eight hour shifts. When the firewatch ended one route he or she would return to the origin of the route and start again, expected to complete seven dedicated rounds on each eight hour shift. Firewatches served a crucial role in the safety of the plant. A fire, no matter how small, could be devastating to a nuclear plant, its production, its employees and the community. Though vitally important to the protection of the facility, firewatches were typically high school dropouts, retirees and other people who were between jobs. In other words, they were people who did not have much at stake with their employment and were looking for something to occupy their time while they collected a modest paycheck all the while waiting for a better job to come along

It was not difficult for these hired sentinels to perform their duties. They were required to initial sheets of paper at various check points ensuring that an examination had taken place. The sheets were similar to those one might find in the bathroom of a fast food restaurant requiring a check for cleanliness. The firewatches were paid slightly better than the employees of a fast food restaurant but, only slightly. Despite the simplicity of their tasks, the firewatches came up with elaborate methods to avoid completing their chores. They often spent more energy devising and employing sophisticated schemes to account for their routes instead of completing the rounds honestly. When they were not performing their duties they generally were up to no good. Like the guards, many found remote hideaways to spend their shift sleeping. Others took drugs. It was part of my responsibility to find firewatches not performing their jobs. Consequently, it would be an understatement to say I was not on the Christmas card list of the firewatches. Regardless of their opinion, I did my job.

I had been at the plant approximately one year but, with each passing shift, I grew more disenchanted and disillusioned. At twenty-three, I hadn't envisioned working in basically what was a glorified factory and I hadn't anticipated I would be doing it for the next thirty-five years of my life. I had been functioning satisfactorily, catching a guard or a firewatch in violation of some policy or another and I was gradually acquiring a reputation for an ability to perform my job well. My boss liked me and nominated me for a raise. I had a secure position but, after only a few months, I realized it was not a career. When the Drug Enforcement Administration contacted me and expressed an interest in interviewing me, I was ecstatic I would be finally given the chance to put my CJ Degree to work. It was a position where I would be paid to ferret out real criminals, even if they were just drug dealers.

3

It had taken the DEA nearly two years to process my application. During that time, I had honestly forgotten that I had ever even submitted it. I regarded my efforts to gain employment with a federal government as having failed. Then unexpectedly, I received a succinct one page letter stating the DEA Recruitment Coordinator would like me to call her in the DEA's office in Philadelphia. I hastily called the following day and was scheduled for a panel interview by Friday of the same week. I hadn't even known what a panel interview was but, I had only three days to prepare for it. I went to the library that evening and researched any information I could find about the Drug Enforcement Administration.

I was disappointed to learn there wasn't much available reading material regarding the agency. I uncovered a few articles in the periodical section but, most of those focused on the criminals and traffickers the agency had investigated. I came across a synopsis pertaining to the formation of the agency which attributed its creation to former President Richard Nixon who signed an executive order creating the Drug Enforcement Administration in July of 1973. The establishment of the DEA effectively abolished three separate agencies, the Bureau of Narcotics and Dangerous Drugs, the Office of National Narcotic Intelligence and the Office of Drug Abuse Law Enforcement. The DEA's purpose was to consolidate all of these federal anti-drug forces into one unified agency. I xeroxed the information, memorized it and prepared myself to expound upon it if asked but, I was still not content with the general limited information I had acquired. I knew I needed to learn more about the agents and the requirements of their position. While searching the periodical index, I discovered an article which linked Elvis Presley and the DEA. I found this prospect intriguing and immediately sought it out. Fortunately, the article was a Time magazine piece and my modest library carried the edition on microfilm. I had hoped to find a juicy article attributing portions of Elvis' financial empire to have been built on his association with Colombian Drug Lords but, instead, I found a brief column about Presley's fascination with law enforcement. As a favor, then President Nixon, apparently rewarded Presley with a special appointment to the DEA. Presley was given official credentials as a Special Agent of the Drug Enforcement Administration, the only individual to ever have received complete and authentic DEA credentials without having been trained and officially sanctioned by the DEA Administrator. The brief article was not complimentary of Presley or the DEA and described the association between both to be a farce.

Having failed in the periodical section, I turned to the librarian. I did it with a great degree of doubt, regarding him by his appearance as little more than a bookworm who probably knew very little about law enforcement. Desperate, I asked him anyway. He informed me, as expected, he knew nothing about the DEA and sarcastically added he didn't care too learn much more. Before elaborating on the reason for his disdain, he recalled reading a book about their particular efforts in Southeast Asia and said he might be able to locate the title and determine if the book was currently in circulation in one of the libraries' branches. He returned to his disorganized desk and inspiredly attacked an antiquated desktop computer that sat teetering on top. I was impressed by the verve with which he pursued the task and after a few moments was delighted with his revelation the book was currently in the same library in which we stood.

The Underground Empire was a well researched manuscript by author James Mills, published by Doubleday, which catalogued international narcotics interdiction efforts. The contents of the book documented the commingling of crime and government and reported how internationally organized drug distributing syndicates functioned and its implications on U.S. domestic drug policy. Initially, I found its contents intimidating but, I managed to complete it in three days. The non-fictional work consisted of recollections and memoirs of agents investigating and infiltrating sophisticated and organized drug traffickers in far away countries, work I rationalized, I would never be capable of completing. How could I, never having been out of the United States and with no ability to speak a foreign language. The book about DEA Agents and their furtive global endeavors seemed even more fascinating than the hyperbole of predictable television drama and I had to admit, as I delved more into the journal, the interesting investigations conducted by the DEA enthralled me and I found myself intrigued by the lives of the agents I read about. By the time my scheduled interview had arrived, I had completed the book, something I had never done with such a lengthy essay in so short a time. With the compelling information very fresh in my mind, I felt confident I could impress the people who would interview me with my knowledge of the Administration and its far reaching and consequential performance.

∗

I sat alone in the comfortless waiting room surrounded by empty plastic chairs. I had expected to see other people, perhaps other interviewees but, there was no one else but me. Whether by design or not, over an hour passed between the time I arrived and the interview. The delay gave me a lot of time to fidget and worry. When called, I was guided down a narrow, poorly painted hallway, past a room which had a slanted fingerprinting stand and a mug-shot camera in it. Adjacent to that was a holding facility with dimly-lit and constrictive gray cells. A second room nearby contained instruments that looked, based on my brief glimpse, to be audio and video recording equipment. I tried to obtain a prolonged look but was permitted only a peek as I followed the man who escorted me. I was led to a conference room which housed a long wooden rectangular table with one uncomfortable-looking metal folding chair sitting at the end nearest the door. Before I noticed anything else, I saw a revolver lying on its side with the barrel facing the vacant chair. I turned and observed four men seated at the opposite end of the table. All appeared professional, confident and successful. I said "Hello" but, no one responded. One, a young, black muscular looking man nodded but, offered no audible reply. He was seated furthest to the left. I was shown the seat and told to sit in it. I tried to appear undaunted but, I was quaking inside. I was grateful the table covered my knees which I could feel were quivering slightly.

The man furthest to my right, some twelve feet away across the long table, spoke first. He introduced himself and his counterparts. All were special agents. I repeated their names in my head, desperately hoping to remember them. He no sooner finished the introductions when he requested me to pick up the revolver in front of me. I hesitated and he requested me to do so a second time in a demanding tone which exuded impatience and disdain for timidity. I reached for it wondering whether he was going to instruct me to place it against my head. The whole proceeding was so intimidating, I might have done it if I had been directed. He asked me to hold the gun in my outstretched hand and squeeze the trigger. I thought his directive was a clever trick to determine if I was reckless or unsafe so, I immediately declined.

"Mr. Connors, the gun is unloaded. Please do as I say."

I looked at the weapon. I had held revolvers in my hands and twice had fired similar weapons. On both occasions, I had been at a firing range where I distinctly recalled the instructor cautioning the participants that a weapon should never be "dry-fired." That is, pulling the trigger of a gun assuming it to be unloaded. Nevertheless, I followed their instructions and picked up the pistol. I kept the barrel facing the wall and decided I would be best served making sure the gun was unloaded. I released the lever which opened the cylinder and checked to see if it was devoid of rounds. It was. I looked at the faces around the room hoping to find satisfaction in what I had done. Instead, I found neither encouragement or contempt. Their faces remained devoid of emotion, differing only in pigment.

"Mr. Connors." The same agent spoke, "if you are ever going to become an agent you better learn to trust an agent. Someone at this table might be asked to safe your life one day."

"Besides," another agent added, "you think we would be stupid enough to give someone we never met before a loaded weapon. Especially someone who looked as naive as you."

His sardonic remark produced assorted chuckles. The first agent, a fit, well-coifed white man of thirty-five or so requested me to hold my arm out with the weapon in my dominant strong hand. He instructed me to pull the trigger as many times as I could for a period lasting one minute. After completing the task, I was asked to switch hands and repeat the process. The test, I was told later, was to measure the trigger pull strength of each applicant. Someone who could not successfully demonstrate they had the capacity to utilize this most rudimentary firearm was given a brief interview and then immediately dismissed from consideration. I evidently passed the first exam because my interview continued and lasted close to two and a half hours. The standard questions about my background, schooling and work experience comprised only a small portion of the interview. Instead, the main focus consisted of an examination which included hypothetical situations and open-ended questions about how I would respond and react to certain situations. The presentation of inquiries spanned moral analysis about whether I felt I could kill someone to transcendent questions having to do with a partner who had been cheating on his wife. They asked me questions about my opinions about subjects ranging from marijuana use to corporal punishment. They asked me if I liked women and if I considered myself a good person. The style of the inquiries prohibited simple "yes" or "no" answers and was designed to elicit elaborate opinions. The questions were intended to expose the applicant's true feelings, thoughts and emotions. I remember the method succeeding for I found myself answering questions I had never really given much thought to and I had to do it in such a way as I appeared to have formulated intelligent thought regarding the matters. There was no way one could answer the questions "right." There were too many designed to evoke views and perspectives. After having been hired, I know what the agents were trying to accomplish. The rigid screening process had already determined me to at least be considered a candidate but questionnaires, applications and resumes never can communicate what a person actually believes. Only a meeting can accomplish that and the real purpose of the panel interview was to ascertain if the DEA Agents in the room could work with me, could I be compatible professionally and personally and above all else, whether they could trust me.

I specifically remember being quizzed with one scenario.

"Suppose your partner had some financial problems. Say his son was ill and his medical coverage had not been covering the cost of his pills. The operation was paid for and so were the doctors but, the price of the pills, and you know how much they can cost these days, are so exorbitant that he simply is having trouble meeting the payments…"

Another agent added, "And he told you his wife is thinking about divorcing him, she wants the house and him out of it, and she is planning to leave him with nothing but his dog."

"Basically, everything's going wrong for the guy, " The first agent continued, "and that sick son, he's your Godson. And you are on a search warrant with your partner and you see him pick up some gold coins out of a coin collection. You know they are worth some money. What are you going to do, Connors?"

"I would try to lend him some money." I responded, thinking it would have been the compassionate thing to do and an idea which would enable me to discreetly skirt the question. It didn't work.

They laughed. "No, Connors, you've already given this guy a couple thousand bucks. He hasn't paid you back and let's face it, you don't have the kind of money yourself to be throwing two and three thousand bucks around. Now, you see your partner stealing. What are you going to do?"

I thought about what they wanted me to say. What the "correct" answer should be. I formulated the beginning of my answer before another agent interrupted.

"Are you going to turn him in?"

The manner of his inquiry didn't express happiness or contempt with such a decision. However, the thought of "turning him in" did not appeal to me.

"I wouldn't turn him in."

"You wouldn't?" The agent replied, this time in a manner that echoed scorn. "Why the hell not, he's a thief isn't he?"

"I would confront him first." I responded. "I would tell him I saw him do it and ask him to put it…"

Another Agent interrupted, "Suppose he tells you to go fuck yourself."

I thought about the predicament. I no longer tried to conceive the right answer and instead felt betrayal at a partner who would do such a thing and so disregard my feelings. "I'd tell him I saw him do it and I did not like it."

"That's it?" The black agent asked.

"No, I would go to my supervisor." I hesitated a long while actually considering what I would say. The agents allowed me time to formulate my rebuttal. "I would request a new partner."

"Why, Connors. He's a thief. His actions are not only jeopardizing his career but, yours as well. A loose cannon like that is dangerous for everybody. Are you content to just make him someone else's problem or don't you think it would be best concerned for everyone if you turned him in."

I thought about it and agreed. "Yes, he should be turned in. I feel I couldn't trust him anymore and his actions were betraying my trust." The answer was truthful. After considering the audacity of a partner who couldn't care less what I thought, I really felt that way.

The interview concluded with the agents informing me I had scored well and would probably be hearing from the agency within a few weeks. I was pleased and left the DEA Office proud. I reconsidered my responses to some of their probing questions and I honestly felt a sense of self-affirmation in that what I said was really the way I felt. I was an honorable man and I could be expected to uphold the law. If I had to save someone's life while risking my own to do so, I would do it. I had surprised and impressed myself. In addition, I was completely intrigued by the men in the interview room. I left obsessed with the idea I had a chance to become one of those men. I desperately wanted to become an agent, a DEA Agent.

When the Drug Enforcement Administration decided I was a qualified applicant, they assigned me a date to report to the DEA/FBI training Academy at the Marine Corps Base in Quantico, Virginia. When I arrived, I was physically and mentally ready for the challenge of the academy and I was fully resolved to become a DEA Agent along with the other forty students who had been assigned to my class, BA-063, Basic Academy Class 063.

The thirteen week school was not as rigorous as had been predicted by my recruiter. I was tenaciously determined to succeed and was not going to be deterred. The pace was hectic at times but, certainly not unbearable. A typical day involved two hours of physical fitness training which included demanding activity like wrestling, boxing and running.

We also had six hours of classroom training which consisted of courses pertaining to criminal law and procedure and drug identification. The curriculum also included two hours of firearms training with various ordnance including shotguns, rifles, and automatic weapons. By the end of the day one was tired but still capable of a couple hours of study, a movie in the film room or a beer or two at the Board Room, an on-site bar for students, visitors and guests of the FBI Academy.

Basic Agent Class 063 incorporated thirty-six men and four women. The trainees came from a diverse background with approximately one-half having had prior law enforcement experience. Most were Caucasians with about twenty-five percent African-American and Hispanic. There were two Asians, one of whom was a female. I liked most of my classmates and respected all of them with the exception of one, a recruit who was eventually expelled for cheating on an exam. He had compiled a small index card containing information pertaining to a criminal law test. His "cheat sheet" was presented for the class to see and it was filled with so much information, it was barely decipherable. It looked more like microfiche and I did not know how he could even read it. Upon its discovery, many members of the class found its existence among us particularly disparaging. We were troubled a fellow classmate in the DEA Academy was caught cheating on a law exam. It was embarrassing to the student and to us and we all supported the decision to expel him. In addition to the cheater, three people succumbed to the requirements of training. Two recruits failed to pass their firearms prerequisites while another student broke an ankle during a four mile jog through the woods that surround the institution.

During the training academy, there existed a great deal of camaraderie among the pupils with a considerable effort made by the instructors to instill a team concept based on the virtuous qualities of pride, commitment and integrity. Everyone helped each other utilizing group strengths to overcome individual weaknesses. We were taught to work and succeed as a unit and any failure by one reflected a failure by all. Every member of the class realized how fortunate each was to have been selected to this academy class from a pool of literally thousands of applicants from all over the country. It was vitally important to the success of the DEA mission to weed out those who could not make the grade. Physical limitation or deception would not be tolerated and incompetence was considered a disgraceful and intolerable offense.

When I walked across the stage in the facility's auditorium at the conclusion of the training, I was as proud as I had ever been in my life. I had accomplished something which I had worked hard to achieve. Fortuitous luck had brought me to the attention of the recruiter but effort, perseverance and desire had propelled me to the Administrator who handed me my gold plated DEA badge and credentials. On December 22, 1989, I was officially commissioned a Special Agent of the Drug Enforcement Administration.

I reported to my first permanent post of duty, the Chicago Field Division, one of the geographically largest divisions in the DEA. I brought with me all the inspiration of teamwork, effort and integrity that had been progressively infused in me during the 13 week academy. I realized only a few months into my career that these dignified notions were set aside in favor of personal achievement and recognition or neglected due to political infighting or favoritism.

4

I had been an agent for two weeks when I was asked to perform my first undercover role. Naturally, I was excited. The undercover task is the essence of narcotics enforcement. At least, that's the public's perception and since I had only been an official federal agent for half a month, it was mine as well. The notion of duping someone into believing I was a drug dealer was going to be serious business. It wasn't play-acting as it had been in the academy. The proposition was real and I had to consider the distinct possibility my first undercover role could be my last. Though it was a dangerous proposition, it was my first chance to prove I was worthy to have a gold tinted federal badge. Though admittedly nervous, I was stimulated by the opportunity, until I found out the details.

I was told to buy a quarter ounce of pot from a 17-year-old kid.

Another agent, Tom Kerrigan, had asked my supervisor if he could use the new guy, me, for an undercover purchase. My boss thought it would give me a taste of what was to come and I agreed. I can't believe or at least didn't want to believe he knew the actual assignment he had volunteered me to perform. I know Kerrigan had asserted the buy would be a small one designed to gauge my ability as an undercover. It wouldn't be fair to send me or anyone else out on the street to negotiate a multi-kilo deal. Without any previous experience, I would have been recognized as a cop immediately. But I certainly didn't think I should be sent out to buy a fraction of marijuana. I wondered if this was the kind of case the DEA typically worked. If so, I wondered how many people similar to the ones I used to hang out with would I end up arresting? I couldn't believe the DEA had to test my faculties by sending me out for a quarter ounce of weed. Hell, I could have gotten a pound of weed at gym class in high school. I wondered if this were the type of case I would be working as an agent until I learned the true motivation behind the buy, an incentive which had nothing to do with drug enforcement at all.

Tom Kerrigan was a senior agent. As such he supposedly should have the experience to guide young agents in their career. He was expected to train us, show us the ropes and mold novices like myself into becoming proud, capable federal agents. This hardly seemed a promising initial step. I was to learn later, Kerrigan was considered a moron, an arrogant man who was one of the most self-serving agents in the office.

Apparently, before coming to the DEA, Kerrigan, I learned, had once been a member of the Illinois State Police. He maintained close ties with the ranks with which he formerly worked including a detail known to the DEA as the Northeast Metropolitan Enforcement Group. We called them NEMEG and their priority was drug cases. Kerrigan claimed my purchase of a quarter ounce of pot was in furtherance of an investigation NEMEG was working on against big time suburban marijuana distributors. When I delved further into the case, I found out the target, the 17-year-old kid, had been involved in a car accident with one of the NEMEG's investigators. Apparently, someone from NEMEG had been out boozing it up all night and forgot that red traffic lights should be obeyed by all motorists, not just those without the privilege of badges in their back pocket. The inebriated cop cruised right through an intersection and broad-sided a car which happened to be driven by this 17-year-old kid. The teenager was coming home from his shift at Taco Bell and was sober. The kid was alright but upset about the car accident. He rightfully accused the driver who hit him as being drunk. When the police arrived at the scene, the driver who hit him identified himself, rather boisterously, as a cop. The police tried to resolve the issue at the scene and have someone discreetly take the cop home but, the kid accused the police of hiding the fact the driver was drunk. The teen didn't let it go and filed an accusation of corruption against the suburban force where the accident occurred. He wasn't prepared to let the issue die so the NEMEG Agent who hit him concocted the plan to buy dope off him to soil the teenager's integrity.

It was a farce.

I had agreed to meet the kid at the Taco Bell where he worked. I hadn't even spoken to him. I had been told the deal was already arranged by a Confidential Informant. I kept my feelings about the necessity of a CI to buy a quarter ounce to myself. I went along with the deal because I had already agreed to do it but secretly, I hoped the kid wouldn't show up. He did, at exactly the time he was supposed to, 3:30 PM after he had gotten out of his last class. He found me because he was told I would be in a Jeep Cherokee. He was on a skateboard. He circled my vehicle three times before he stopped and addressed me.

"Are you Tony?"

That was the name I was given for the role. I didn't choose it, Kerrigan gave it to me. I didn't like the name and the more the ridiculous deal unfolded, the more I detested it.

"Yea."

The kid stood there. He didn't come forward. Instead, he looked from side to side. He certainly didn't carry himself like a member of some distribution network. He was just a kid on a skateboard whose obvious apprehensiveness would have precluded him from pilfering a candy bar off the countertop of a blind merchant's store. I waited.

"Are you sure you're Tony?"

It was nonsensical, "Yea! I'm Tony!" I demanded, "Come here will you!"

He dismantled the board, expertly flipping it up into his hands with an adept kick of his heel. He moved toward the car.

"You have something for me?" I asked.

He stopped abruptly, "No, why?"

Though I was disappointed at the assignment, I certainly didn't want to fail on my first undercover attempt. I couldn't let this naïve kid figure out I was a cop. I scrambled to reassure him. "I thought you were supposed to meet me. Frankie sent you right."

Seemingly relieved he responded, "Yea. I guess so."

"Well…."

He looked around again and then cautiously walked up to my driver's side window. He backed away then proceeded around my car to the other side. I was perplexed. I watched him as he walked up to the passenger's side. He was about to knock on the window but I lowered it.

"What are you doing?"

"I don't know who you are, man." He said almost apologetically.

"I know but here I am" I offered. "We both know Frankie right." I pushed my coat away making sure it wasn't covering the transmitter I was wearing. A transmitter recording a ludicrous conversation with a 17 year-old scared kid. He looked into my car as I moved and his eyes grew wide.

"What the fuck's the matter?"

"You got a gun?" He asked.

"A gun? I don't have a fucking gun!" I didn't, at least visible. I had tucked it under the seat. I didn't expect it would be needed for this deal but, I had it in case something happened on the way. I looked at the floorboard to make sure it hadn't slid out when I parked. It had.

He confessed, "I think I should tell you I ain't got them."

"Them what?" I asked. "You don't have what?"

"I don't do this."

"Do what? Just give it to me. I'm not gonna rip you off. "

"That's what I'm trying to tell you." He said. "I told Frankie no!"

"You don't have the quarter ounce?"

"Quarter ounce?"

"Yea, the fucking quarter ounce!" I yelled disgustedly.

Frankie told me to give you two joints."

"Two joints? You're supposed to have a quarter ounce.:"

"I don't know where you can get a quarter ounce." He hesitated, pondering something then asked directly, "Frankie sells ounces?"

"You're kidding me aren't you?"

The teenager shook his head. He looked to the right then pulled the inside of his pants pocket out revealing nothing but a crumpled single dollar bill. "I told you, I told Frankie no."

I was really annoyed. I was embarrassed that I had been asked to do this and now, I was mad at the kid who made me look foolish. The thought of two surveillance cars watching all this folly further perturbed me. Kerrigan hadn't even shown up. Instead, he sent me out with two NEMEG Agents for back up.

"You mean you don't have any pot."

"I don't get involved with marijuana. Frankie told me he'd kick my ass if I didn't deliver something to you. I told him he would have to beat me up then. He gave me the joints but I threw them away." His voice cracked as he spoke, the last few words spoken as if he hadn't completed puberty.

I laughed, and added, "Say no to drugs, right dude."

I put the car in drive and drove away. The episode was my first flagrant experience with the bureaucracy, self-serving and corruptness of my fellow agents. It was long forgotten by the time I had experienced my last.

5

The Chicago Field Division, was headquarters for all Federal Drug Enforcement related activities for the Upper Midwestern United States with dedicated coverage in Illinois, Indiana, Wisconsin, Minnesota and both Dakotas. Our region was overseen by Kenneth Starr, the Division's Special Agent in Charge or SAC as he was usually called. His position was to serve as a territorial administrator and perform liaison duties with the leaders of other federal, state and local agencies for the purposes of relations and coordination. Though he possessed a reputable title, he was mainly a figurehead. Most, if not all, the major decisions were made by the Associate Special Agent in Charge, Frank Black. Black was a menacing and intimidating man who wasn't physically large but despite his advanced middle age, maintained a remarkable degree of physical fitness. He was known to run eight miles every other day while continuing a daily regimen of grueling one and a half hour workouts followed by thirty minutes beating the stuffings out of a heavy bag. Black boasted he had killed the most people by any active law enforcement officer and staked his violent reputation on an episode which once occurred in federal court. When asked why he had shot a particular suspect fifteen times, a defense attorney was shocked to hear Black's response "Because I ran out of bullets." Black frequently stripped down to his underwear and did pushups and sit-ups in his office. He was a consummate agent who reeked of discipline, authority and testosterone. Black managed the Assistant Special Agents in Charge or ASACs, each of whom were responsible for maintaining policies and all administrative, procedural and investigative decisions for respective departments under their watch. The Chicago Division had three ASACs, each with their own specific duties and responsibilities. One ASAC, Sam Ciangalini, supervised all enforcement related activity conducted by resident offices. The RO's were condensed DEA forces in smaller metropolitan areas in the Upper Midwest. Those offices included Minneapolis, Milwaukee, Indianapolis, Springfield, Illinois and Fargo, North Dakota. The Agency also operated two supplemental offices, called Posts of Duty, in Green Bay and Hammond, Indiana. The Green Bay office targeted clandestine laboratory operators while the Hammond office concentrated their efforts against violent street gangs which were crippling the small communities of Northwest Indiana. The main task of all the RO's and the POD's was to assist and coordinate sophisticated narcotics investigations conducted by overwhelmed and undermanned state and local police departments.

Another ASAC, Quincy Jackson, a seventeen year veteran of the Agency, supervised non-enforcement groups such as support and intelligence. The individuals in these groups did not participate in any enforcement activities like arrests, surveillance and interdiction. Among the large number of employees who made up these various groups was a very small number of Special Agents, who remained armed, but only assisted in compliance activities. The younger agents placed into these groups often were being punished for violating policy like wrecking a G-ride or getting arrested for DUI. The older agents in these groups were employees content to finish the remainder of their careers writing summaries and filing statistical information about narcotics related activity. I would occasionally wander over to their offices to speak with some or seek their wisdom regarding a case. Inevitably, I would have to interrupt one of the lazier agents from a particularly engrossing game of computer solitaire but, I usually came away with competent advice from one of the veteran agents. If they couldn't help me with a specific question, at least I was sure to learn the location of a good delicatessen serving cheap roast beef or pork sandwiches.

The support staff included members of a department called Intelligence. Their duty was to provide information on suspected traffickers. The analysis their unit typically supplied included financial information, professional licenses or business interests, real estate holdings, employment histories and any information which might reveal owned or hidden assets. They also cross-referenced targets with other individuals who were being investigated by our office and attempted to identify their co-conspirators and associates. It was amazing how many violators would list common residences, business ownerships or similar holdings and assets. Intelligence also petitioned other federal, state and local law enforcement agencies for any pertinent information they might possess about potential DEA targets. This included determining if a target was under investigation by another agency, something that a few evasive agencies like the FBI would never divulge. The Intelligence units had access to a vast network of private and public information but, unfortunately, in order to maintain and protect their value and sustain their existence, they exaggerated the significance of their unit by pretending the information they disseminated was extremely difficult to obtain. Their incessant delays in processing and divulging material became more a hindrance than a help. To garner any information at all required the submission of lengthy forms filled with redundant questions. The demand for intelligence was plentiful but, unfortunately, the staff's malaise failed to meet the orders. Though some of the information I might have used was literally available at the touch of a keyboard, I was required to submit a needless array of forms which only served to create paperwork, all managed by employees who otherwise would not have a job. It was a ridiculous system which reeked of self-effacing bureaucracy but, typical of the government and specifically, the Drug Enforcement Administration.

The Diversion Department also fell under the supervision of Jackson. Their responsibility was to investigate pharmaceutical manufacturers, pharmacies, doctors and medical personnel. They monitored the ordering and distribution of pills and medications which were characterized as controlled substances. Basically, Diversion functioned as a watchdog unit for any entity which manufactured, prescribed or distributed regulated controlled substances as classified by federal law.

Some of the other entities under Jackson's purview were the Demand Reduction Unit which supported programs like drug abuse resistance education, more commonly known to kids throughout the United States as D.A.R.E. Also, the Technical Operations Department, which maintained and distributed any special equipment like mini-audio or video recorders for case use, also was part of Jackson's responsibility.

Jackson's portfolio was massive and his groups performed a wide variety of important functions. In the hands of a competent ASAC, it was a significant responsibility. Under the charge of Jackson, the groups' performance was a disaster. My personal opinion of Quincy Jackson's decrepitude was confirmed when I heard he had shot himself in the foot during a surveillance in the late 70's. He had been considered a loose cannon before the incident but, after that episode, someone had the foresight to get him off the street and into an administrative position before he killed himself, an agent or an innocent victim. Remarkably, the derelict shooting turned into a fantastic career move, as Jackson's total incompetence limited positions in which he could be placed which required any degree of intelligence. When the position of ASAC of Support was vacated, Jackson became a superb choice. Jackson was quickly inserted into the post and immediately took full advantage. He generally could be found in the office no more than six hours a day. As a GS-15 with cost of living (COLA) and overtime allowances, (AUO) Jackson was grossing a salary in the low six figures. It was an extremely comfortable salary for a man who did very little to contribute to the success of the war on drugs. However, I also had learned after he had shot himself in the foot, he brazenly sued the Department of Justice for liability. In a settlement eventually reached out of court, he was paid a tax-free lump sum of $25,000 for disability which included compensation for the partial loss of feeling in his foot, incurred as a result of his own idiocy. Consequently, it became a running joke in our office when someone committed a stupid act and had gotten away with it without repercussion, co-workers would remark the individual "pulled a Jackson." As an affirmation of the joke, the person inevitably received a xeroxed copy of the silhouette of a man sitting at his desk pointing a revolver at his own bare foot.

My ASAC, John Caravan, was responsible for all activities conducted by the regular enforcement groups in the Chicago area. There were six groups functioning in Chicago, each designated with a particular area of expertise. Each group was directed to interdict specific drugs and target individuals distributing those drugs. Group 1 worked marijuana and hashish cases. Group 2, clandestine laboratories where the primary violators were white motorcycle gangs and PCP manufacturers, who were often satellites or factions of inner city street gangs. Group 3 investigated heroin traffickers comprised of a wide variety of violators which included Southeast Asians, Nigerians, Middle Easterners and Mexicans. The last 3 groups, of which I was assigned in Group 5, were responsible for cocaine investigations. It was possible for agents in other groups to investigate cases involving substances outside their squad's primary responsibility but, when doing so, they tread on sensitive ground. The cocaine groups enjoyed the advantage of working offenders of any ethnicity because coke dealers came in all flavors where as certain drugs like brown heroin, were the purview of Mexican dealers exclusively. Having such freedom greatly improved the possibilities of case development. I was happy to work in one of the cocaine enforcement groups but, I was disappointed with developments I observed among some of the other agents who I occasionally found attempting to steal, obstruct or impede investigations which targeted common violators. It led to extensive problems especially when it was discovered some of these very agents were hiding information and at times, even divulging sensitive investigative information to informants in order to protect their own cases. Consequently, there existed not only competition amongst rival federal agencies and between federal, state and local agencies but, also amongst DEA agents working in the same office, sometimes even in the same group.

Group 5 was supervised by Bobby Hayes, a reserved and intelligent man of African American descent who had made his bones as an undercover agent. He spent six years with the Gary, Indiana Police Department, starting out as patrol officer in 1968. An astute supervisor recognized Hayes' great potential as a narcotics officer and Hayes was transferred to the vice unit after only one year on street patrol. It was a rapid promotion but, any thoughts fellow officers possessed about Hayes promotion being unwarranted were dashed within one week of his acceptance of the promotion. Hayes was a friendly but very modest man and did not divulge many details of his career however, others who had known and worked with him during his Gary PD days, revealed Hayes was forced to kill a man who attempted to rob him on only his second undercover deal. What was remarkable about the incident was we were told the bad guy fired two shots into Hayes' car seat before Hayes, who had been unarmed, wrestled the weapon's muzzle toward the attacker and fired two rounds into him. The assailant died at the scene. It was a story I never heard Hayes repeat, a display of modest temperance which made me respect him more. Some veteran Agents, particularly supervisors, eagerly recounted violent incidents in their careers and with each telling of the story their exploits would grow more impressive. The tales of a suspect being killed seemed to be favorites among many of both the tellers and the listeners but, Hayes never recounted the affair for my ears or anyone else's in my Group. I had also learned the individual had not been the only one Hayes had killed during his career and there had been, in fact, two others as well. I wasn't as enamored with the fact Hayes had killed three people as were some of my fellow agents. Shooting someone wasn't an act I considered heroic but, I had no doubt Hayes had done it each time only as an act of self-preservation and would have chosen any other alternative had it been available to him. I respected Bobby Hayes for that quality as well as many others.

Hayes spent six years working for the Gary Police Department, five of it as a member of the DEA Task Force working in joint cooperation with the Indiana State Police. Hayes did such a fine job with the Narcotics Unit, he was asked by the DEA to consider becoming an Agent. I was told he had never even filed an application but, as soon as he decided, he was placed right into a DEA Basic Training Class. Hayes spent the bulk of his career in New York City where he developed some legendary drug cases. Hayes was hit once in the right thigh in a shootout which left two policemen dead. Again, all of this information was relayed to me from other people who had known Hayes throughout his career.

I had known Hayes for two years, meeting him when he had been transferred from St. Louis to finish his career as the supervisor of my group. Initially he had been difficult to speak too. I assumed he wasn't impressed with any of the Agents under his charge given the considerable exploits of his own career and the uninteresting ones of ours. I ignorantly assumed since he was a black man he would extend more consideration to fellow black agents working for him. Consequently, I didn't make much of an effort to get to know him during his first few weeks. In retrospect, I suppose, I was intimidated by him and his feats as well as prejudiced by my own ignorance.

Early into his tenure as my supervisor, he called me into his office and I could tell by the tone of his inflection, he was not happy. Prior to that day, there had been no conflicts with anyone in his group. Others recognized I must have done something wrong, when all heads raised after the announcement, "Connor, get in here."

I hadn't been in the building for most of the day and in fact, had just come in and sat at my desk. I didn't feel most people even realized I had entered the room, let alone Hayes, whose separate office entrance offered no view of my desk. It was as if Hayes sensed I was there, or had simply assumed I better have been. I rose from my desk and shrugged my shoulders as Chad Jennings, my partner. asked, "What did you do?"

Again, I threw my hands up indicating oblivion as some of the other agents seated at desks, watched me. I proceeded toward the office sensing everyone's silence behind me as I walked through the portal of Hayes' office.

"Close the door, Connor." I didn't bother to correct him about the fact my name actually ended in an "s." He had been calling me "Connor" since his first day. As I followed his direction and closed the door I thought briefly about the disappointment my group mates would have if they couldn't hear Hayes berate me. "You submitted this 202 for Simeon Reed, right."

The DEA-202 was an obligatory personal identification form we filled out with information about people we arrested. It was a standard DEA form and I had typed it two days after processing Reed for delivery of a kilogram and a half of cocaine.

"Yes, sir."

"And you filled it out correctly, Connor?"

I was sure I had, the form was very simple and required basic information like name, age, date of birth and so on. I believed I couldn't have screwed a simple form like the 202 up unless Reed had supplied false information or identification. With great hesitation, I responded to his question.

"I think I filled it out right."

"You think." Hayes. said, pronouncing "think" with emphasis like a question rather than a remark. "This section, eight…race, you see that." He handed me the one page form pointing at the section.

"Yes."

"That section labeled race, what you got in there?"

I looked at the form. "African-American," I said.

"What color is Mr. Simeon Reed?" Hayes asked, quizzically.

I felt the answer was obvious but, I couldn't figure out his line of questioning so, I furled my eyebrows and did not respond.

"Connor, what color am I?"

My first thought was Hayes was some kind of race-bater and he was trying to trap me into saying something offensive.

Hayes held up his right hand, with the back of it facing me. "Connor, are you too unobservant to know I'm a black man."

"No."

"And what color is the back of Reed's hand, is it black too?"

I scrambled, "Yes, sir, he…well, of course it is."

"Then what the fuck you got African-American in there for. Do I look like some African to you. What, do I got trinkets and robes on?"

Confused but certain Hayes was in a suit, I responded "No."

"Then what you go calling me an African for?'"

I couldn't tell if Hayes was being sarcastic or was asking a legitimate question.

"Its the correct term, I thought, Mr. Hayes. That's what I have been using to describe black people since I came on board."

Hayes extended his arm and gestured behind me. "Open that door."

I rose and opened the door and began to walk out.

"Where you going, Connor? Sit back down." He sighed then announced, "McKey, get in here."

Rasheed McKey was another black agent who worked in the group. He came in quickly and I assumed his swiftness in entering was facilitated by the proximity with which he had been to the door when summoned. His efforts to hear what I was being railed at only succeeded in having himself drafted into the fray. Hayes' uncanny ability to sense things and situations would be something I would observe several other times during my career. McKey walked in but, did not sit.

"McKey, when you fill out these 202's what do you put in section eight, when you arrest a brother?"

McKey looked at the 202 which I had been holding. "African American, boss."

"Alright, McKey." He motioned for McKey to leave which he gladly and eagerly did.

"I guess you're right, Connors." Hayes returned to the proper pronunciation of my name indicating to me he had known how to pronounce it all along. "I'm done, you have any questions?"

"No, Mr. Hayes." I rose to leave, completely and utterly perplexed.

"Everybody's so God-damned politically correct around here." Hayes offered. "Seems like nobody enjoys working." I turned back toward him as he addressed me again. "Connors, do you like your work?"

I stopped before passing through the door.

"Yes, Mr. Hayes."

"My name is Bobby. Mr. Hayes is my father. OK Connors." He smiled and added, "loosen up a little, kid, you're making me nervous."

٭

There were eleven agents in Group 5, including me. My senior partner was Chad Jennings, a 6'4" WASP from Auburn Hills, Michigan. He had graduated from Eastern Michigan University on a baseball scholarship. His father was a Secret Service Agent and I suspected he had helped Jennings obtain his position with the DEA. I was confused why Jennings had never attempted to join the Service but, I suspected the relationship he had with his father had not been a close one. Jennings was three years older than me and initially reaped satisfaction introducing me as his "Junior Agent." There was no such phrase in the DEA's vocabulary but, that didn't prevent Jennings from using the term often, until after several weeks of having listened to it, I told him the moniker made me feel like a child. Jennings apologized and our mutual enjoyment of sports created a commonality with which we could build a working and friendly relationship. Jennings didn't work exceptionally hard but, had a charming way of relating to people when he wanted too. He also had a keen ability to patronize people who could help promote his career, an ambition with which he correlated every move. In the process, he often disregarded those who couldn't oblige his ambitions, behavior which insulted co-workers who misunderstood his self-confidence and associated his aloofness with arrogance.

We had been partners for about one and a half years when Hayes joined our group as its supervisor. Jennings and I had made some interesting cases but, none that were particularly noteworthy. We both preferred to work white coke dealers in Chicago's Western Suburbs. We made these suspects our targets because we both agreed white informants were easily controlled and usually did what they were told. It was also conducive to concentrate on investigations whose subjects were closer to where we lived and both of us resided in the sprawling suburbs west of the city. I lived in a one bedroom apartment in Westmont, a quaint community about fifteen miles southwest of our Loop offices. Jennings lived in Naperville, a town I had once heard described as Closed-mindedness, U.S.A. but, a place I liked. He had been married for approximately 3 months and I noticed his efforts and productivity had been steadily decreasing since his wedding. Jennings, having been an agent for close to six years, was eyeing other positions with the Agency and was actively pursuing a transfer to the Office of Training in Quantico. Each passing day the promotion failed to materialize prompted Jennings to become more aggravated and less inclined to work. His career temporarily stalled, he became content to allow me to conduct most of the investigative and administrative work and initiate and develop cases as I saw fit. I didn't mind the arrangement because it gave me the freedom to work the cases which interested me. I hoped our new association with Hayes would not impair our techniques but, I was also optimistic I would procure more recognition for the efforts I was putting into cases and their development. Jennings had been quick to report successes to our group's previous Supervisor, Stan Demeter, and often reaped the recognition and accolades from the front office, some of which were probably due me.

Jennings and I were the only two man team in our Group. There were three other teams, each consisting of three agents. Desmond Brokenborough was the senior agent of a three team unit that consisted of Brian Sullivan, my closest friend in the Agency, and Sandy Foster. Sullivan was my age and was also from the East Coast. We often assisted each other on our respective cases and enjoyed getting together outside of work to go to ball games and have a few beers. Their third partner, Sandy Foster, was a friendly person, played a mean piano and was a marathon runner. Unfortunately, she was not much of an agent. She came from a small town in Western Illinois and seemed to be very naive about the mean streets of Chicago. We all looked out for Foster and favored her whenever possible, particularly when she had a gun in her hand. She could shoot well enough on the firing range but, we were leery of the judgment she had exercised in real street situations. One time we had conducted a raid on a house and an individual who we confronted on the porch of the home had been left in the sole custody of Foster. We entered the house and in our haste to secure the premises no one had handcuffed the suspect. When the guy realized he was alone with Foster, who he outweighed by more than one hundred pounds, he simply pushed her across the wooden porch, fled down the steps and up the street. In recounting the episode, Foster stated she warned the perpetrator she would shoot him if he continued running. Foster said the guy replied, "Go ahead, shoot bitch!" Foster responded by firing two rounds, both of which fortunately struck a wooden support beam only three feet in front of her. Though I might have done the same thing if I had been called a bitch, Foster had acted recklessly and had no grounds for shooting at the unarmed fleeing suspect. We managed to quell the episode before anything was reported. Our deferment nullified the need for an internal investigation which certainly would have resulted in disciplinary action against Foster. Fearing reprisals, we never sought the individual who had fled.

Brenda Xavier led another team. Xavier was the senior agent in our group, having spent nine years as an agent, six of those in the Chicago Field Division. Xavier was an intelligent and driven agent but, she had no qualms about offering her opinion and advice, even when it was not requested. Xavier was always seeking the opportunity to enhance her career and acted as the back up supervisor when Hayes was away or out of the office. She was the type of person who delighted a position of authority and would occasionally abuse her temporary powers. Personally, I liked her but, professionally I would never trust her. She especially was fond of ordering around her two less tenured agents, Phil Vreeswyck and Carlos Perez. Both Vreeswyck and Perez had been on the job a year or so less than me but, both were a few years older. They were nice guys and dedicated agents. Perez was an ex-Chicago Cop and Vreeswyck a former Marine who served at diplomatic posts as an embassy guard around the world.

Our fourth team was led by Jim Walker, an egotistical man who I had avoided earlier in my career. I found him to be a conceited and self righteous bore who relished the power and authority of a gun and a badge. He was an individual who loved to intimidate people. I thought his unenlightened views made him a dangerous agent. He regularly carried two guns on his person, even in the secure environment of our office. On raids I often saw him in possession of three guns, two of which were on belt holsters and a third tucked under a pant leg on an ankle holster. He also occasionally carried retractable batons, maces and pepper sprays, a variety of knives and any other weapons he could get his hands on. His favorite magazines were violent rags like Soldier of Fortune and far-fetched crap like True Detective. He mail-ordered all kinds of gadgets and once even purchased a blow gun through a special foreign mail order catalog. As a Christmas Pollyanna gift, he gave me a 5 ½" serrated, stainless-steel knife with a pearl inlay which I convinced myself to be a thoughtful gesture from an otherwise barbarous man.

Walker had been a DEA Agent for seven years and openly expressed one of his career goals was to survive a gun battle, preferably on a crowded street so his exploits could be witnessed by members of the public. He once confided in me he hoped if he were to die young, he wanted it to be on the job so that his name would be emblazoned on the DEA Memorial to those killed in the line of duty. Scary.

Walker tutored two agents under him, Bernard Sharkey and Rasheed McKey. McKey was a native Chicagoan, having been reared in Chicago's tough south side suburbs. McKey was a former Harvey, Illinois policemen who was more interested in the paychecks and the ladies he had on the side than federal law enforcement. He had been an officer for close to five years when he joined the DEA. After graduating from the DEA Academy, the appeal of investigating and arresting the nefarious had dissipated. McKey was more interested in the respected status he acquired as a federal agent. He enjoyed the additional income the job included and spent large portions of it on the girlfriends he maintained, all of whom were unknown to his wife. Sharkey, only a year on, constantly reminded people his name was Bernard which only resulted in the nickname Barney sticking to him from the first day he protested the unwanted moniker. He had graduated from a small community college with a degree in Physical Education. At that time his aspirations had been to become a phys-ed teacher. Apparently that goal had been derailed for reasons unknown and he obtained a position with the Illinois Department of Highways as a toll booth collector.

There are many toll roads in the Chicagoland area. Consequently, as law enforcement officers who frequently use the roads, federal agents are supplied passes with which they are permitted free access to pass through tolls without paying for them. Apparently, Sharkey accepted many of these passes from one of our veteran agents as he traveled to and from work each day. One day, Sharkey struck up a conversation with the agent at a toll booth during congested traffic caused by an accident. Out of that encounter grew some kind of social relationship during which time the agent utilized some favors and positioned Sharkey for an interview. Remarkably, Sharkey was accepted into the DEA Academy without any education or experience pertaining to criminal law or procedure. Though my experience had certainly been limited, at least I possessed a degree in Criminal Justice from an accredited University.

The peculiar thing about the affair is that the agent who was instrumental in getting Sharkey on board was eventually placed on permanent disability for mental disorders relating to paranoia and schizophrenia. He confided in a former wife he was headed to Washington D.C. to "meet the President." His former paramour called the Secret Service who picked him up at BWI Airport waiting for his luggage which contained his DEA issued sub-machine gun and a half dozen boxes of ammunition. Last I heard, the former agent was in the landscaping business, living comfortably on a disability plan which pays him 75% of his last yearly salary, $62,000, until he reached retirement age. Given the profitability of his diagnosis, I had often wondered just how crazy he actually was.

Sharkey was intelligent enough to understand Walker's abrasive style would never help advance his career. Unfortunately, Sharkey failed to develop his own technique of developing investigations. He started with several good cases and then without explanation, had started to slack. I attributed his languor to his unhappiness with slow promotions and a general resentment of Walker's perceived superiority. Walker, Sharkey and McKey did not work well together and did not seem to enjoy each other's company. There was no cooperation on either's part and their cumulative work productivity would be something I suspected Hayes would eventually be forced to address.

6

Most people who didn't know me well were surprised when I informed them I was employed as an Agent of the Drug Enforcement Administration. Almost all of them initially did not believe me either. They expected to see someone who matched their notion of a narcotics agent based on what they had seen on movies and television. A smooth talking slickster with a polished rap, flashy clothes and a ½ carat diamond stud post embedded in the left ear. That stereotypical image, or the other common one of a pony-tailed, fu-manchued biker with scraggly denim clothes and dark sunglasses. Undeniably, there existed agents who deliberately coiffured themselves in this manner in an attempt to mirror a character they had seen on some overblown film drama however, their decision to dress that way was a personal choice that had little effect on their ability to successfully perform the job. Those few agents who paraded around the office with earrings and sunglasses were generally regarded as people who had become consumed in a misguided belief they had to look that way to outwit seasoned dealers. I believe about half of the agents who adopted this philosophy were considered successful. The vast majority of us resembled people one would find in any typical work-place environment. They were unassuming and natural people who looked more like accountants, salespeople and technical programmers and, in actuality, the same type of people who were making a tremendous amount of money selling drugs. Most of the younger agents were recently married and starting families. The older ones reflected the demographics of their generation with some divorced while others struggled to finance children through high school and college. Many of the agents, old and young, were athletically inclined and most generally lived wholesome and clean lives. They were men and women raised in hard-working, honorable middle-class families. They were educated, bright people with strong wills and clear visions. The agents I came to know and work with were decent and often dedicated, most to the mission of the DEA but, all dedicated at least, to something. Most exhibited an inner fortitude, an ability to set goals and achieve them. It was a trait I admired and as a member of the DEA organization, I hoped to manifest. The majority of agents fostered and clung to a virtuous principle that they offered a valuable service to the community and the nation. It was a noble endeavor to slow the plague of drugs and it was a commitment I adopted as well.

I realized early in my career, revealing yourself to be a DEA Agent often elicited a response of some kind. If I were to tell someone I was an architect or a banker, a stranger might be inclined to express an interest or share a related story about the profession. They might mention they knew someone who did similar work. A person would not usually risk being considered rude or impolite and offer an opinion about the validity of someone else's career. However, I encountered opinions anytime I told someone what I did for a living. Generally, the response was favorable but, occasionally it was not. Drugs and their use was, and has been, a debated topic in America for several decades. The safety and legalization of drugs evokes passionate convictions from those who are both pro and con. The people and groups who support and use drugs themselves often feel prosecuted both figuratively and sometimes literally by the government for participating in something they feel produces harmless consequences. They believe narcotics interdiction is nothing more than a government plot against its own people. On the other hand, people who vehemently oppose drugs often have their own agenda to promote, usually basing their stance on religious or moral issues. There also exist individuals who have spent parts and sometimes most of their lives abusing drugs. When they appear in public crusading against its use, I feel their motives are little more than self-serving. I always believed it was particularly dangerous when popular figures like athletes, musicians and actors promote themselves as people who have tried drugs and experienced its perils first hand. I can't think of anything more effectually damaging to a young person than being told that his hero, a person he or she has admired and been inspired by accomplished some of their wondrous feats under the influence of drugs or alcohol. Sadly, there doesn't seem to exist a celebrity interview any more in which the subject fails to admit to the use of drugs. These cavalcades of celebrities are barraging our young people with the idea drugs won't really hurt in the long run and it is a terrible message to send to the future sustainers of our country.

The nature of my job promoted controversy and though some did not, most people were unable to resist making some comment on drugs and my position when informed. I had an opinion about drugs too and, of course, it was influenced by my job. I would have been a hypocrite, employed as a DEA Agent, if I condoned drug use and supported its legalization. I did not but, even after I had been an agent enforcing controlled substance laws for over three years, I didn't think its use should be considered a serious criminal act. However, I did detest the individuals who profited from its distribution. If people could understand how profitable drug dealing was, I believe, even some users themselves would give up the drugs, just out of stubborn jealousy. Despite the occasional bulk seizures sporadically chronicled on the evening news most people don't comprehend the hundreds of millions of dollars in income drugs generate in the United States. A great portion of that money ultimately is filtered out of the country, enriching foreign nationals who are reaping huge profits while their products pollute the most vulnerable citizens of the United States, particularly its poor, diseased and crime-addled. If those were the only people suffering at the hands of drug traffickers, America could probably maintain its position as one of the greatest countries in the history of civilization. However, as drugs have seeped across the classes, infiltrating the mass work force while tantalizing and contaminating the fertile minds who hold the keys to the nation's future, our society undeniably has begun to exhibit the severe ramifications. Its a fact most crime in America is directly attributable to drugs. In desperate response, our republic has reacted by demanding politicians introduce and enact laws which call for the swift and certain punishment of drug dealers. The plain truth is the peddlers are far from the only individuals benefiting from the bane of chemicals being bought and sold from urban ghetto corners to the corporate offices of executive America. There exist hundreds of "legitimate" enterprises which cater to the narcotics business and indirectly reap income and mass fortune from it. The individuals and executives of these organizations have elected to turn a blind eye to the means as long as the end is profitable. For example, respected lawyers who fight prodigiously in local, state and federal courts for their recidivist drug dealing client's freedoms solely for the purposes of collecting gigantic and lucrative retainers and then ridiculously justifying and veiling their motives by claiming their representation ensures justice for the wrongly and indiscriminately persecuted. The attorneys stand in a long line which includes automobile dealers and real estate brokers, bankers, financiers, tax-prepares and accountants eagerly finagling rules and regulations which control misapplication of revenues and funds so they can protect and launder illegally obtained monies, all in order to garner their ridiculous commissions. Communications companies have exploded with paging and cellular services which have facilitated and catered to the clandestine world of drug trafficking, especially in poorer, drug infested neighborhoods. These companies have openly flaunted their pursuits contracting much of their business to small, private corner-store operations which provide discreet, unidentifiable services which ultimately filter millions in revenue back to the mega-conglomerate communication companies who continue to mass produce better services and more sophisticated equipment. There even exist subtle attempts to capitalize on the narcotics trade by small ventures like pharmacies who often quadruple the prices of inexpensive products like Vitamin B and Inositol, common adulterants used to dilute cocaine. Hardware stores and supermarkets operating on the outskirts of well known drug dealing neighborhoods actively stock exorbitantly priced pots and pans and an odd but, wide variety of metal and plastic strainers which are used solely for the convenient manufacture of crack cocaine. All of these enterprises and countless others, furtively and quite happily, profiting from the drug trade.

Law enforcement organizations themselves are as guilty as any profit seeking company. They have opted to chase the cash cow conceived by the drug trade. There is certainly a large contingent of federal, state and local agencies who openly promote and demand narcotics investigations for the exclusive purpose of seizing cash and related assets to supplement their budgets. Homicide, rape, robbery and other violent crimes do not yield seizures when suspects are investigated or even apprehended and as a result, there has been a sad decrease in the focus of agencies supplying manpower to solve these types of crimes. Instead, enforcement administrators have ignited a mad rush to capitalize on the trend of enriching budgets through broadly worded seizure laws designed to grant law enforcement agencies the sweeping authority to seize cash and assets for the benefit of their department's cash journals.

*

With my appointment to the DEA, I noticed some of my longtime friends began to drift away from me. Some of them continued to use drugs and I supposed they were uncomfortable sustaining a relationship with me. I hoped they wouldn't think I would ever arrest them for smoking a joint or snorting a line. The DEA didn't imprison people for personal use quantities anyway but, to anyone who uses drugs, a DEA Agent is as welcome as a burrito fart in a stalled elevator. Just the same, I could no longer be around drugs and I was forced to sidestep places where people openly used it. What surprised me was to lose friends who I had not suspected had anything to do with drugs. Later, I was to discover some were involved in reaping the profits of distribution. I learned some were small-time dealers themselves or, as their own careers advanced, were people who indirectly profited from the sale of drugs. They turned out to be the same car dealers, real estate people and lawyers. As my career progressed, I hesitated to let anyone who didn't already know I was an agent find out.

Consequently, though I was very proud to be a DEA Agent, I learned it was much easier to lie to people about my job. To avoid disparaging remarks about my profession or the need to explain or recount episodes during arrests or raids, I assumed the role of a copy machine repairman. Nobody ever expressed an interest in that position. Sometimes to amuse myself, I would claim I was a flaming barrel jumper in the Ice Capades. I formulated a whole story about it and I actually found strangers presumed it more plausible than employment as a DEA Agent.

It was difficult to proceed through life without people knowing what I did for work. Casual girlfriends, neighbors, the dry cleaner, the grocer, the mechanic, people you get to know on a social basis ordinarily want to know about superficial things and one of the most basic items discussed is your livelihood. It's a natural progression. As an amicable and proud person I found it extremely difficulty to lie about myself. But, I did. There were some agents who didn't want anyone to know about their position and found lying to be a convenient method to not only disguise their employment but, an essential technique to insure their safety. Seeking retribution, the Cali, Columbia Cocaine Cartel had placed a million dollar bounty on the head of any DEA Agent after they had lost a series of very valuable cocaine shipments in the late 80's. A few agents in our office considered this threat seriously. They took circuitous routes to and from work, installed high tech and expensive security systems in their homes and would occasionally double back during lunch to see if anyone was following them. I viewed these measures as overly cautious and bordering on the absurd. All a potential assassin had to do was find our address in the white pages, come to our offices in the Dirksen Federal Building, take a public stairwell to the fifth floor and wait in the lobby. There, the assailant could easily identify any number of DEA Agents who walked in and out through the main, clearly labeled, double-glass doors. From there, an agent could easily be followed covertly to our public parking garages, the public cafeteria or across the street to our physical fitness center in the basement of another federal building. It would not have been difficult to take one or any number of us out. Regardless of the ease with which it could be carried out by even an inept killer let alone a hired professional, a few agents haughtily believed they were earmarked for assassination and lived their lives accordingly.

Either way, I hated pretending I was someone else. It was not conducive to building strong relationships, either with friends or romantic interests and consequently, I ended up socializing with people with whom I worked. Some became close friends but, unfortunately, I failed establishing many relationships which were not law enforcement related. The people I did meet outside of work often were intrigued to discover the truth about my job if I elected to disclose it. There were occasions, many occasions actually, the work was dangerous and people were anxious to hear me relate the details of an incident which had occurred. When discussing those events, I always left out the paperwork chores which were required at least a couple days a week. Everything we did had to be documented on some type of triplicated government form and there were times the bureaucratic requirements overwhelmed me and made the work almost unbearable. If the information was case related, it was categorized on a DEA-6, a report summarizing activities related to an investigation. I was required to write DEA-6's when I was involved in any type of enforcement action like an interview, an arrest, a surveillance or the service of a warrant. Some agents wrote 6's on virtually anything even though the reports were only necessary for enforcement related activity. Submitting excessive reports was done to accomplish one goal, pad a case file. I found it to be an amazing fact that some agents had case files three to five inches thick but, had made no arrests or seizures. On one occasion, while researching a case, I found a DEA-6 consisting of a wordy, three paged report about an agent who had received an obscene phone call at work.

If our paperwork load had centered only on investigative related efforts, I would have been content. Unfortunately, that was not the case. A government form requiring documentation of some kind was required for everything that was attempted or accomplished. If one wanted to change the oil on the government car, a DEA-349a was required. If a "AA" battery for the pager you were issued died, you needed to fill out a DEA-12 for a new one. Your bi-monthly case summaries went on a DEA-352. Expenses went on a DEA-39. Approval for the use of recording devices, a DEA-52. A request to pay an informant, a DEA-15, a signature proving payment of the funds, a DEA-103. There was even a form which was used to request more replacement forms. There existed an administrative form for virtually every undertaking. The dockets all required at least two and sometimes three signatures for complete approval. If one of the persons whose signature was required was unavailable, the task could not be completed or the item requested could not be furnished. These records and the protocol by which they had to be completed utterly frustrated me. The bureaucratic requirements hindered my efforts to do what I really enjoyed, the enforcement action. I loved to conduct surveillances, watching people and following them. Arrests and particularly the buy-bust deals were my favorites.

Snatching people off the street and arresting them in the middle of a drug deal was exhilarating. I especially was fond of serving search warrants too. Pre-dawn raids on the residences of unsuspecting drug dealers was exciting and fascinating. To be permitted by law to surreptitiously sneak up to someone's front door under the cover of darkness, infiltrate the residence by crashing through the entrance, all the while tossing people and property to the floor and, in the process, granted the authority to kill anyone who might be a physical threat to your life is an awesome responsibility, and great fun !

By conducting raids in early morning hours just before dawn, we judiciously insured a safe raid and usually the arrest of a deep-sleeping suspect. Many of our targets savored lifestyles which usually precluded them from getting to sleep before two or three o'clock in the morning. They often slept until well past noon. The greatest challenge facing us when we intended to arrest someone was not engaging them in violence but rather predicting which night the suspect would elect to sleep in his own home. I use the term "he" because we would rarely aggressively raid a female target's house. Successful female dealers were plentiful but homes where women resided usually included juveniles and there existed no need to alarm or endanger children's safety during these chaotic invasions.

We usually "hit" places after having a cup of coffee and yes, even a donut at a pre-determined meet location. If we were scheduling a raid at about six a.m. we would often meet at a central location about one to two hours before the anticipated activity. There, we would formulate our plans, delegate supplemental responsibilities such as evidence collector, photographer, prisoner transport, and any additional assignments we were required to fulfill. Someone always brought a thermos of coffee and a box or two of a dozen donuts to the assembly and the contribution was always appreciated. It was a habitual routine and one we followed before every activity including the morning when we served a search and arrest warrant on Steve Williams known on the streets of Chicago's South Side as Stevie the Pip or simply The Pip.

The Pip lived in a custom-built $235,000 mason constructed split-level in Country Club Hills, Illinois. The town, a southwest suburb of Chicago, had gained a reputation among federal investigators as a haven for young, black, successful dope dealers. The location of the town afforded the traffickers the security of a small community and an unacquainted and undermanned police force to investigate them. This was facilitated by the convenience of a short thirty minute commute to their "hoods" where they pedaled their product, established connections and engaged in social games of poker, dominos and craps. While the dealers relaxed playing entertaining street games, their workers raked in huge amounts of cash selling drugs ranging from marijuana to cocaine and heroin.

Pip was doing very well for a twenty-five year old man who had failed to earn a high school diploma and only filed two tax returns in his life. The Pip, whose self-reported accumulated income for those two years was a meager $19,451 was the proud owner of a black Chevrolet Blazer, a hunter green Mercedes 525 with rag top and the beautiful house on a quiet street in Country Club Hills. The home had four bedrooms, two and a half baths, a floor to ceiling stone fireplace and a large eat-in kitchen. He had a fully furnished fitness room and a recreation room which included a regulation size oak framed pool table. Furthermore, an informant had divulged the Pip was considering opening a seafood restaurant but, had not yet found a desirable location or more importantly, an individual he trusted enough to manage it.

At 6:15 a.m. on a fall Thursday morning, the Pip had more pressing issues to contemplate.

The raid was executed without resistance. We found the Pip in his Italian lacquered king size bed with a naked and attractive twenty-one year old college student. I hadn't gotten a peak myself but incidental

Polaroid pictures left on a nightstand taken during an amorous interlude had afforded me an extended leisurely period to review her beauty.

I was designated as the evidence custodian for this particular raid.
My duty was to photograph evidence, detail where it was found, secure
exhibits and transport them back to the office for processing. Evidence
collected at raids typically included weapons, drugs, currency, jewelry,
financial records like bank statements and any papers, telephone
records and any other documents that would identify assets and associates in the drug business. It was the duty of all agents to find evidence,
including me, wherever it may exist in the house. When it was found, I
was alerted and specifically for this raid given the task of seizing it.

The Pip's home was lavishly furnished. He possessed superior electronic equipment including a 50" projection television equipped with a
digital satellite system, a laser disc player, a high fidelity stereo video
cassette recorder, a state of the art receiver and a complete sound
speaker system. He bragged the entire unit cost him $12,000, a sum we
estimated he was making in a day and a half. He obviously enjoyed it
while lounging on one of three imported Italian leather sofas which sat
within the circumference of the surround sound stereo system. Despite
his prodigious lifestyle, the Pip had a modest collection of $225 in
Department of Agriculture food coupons in a kitchen drawer.
Apparently, the Pip was not so proud that he would not allow Uncle
Sam to pay his grocery bill. I was always disturbed by such discoveries.
Disgustingly though, they were quite common. Dealers, despite their
staggering incomes, invariably relied on some form of public assistance
like welfare, disability or workman's compensation to supplement their
incomes, often relying on government subsidies because they were so
easily obtained.

We seized a gun, a 9mm Beretta, from his bedroom nightstand. It was
not loaded and the Pip wisely had made no attempt to retrieve it during
the raid. The gun served Pip as a showpiece. Its prominent display

exhorted others to respect his authority even though the Pip probably didn't even know how to fire or even load the weapon properly.

The Pip had no drugs at the residence. When asked if any drugs were at the house he emphatically replied, "This is where I lay my head, I don't keep none of that shit around here." He laughed out loud when one of the agents asked the Pip if he had any needles in the house. Most successful dealers in my experience did not indulge in their product. Most even despised dope users but tolerated them as a necessary nuisance to their business. I viewed the relationship much like professional athletes probably view their fans.

The Pip was also a bit of a jewelry connoisseur. He owned a diamond bracelet, a custom made gold ring which fit three fingers across with diamond studded letters spelling out P-I-P. He had a stylish, Girard Perregaux Ferrari Chronograph and a newly purchased two carat diamond ring which he had yet to bestow on a potential bride. All of these items were inventoried by me and taken to the office in the company of Pip whose rude incarceration had reduced him to just being Steve Williams again. The subject of a lengthy DEA probe which identified Williams as a conspirator in a multi-state cocaine distribution ring, the Pip was transformed from Country Club Hills playboy to a federal prison inmate all by the stroke of a judge's pen and the dedicated work of a couple of my fellow agents.

The evidence was eventually processed back at the office. The pieces were surveyed by a jeweler who was contracted by the Department of Justice to appraise all seized jewelry. The Pip's collection was valued at $24,500. When I considered Williams was on public assistance, lived the life of luxury, hardly paid any taxes on his vast income, sold dope for a living and sported very expensive and some of it very gaudy jewelry, I felt considerably better about having permanently borrowed one of his trinkets. I had been an agent for three and a half years and had not engaged in any criminal activity but, this digression had been my second episode of dishonesty in two months.

Nobody was in the room when I came across the stylish Movado, a diamond bezeled wristwatch. I had found it on a second sweep of the master bedroom. We usually conducted multiple inspections of a location in the event someone missed evidence through carelessness or mistake. I found the watch amongst some pocket change, underwear, socks and house keys. It was nice. As soon as I saw it I knew it was a select piece and it annoyed me that it was left so carelessly among many worthless and trivial items. I immediately considered taking it.

Going through the house a second time, I was jealous of Steve Williams. He was living the good life. He had everything a man of twenty-five or even a retired man of sixty-five might want with the exception of a little fishing and leisure boat. I was filled with covetousness. Williams even had a collection of beautiful young ladies ceremoniously showcased in assorted photographs left scattered all over his house. Snapshots of the Pip mugging in the Bahamas and embracing two tanned and bikini-clad girls in a picture labeled "Barbados '90." He had brand new clothes and at least sixty pairs of neatly kept shoes including leather boots, loafers plus three pairs of Air Jordan basketball shoes which I knew to be priced at more than a $150 a piece.

I looked around his place and figured working the rest of my life I would be lucky to acquire such a nice home with a wardrobe of stylish and expensive clothes. I took a quick inventory of my possessions which included a modest apartment decorated with press-board furniture, a used domestic car and a generic old stereo given to me as a high school graduation present. Reviewing my holdings and comparing it against the Pip's, I realized I didn't own shit but, at least, I would own one of his watches.

I placed the extravagant timepiece in my right front pants pocket for a few minutes. I began to feel paranoid someone might notice its round indentation against my thigh. I also wondered what might happen if

Williams decided to make an issue of his jewelry and demand a receipt for his property. It was customary for the DEA to issue a receipt for any and all seized property, a DEA-75.

I decided it would be wise to return to my car and put the watch there. I told a few agents I was going out to my vehicle to place my raid jacket and some other equipment in the trunk. There was no need to but, I just made sure I told somebody. My mind raced with thoughts of being discovered. A sting, a trap set by zealous agents of the FBI to ensnare a dirty federal drug agent. I knew this concept was ridiculous. It was our case and no one but the agents who had investigated it knew we were going to be at Pip's home that morning.

I placed the watch in my glove compartment and instead of feeling apprehensive, I felt a sense of agreeable comfort. I did not mislead myself to believe I was completely justified in stealing the watch. I knew I was not. However, I felt like I had taken something back, a small trophy for myself that symbolized to me, a good law-abiding citizen who tried to live by the golden rule would still prosper over the conniving dope peddler. It was a convenient rationalization for a thoroughly dishonest act.

7

Work progressed routinely over the course of the next couple of months. During that time our enforcement group had conducted numerous arrests and seizures, averaging about three apprehensions per week. Two of the most recent cases Jennings and I had put together included the arrest of a white guy who had used his girlfriend to deliver a kilogram and a half of coke to an informant. Upon arrest, both immediately expressed an interest in cooperating. Unfortunately for the female the only drug dealer she knew was her boyfriend. Unable to set anyone else up, she plead guilty and prayed for the mercy of the court. Her lover knew considerably more dopers as he had been functioning as a multi-kilo dealer for six months prior to his arrest. He immediately began working as a defendant informant and arranged for two deliveries from previous sources while out on bail. Though he was obviously the experienced drug dealer, his cooperation led to a reduced sentence, even less than his estranged accomplice whose relationship he terminated shortly after his arrest. Both were looking at least a mandatory minimum sentence of five years. At twenty-seven and twenty-five respectively, neither the man or the woman would view their dope dealing adventures as having been worth it.

I had also garnered enough information to obtain a search warrant on an apartment where we seized three kilos of cocaine and two ounces of high grade black tar heroin, a potent opiate which bears a resemblance to caramel candy, only darker. It is primarily distributed by Nigerian traffickers. The suspect, a middle aged Pakistani, had not been home when we executed the search warrant and upon learning of it, had fled, perhaps home to his native country under an alias. He was considered a DEA fugitive. I also assisted several other cases within our group and I had made no active effort to steal anything since the watch. I was still very eager to do the job I was being paid to do and I still believed it was an incredible amount of fun, despite the bureaucracy and the corruption. On the street we were our own bosses. Bobby Hayes was not an overbearing supervisor who hovered over our heads threatening or imploring us to make cases. Hayes was satisfied as long as he felt each agent was extending his or her best effort trying to put dope on the table and people in jail. After I had given Hayes the opportunity, I found our relationship blossomed into a casual friendship as well as a professional association. I liked working for him and he reciprocated my respect by extending me latitude in the style and scope of my investigations.

I had invested about four weeks of work in the investigation of Nunzio Maldonado. I had been introduced to Maldonado by an informant who described Maldonado as a Hispanic dope dealer who was selling ounces and quarter kilos of coke. Maldonado was thirty and was officially unemployed, deriving all his income from dope sales. He was not living luxuriously by any means, owning an '85 Camaro while living on the second floor of a two-flat owned by his parents in a predominately Hispanic neighborhood. My impression of Maldonado was that he was a middle man who brokered deals between an insulated source of cocaine and established customers who needed product. With the help of my informant, I had convinced Maldonado I was a wealthy kid from Chicago's north suburbs who would pay top dollar for quality cocaine.

I met Maldonado for the first time in a parking lot of a busy hot dog and beef stand in Cicero, a small town southwest of Chicago where Al Capone used to call headquarters. The community had lost a considerable amount of its glamour since Capone and his gang had been unceremoniously removed by the Criminal Investigative Division of the IRS. The once popular suburb of Chicago had been transformed into a place for mostly low-income renters and transients. Its main intersection, at Cicero and Cermak, was saturated with hotels with orange doors and purple railings, meretricious colors which always seem to beckon truckers and johns.

The informant told Maldonado he knew a guy named Mark who was interested in an ounce. Wisely, Maldonado told the informant he didn't want to meet me and that if I wanted an ounce I should give the money directly to the informant, Danny, who would be delivered the ounce later. Ideally the DEA and any narcotics enforcement unit, attempts to utilize an undercover agent whenever possible whose goal is to negotiate directly with the suspect. Maldonado was prudent in his decision not to meet me but, I told Danny to tell him a story which led Maldonado to believe I didn't trust Danny with a large sum of money. Danny was an eccentric type and at that time, an unemployed bartender whose frequently strange behavior wouldn't make such a tale so unbelievable. If Maldonado was reasonable and particularly if he was greedy, he would understand. I instructed Danny to emphasize I had some money and Maldonado could make some big bucks off me because I was a spoiled guy who had a wealthy daddy. Enticed by the money, Maldonado finally agreed to meet.

In undercover roles, I relied on being myself. I did not feel acting like some two-bit movie character or worse, Tony Montana of Scarface fame, was a presentable facade to convince an experienced dope dealer I was a player. I knew traffickers came in all flavors including poor blacks, wealthy Asians, middle-class whites, Arabs, Latinos and so on. To ensnare Maldonado I would use the same technique which had been successful in the past. I assumed the role of Mark, an average guy with a little extra money who just wanted to buy some coke and turn a decent profit.

Maldonado arrived at the beef stand in his Camaro. There were two other surveillance vehicles watching me. I hadn't anticipated any trouble and I also did not foresee Nunzio Maldonado would sell me an ounce of coke that day. I expected him to initially feel me out and try to determine if I was a cop. After Maldonado parked, he walked up to the truck I was in, the Jeep. He entered as the informant moved to the back seat. Maldonado did not extend his hand to meet mine when I had offered it. He sat in the front seat and stared straight out the window. I noticed he was clean and well-groomed and sported a Chicago Black Hawks hockey jersey, an odd choice of clothing for a Hispanic unless he was affiliated with a gang. I was not aware of any groups whose colors were red and black but after considering his choice of outfits, I reasoned the cut of the jersey made it a perfect top to conceal a gun tucked in the waistband of his pants. He talked to the informant about me as if I wasn't there, speaking out of the side of his mouth while doing so.

"This guy alright ?"

"Yea." Danny replied.

"Where's he from ?" Maldonado asked.

I said "North." as the informant said "Chicago." I quickly added "Near the north side of Chicago but, really in the suburbs." Maldonado did not respond and instead scratched his chin and announced, "Something ain't right."

There was an anxious pause before Danny spoke up. "Nunz…you always say that! And every time everything is O.K. Look man, he needs an OZ.. and I thought you could give it to him. He has got some money and he needs it soon."

Maldonado continued to remain stoic, staring out the window while refusing to acknowledge me. "How much does he got ?"

"How much is an ounce ?" I asked but, there was no reply, at least one directed toward me.

"Danny, how much does he got ?" Maldonado ignored me and turned awkwardly around to his right, swiveling in his seat to address Danny.

"You said an "OZ" would be eleven hundred. That is what I told him to have ready." Danny said, confirming a price we had already agreed upon. I had recorded two previous phone calls between Danny and Nunzio and Maldonado had told the informant an ounce would be $1,100.00. The cost was high in Chicago at that time. If I was a budget-minded cocaine customer, I could probably find an ounce for $900 maybe $950 but, definitely cheaper than $1,100.00. For the initial buy I would pay the higher price. I intended to explain this to Maldonado but Maldonado rejected the possibility of any discussion with me.

"He got it with him ?" Maldonado asked.

I had received approval from Hayes to make the purchase but, I didn't expect Maldonado to ask for it. Foolishly, I had left the money with Chad Jennings and in my rush to pick up the informant and meet Maldonado, I had neglected to retrieve it. I offered a tentative excuse to Maldonado, "The money is close by."

Maldonado slowly turned to the left finally making an effort to acknowledge my presence. "Then why the fuck am I here ?"

Danny strategically interrupted, "You said you just wanted to meet him." Danny looked at me with a perplexed grimace, no doubt wondering why I said I didn't have the money when I had told him on the way out I had it. Still, Danny didn't give it away. "You said you wanted to meet him Nunz and we didn't know you wanted to do it today. You can't expect us to drive around here with eleven hundred bucks do you ?"

Nunzio Maldonado was silent. He looked straight ahead again. He gave me plenty of time to size him up. He was a macho Hispanic. I reasoned he had to be in charge of everything and I recognized by the derogatory manner in which he addressed Danny he didn't like or respect him. Consequently, I was certain he regarded me with even less approval. It was a perception I would be forced to change. He didn't have to like me but, I had to make him respect me. I thought quickly. I would play subservient to his ego but he wouldn't run roughshod over me. I would play the role of a whore but I would be a respected whore.

"Look, I can get the money real quick." I said cautiously. "Money is no issue with me, I got some money. But I don't have it right here. I don't know you like you don't know me and I wasn't going to bring money down here so you could rip me off !" I tried to play to Maldonado's ego to make him feel I was slightly afraid of him and it worked.

"If I wanted your money," he hesitated, "what's your name?"

"Mark."

"Mark" He wryly smiled, "I would have your money. I don't need to rip nobody off." He turned toward Danny, "Still, don't fuck around with me. If you were serious you would have the money. Danny, don't play games here, I don't have time to play fuckin' games."

I thought to myself this pastime is all Maldonado ever does. He plays this game every day, all day.

"I can get the money in thirty minutes." I told him. I could have gotten the money in two minutes if I walked across the street to Jennings' car and got it from him. The front of my car was facing Jennings who I noticed was stuffing his gaping mouth with one of the beef stand's lunch specials. Though he was as white-bred as a man could possibly be, he loved catfish sandwiches and the stand we were negotiating at specialized in them. I was thinking Jennings' position was too close and Maldonado was going to make him as a cop but, Maldonado did not.

"Meet me here in twenty-five minutes" Maldonado said. He wanted control so much he deliberately shaved off five minutes of my time. Though he had the dope and gave the directions, I knew by agreeing to make a concession and come back, already I was gradually assuming the control he desperately sought.

"No problem." I said.

Maldonado pulled the handle of the door. As he exited he turned to the informant, "Don't fuck me around Danny, you know me, you know what I can do." He left before Danny could respond. He got in his Camaro and drove away. There wasn't enough surveillance vehicles to follow him and I judged an attempt to shadow him might be premature so we allowed him to depart unmonitored.

I let him leave then, left myself. I was followed too closely by Jennings. As I drove, I pulled the radio from under the seat and radioed Jennings, telling him I needed the money. We met several blocks away in an alley. Jennings gave me the $1,100 while I ribbed him about the sandwich. I told him Maldonado was going to sell me the ounce and I didn't expect any complications. I added I believed Maldonado was unpredictable and since my feeling had been that he didn't like us, I told Jennings, "watch my back, just in case." We talked about general topics including the Bulls game for several minutes, wasting time. Twenty minutes elapsed then Danny and I returned to the beef stand.

An hour passed while we waited.

Maldonado finally showed up in the same car, the Camaro. After parking in the cinder-stoned lot, he exited the car and walked over. Danny got out of the front seat and started for the back.

"Stay there, I'm not getting in. Where is the money?"

"Where is the stuff ?" I replied and the game began again.

"Its close by." He chuckled then scolded me, "You don't see nothing until I see the money. If I don't see money, you don't see nothing."

I removed the rolled up bills from my pocket. I had deliberately taken out the money is denominations of $20 notes. I always did this. I hoped to appeal to greed and I always believed fifty-five twenties looked like a lot more money than eleven hundreds. I thumbed the money for Maldonado to see but the sight of the verdant wad didn't faze him.

"Count it out." He demanded.

"Its there!" I said.

Maldonado emphatically replied, "I said count it. Count it in front of me on your lap."

It was another power play and to reassert my dominion, I refused. "No, I said its there." The volley proceeded, back and forth.

Maldonado reached inside the right front pocket of the windbreaker he was now wearing over the hockey sweater. Before I could react he pulled out the ounce. He conceded, throwing it on the floor of the front seat but, still within his reach. This was the tensest and most dangerous point of any narcotics transaction. The exchange of the dope for the money. Maldonado could very well have pulled a gun on me and robbed me. That fast. I didn't expect him to rob me but he could have. He could have shot me right there. Convenience stores and gas stations, even banks, get held up for less than $1,100 and people often get shot during these violent robberies. However, in the dope business eleven hundred dollars is pocket change and even a man as impatient as Maldonado was not going to shoot somebody for pocket change.

"Give me the money. Give me the money." Maldonado repeated, failing to conceal his own nervousness. He also knew this was the precarious moment he would be arrested if I was a cop. The police could not afford to buy ounces in Chicago. The DEA could but, Maldonado never considered me to be a DEA Agent. He probably thought he was too small a dealer to draw DEA scrutiny. He probably should have been right but, I was willing to develop the case if we could get a larger quantity out of Maldonado. That was the goal, appeal to his greed, bust him then turn him into an informant.

I handed the balled up money to Maldonado. It went immediately into the same pocket the ounce came from. A visibly relieved Maldonado looked around. There were no police. He was free to sell more dope. I wondered how often he completed these pressured transactions during a typical day in his life.

I picked up the ounce and threw it into the glove compartment. I examined it briefly as I did. It appeared chunky. I said to Maldonado , "It looks good."

Relieved freedom was still his and content he made $200 in profit for four minutes worth of work, he bragged, "Of course its good, Danny knows I always have the best."

"Yea, Nunzio, that's why we're here." Danny agreed.

I wanted to elicit conversation from Maldonado but, I could tell he wanted to leave, assuaged he had weathered another introduction and satisfied he had established another dumb customer.

Look, if this is good I'll call you for more. I can do more, can you ?" I asked

Maldonado replied, "Call Danny, Danny will call me. I'll let you know." As he walked away he said, "It all better be here, all of it." He patted his windbreaker.

"It was." He did not hear me. I noticed his hand remained in his right coat pocket, caressing the money he had received. Maldonado had completed these deals a hundred times but, the feel of the money in his hand always sustained the same powerful appeal. I would soon know the same wonderful feeling.

*

The manual prepared by the Drug Enforcement Administration's Office of Training defines confidential informants as anyone who provides information of an investigative nature to law enforcement. The manual classifies informants in four groups. These groups are (1) the average citizen, (2) fellow law enforcement investigators, (3) demented or disturbed persons and (4) criminals or criminal associates.

I had a simpler method for categorizing an informant, a good one and a bad one. The average citizen could never be considered an informant because most individuals knew very little about high level narcotics traffickers. They might hear rumors or maintain suspicions but, very few of them possess intimate knowledge of traffickers' resources, methods and patterns. When I use the term traffickers, I'm not referring to the guy who sells a couple grams at the corner bar. They are typically the bottom feeders on the list of those who profit from the drug trade. Not to say they do not make money, they do, but, they are not the people reaping huge profits like the multi-kilogram suppliers.

As my career with the DEA progressed, I observed a pattern develop where fellow law enforcement investigators did not share information. When they did it usually was for self serving purposes. Agents working narcotics cases, particularly at the state and federal levels, rarely provided information or intelligence unless they themselves had something to gain. The fact was, narcotics investigations were typically interesting and exciting work. To be assigned to a narcotics investigative team, whether as part of a federal or state agency, was considered a perk for most law enforcement officers. To remain in the narcotics unit, one had to manufacture cases and produce statistics. If one were to give away information, he or she might lose the chance to maintain jurisdiction over an investigation. This was particularly true of state agencies. They often refused to assist or participate in investigations unless their agents were officially deputized to be part of a federal task force. Then, those officers would become part of an investigative team but, more significantly, their departments would share in the remunerative seizure of assets which was becoming, in the early 1990's, a top priority even more than arrests. Narcotics traffickers make money, lots of it. Staggering amounts in fact. Seizing parts of that cash cow enabled agencies to supplement and fund their budgets to purchase better equipment, hire more personnel and upgrade the deplorable and substandard environments in which many police departments functioned. It was no secret the DEA had been seizing more in assets than had been budgeted to the agency. The DEA was the only federal law enforcement agency that was functioning in the black, bringing in significantly more money than it spent. Consequently, the DEA began to acquire better facilities, improved equipment, investigative tools and also, attracted and recruited more qualified applicants. This development caused great consternation among many federal agencies, especially with the Department of Justice's Golden Child, The FBI. As a move to acquire some of those easily seized assets, the Federal Bureau of Investigation began to actively pursue drug investigations, going so far as to set up their own narcotics unit within their agency. The success of the FBI's operations led other agencies to create their own drug units. Consequently, US Customs, The Bureau of Alcohol, Tobacco and Firearms, the U.S. Marshals Service, US Border Patrol as well as count-less other agencies set up investigative divisions whose foremost pur-pose was to concentrate on narcotics interdiction. Ridiculously, even such obscure agencies as the Department of Wildlife Conservation began to investigate drug trafficking organizations, supposedly those traversing federal forest preserves. With each agency's desire to get the assets first, agency personnel resorted to shameful tactics which included concealing investigative information from each other. The very reason President Nixon created the DEA in 1973 was to consolidate federal drug interdiction efforts and already by the 90's the system was being abused and circumvented.

Each agency attempted to protect their informants, the good ones anyway. Unfortunately, the best ones were usually some combination of categories 3 and 4, demented criminals. My partner, Chad Jennings, often said, "You don't get swans from sewers." He was referring to informants and their penchant for criminal behavior. A good informant knew his way around drug dealers because he was one himself. He knew the lingo, the nightclubs, the hookers, the vacation spots, the smuggling techniques, the routes, the safehouses, everything. The informant knew the ins and the outs, and the ins were always very criminal. A barber would not make a good informant but, he would be the person I would see if I wanted to get my hair cut. And if I wanted to learn how to cut hair, which scissors and razors to use for particular styles, a barber is who I would seek out to teach me. To learn about, to understand and investigate drug dealers, the DEA and any other investigative agency must seek out drug dealers to instruct them.

The motivation for someone to become an informant is easily understood. Just as the investigator's motive for providing information was self serving, so too was the informant. I can say confidently, there doesn't exist a good informant within the ranks of the DEA who is providing information because they are concerned about the effects of drug trafficking on the community.

There was one, at least, I suspected as having been legitimately concerned about her neighborhood, at least initially. She was an employee of American Airlines at O'Hare Airport who was providing information to us about individuals purchasing round trip tickets with cash to destinations which were well known havens for drug traffickers. Chicago to New York and Miami were preferred flights of traffickers who were returning large sums of cash to awaiting Colombian sources. Chicago to El Paso and Houston were returning large sums of cash to Mexican organizations. Chicago to Bangkok, Thailand via San Francisco was a well-established route where couriers would be sent to pick up quantities of heroin to smuggle back to the U.S. Certainly, most of the people who were on flights like these were not drug traffickers. However, it is very rare for average citizens to walk up to ticket counters carting only one bag and purchase round trip tickets to destinations with their return flight occurring only a day and often only hours after they arrived. Obviously, business people made travel arrangements like that often however, they usually wore business attire and had their tickets and reservations prepared in advance by reputable travel agencies. Only a drug courier dressed in a sweatsuit or jeans takes a 23 hour flight to southeast Asia with one piece of carry on luggage, stays for a day and returns on another 23 hour flight. Our ticketing agent was cognizant of drug traffickers' modus operandi and had been informally trained by her controlling agent which particular idiosyncrasies and habits to recognize. She called our airport detail every time a peculiar purchase was made by a skittish passenger. This arrangement lasted approximately one and a half years, with the ticketing agent providing information for at least twenty cases which resulted in large cash and drug seizures. Initially, she had called the DEA out of a sense of civic duty. However, after she had been financially compensated for her cooperation she became motivated to actively pursue couriers. The employee had quite a side business going on and had received well over $100,000 in payments and indemnities for her information. She was very content with her rewards until an agent had told her she was entitled to as much as a 25% cut of seizures she helped us make. He apparently went on to divulge that one of her most recent cases resulted in the seizure of four kilos of heroin from a person entering San Francisco with the contraband cleverly concealed in pouches attached to her body. During her internship, the ticketing agent had adopted quite an interest in drug trafficking and knew a kilo of heroin was worth approximately $250,000 in the U.S. With four kilos seized she easily calculated she was entitled to a quarter-million dollar reward for that particular seizure. When she presented her case to her controlling agents, they told her she was not eligible because her information had only assisted and not led directly to the seizure. It was a lie but, a lie she could have lived with. After all, the information she was providing was a direct violation of American Airlines' policies pertaining to confidentiality about its customers and if found out, she would have immediately been terminated. Since she was only making about $26,000 a year as a ticket agent, she, in my opinion should have been very content with the supplemental income she was deriving from her information. However, she became greedy and decided to go to the other side. She confided in an individual who was a Colombian male who purchased a quick trip with cash from Chicago to Miami. Evidently she told him what she was doing and divulged to the man he would be a perfect candidate to call the DEA on.

It was a tragic mistake. Apparently, her plan was to gain the confidence of drug traffickers and assure them that they should make their ticket purchases through her. The scheme worked for a while with dealers instructing their couriers to purchase seats strictly through the ticketer called "Blanca". Unfortunately for Blanca, the DEA conducts random profile stops at various high traffic airports and often does so without the assistance of an informant. One such stop was made at New York's Laguardia Airport, netting a Colombian national in possession of two pieces of luggage which contained $1.5 million dollars. His ticket had been issued by Blanca. Misconceiving they had been set up, the Colombian response was swift and violent. The Chicago Tribune's headline ran "Random Act of Depravity in Schaumburg." The article described the gruesome death of a local female employee of national airline, a 27 year old mother of one, who the paper stated was apparently randomly selected and tortured while spending an evening at home. Her body had been severely beaten, she had been raped and sodomized and as a final gesture of particular disdain, her breasts had been severed and her eyes had been scooped out, according to the coroner, while she was still alive. The horrified public was informed there were no suspects and many sleepless nights followed by residents of Schaumburg and surrounding Northwest Chicago.

Though an informant's motives will always be self-serving, they still manifest themselves in different ways. The leading motivation is greed. Money can be made in the drug business, that is obvious. Money, serious money, can also be made turning in people in the drug business. And as I mentioned previously, you have to be in the business to know the business. One doesn't necessarily have to be an active dealer, trading drugs for money, but, the person must have distinct knowledge like a courier, a money launderer or a person who utilizes their specific expertise to conceal, transport or distribute dope. They also have to have the ability, through one means or another, to provide intelligent, decipherable and reliable information. This is where the demented usually came into play. An individual whose main motive to become an informant is money, will not live long enough to enjoy it. Its that simple. The charm of fast money often kills. The desire for success often incites risks that one might not otherwise consider taking. An agent, not just a DEA Agent but, any investigator, particularly one employed in narcotics, is going to let the informant assume most of the risks. Some agents, and I wasn't one of them because it was unethical and an outrageous lie, told informants they should expect to reap large rewards for their cooperation. Most of the awards took months to process and had to be approved by several bureaucratic departments within the DEA before cash awards were disposed. I'm not contending that large awards were not paid. There existed several occasions when individuals left our offices literally carrying a paper bag full of money. Cash rewards for a single case of twenty, thirty even fifty thousand dollars were rare but, not completely uncommon. However, I also was aware of several instances when a cash reward was paid to an informant's next of kin rather than the informant himself. The truth of the matter was if an informant could put together a case by himself and come away unscathed, great. More times than not however, the informant's prosperity required the support and direction of the controlling agent. The reason being, it was after all, the agent who determined the success and consequently the reward. I know that if I could convince an informant to extend himself, even if it meant taking extra risks, I would. I am proud to say though, I never requested an informant to go so far as to completely put himself "on front street" as some agents called it. Front street is an avenue no one, especially an informant, wants to be found walking on, where there is no other person left to take the blame for the set up than the guy standing in the middle of the road. I can say I knew of at least one instance within my group where an informant, following the specific direction of his agent, was killed as a result. Before killing the informant though, the persons responsible elected to murder his nine year old son. I knew this type of neglect would happen again and, it did.

Other informants were motivated to knock out their competition. They called the office under the guise of hoping to fulfill their "civic duty." These people were often as transparent as sandwich baggies. Quite literally, they provided information about their rivals, seeking to have them arrested so they could take over their territory. I didn't care for such informants but, would gladly sign them up and work with them, again for my own benefit. After the competitor was arrested, they assumed control, and I would expect to see another individual show up and attempt to pull the same scheme on him.

The best informant, the one who I felt gave me the greatest chance of success, was the defendant informant. These were people who were facing lengthy criminal sentences as a result of their own criminal activity. My overall experience with the criminal justice system was limited to drug cases but, I couldn't imagine any person more unwilling to go to prison than drug dealers. There were no "stand up guys" in the drug world. All of them and I mean every defendant I ever participated in prosecuting, expressed some interest in cooperation in return for considerations. I'm pretty certain most of the defendants prosecuted by the DEA have considered and provided some type of information to the DEA, in return for concessions regarding their prison time. I've seen longtime friends set each other up, I've seen wives rat on their husbands. Unbelievably true, I've participated in a case where a father sought to set up his only son. Without a doubt, there is no more cowardly a person than a successful and wealthy drug dealer facing a long prison term.

Unfortunately, the greatest motivation for a defendant informant, the desperation of a long prison term, also was his greatest detriment. A defendant informant is usually incarcerated. Word of an arrest travels quickly through the drug world. As soon as someone hears about the arrest of a confederate, all the smart dealers immediately insulate themselves and attempt to sever all ties to the defendant. Fortunately, that is not often easily accomplished. A dealer who has been working successfully for a period of time with an individual, whether he be a source of supply or a customer, tends to have trouble replacing the individual. Remember, the DEA is not typically investigating street level dealers. When someone is purchasing $50,000 of cocaine per week and suddenly that person is not providing the cash anymore, the loss of income hurts. The defendant informant is encouraged to play upon that loss of business and pressure the unwitting into reestablishing trust. It sounds incredulous but, cases are made every week with informants arranging deals from prison. The bad guys just can't resist the money and it's the money which leads everybody down the drain.

*

The investigation of Nunzio Maldonado continued for a month after our initial meeting. A week after I had been introduced, I met Maldonado a second time. Danny, the informant, had arranged another ounce purchase and had been able to convince Maldonado to meet me alone. It was excellent work on Danny's part.

My intention was to deal directly with Maldonado. I wanted to "cut the informant out." Ideally, the undercover agent tries to accomplish this so the business with the dealer is uninterrupted by the existence of the informant. Police do this so that the informant may ease himself out of the negotiations. That is, allow the agent to assume control. The agent may, in turn, attempt to introduce another undercover agent into the negotiations and that new agent will be the man who ends up arresting the suspect and testifying against the defendant in court. This is designed to try to protect the identity of the informant and is common DEA procedure however defendants, despite the admirable intentions of investigating agents, can usually figure out quite easily who ultimately was responsible for the set up.

Danny didn't really care if he was exposed as an informant. He was working strictly for the income and was setting people up all over Chicago. Some were even casual friends and most of whom he had met during various stints as a bartender at nightclubs all around the United States' third largest city. He had no fear of reprisal and was gathering money for a move to California to start a new life. I could have been content to permit Danny to run wild and use him until his luck ran out. Some agents would have done just that but I felt an obligation to implement the best strategy to protect Danny as much as possible. As he negotiated more deals, his conduct became reckless and worrisome and I didn't want his death on my conscience.

My intention with Maldonado was to make another small buy and then convince him I was interested in a larger purchase. I hoped to push Maldonado to a quantity that would allow us to prosecute him federally. Chicago was within the United States Federal District of Northern Illinois and the United States Attorney's Office would not prosecute any defendants who delivered less than a half kilogram or 500 grams. In a smaller district, like the Southern District of Illinois which encompassed smaller Springfield, the Feds would be glad to prosecute a multi-ounce dealer. However, in Chicago, ounce dealers were crawling out of the woodwork and I would never consider presenting a federal case based on two one-ounce deliveries. I settled on attempting to have Maldonado deliver a half-kilogram. A half kilo was slightly more than a pound of coke. I had purchased one ounce and had set up a second ounce delivery from Maldonado and it would take considerable effort to convince him he could trust me enough to sell a half kilo to me.

The second deal went much like the first. I met Maldonado in a restaurant, this one only two blocks from his home. Of course, Maldonado did not know I had identified his residence. I had subpoenaed the beeper number supplied by Danny and discovered Maldonado's bills were being sent to a post office box. The mail drop was rented by Maldonado who foolishly listed his own address as a point of contact in renting it. Disseminating the information and determining the location of his residence was a half hour's worth of work and it took that long because I had to type the subpoena myself before faxing it to the appropriate companies.

I agreed to meet Maldonado in close proximity to his home because I assumed Maldonado was distrustful of me. I also believed Maldonado would feel safe setting up a deal in his own surroundings. I didn't believe I was conceding anything in meeting Maldonado near his home. Contrastly, I believed him requesting a meeting near his home was evidence he maintained a concern about me. Caution is a good trait in dope dealers and it was a virtue I respected.

I went to the restaurant Maldonado instructed Danny to send me to. It was a little corner Mexican place specializing in burritos, enchiladas and tacos. I arrived earlier than expected because I wanted to be there before Maldonado walked in. I was hungry so I ordered a burrito. Jennings was one of two surveillance agents who entered the restaurant as well. He must also have been hungry because he ordered a taco platter and a burrito. It seemed my partner always enjoyed a healthy appetite. This time he sat with his back towards me, talking to Phil Vreeswyck who sat facing my table. Other agents had established surveillance at Maldonado's house in an attempt to follow him if he went to pick up the dope from his source. I was advised over the radio just before I entered the restaurant Maldonado was probably not home because his car, the '85 Camaro, was not parked outside.

I was seated in the restaurant and waited for my order. I acted like anyone else might act in a restaurant. For all I knew, others might be negotiating dope transactions as well. About twenty minutes elapsed before Maldonado arrived but he arrived on time. His punctuality indicated to me an eagerness to consummate another deal and I thought the indication provided me more confidence to believe I could bump up the amount I was interested in purchasing. As he walked in, my food was delivered by the waiter. Maldonado spotted me and walked straight to my table.

"Hey Mark, what's up?" His attitude was more relaxed and even casual.

"Hey, I just ordered some food, I just got here." I answered.

"I know, I saw you walk in," Maldonado caught me off guard with that revelation. I wondered whether he had made any surveillance agents. Two agents sat three tables way and I tried to recall whether we had all come in together. Jennings and Vreeswyck's race would not be suspicious since it was not odd to find Caucasians in the Mexican neighborhood we were in. The restaurants that dotted the neighborhood were all known for their cheap but tasty food. I thought about the likelihood Maldonado might remember Jennings' face at the beef stand but I reasoned that possibility was remote.

Maldonado looked around the semi-crowded restaurant. He spoke. "I see you're having the burrito, they are good."

"Yea, they are big, you want one?"

"No, I just ate." Maldonado looked at the table and noticed I did not have a beverage. It gave him the opportunity to suggest I order something. "Why don't you have a beer, a beer tastes good with those."

His suggestion was a ruse designed to cleverly determine if I was a cop. I am sure he reasoned I could not order a beer if I was a law enforcement officer meeting him in an undercover capacity. It was an absurd myth to which many inexperienced and misinformed dealers clung, incorrectly believing a policeman could not consume alcohol when on duty even if acting in an undercover capacity. An agent is permitted to do anything considered legal activity to protect the undercover identity, including drinking alcohol. I thought about a nice cold beer and since Uncle Sam was paying for my lunch because I was acting in an undercover role, I replied, "That sounds like a good idea. You want one?"

He said, "No." He looked at me as I motioned for the waiter. I ordered a Corona beer. Pleased contentment swept across his face and he appeared very satisfied I was not a cop. I could tell by his posture, as he became even more comfortable. I almost was disappointed. I really enjoyed the undercover role and welcomed it as a challenge. Now, I realized Nunzio Maldonado was a novice and he would not be as difficult to ensnare as I had previously imagined.

Our conversation quickly focused on my money. I casually mentioned I had some cash to invest in Nunzio's "business." He liked the sound of my tone. He wanted to think of himself as a businessman, not a dope dealer. He also wanted to make more money and I knew he viewed me as a guy he could ride to the bank. He was charging me excessive prices for the cocaine. He wanted another $1,100.00 for this ounce. I told him it was too much. I figured he was probably paying $900.00 for the ounce and turning around and selling it to me at a two hundred-dollar profit. If Maldonado did this five times a day with weekends off, which would be a conservative estimate, he was a man making $5,000.00 a week, tax-free. However, I did not suspect Nunzio Maldonado was making five thousand dollars a week because he didn't know many people like me, a guy who would pay $1,100.00 for an ounce of coke that was selling for no more than $950, probably as close as the next table. But now he did and I was prepared to seduce his greedy libido with an alluring proposal.

"You know I got rid of that package very fast last time." I cut it in quarters and turned a quick buck." I continued, "It was good shit." I was lying. The ounce he gave me was analyzed to be only 63% cocaine which meant he, or someone else, had diluted the package considerably. Most of the coke we were seizing was at least 80% and some ounces were even more, numbers which indicated cocaine was plentiful in Chicago. I offered my unwitting approval of the quality of the coke as an indication I didn't know what I was talking about. I hoped Maldonado would catch it and view me as a buffoon. I reckoned he did when I observed a slight smirk cross his face. I added, "This one, I imagine, will go just as quick. Do you have it close ?"

He smiled, "Oh yea. Lets go outside."

I did not want to go outside because I did not want to be expected to travel in a car with Maldonado. I wanted him to retrieve the ounce and deliver it to me. I was hoping the outside possibility existed he would have to go to his source to obtain it, since we were so close to his residence, I hoped he might even travel there to pick it up. I said, "No I'll wait here, I don't want to go anywhere."

"No, no, no. We will go in your car. We'll do it there." Maldonado reiterated.

"No. I'll wait here, you do what you got to do." I wanted him to go get the dope and have surveillance follow him back to his source. This would be ideal for the investigation. Follow Maldonado back to his source of supply then hit the place on a search warrant the next time we consummated a deal.

Maldonado's frustration mounted, "Not here, man, I'm not going to give it to you here." He paused and slipped back into his mode of paranoia and suspicion. "Are you a cop because if you are, you're dealing with the wrong person. I've got friends…"

Maldonado turned quickly and inspected the patrons. He was making a wise assumption but, was speaking foolishly. I realized Maldonado had the ounce with him. I had incorrectly planned Maldonado would go get the ounce. Like the first deal, he was prepared to sell the ounce right away. The questions and the interrogation were all a facade. Maldonado had been conducting his dirty business without repercussion for so long he had become lackadaisical and his keen instincts had been dulled. He acted boldly with little regard for police investigative techniques. His threat was a feeble-minded remark and it would become an issue because I was taping the conversation with a cleverly concealed mini-cassette recorder. I was confident the recording would be audible.

"Oh, you got it with you. I thought you wanted me to go somewhere." I decided it was acceptable to go out to the car but, I wouldn't go anywhere with him. I drank the last few drops of my beer and left a half-finished burrito. We walked to the car. Maldonado drifted to the passengers side as if to get in. I opened my door and pushed the automatic door button. The button released the lock and Maldonado climbed in.

"Drive around." Maldonado said excitedly. He looked behind through the rear window. If he was looking for police, if he really knew what he should be looking for, he would have seen the surveillance agents. He did not, however.

"Nunzio, I said I'm not going anywhere." This was a common sense decision. If we started to move, the possibility existed that surveillance would not be able to remain with me. I held out that they had noticed Maldonado was as fidgety as a whore in church and would be trying to detect surveillance. Furthermore, I could not let Nunzio dictate the specifics. He had to give me the ounce right away if he had it. "C'mon Nunzio, just give me the thing."

"I don't like it here." He replied. "Something ain't right."

"I'm not going anywhere, like I said."

Tempted by the profit he expected to reap, he conceded, "Alright, let's do it." He reached inside his jeans, into the crotch area. I tensed briefly as he fumbled in his waistband briefly before pulling out the white baggy containing the cocaine. I didn't appreciate his choice of a hiding place but I couldn't complain. It was an accepted spot to conceal dope.

"Here." He handed it to me and he immediately demanded, "Give me the money!"

I took the cocaine and leisurely examined it in my lap in an effort to appear as if I was analyzing its quality. I hoped its texture was chunky. Otherwise, I didn't know what I was looking at. I've handled cocaine dozens of times but, I was much like Maldonado with his futile effort to find police. I wasn't sure of what I thought I was supposed to see. I didn't know if it was 63% coke or 13%. Regardless, I accepted the package and handed Maldonado the small bundle from my pocket. Twenty-two fifties. This time he counted it in front of me as I hid the cocaine under the front seat of the car.

"Its all there, just like before." I assured.

Maldonado was not paying attention to me. I saw him mouthing the words "three hundred, three fifty, four..." as he counted.

I decided to submit my audacious proposal. "You know, I can move a little more. I don't want to have to come downtown like this every other day or two to buy an ounce. I would like to be able to get something a little bigger. And cheaper, of course."

Maldonado heard me this time but waited until he finished counting. "We'll talk about it. You got a pen, I'll give you my beeper. But listen, Mark, if your setting me up you will regret it. I don't get set up. I ain't been busted for a reason and its because of who I am and who I know." I nodded my head in a fraudulent gesture of respectful acknowledgment all the while recognizing Maldonado was a farce. I was inside his house and his greed would never let him throw me out. He had made two deliveries to me. Though his sales to me were not significant enough to prosecute federally, Maldonado would still face considerable jail time if I were to proceed with a state prosecution. Each of the two deliveries was punishable by three-year sentences if he was found guilty in the state system. Any delivery of eight grams or more of cocaine is punishable by a term of up to three years. Any further offenses are punishable by three additional years to be added at the judge's discretion. Maldonado could serve six years in prison for the fifty-six grams of granulated powder he had delivered to me over the course of our two meetings. Maldonado was now in this thing for the long haul. He would make his tidy fortune from me or he would go down in flames. I reasoned his idle threats were futile attempts to cling to some degree of control. By selling me the first ounce, Maldonado had committed his trust to me. The second ounce delivery solidified our bond and although Maldonado didn't recognize it, the completion of the transaction placed me in charge of the next decade of his life.

*

I was busy during the Maldonado investigation. In addition to my responsibilities connected with that case, I conducted numerous surveillances and assisted on several other agent's investigations. Many fellow agents were known for their selfish habits and refusal to aid any case that wasn't there own. Conversely, I was always willing to help everyone out, including agents in other groups. I had a good reputation for my willingness to accommodate other agents and I counted on that reputation if a question about my integrity was ever raised.

Gradually, my work habits began leaning toward self-serving efforts to grant me opportunities to broaden my thieving endeavors. Though I remained dedicated to the interdiction of drugs, I found myself eagerly searching for a fair field to pick up a valuable trinket. During an arrest of a white suburban cocaine dealer, I had managed to pick up two one ounce gold South African Kruggerands and another fashionable wristwatch from a nightstand.

I elected to keep the gold coins hoping they would bring me luck. I just liked the thought of owning them and the concept of pirated treasure intrigued me. I had other plans for the watch. I decided to try to pawn it even though I had never pawned anything in my life. I had no experience negotiating with pawnbrokers and fortunately, never had any reason to. I always thought of pawnbrokers with the stereotypical perception of sleazy con men who existed day to day for reasons only God knew. But now, after deciding to pawn the dealer's watch, they would become my confederates.

Before going to the pawns, I attempted to find out what the watch was actually worth. It was a Cartier with a diamond bezeled face and I assumed it was expensive because of its quality name and its shimmering appearance. The guy who owned it was a white kid from Chicago's Southwest suburbs. He made the mistake of trying to buy a kilo from one of our undercover agents during a reverse narcotics sting. The reverse operation was when we posed as the dealers capable of selling kilos to unsuspecting customers. It was another myth fostered by ignorance that the police were not permitted to pose as the dope peddlers. Defense attorneys often argued entrapment but, it was invariably difficult to convince a jury the government lured an individual into arriving at a predetermined location with a liberal amount of cash. Though some members of defense counsel were shrewd, I had yet to meet one who could effectively persuade a normal jury pool made up of laborers, housewives, fathers, television repairman, cashiers, sisters-in-law and so forth that a wrongly accused defendant met an undercover agent with tens of thousands of dollars of his own money because he was enticed by the government to engage in an act he wouldn't normally consider, like purchase drugs. Regular people just didn't believe it, especially when the defendant would not be able to furnish any evidence how he came to be in possession of such large amounts of currency. I didn't expect the suburban doper to be able to prove his case either especially when he showed up with $22,000 to buy a kilo and receive a second one on consignment. He was adroitly relieved of the money and arrested. The money was forfeited to the U.S. government. We subsequently searched his house and found some dope paraphernalia including scales, baggies, rubber bands and dilutants. The whole melange was confiscated and placed into evidence. I took the Cartier and the Kruggerands when someone else was collecting the exhibits. Just picked it up and threw it into my coat without a thought of remorse.

I was nervous looking at similar watches in jewelry stores. I was anxious and assumed someone was watching, aware of the indiscretions I had committed. I felt extremely uncomfortable asking about the prices of the watches. I just assumed the sales staff knew I couldn't afford any of the expensive items I was inquiring about. I realized I was being to cautious. It was my conscience, in truth with which I was wrestling. I found out the watch retailed for $1,200. Though I expected the watch had cost more, I estimated I might get as much as $400 for it in the pawns.

I walked into my first pawn shop with the watch buried deep in my pocket. I just wanted to get a feel of the place. I examined a variety of watches manufactured by various designers who each seemed to have their distinct styles. I did not find anything which resembled the Cartier I possessed. I saw the inflated prices of some of the items and the asking rates were higher than I had anticipated. I thought that was a promising development. The shop was crowded so I loitered about hoping to hear a little banter between a salesman and a customer.

An employee approached me. He saw me looking at the watches and assumed, I suppose, that I could afford a second hand one. He asked what I liked but, I was there to sell not buy. Apprehension prohibited me from offering my item which I realized I did not have the guts to try to sell. We engaged in small talk about the watches and other jewelry. I ultimately walked out never having offered the watch for sale.

I went home that afternoon with the watch. I threw it into a sock then placed the sock into the crusty thumb of a worn out ice hockey glove. I placed the glove in a dusty box with its mate in the storage locker in the basement of my apartment building. It rested in the same place where I had placed the other watch purloined from the Pip. The storage locker, nothing but a wooden frame encased in chicken wire, seemed the most unlikely place to find anything of value. There was a cheap lock on the door of the locker which could have been broken off by a sickly third grader. After I put the watch away I wondered if I really had the stomach to live on the other side. I reviewed the ease with which I had acquired the jewelry and the coins and reasoned it was accomplished too smoothly to forsake any future plans. I just had to redefine my objective. I considered the twenty-year old punk who had $22,000 to buy a kilogram of coke. He had dropped out of high school and after listening to Brian Sullivan interview him, I deduced he didn't have enough brains to blow his nose. Yet here he was, tooling around Chicago with twenty-two grand in his car. I certainly was smarter than him. I concluded if I was going to succeed, I had to focus on things which could not be traced to me. I decided to consolidate my efforts on the acquisition of cash.

*

I didn't wait long to call Maldonado after his second delivery of cocaine. Though we had not managed to identify his source, I anticipated the source would be required to get involved if a large amount was requested. I reasoned if the source was wise, he wouldn't trust Maldonado's ability to consummate the deal. I wanted to tantalize Maldonado with my urgent need for more cocaine and cajole him with my willingness to pay a premium price for it. I paged Maldonado to an undercover phone in the DEA office which was specially installed by the phone company to be listed to any number of subscribers we chose. If he were to try to use caller ID to trace the number I selected a code which would announce my call as having been placed from a pay phone outside a near north side laundromat. Maldonado called me back almost immediately.

"Hello."

"Hey, what's up ?" Maldonado asked. He was not interested in my reply. Before I could answer he spoke. "Listen, I told you I wasn't fucking around. Your address is Fifteen-O-Five Euclid Avenue, in Arlington Heights."

I was silent. I lived in Westmont and didn't know anyone in Arlington Heights. It didn't immediately strike me to what he was referring.

"Your license plate, one-nine-two-five-five-seven, is registered to Walter Madison, 1505 Euclid Street. You said your name is Mark but, its fucking Walter."

"Huh?"

"Your name is Walter." Maldonado repeated.

Thankfully Maldonado had given me time to realize what he was talking about. He had evidently memorized the license plate on the Cherokee I was driving. He must know someone who had access to motor vehicle information who had supplied him with my registration. It could have been an employee of the motor vehicle department or a private investigator but, it also could have been a cop.

"My name is Mark," I tap-danced. "My old man's name is Walter. The car is registered to him. Its registered to him because it saves money on insurance."

Maldonado's tone reflected confidence. "Yea, well like I said, I know people and those people say you ain't right."

I had to assume a demeanor of annoyance. It wasn't difficult because I actually was irritated and I had to counter Maldonado's surprise assault. Maldonado was smarter than I imagined. Obviously he had made some efforts to protect himself and had made good on his promise to check me out. I hadn't been prepared for the registration information because I never considered it to be important. We often drive many different vehicles in the DEA and frequently changed cars. The registrations also change and its virtually impossible to remember which plates are on which particular car.

"Look, I am cool. If you don't trust me forget it." I bluffed, "Let's just forget the whole thing if you think I'm a cop," I said.

"If you're a cop that house is gone. I'll blow it sky high. Say good-bye to fifteen-oh-five. Everyone will go 'cause I don't play no fucking games." Maldonado boldly promised.

I was astonished by his degree of vengefulness. If I was a cop, I assumed, he would want to stay as far away as possible from me. Instead, he was defiantly threatening to blow up my house and kill family members. I determined his behavior were the threats of an amateur, a man who was is in over his head. Big time dope dealers don't need to make threats like that. They exist on their instinct and when something smells fishy they just back off. I thought besides, wouldn't it be rather stupid for an undercover cop to have his registered license plates on an automobile he was using during an undercover operation. I posed that question to Maldonado.

"I don't know if you're the police or not. My friends who know these things say your not straight up. Whatever you are, cop or mother-fucker, that house will go up if I am ever arrested or ripped off."

The remark about being robbed suggested Maldonado still wasn't certain what I was and since there remained an opportunity, I pursued it. I tried to assuage Maldonado and presented him with the proposal I had been considering. "Look, the reason I called was to ask about a big-ger item. I'm not in this thing to get killed. I say if you don't want to make money with me, fuck it. Forget it." I hoped to appeal to his greed again. I did not know how much information Maldonado's friend was able to garner from the Department of Motor Vehicles but, I suppose depending on his degree of access, he might have been able to find out the car was actually owned by the Drug Enforcement Administration. Our vehicles are registered to fictitious people all over Chicago and its suburbs. The people's names are completely bogus but, the addresses do exist. They usually are large apartment complexes or downtown high-rises with many individual units. Occasionally, the address listed on the registration will be a specific residence. The Illinois Department of Motor Vehicles attempts to make it difficult for someone to trace the ownership of our cars but, it can be deciphered with some degree of research. I did not know to what levels Maldonado's accomplice had access so I decided to ascertain right away if Maldonado knew for cer-tain whether I was an agent or not. " I just want to make money." I offered. When Maldonado responded, I knew he did not know.

"Money is what I am about."

Relieved, I encouraged Maldonado, "Then let's make money and for-get all this bullshit. I want something of greater weight. Can you do..."

"Call them rolls of carpet," Maldonado interrupted. Like many dope dealers, Maldonado used code words to negotiate drug deals. It was another misconception, probably perpetuated by a $50 an hour storefront attorney, the use of code words would exonerate dealers in instances where the calls were being recorded. In this case, Maldonado was being recorded and of course, the codes did not acquit him or any other dealer who used them.

I had decided to press Maldonado to substantiate what quantities he was capable of delivering. Our investigative budget would not permit me to buy any more cocaine besides, it would serve no purpose. Maldonado, by virtue of his two deliveries, was facing considerable jail time. I knew it was early to propose a large amount but, I hoped Maldonado would see dollar signs. "Then I'm interested in one big roll of carpet."

There was silence on the other end. Had I jumped too far, scaring Maldonado with my desire to purchase a large quantity so quickly? His silence had indicated I had.

"No way. You are a cop. I knew you were. You are not right."

"I am not a cop. You would have been busted by now, a week ago." I responded. "Man, this is getting old. What cops buy ounces of coke? I just need a bigger amount. The two ounces went right away." I pleaded my argument.

"Call the ounces rolls of carpet, you dumb mother-fucker." Maldonado shouted into the receiver. "Don't make that mistake again or I will hang up."

I knew for certain I had him. Nunzio would have hung up if he hadn't clung to the chance of making some big money. I persisted, "I need one, I've got about twenty-five, twenty-six thousand for one." A ridiculous sum to pay for carpet and too much to pay for a kilogram., I thought. "I've got a partner who is helping me out."

"I am not meeting anybody. Just you and me." Despite his hesitation, Maldonado's greed anchored his interest. Twenty-five thousand dollars was at least two thousand dollars too much to pay for a kilogram. I knew it but more importantly Maldonado knew it. I suspected Maldonado sold his coke on consignment, a typical method employed by smaller dealers with less capitol. Maldonado picked up his coke, sold it and relinquished a fixed payment to his source, like the Mexican in the Cutlass and so many hundreds before him. Anything Maldonado made on top of that was his to keep as proceeds. The extra money from my proposed deal would be clear profit for him. He might make as much as $4,000 or $5,000 off this deal especially if he diluted the coke. I knew it would be too good to pass up.

"I'll check with my end." Maldonado said, acknowledging without realizing he was admitting he had a source who controlled larger deliveries, a fact I suspected all along. "I'll get back to you."

"You can page me." I gave Maldonado my beeper number. The call, fully recorded, was terminated. Only two hours later, Maldonado paged me.

I returned the call.

"Hey," he excitedly answered.

"This is Mark"

"Who ?"

C'mon Nunzio, I thought. You know who this is. This is the down payment on your new car.

"Its Mark, you just paged me." I said.

"Oh yea Mark, I have got what you need."

"The whole thing?" I asked.

"No, a half a roll."

"A half of a roll, I don't want a half-of-a-roll." I replied emphatically.

"I mean a half of a kilo. A half kilo." Maldonado was so excited he had broken his own rule.

I was satisfied with the amount. I knew if Maldonado delivered a half kilogram of cocaine, 500 grams, I could threaten to prosecute him in federal court, a prospect which would motivate him to become a zealous informant. Nevertheless, I played it conservatively and expressed disappointment I could not obtain a larger package. "I really need a whole roll. That's what I was hoping for."

Maldonado, who's last call had reflected the demeanor of a tough intimidator quickly transubstantiated into a desperate salesman. "I know but on such short notice, its all I could get. Do you want it ? Its good stuff. " He begged, "I mean you are not going to get this type of quality on such short notice."

The beseeching pitch didn't include an ounce of truth, so to speak, but, I let him plead for my consideration.

"How much ?" I asked.

"Fifteen."

"Not today or any day." I said. Maldonado knew fifteen thousand was an exorbitant price to pay for a half kilogram even if it was totally uncut cocaine. I balked, "That is way too high."

Maldonado was disappointed but, I think, in some way relieved I would not agree to that price. Some cops who assume the undercover role agree to virtually any requests by a suspect and those who do often give themselves away to be police. Maldonado retracted the initial price and countered with another offer, "Fourteen-five."

"Fourteen is too high." I shot back. The going price in Chicago at that time for a half-kilo was no more than $13,000 and I had to keep that in mind to make my negotiations at least appear legitimate. A half-kilo of close to pure cocaine would produce slightly more than seventeen whole ounces. If a dope dealer diluted the coke with 25% adulterant or cut he would then have twenty-four ounces of street level cocaine. Selling his dope in ounce quantities for a fair price of $900 an ounce a dealer would make $22,600, an $8,600 profit on an investment of $14,000. No broker despite experience, savvy or even inside information has ever consistently delivered such numbers. And it could be done quickly and easily. Perhaps in as little as an afternoon.

"Fourteen is as low as I could go."

I guessed he was probably responsible for $12,000 maybe $12,5 for the half kilo. Maldonado would still be making a decent profit if he consummated the transaction. If he really protested, I would offer $14,5. I knew that it would not matter what amount we agreed upon, Maldonado would never get it.

"I'm not paying anything more than fourteen and the shit better be good for that much!"

"Fourteen" He affirmed, "but you're killing me."

I hope I won't have to, I thought.

"Alright, " I validated the price and to appear convincing added, "I'll need two hours." I needed the time to formulate a game plan for my supervisor's approval. Furthermore, I had to find enough agents to throw together an arrest team.

"That restaurant again. In two hours." said Maldonado.

After the telephone call, I immediately contacted the Arlington Heights Police Department and had an officer verify the address at 1505 Euclid Avenue. I was fearful Maldonado would make good on his reckless promise to blow the house up regardless of whom lived there. The Arlington Police enthusiastically checked the address and the responding officer called me back a half-hour later to tell me the address housed an unobtrusive antiques dealer who had been operating a small shop for years. She zealously proposed surveillance by her department's narcotics unit but I assured her it was not necessary. I tried to convince her it was for information purposes only, with the reason being I needed the info because the address had appeared in a telephone book we had recently seized. Nevertheless, I'm certain the antique shop was periodically watched for weeks after my inquiry.

A flashroll of $14,000 was needed to present to Maldonado. A flashroll consisted of DEA money that an agent would sign out after receiving approval from a supervisor and the ASAC. It was used to show the dealer during a deal and it was never to be spent or worse, lost. The agent who signed for and accepted the flashroll would be completely responsible for its safe return. $14,000, to most, is quite a sum of cash to be hauling around however, by DEA standards, it is not considered a large sum by any means. I had participated in a deal where we had used a flashroll of $2,000,000, all in one hundred-dollar bills. That was a lot of money. To obtain it, the Chicago DEA Office was required to contact DEA Headquarters in Washington. After receiving approval, Washington wired the money to the First Bank of Chicago who took several hours to prepare the money themselves. When it was ready to be picked up it took six agents, three of them literally toting two suitcases of cash each to haul the money two blocks from the First Bank of Chicago to the office. The other three agents guarded the money but, did so as discreetly as possible. Its ridiculous when one considers it but, due to the lack of parking facilities at the Loop located Bank of Chicago, we hand-carried the money beck to our office. As we passed a crowded lottery stand, I couldn't help but chuckle at the irony.

It is DEA policy to serialize a flashroll, which means recording the serial numbers of each bill. Serialization is done in case portions or all of the money is lost or stolen. If found, the bills will be checked against the serialized list. Naturally, every agent fears losing any money and utilizing the serialized list. Serializing the money is a monotonous process. It can be accomplished in one of two ways, by handwriting each serial number on pages which requires quite a bit of tedious effort and patience or Xeroxing the bills at a copying machine, usually laying fifteen bills out at a time. The day we flashed two million bucks we had every copier in the office churning out 8" by 11" copies of 100 hundred-dollar bills. It took awhile because we had to copy 20,000 $100 bills. I wondered what the Secret Service might say had they known about our mock counterfeiting ring.

I never had to serialize the $14,000 because I never received it. The ASAC, Joe Caravan, was not around to sign or authorize the approval form. His secretary said he was at a meeting but, I suspected he was at a discreet bar near the office called Charlie's. Some of us, including me, had dubbed Charlie's the "Wax Museum" because the same people were in the saloon every day occupying the same seats around the warped, tired old bar. Though Caravan didn't have a drinking problem, one of his closest associates in the US Marshals Service did. Caravan was trying to help the guy through some marital problems and had been consoling his friend a couple times a week in Charlie's. Bobby Hayes told me to go over to the bar and get Caravan's approval. I told Hayes I had attempted to but, couldn't find him. I didn't think it was a good idea to walk over there and disturb Caravan in the middle of personal business. Instead, I figured I would rely on cunning to trick Maldonado into believing I had the money.

I headed out with most of my fellow groupmates to the restaurant to meet Maldonado. I had my gun and my looks but, no cash to flash. I would be forced to dazzle Maldonado and I wasn't completely confident I could pull it off. I warned my groupmates about Maldonado's threats.

I met Maldonado as planned, in the same Mexican restaurant where I had purchased the second ounce of coke. Unlike the previous meeting, there was no small talk at all. Maldonado wanted to see the money and I wanted to see the cocaine. The meeting was tense and we argued. I ascertained Maldonado wasn't accustomed to the types of deals that involved this much weight and frankly, his nervousness made me uneasy. Our negotiations paralleled a game I played as a child with a female neighbor. We used to play in her garage, each of us urging the other to pull down their pants. One would, if the other went first. I can't remember if either one of us ever did pull down our pants but, I knew the contest I was playing with Maldonado was considerably more dangerous than "Show me yours and I'll show you mine."

"Don't fuck around, Mark." Maldonado warned, repeatedly. I replied in turn, attempting to show equal displeasure with Maldonado's stonewalling. In most cases, its accepted practice for the money to be displayed first. There was more dope than there was money and the cash was harder to come by so the money was always more important. After about thirty minutes worth of bickering, during which time Maldonado should have figured I did not have the money, we walked outside. Maldonado was frustrated with my stubbornness and finally instructed me to look inside the cab of a beat up red Ford pick-up truck parked at the corner. Guarding the truck nearby was another Hispanic male dressed in an old coat who I had never seen before. He stood near the front of the truck with his arms crossed. He looked neither imposing nor mute, just another person hanging in the neighborhood, looking for an opportunity. With Maldonado's implied consent, the "guard" allowed me to approach the truck. He offered no direction or resistance as I peeked inside. The cocaine was inside a brown paper bag stuffed between the truck's two bucket seats. Inside the furrowed bag there was ten baggies each containing presumably an ounce of cocaine. There also was a white chunk of cocaine in the shape and size of a bar of soap. It looked like a piece broken right off a kilo and combined with the ten ounce packages, it seemed like Maldonado had hastily put the package together. Its condition did not impress me but it didn't have to. All I had to do was make sure it looked like coke and Maldonado was finished.

I walked back toward the restaurant, approaching Maldonado, who had remained outside, scrutinizing vehicles. As I neared him, I removed a red handkerchief from my pocket, the pre-arranged arrest signal and one of the oldest and most obvious cues in law enforcement. I blew my nose into the handkerchief and expected the arrest team to come barreling out of the van. Instead, nothing happened other than I had a hankie full of snot in my left hand. Maldonado acutely recognized the scarf as a signal. It was obvious to everyone but my fellow agents.

"Mark, if you're setting me up with that fucking scarf you are a dead man." Maldonado threatened.

No response. Seconds pass by like hours when you are an under-cover agent who has given the arrest signal and there is no response. We had been trained the undercover agent never, absolutely never makes the arrest. The reason for this is simple. The dope trade involves tense negotiations and clandestine deals. Occasionally deals go south and one person turns on the other with their motive being robbery. In this case, as in all undercover deals, Maldonado didn't know I was a cop. If I were to pull out a gun and try to arrest him he might try to defend himself fearing a robbery. It certainly is reasonable for a person to protect himself. An arrest team composed of individuals bearing distinctive police clothing or badges at least gave Maldonado and any other suspect a reasonable clue the police were actually involved. I had nothing to identify myself as a police officer and being outnumbered two to one with the adversaries on each side of me, I decided not to try to make an arrest. I elected to improvise. "I'm not setting you up, C'mon, I'll show you the money." I nervously offered as I stalled for time. I held the conspicuous brown bag containing the coke in my right hand while I wondered why no one saw me carrying the handkerchief or the dope. I walked toward my car, passing our surveillance van with the inattentive arrest team inside. A few feet away from Maldonado but, with him unable to see me, I held up the handkerchief, opened my eyes real wide and waved the handkerchief at the van window. Maldonado's criminal intuition finally ignited and he started to walk fast, the other way. Finally, the surveillance van's cargo door swung violently open as Maldonado initiated the first stride of a full sprint. Agents crashed out of the van and began the pur-suit of Maldonado. Maldonado reached into his pocket and extricated something, throwing it under a car as he ran. Sixty yards later, he was swarmed under by a gang tackling trio that included two of our more physical agents, Jennings and Jim Walker. The clobbering tackle would have made any football team's defensive line coach quite proud. The other Hispanic confederate of Maldonado, who was identified during processing as Eduardo Villareal, just stood there in motionless terror. He quietly gave himself up but, he too was knocked down onto his ass by a couple of agents. Dropping someone was always an exciting part of an arrest and a tacit surrender usually did not prevent a good hit.

Brenda Xavier, part of the tardy arrest team, retrieved the item Maldonado had tossed under the car. It was a loaded and cocked .22 Derringer containing two bullets ready to be unloaded into an unfortunate victim. Brenda walked over to me and held out her hand to show me the weapon.

Inappropriately amused, she proposed, "This is what he had." Looking around at the interested but small crowd which had quickly gathered she added, "This could really hurt somebody."

"Yes, it could." I said, derisively. "It's a good thing he decided to throw it away."

8

I was completely enjoying the prestige and power associated with the DEA badge and the gun. I had been on the job now for over four years and was beginning to take full advantage of enjoyable perks that were offered us. Chicago Stadium was a favorite destination as we habitually attended Bulls and Hawks games, all for free. Unfortunately, there rarely was anything else at the stadium in which I was ever interested. The circus came around and occasionally a concert but teased lions, chained elephants and hobo clowns never appealed to me and the last few concerts I attended had left me with a contact high and a headache from all the reefer being smoked. Sports is what I enjoyed most and we often went into Wrigley and Soldier Fields to see ball games "on the arm," a term one of my fellow agents used to describe admission gained solely with the presentation of the badge. It worked other places as well. I saved over $25 a month on waived cover charges at local bars and Chicago's notorious and bombastic nightclubs. The free admittance was granted with the unwritten stipulation that any police in the establishment would offer assistance to bouncers if a patron or two became unruly and had to be physically removed. It had been my experience though the most unbridled customers were often the police themselves.

One of my best friends in the office was Brian Sullivan. We had quite a bit in common being single, the same age and both having been reared on the East Coast. We shared many of the same interests, which included sports, carousing, good food, boozing and other sordid endeavors. Though Sullivan was a partier he also was a dedicated agent and was respected in the office for his work ethic. Unfortunately, he had been in an investigative rut and had resorted to the use of some very questionable informants to generate some cases. He had been debriefing and recruiting unreliable and suspicious informants, contacting people he had put in jail and conducting surveillances on his own hoping to get lucky and be present when a development occurred. I admired him for his tenacious and persistent efforts and recognized the fact Bobby Hayes did not make his recent lack of success an issue.

Sullivan was dealing with one snitch in particular who was the object of everyone else's disdain, an unemployed and for lack of a better adjective, smelly West-sider named Tyrone Jones. There wasn't an agent in the group who believed Jones was connected or trusted enough to initiate DEA caliber dope deals. He simply didn't have the charisma or the swagger to promote himself as a legitimate player. Furthermore, Tyrone Jones was known on the street as "Pistol Face" because, as he himself admitted, he was ugly. His face was flat and his complexion so dark his skin took on a purple hue in the sunlight. His nose was pushed at an upwards angle towards his left eyebrow, a characteristic which made his face look like it was perpetually pressed against a plane of glass. His crude personal hygiene habits did not endear him to anyone either.

Tyrone had set up a deal for a quarter kilo on Chicago's North Side. A quarter kilogram of cocaine sold for about $6500 at this time in Chicago. The suspect, known to Pistol Face only as Chris, wanted $5,000 from our undercover agent, who was going to be Sullivan. Everyone had their doubts about the deal but, after Brian made an undercover call to Chris, the deal actually sounded like it might go. Undercover calls were usually a great gauge of the reliability of a dealer and if the suspect made ridiculous promises or excessive demands one could usually assume he was a "wannabe" dope dealer who possessed neither the experience or the wherewithal to produce the goods. Sometimes immoderate assurances were an indication the person on the other end was a cop, also trying to make a case. That happened occasionally where you had two cops from separate agencies each negotiating for a deal between each other with neither aware each was trying to set the other up.

The telephone call to Chris was taped, as virtually every undercover call is. The agents in the room reviewed the recording and agreed Chris' presentation and attitude sounded like he was a bona fide doper. Tyrone was very happy that he had finally came through. He had been quite zealous trying to set up a deal but had yet to be successful. More importantly, since he had not yet completed a transaction, he hadn't been paid any rewards or expense monies. The only doubt in Sullivan's mind as well as our supervisor's was the cheap asking price of the product. Chris price, $1,500 off the generally accepted market price, produced some degree of suspicion.

Surveillance was set up on a brick, three-story apartment building at the corner of an otherwise unassuming street in Northwest Chicago. The building was supposedly Chris' residence. It was a racially mixed neighborhood but, predominately white. I was alone in my car as I preferred to be when "tripping" was anticipated. Tripping was defined as moving to a second or third location to acquire the dope. We discussed in our briefing the possibility Chris may not have the cocaine in his possession and he would probably have to go to a location nearby to cop his product. The move would afford us the opportunity to follow Chris and maybe identify his source as we hoped to do in all instances. Sometimes we were fortunate in this endeavor however, the more experienced violators outfoxed or outmaneuvered us by insulating themselves with drop points and deliverymen.

Sullivan drove to the location in the company of Pistol Face. Jones exited the undercover vehicle that by coincidence was the same Jeep Cherokee I had used on my deal with Nunzio Maldonado. Jones rang one of the buzzers on the frame of the doors. A white male who looked to be about 20 years old exited. The guy looked like your average head-banger, long brown hair in a slight frame clothed in a black Iron Maiden T-shirt and a red checkered flannel whose tattered sleeves had been sloppily cut off. This was Chris. He spoke to Tyrone for a short while and then followed Tyrone to the undercover car, seating himself in the back seat. Adrenaline flowed. This was the point where any number of things might occur. Ideally, Chris would show Sullivan the coke and Sullivan would give the bust signal. We had previously agreed a visual signal would be the successive glow of Sullivan's brake lights which he would induce by gently tapping the pedal several times. There was no intermittent glow of red lights and there were no signs of fighting or struggle so we assumed they were engaging in small talk, certainly acceptable behavior by any strangers conspiring to trade $5,000 for 250 grams of cocaine hydrochloride. Phil Vreeswyck was in position to monitor the "kel." The kel was the radio transmitting equipment Brian was wearing. Brian was wired and Vreeswyck listened to the conversa-tion. Despite its sophisticated technological circuitry, sometimes even at close ranges of thirty feet or less, the kel didn't function properly, its frequency disrupted by a varied degree of common items like cellular phones, household appliances and CB radios. The kel was not reliable and served only to enhance our investigations. What we relied on mainly was our observations and our instinct to determine what was happening and for Brian and any undercover's safety, what might hap-pen. Fortunately, on this occasion, Vreeswyck could hear the kel clearly and he announced over the radio Chris did not have the package. He added they were feeling each other out which allowed me to relax momentarily.

After a few minutes, Chris left the car and returned to the building. Although Sullivan didn't tell us we were assuming Chris was going to retrieve the package. I recharged my head and concentrated on where he was going. We had the apartment building's entrance monitored by surveillance but there were several housing units in the tenement and there was no way of knowing exactly which apartment from which Chris would obtain the cocaine.

A pair of similarly dressed young white males exited the building wearing the same style of clothing as Chris. They paid no attention to Brian. However they curiously chose to remain outside and in the area of a driveway, slightly west of the entrance to the apartments. They loitered about and eventually were met by a black male who had come from an older Ford Mustang which he had parked across the street. I suspected all three were involved. I ran a 10-28 check for license and vehicle registration of the Mustang. It was reported from our base station the vehicle was owned by a Willemina Ford, at an address close by our location. I made a note of it and reported its appearance to the members of surveillance. There was other pedestrian traffic in the neighborhood as well since it was three-thirty in the afternoon. A lady had passed by towing an adolescent child and an older gentleman exited the apartment rolling an empty cart. He was a resident, I supposed and the woman a neighbor. I summarily dismissed them both as not being involved.

Suddenly, Chris came back out and approached Brian's undercover vehicle. He was not carrying anything and had made no motion toward the three individuals gathered outside his building. There was no signal of brake lights. Chris chose not to enter the vehicle but instead, only remained at the passenger side talking to Pistol Face, occasionally leaning into the car to emphasize something to Brian. After a few minutes, he returned to the apartments.

There was no transmission of the kel. Vreeswyck advised us he heard nothing but static. I assumed the fact that Brian remained was an indication he felt comfortable Chris was trying to get the dope but, I wished the housewife who was heating leftovers in the microwave or the teenage girl blow-drying her hair would hurry up and finish.

The black guy from the Mustang was gone. I had temporarily stopped watching the three young men in front of the building and now there was only one left, a dirty-blond haired, white teenager who walked toward me. He glimpsed briefly in my direction. I pretended to read a newspaper but I'm sure he identified me to be a cop. I watched him through the rear-view mirror as he glanced back over his right shoulder. He spit defiantly but continued on his way. I hoped he did not return and if he was involved and had known Chris was attempting a cocaine deal, he would surely alert the dealer narcs were outside.

A vehicle apparently arrived from the north side of the street away from my view. One of the other surveillance agents observed it and notified us via the radio. The driver, a short Hispanic male, exited his car and walked directly toward the apartments. He entered after being buzzed in through the security system. He was only inside approximately two minutes, plenty of time to drop off a quarter kilo of coke. We reasoned he probably was the source and as he left he was followed away by myself and another agent, Rasheed McKey. He had no license plate on his car but instead, a licence-applied for sticker, a common idiosyncrasy among traffickers who change automobiles frequently. He drove two blocks south and made an unexpectedly quick left turn. I sped up to continue to follow him but, I was impeded by oncoming traffic which prohibited me from making the same turn. The other agent, Rasheed McKey, was behind me. A parade of rush hour vehicles drove by as I waited to make the left turn. I desperately tried to monitor the progress of the vehicle we were following but I had lost sight of it. The Hispanic hadn't driven three blocks and I had lost him.

After making the turn, I tried frantically to pass traffic which proceeded routinely along the avenue. I weaved through three cars attracting some attention from at least one irate driver who blew his horn and paid tribute to his government at work by flipping me an obscene gesture. In spite of my efforts, I couldn't find the vehicle. I was too flustered at the loss of the Hispanic to engage in a traffic altercation and I had no alternative but to abashedly confess to the rest of surveillance I had lost the Hispanic.

I returned to the location of the deal as hastily as I could. I surmised the transaction would take place quickly if the unknown Hispanic had given Chris the coke. I was able to park in my original location which afforded me the same excellent view of the apartments. Chris did not immediately exit however and the announcement was a clue we were going to continue doing what we always did on surveillance, wait.

The old man I had previously observed with the shopping cart returned with a bag of groceries. Other people passed through the neighborhood, most if not all incognizant of the narcotics negotiations taking place around them. I fiddled with the FM stations, searching for a familiar song. Approximately forty-five minutes had elapsed since I had lost the Hispanic. There had been other traffic entering and exiting the apartment. I had paid some attention to the individuals but reasoned the source of the cocaine was the Hispanic who I had failed to properly identify. As time passed, I paid less attention to the people coming and going and fought the inviting impulse to rest my eyes for a few seconds.

We had been at the location for an hour and a half. Chris exited just as Hayes was about to suggest sending Tyrone into the apartment to identify the reason for the delay. Chris approached the vehicle with nothing identifiable in his hand. He did not enter the vehicle but seemed instead to get close enough to yell something to Brian and Tyrone. Again, he returned to the apartments. I had now felt better about losing the Hispanic. Apparently, he had not been the source as I'm certain if he had been, Chris would have consummated the transaction.

Subsequently, Vreeswyck revealed the kel was coming in better and Sullivan announced Chris promised the package was on its way. The message confirmed I had probably not lost the source. I was relieved and certainly less embarrassed. We waited while I focused more determinedly toward the apartment's entrance. A woman exited with two toddlers. She was not involved. The mailman came. I watched him carefully. I determined he was delivering only mail. Twenty-five more minutes elapsed. I was thirsty and needed a stretch, so I notified my partners I was going to get a soda pop. I left and returned and still nothing had happened.

Approximately two hours and forty-five minutes had elapsed since we had first arrived. Chris came popping out of the apartment, still nothing in his hands. It was his fourth visit with Sullivan. We were all pretty frustrated at this point and Hayes was about to call the operation off just as the brake lights intermittently glowed. The bust signal. I threw the transmission in drive and traversed the hundred or so yards to the rear of Brian's car. I was careful not to collide with any agents who might be coming from other directions in cars or on foot. Within seconds, Chris was prone on his stomach. He screamed as his right arm was pulled forcefully around his back to meet his left wrist. Chris was placed under arrest and put in the back seat of a car before there was a chance for any type of crowd to develop. A few curious neighbors milled around to see the cause of the commotion but most were too confused to understand what had transpired.

I remained outside as my supervisor questioned Chris. Hayes wasn't physically intimidating but under the right circumstance, he could terrify any man. Having just had automatic weapons placed against his head and being violently dragged to a car where he sat being questioned presented Hayes with the right circumstances to question Chris. As Hayes garnered a quick confession from Chris, Sullivan was using a portable test kit to analyze the quarter kilo Chris had delivered. Chris had removed it from the small of his back when he had entered Brian's vehicle. The package was actually eight separate bags of white powder, each placed in its own transparent sandwich baggie. Sullivan commented the cocaine looked extremely powdery. I moved closer to examine it while Vreeswyck questioned whether it was really cocaine at all. As I came closer to see the packages, Hayes yelled from his car, "The shit ain't real."

Sullivan looked at each package which contained white granulate, all bearing similar consistency. However, none of the chunky particles were present which were characteristic of real cocaine when it is left in ounce form. At least, high grade cocaine.

Cocaine is commonly shipped into the United States in kilogram packages. The cocaine is usually undiluted in that form and is up to 98% pure when it arrives in its 2.2 pound parcels. As the cocaine is broken from its kilogram packages into halves, quarters, ounces and so forth, it passes through many hands with each person controlling it determining how much cut or adulterant to add. As it progresses from kilogram to personal use quantities, it is diluted to increase profit margins for the person who sold it. It is a certain fact the guy who ends up snorting a line off a coffee table in Tulsa, Oklahoma is not snorting the same product which left the arcane, makeshift lab in the extraordinary forests of the Andes Mountains. Along the way, it has been diluted with everything from Vitamin B to baby powder. I had once arrested a dealer who was using hair spray and, on occasion, Lysol to lump his cocaine and make it chunky, making it appear like it was high grade coke. He called his process "Rerocking for the Rockheads." It was a general axiom, the more dilutant mixed into the cocaine the more powdery it becomes.

In this particular case, the alleged cocaine was completely powder. More specifically, Chris admitted the powder was Bisquick, the flour used to make pancakes and dumplings. Apparently, while nine federal agents waited patiently outside, Chris studiously weighed out eight ounces of Bisquick, wrapped the flour in baggies and attempted to sell the stuff which he purchased for less than two bucks a pound to the U.S. government for approximately $620 an ounce. Truly an American entrepreneur at work.

We suspected Chris may have the real thing inside his residence, so we requested he grant us the opportunity to search his home. Completely intimidated, he consented. Only three of us went inside B202, the second floor apartment where Chris admitted he lived. We found the scale he had used to weigh the flour on the kitchen table. He had spilled quite a bit of his valuable flour on the floor while concocting his little scheme. We were all disgusted but, I managed to extract a little humor in the situation though I was perturbed I had wasted most of the day assisting the deal.

Desmond Brokenborough found several boxes of sandwich baggies and a bag of multicolored rubber bands in a kitchen cabinet. Evidently when not swindling his government, Chris engaged in some legitimate trafficking as well. We heard from outside Chris had admitted to Hayes he dealt grams and eight balls of cocaine but was not capable of selling ounce quantities. For shits and giggles, I decided to search Chris' bedroom. Meanwhile, Brokenborough reported Chris denied there was any cocaine inside his apartment, a unit which he shared with a younger brother and his mother who fortuitously, were not at home to witness the spectacle of Chris' arrest.

The whole apartment was unkempt and disheveled and Chris' room was the worst. It was littered with clothing, magazines, coins, dirty laundry and audio cassettes. I found a small carton of lubricated condoms in Chris' top drawer along with several papers containing phone numbers, mostly girls, some discarded batteries and a mistreated Panasonic Walkman. I continued to fish around the drawers, more out of curiosity than an attempt to acquire evidence.

As I searched the third drawer, I came across a balled-up white winter sock which looked distinctly out of place in the drawer containing more of his swarthy cotton concert shirts. I unfurled the sock and found one crisp $100 note inside. I immediately considered taking it and before my conscience had a chance to engage my psyche in guilt, I placed the bill into my pocket.

I found nothing else. I was more interested in leaving with my supplemental income. Chris was arrested and transported to our DEA office for processing. Though he had not delivered real dope he was still guilty of some violation of a state crime deeming it illegal to attempt to defraud or deceive a government representative. The statute was adopted to protect misinformed and incompetent controllers from being duped by disreputable contractors but, we employed it to protect our pride against humiliating escapades like we had just endured. He probably wouldn't get more than probation, I surmised.

After I had gotten back to my car, I removed the lone hundred dollar bill from my pocket to examine it. I was delighted to discover the crisp bill was so fresh that there was a second bill stuck to it. I congratulated myself stealing two hundred bucks had been so easy but, privately, I wished he had more.

I came home that evening and felt absolutely no guilt for what I had done. Quite conversely, I believed I had punished Chris for wasting my time and the effort of other agents during the whole preposterous episode. I reasoned the action I had undertaken served the taxpayers of America by providing encouragement he not try something so bold again. The justifications turned to excuses as the evening progressed. About 1 a.m., while watching late night nonsense television, I recognized with this carefree and deliberate theft I had indisputably leaped over a border, a boundary that I had taken an oath to never traverse.

All of my life, I had lived an honest life. I came from a home of hard working and honest parents. My oldest brother had chosen the same path. Contrastly, I loathed the philosophy of my middle brother, who chose to shirk responsibility whenever possible. For all the petty and ridiculous offenses he had committed through the years, like stealing bicycles and petty shoplifting, he had never attempted what I had now done a fourth time. I thought back to childhood and could not recall even one instance where I had stolen so much as a lollipop from a merchant. I had never filched a red nickel from any employer for whom I had worked. Nothing. Now by my own volition, I had entered a realm of crime that not only would embarrass myself, my family and my agency but, would also result in severe repercussions if I were ever to be caught.

As the evening turned into morning, I recognized this theft was different. I was honest enough with myself to be able to comprehend I had entered a domain where some reckless policeman travel. I was officially a "dirty" cop.

That restless night passed as did several more. My realization did not wane. I knew what I had become and quite frankly, I accepted it, fully acknowledging to myself I had become corrupt. I was prepared to live with my new label but, even more determined to make it a worthwhile enterprise. My priority was to ensure no one else found out.

9

In our office, like other corporate offices throughout America, people enjoy gossiping. Coworkers make sport of talking behind each other's back, rehashing professional failures and offering opinions about personal issues and private lives. The Drug Enforcement Administration was no different. In our predominately male office, the talk centered around other agents and cops. Many of the stories were light-hearted and involved tales of individuals being caught in embarrassing or inauspicious circumstances, usually following an evening of drinking. Occasionally the subject of a cop or an agent who had been discovered corrupt would be discussed. I liked to chat about these people as much as anyone else. After all, if there was ever an innovative way developed to catch these people, I wanted to be aware of it. It seemed there never was. There was, however, a common trait which always seemed so prevalent among the crooked cops and it was how unfathomably stupid and careless their behavior had been which led them to being caught.

One story that made the rounds in the DEA was the group supervisor from Boston who managed to get himself busted bringing a 20 kilogram cocaine shipment from Miami through Boston's Logan Airport. Apparently, he convinced an informant to set up a deal where he traveled to Miami, picked up a small load of cocaine and loaded it all into a suitcase. The agent then planned to fly the coke up on a commercial airline flight with the cocaine dutifully packed in his luggage. He believed no one would suspect a DEA Agent to be transporting cocaine and even if his activity did come under scrutiny, he planned to convince officials he was traveling with evidence for official business. The Boston police would verify his identity and he would be on his merry way with over $400,000 worth of cocaine. The agent was right, he could get away with it and in fact, had already made one successful trip. A few weeks prior to the day of his apprehension, the supervisor, a guy with an Irish name, made his initial run and triumphantly returned with five kilos of cocaine which he delivered as planned to the patiently waiting informant in Boston. The federally employed courier was paid a meager $5,000 for the inaugural effort.

The problem with the entire scheme was it relied on the informant to initiate the meeting, arrange for the transportation of the cocaine in Miami and receive it in Boston. Anybody with any degree of experience will tell you, an informant is an informant for a reason. He has a motive that is always beyond good intentions, plain and simple. Always.

Upon the initiation of this confederacy, the agent broke a cardinal rule between agents and informants. He totally trusted the informant. The shrewd snitch however did not trust his emerald isle born accessory. The informant sensed this profitable arrangement was too good to be true. The transportation of the contraband seemed too easy and the informant smelled a set up. Though the DEA Agent was in it for the money as much as the informant was, the snitch panicked and his paranoia eventually led him to approach the Federal Bureau of Investigation who probably were initially weary of an informant telling such a relatively bold tale about his DEA accomplice.

Skeptical at the outset, the FBI nevertheless initiated an investigation based on the provocative revelation and the agent was eventually snagged in Boston with only his second tidy little load. When the federal government examines one of their own they usually pursue the investigation with zealous and unwavering conviction. With that investigation, the FBI utilized every resource they possessed and successfully built an air-tight case against the suspect. The federal defendant had no alternative but to plead guilty and beg for leniency. Clemency was never considered and the former agent who was making close to $90,000 a year is currently serving a rather lengthy and uncomfortable federal prison term while his trusted informant continues to ply his craft, now under the control of an agent of the FBI.

Reviewing the information, I was absolutely amazed how dim-witted the Irishman was, as well as the countless others who had been investigated, apprehended and prosecuted. There were hundreds of stories about police who robbed dope dealers. Their corrupt behavior was often obvious, at least the ones I had heard about. Police officers with families don't make enough money to purchase luxury cars, jewelry and extravagant vacation lodges, no matter how much overtime they log. When they began expending extravagantly with some of the monies they had pilfered, they were easily identified, if not by jealous co-workers then at least, suspicious neighbors.

Another prevalent method of corruption employed by dirty cops occurred when they seized cash during an arrest. Some dirty cops took whatever they wanted for themselves and then cut the suspects loose. Police didn't understand some of these people were responsible for the cash which was stolen from them. The suspects simply couldn't forget about the loss of the money because they had to pay it to someone else. It wasn't "their" money which was stolen. If they had been properly arrested and their cash seized as evidence documented within an official police report, the suspect could show a person whose money was supposed to be delivered that the police had really seized it. When law enforcement officers robbed dealers, the dealers often had no alternative other than to approach internal investigators or the FBI about the loss of their monies. An investigation would inevitably ensue and if enough evidence was established, and often it easily was, then arrests would be made. On other occasions dirty officers attempted to work out a deal where the suspects whose dope they stole would be asked to meet them later and buy the stuff back at reduced rates. The cops who utilized this method, in my opinion, were brazen and extremely reckless. Eventually, if they did this enough times, and greed would encourage them to do it often if they had gotten away with it once, they became the victims of violent reprisals. A dope dealer is only going to be ripped off so many times before he chooses another method of income or considers another option to solve his problems. Chicago, like other cities and towns across the country, also had its share of officers accepting protection money so dope dealers could conduct business under the protective umbrella of watchful policeman.

Though there were avenues corrupt officers and agents could pursue, the local and state police and federal agents I knew, all of them through the first four years of my career, were not corrupt. They were honest. Though selfish at times, they were good people who believed in the righteousness and importance of what they were doing. There exists a dire need in society for people to uphold some type of moral standard and many cops believe they are the only ones left who can do it. I felt I was one of these people until I realized I had crossed the line. I wondered if I was alone in my perverted endeavors. I realized I was not only a week after I had committed my theft of $200 from Chris' dresser drawer.

*

Every couple months, the local news stations will televise an impressive raid complete with live reports and filmed footage of heavily-armed police officers breaking down doors and shattering glass with sledgehammers and battering rams. In actuality, large, multi-agency raids where hundreds of law enforcement officers from various federal, state and local police agencies swoop down on a community conducting observable arrests and seizure of property serves little purpose other than media grandstanding. The raids don't accomplish much in the realm of protecting the municipality because usually the offenders arrested, many of whom are paraded in front of television cameras, are little more than petty criminals wanted on misdemeanor charges. These individuals are often out of jail and out on bail before the videotape is run on the late evening news. Nevertheless, the media loves it, law enforcement chiefs relish the exposure and the chance to make public speeches and the taxpayers are satisfied by it, so of course, the ridiculous practice continues.

From solely a safety perspective, the operations are dangerous. Typically agents from different agencies are sent to a location to serve a warrant, arrest a suspect and search the premises for illegal contraband and information helpful to an investigation such as phone records, photographs and other documents. Typically, assignments are divided so each agency participating is represented during the operation. Usually there will be a DEA Agent responsible for seizing dope evidence, A BATF Agent for guns, An IRS Agent for monies and financial records, A US Marshal if the suspect was a federal fugitive and any local or state police who maintain an active interest in the investigation. There may be others too, like reporters, photographers, informants and virtually anyone else who might have a stake in being present. Once, our group was directed to bring along a Hollywood actor who was preparing himself for a made for TV movie role. The actor requested to accompany us on as many raids as possible during the week he was visiting Chicago preparing for the part. After he experienced the very real danger and unexpected chaos of his first raid, he elected to wait in the comfort and security of a patrol car and watch. The practice of inviting people who don't belong and combining unacquainted individuals into raiding units makes for establishing wonderful new friends and gregarious photo opportunities but, is fool hearty in the name of safety. People bursting into a unfamiliar house with varying degrees of weaponry who do not know each other and have no ability to perceive how each one might react does not make ideal conditions for the execution of a secure raid.

I participated in the execution of many federal search warrants and my preference was to work only with the DEA Agents I knew. Still, we all were required to assist when the office put together these media extravaganzas. They were humorously referred to as "Dog and Pony Shows." During one particular pony show, I was assigned as the team leader of seven agents. Our assignment was to arrest a Latin Eagles' Gang Leader wanted for conspiracy to distribute marijuana and cocaine and related gun charges. He had a notorious reputation for violence. My team consisted of two agents from the BATF, one of whom I had met on a prior occasion, an INS agent because the individual we planned to arrest was an illegal alien from one of the Central American countries, a US Marshal and two police officers from the town where he lived, Villa Park, Illinois. Of the members on my team I knew only one, Mike Kamenski. I had met Kamenski, one of the two BATF Agents, during a golf outing for the benefit of a slain Chicago Police Officer. I had gratuitously exchanged business cards with him over a few beers once. To my surprise, Kamenski had actually called me shortly thereafter and I was able to provide him information from our DEA computer data base about a potential suspect in one of his investigations. I remember he had been grateful for the unanticipated assistance.

He approached me when he saw me, "Hi, I'm Mike. Remember me…from the golf outing? We are on the same raid team."

I smiled, acknowledging he was correct. "Hi," but before I had closed my mouth I began assessing his skills, his judgment and his courage. As my team came together, in the rear of the large meeting room as we were instructed by the coordinator, I noticed others conducting the same analysis. Each officer evaluating the members of the raid team for competence and ability. Each appraising the other who may be called on later that day to save a life. As the assigned team leader, I introduced myself and gave a brief explanation of our assignment. Everyone had been supplied a handout describing the violator and the charges for which he was wanted. Consequently, each of us knew more about the suspect and his background than we knew about each other and with his barbarous background well documented, we knew at least, the suspect could handle a weapon. I suggested a location where we should meet near the target's address and everyone agreed it was a wise choice, far enough from the house to assemble yet close enough to not be required to travel far.

An hour later, we were all together again at the meet spot, in this case a convenience store two and a half blocks from the suspect's home. The common practice of picking a meet spot leads to the creation of considerable interest among the public who often see us preparing for the raid. Customers of the store usually gawked as we placed our raid gear on. Typical raid equipment is too cumbersome to drive around while wearing so we usually waited until we were close to the target's house before putting it on. The holsters, the weapons, the bullet resistant vests and the utility belts with knives, flashlights and extra munitions magazines served to create the impression we were preparing for the Armageddon. The customers had to wonder what prospect conjured the need for apparent soldiers parading around in the parking lot with automatic weapons. The fact they possessed only muffins, newspapers and twelve ounce coffees had to concern them. It had not happened yet, but I waited for the day when we would meet at a location, perhaps a fast food parking lot, and the intended suspect we were planning to arrest was already inside happily munching on a sausage and egg croissant speculating on what the fuss was about.

As we gathered, I devised an entry team. I remembered Mike's name so I told him he would enter the house with me through the front door. Based on his reaction, he didn't look enthused and I felt a wave of regret for having selected him. Then I decided to spite his noticeable apprehension and not offer him the chance to change. He spoke up and suggested I also place his associate from the BATF on the entry team. Kamenski probably maintained the same reservations about me and since he felt comfortable with him, I agreed. I asked for any volunteers and the two Villa Park Policemen stepped forward eager to accept the challenge. They seemed enchanted by the whole affair which I came to accept as a risky proposition designed to placate publicity seeking administrators. So, we had our entry team, none of whom had ever worked together. I determined the five of us would smash down the front door and enter a house we had never been in, each of us armed with weapons easily capable of ending several lives, including each other's. I directed the remaining two agents to secure the perimeter, stand outside the house monitoring its sides and rear in case the suspect attempted to flee out the back door or a window. Their responsibilities were significant. I asked them not to enter the house until told to do so. Police obituaries are filled with reports of officers having been shot dead by other cops entering a raid site from an opposite direction, startling each other in a dark room and then engaging in a crossfire. The US Marshal and the INS Agent agreed to remain outside and seemed relieved they had been assigned to locations on the exterior of the house. I did not feel confident about them and believed of the group I had, by sheer happenstance, I managed to pick the best people to accompany me through the front door.

The raid, which was executed precisely at the predetermined time of 7:30 a.m., progressed without incident. We gained entrance, apprehended the slumbering suspect and secured the residence. No one was injured and we proceeded with a complete and thorough search of the two story townhome. Some looked cautiously, expecting booby-traps, I supposed. I was more aggressive in my search and discounted the gangbanger would have been clever enough or even concerned about police to the point of installing booby-traps. During raids of offenders like the gangbanger, I considered myself a "ripper." If a family did not live in the home being searched, that is, children did not reside there, I would scour everything. I enjoyed the privilege of sifting through people's property, examining their possessions and probing their lives. It was amazing the unusual items one would find and I have to believe an interesting book will someday be written about the revelations and startling discoveries made during search warrants. It was fun for me to be able to ransack homes, overturning furniture, breaking down walls and prying open electronic equipment attempting to find a couple grams of coke. I will admit I was not always a complete asshole about it. If I suspected contraband was concealed I would search as thoroughly as possible. If I did not like the suspect or he had a particularly long or violent criminal history, I would take the time to destroy some of his property, all in the name of justice. Before doing so, I always gave the suspect an opportunity to tell me where their dope was hidden to preserve their property. When the individual elected not to accept my invitation to save me the hassle of finding it myself, I went to work. Despite my valiant efforts I have to admit I never found anything illegal sewn into furniture but that never stopped me from ripping apart some very attractive living room pieces.

On this particular raid, the suspect lived by himself in a poorly constructed but, well-furnished home. He had an arrest record which included some twenty-nine arrests ranging from petty crimes to armed robbery, assault and attempted murder. I judged him to be nothing more than a punk based on his lengthy criminal history and I didn't like him well before I had ever met him. Slitting his JBL speakers and his leather love seat gave me some fleeting satisfaction. When he saw me throwing his clothes and his precious shoes around, he really got pissed off. He yelled at me in Spanish and although I did not understand what slanders he was making, I was secure in the knowledge that it was most likely very derogatory and insulting. I respectfully removed some framed photos of his parents and a young boy who I suspected was his son. Then, I delightfully dismantled the projection television the framed photographs had been displayed upon. Once $300,000 had been recovered from the cabinet of a fully functional projection television so I never let the opportunity to break one open pass by. Especially, since I felt I had an obligation to my employer, the Department of Justice, to conduct the most thorough inspection of his residence as possible.

Finding nothing during my search, I made my way up to the second floor where I observed a trap door in the master bedroom. I heard rustling in another room and assumed the orderly bedroom and the area above it had not been searched so I made my way into the crawlspace. Attics were commonly used to store pound quantities of marijuana and other contraband. Since the person was suspected of dealing marijuana as well as cocaine, I figured it would be an excellent place to stash his weed. I assumed since I could not smell any odors like pot, there probably wasn't any significant amounts up there but, I went up anyway, also concentrating on the smell of money too, since my sinister desires were now starting to bloom completely. I creeped on my chest along the rafters which were all dust covered. The moldy and undisturbed state of the attic yielded evidence no one had been up there for some time. Nevertheless, I lifted insulation, probing with my hands and fingers, paying careful attention for any exposed nails or staples which might lacerate me. There was not much room but I still was able to crawl along on my belly. I poked the darkness with my small flashlight which provided me some degree of illumination in the bulbless crawlspace.

I reached the end of the attic, having crawled a distance of about twenty feet. Having checked its length, I suspected the resident had never been up there. As I shimmied my body to turn around, I heard the faint voice of one of the Villa Park Policeman who had accompanied me into the house. While laying over what I presumed was the kitchen, I could hear him apologizing to the suspect about my conduct during the raid. I quietly listened.

"You know these federal guys. They think they are so fucking bad. They think they know everything and their shit don't stink. He did not have to do that, man. Cut your couch and slice it up like that, man."

"He a real asshole, man." The suspect said in broken English, rendering an opinion which I had heard before.

The cop sensed he had gained the affections of the imprisoned suspect. I listened and was briefly aggravated but, I realized this officer would meet the individual again. He would have to deal with him or perhaps his family members or gang affiliates sometime in the future. I would never see the guy and I could treat him accordingly. The cop did not have my advantage and consequently was more concerned with the bad guy's opinion of him than me. I knew at the end of the day I would exchange business cards with the Villa Park Officer and if he could help me in the future and cared to, he would. And if I was inclined to help him if he called, I might but, beyond that, we would probably have little, if any, interaction ever again. The cop, on the other hand, would meet the defendant again and perhaps many more people the defendant knew in the locale he policed. I listened a bit longer but the conversation shifted to people in the community whom both were acquainted. I turned myself around by shimmying into a U-turn. I crawled to the ladder, breathing small particles of dust as I went. I approached the small threshold and was surprised to acquire an angled view of Kamenski, the BATF Agent, opening his pants. I stopped immediately and watched, judging from his actions and his glance toward the door, he was behaving peculiarly. I noticed his pants were open, unbuckled with the zipper pulled down. He pulled at the band of his underwear. It was a clumsy jerking motion wrought with nervousness and anxiety. The elastic band stretched then snapped back against his waist. He awkwardly cocked his neck giving him what I perceived as a view of the hallway. Simultaneously, he pushed his holster belt with his left hand. He strained to pull the polished black leather upward. He muffled the grunt which emitted from his throat as he squeezed the belt around his diaphragm. He had no idea I was only a few feet above him. He pulled his underwear down and out. Embarrassingly, I briefly looked away as I could see his genitals from my perch above. He cocked his head again and with his right elbow, he pressed the holster high against his rib cage. Then with his left hand he delved into the second drawer of the open dresser he stood before. He reached in and pulled out three small transparent bags. He did it awkwardly and one caught the corner of the top drawer causing it to rip open and spill its white powdery contents all over the front of his raid jacket. He thrust the three packages into his groin, letting go of the underwear band and the belt. The three bags of cocaine disappeared into his pants and he began to zip up his pants not realizing one of the bags had torn. He glanced down.

"Fuck." He uttered, quite audibly and surely louder than he had meant. He brushed himself wildly, recognizing he had ripped open one of the bags. The illegal granules went everywhere, in all directions. It was as if a baker had sneezed into a large pan of baking flour. Kamenski panicked and I felt my adrenaline begin to surge but surely not as much as his as he stood swinging his arms violently attempting to dismiss the cocaine powder which clung to him like miniature scarlet letters. He reached into his underwear to extract the source, the broken bag. He flung it to the carpeted floor which served only to scatter the illicit specks over almost a quarter of the room. The small bag spewed its contents everywhere like a child shaking a beach blanket inside the house and the illegal powder was blatantly evident against the red plush carpeting of the bedroom. I reasoned he was panicked with fear that he might be discovered and he was desperately attempting to rid himself of the glaring evidence of his theft. I thought about the fact he was armed and I was laying above him, watching. I had to bare myself but, it must be done in a way as to not startle him. I had to act as if I had seen nothing. As he danced about wildly, I was perched above him, prone and basically defenseless against his panic. If he suddenly looked up he would see me. I deliberately made a loud noise, kicking the wood stud near my left foot. Avoiding his eyes, I hoped he heard and consequently, seen me. Looking behind me, I pretended to have my right foot caught and I struggled to remove it.

"God damn it." I said loudly.

He must have known my existence by now but, I wanted to give him every instant he may need to gain his composure and to formulate an explanation.

I fumbled around for some thirty seconds making obvious noise but making no attempt to look down, into the room and at Mike.

"God damn." I said again emphatically.

"Mark?" Mike's startled voice exhibited surprise but, my deliberate delay had given him time to think of some excuse. "Hey, I found some cocaine." His voice failed. He gulped hard enough for me to hear. "I mean, I just found this and as I went to look at it and this fuck, I mean, this stupid fuck didn't have the bag tied. It spilled on me, all over me and the room and the fucking shit is all over me."

Trying to deflect and mask my concern, I replied, " I think I'm stuck up here on a nail." I had hoped to sound nonchalant at his discovery. "Yea, I'm stuck up here." I kicked at the floor, hitting the ceiling above his head. "I'm, there…I am free. Friggin' nails. I didn't find anything but," I hesitated, "you got something?"

It was horrible acting. I descended the small wooden ladder and finally looked at Mike.

"What happened to you ?" I asked.

His face was flushed. His brow sweated. He had been caught and he must have recognized that I knew.

"I found…were you up there ?" asking the obvious question while he continued to draft his alibi.

"Yea, I was up there. I always check the attic with these guys." I said.

"I found an ounce. I guess it's an ounce. Maybe its more than that the way its all over the place. It was in the drawer and I pulled it out. It went all over me." He shook his head and wiped his perspiring face with the left sleeve, leaving a small culpable streak of residue across his forehead. " I guess I pulled it out upside down or something."

I replied, "You must have. It's all over." I brushed his face while I hunted for the words to reassure him, to calm his racing head. I did not know what measure he might take to extract himself from the critical situation. "Well, at least we got some dope. Don't worry I'll scoop it up. I'll seize this whole fucking carpet if I have to and let the lab collect the residue."

I sensed a twinge of relief but, it might have been my own. I jokingly made reference to his cocaine-soiled raid jacket, "Mike I may have to seize your jacket, too."

He tried to smile but, it was a helpless grimace.

"Mike, brush it off onto the floor, as much as you can. No big deal. At least we got dope."

I hoped he was reassured. I watched him disgustedly push the flakes off his coat and his sleeves. His face translated into an ashen pale color. I attempted to appear preoccupied with the collection of evidence. Stupidly, I blurted out, "Is there anymore?"

The query left him no option. There was no where to go. He couldn't very well say, "Yea, right here in my crotch. Two more ounces."

What I had inadvertently done was create a confrontation. He might possibly construe my off-handed remark as an accusation. I wanted to diffuse the situation and prove I had no plans to confront him. What he was doing was on him. His own conscience would be his executioner and I had no notions whatsoever to question him about what I had observed. I presented him an invitation to leave.

"Mike, go wash off, before you breathe that in and fail your next piss test."

He stopped brushing. He looked up. "Yea." He could no longer resist. "How long were you up there?"

He turned and walked out not having waited for my reply. I heard the toilet flush, several times.

IO

Kamenski's theft had been the most blatant act of dishonesty or corruption I had observed. Of course, I viewed my own thefts as having been considerably less debased. I had stolen a few pieces of jewelry and had done little more than fall into a few hundred dollars. Kamenski, on the other hand, was desperate enough to have actually resorted to stealing dope. I wasn't sure if he was using it or selling it but, I suspected he had developed a Coke Jones, a street slang for a dependency. I reasoned his addiction must have been severe if he was willing to risk his career to steal three ounces of meaningless white powder. He must have had the opportunity to seize bigger quantities of the stuff, after all, the BATF was an agency notorious for pressuring their agents to conduct more narcotics investigations. Chicago's streets were teeming with distributors of coke and I couldn't imagine Kamenski was forced to steal ounces to feed his habit when it was so readily available for purchase on the streets. Seemingly, every neighborhood had prevalent cocaine dealers with some wards featuring kilogram dealers operating on the same block. Certainly buying dope had to be safer than resorting to stealing it.

My groupmate Phil Vreeswyck had found an entire precinct which sustained a thriving horde of kilogram dealers. He had been working a joint inquisition with Investigators from the Cook County State's Attorney's Office. Their office, like so many others, maintained an independent narcotics division and Vreeswyck had established a bilateral and cooperative working arrangement with the unit. Vreeswyck, working closely with one of the Cook County's lead investigators, believed he had identified the residence of a significant cocaine dealer supplying Chicago's violent Harrison district.

The Harrison District, a six square mile area on Chicago's West Side, has the appalling distinction of being one of the most dangerous places for human beings on the face of the earth. It's a tract of land which is a blistered spread of despair, poverty and unemployment with slightly more than 92,000 inhabitants. By the time Vreeswyck's investigation had concluded, there were 93 people murdered in the area over the course of just one year, a figure which surpassed the total of fourteen individual states' homicide rates for 1991. In a time where statistics often fail to demonstrate the carnage and torment of violent crime, the fact that one out of every one thousand people in Harrison could expect to be stabbed to death or gunned down in cold blood was a startling and very undeniable reality.

Not surprisingly, the Harrison district is one of Chicago's most feared neighborhoods. It is a crime haven where dope is literally more readily available than milk and bread. Convenience markets indigenous to most American neighborhoods are frequent targets of armed robberies in Harrison and consequently, are not plentiful. Gas stations, video rental shops and other commonly accepted neighborhood stores also do not operate in the area. Instead, people offer any items of value they have by placing them for sale or barter in front of their storefronts, homes and apartments. Mattresses, boxsprings, end tables, lamps, even toilets are readily displayed on lawns, porches and in yards. The articles have some value in the barren neighborhood but inconsequential enough to merit robbery. Usually. In stark contrast, liquor stores are abundant but are forced to operate behind cages and bulletproof glass. The proprietors of these businesses are also often robbed. However, the alcohol business is so lucrative in down-trodden Harrison, merchants take the risk, often paying a bodyguard as little as $20 or as much as $200 to escort the owner out of the neighborhood with the day's receipts. Devoid of legitimate business, Harrison's top commodity is, not surprisingly drugs and specifically, crack cocaine.

Many of the agents in the group scoffed at Vreeswyck's notion the violator he was targeting, Melvin Rush, was the biggest crack dealer in the area. There was so many, picking one and saying he was the biggest was equivalent to reaching into a bag of shelled peanuts and with the first try, selecting the one with the largest nut inside. Crack cocaine was sold on virtually every street corner and gangway in the six square mile area of the neighborhood. The narcotics trafficking was usually uninterrupted and flowed around the clock with sales only temporarily disrupted by a random drive-by shooting. Police had no effect on the flow of distribution. Though they were occasionally a law enforcement presence, the dealers operated openly and with little regard for their authority. The beleaguered police's main purpose in Harrison was to attempt to suppress violence, not dope deals. Even drug dealers wanted to ply their craft safely and since there existed so much brutality with all the murder and robbery, the police were confined to responding to and investigating only the most serious crimes. There was simply no time or manpower to handle drug interdiction. It was a plain fact even dedicated and honest police officers could not smother an undertaking which provided so many of the people in the neighborhood a reliable livelihood. With crack cocaine so abundant, few agents, including myself, believed only one person could be supplying the entire area with crack cocaine. Despite the repudiating opinions, Vreeswyck admirably persisted with his investigation of Melvin Rush and eventually was able to convince a Cook County Judge to issue a search warrant based on information obtained from a reliable informant. The confidential informant claimed that Rush was stockpiling cocaine in a posh apartment in the upscale and revitalized Printer's Row section of Chicago's downtown loop. It was there, from his secluded and private apartment, he filled the streets of Harrison with crack cocaine.

I volunteered to meet Vreeswyck and one of his partner's, Carlos Perez, one morning at 7 a.m. near Rush's residence. Vreeswyck's senior partner, Brenda Xavier, had been uninterested in assisting Vreeswyck since he had not followed her direction in the investigation. Vreeswyck had also been guilty of selfish behavior and had listed himself as the sole case agent on the Rush investigation despite the considerable assistance Perez had offered. I wasn't interested in the politics of the process but, I was interested in the potential. That is precisely the reason I volunteered to help Vreeswyck and met him, Perez and several members of the Cook County Investigators team to execute a search warrant at Rush's seventh floor, two bedroom apartment which was, coincidentally, located only four blocks south of our offices.

Rush was asleep in an elaborately decorated bedroom when we arrived. He must have fancied beasts of the field since many of his possessions were styled in the color of animal hides. His sheets were zebra skins, his underwear leopard, his boots snake and his couch, a rich chocolate leather. He even possessed a large, ostentatious polar bearskin rug. The lumpish pelt looked ridiculous in his small living room area where the sheer size of the item compelled the polar bear's head to be left absurdly exhibited under an end table.

Briefly amused, we began searching the apartment thoroughly. An informant had told Vreeswyck that Rush concealed kilograms of cocaine in the utility room's ventilation duct above his washer and dryer. The vent, upon removal of its cover, was discovered to contain nothing but dust. Only spiders and ghosts had been inside that duct since it was installed by the builder. Regardless, we searched for cocaine, in the metal conduit, in cabinets, under rugs and everywhere else and though we found no cocaine, the service of the warrant proved to be very fruitful.

Rush had money scattered, literally, all over the apartment. There was cash in every drawer in his bedroom. There was a pile of five dollar bills in his sock drawer. The hoard was neatly arranged in order, and was about eighteen inches long. Rush had currency of various denominations in his underwear drawer. Fives, tens, twenties and fifties tossed haphazardly among his silk undergarments. Two drawers contained three shoe boxes each. Each shoe box contained piles of cash wrapped with a variety of colored rubber bands. Somebody stopped and counted one pile. It contained $4,500. Just one pile. In one shoe box, there was eight piles. In another thirteen. Still two others contained seven and eight piles of cash. The mother lode was concealed in a medium sized black gym bag found in a living room closet. The nylon satchel held fourteen bundles of cash, neatly organized in denominations ranging from $5 to $100 bills. Each bundle contained exactly $20,000.

A search of the living room and the dining room also yielded money. Even the kitchen had currency concealed in drawers, cupboards and under the sink. The money was in paper bags, plastic bags and small boxes. Rush had $3,800 in a plastic lunch box emblazoned with the popular children's character Barney on it.

When people see that kind of money they often get excited. I know I was. I can only offer my own opinion but when I meet someone, even a dope dealer, who has access to that amount of money, I am impressed and envious. No one could deny Mel Rush was a bona-fide success in his chosen enterprise. He had the mental capacity and the business acumen of any successful entrepreneur in America. Making his money so boldly and illegally, one could argue Rush had taken strikingly more risks than Don Trump, Lee Iacocca or other respected magnates who often hide behind high priced tax attorneys and praetorian accountants to build their paper fortunes. Rush, on the other hand, was out on the street, sticking his neck out in order to succeed. His financial liquidity provided ample evidence he had.

Someone decided the money should be pooled onto the granite coffee table in the living room. At the beginning of the raid we were careful to photograph places where each container of cash was found but, so many of the agents were finding caches of cash, we lost track. Toward the end, bags, boxes and loose bills were just being thrown onto the table. Counting money is a tedious task and there was simply too much of it to compute at the apartment. Vreeswyck, who was so thorough an agent he carried it to the point of irritation, was upset the search had become so disorganized. He insisted that more care be exercised in procuring photographs of the money and documenting locations where each box and bag was found but, few listened and the giddy seizure of cash continued.

Rush was completely unfazed by the actions taking place around him. He sat stoically, apparently more concerned about how we found out where he lived rather than all his cash he watched being confiscated. One of the investigators asked Rush how he could remain so indifferent. Rush shrugged his shoulders, then finally offered, "That's Christmas money. Your peckers are all hard and that money is what I use to buy Christmas presents." He paused, "Hey mother fucker," he addressed Carlos Perez, "grab a pile and buy your daughter something nice for a change." Perez, as luck would have it, had a daughter who had been diagnosed with autism and the remark enraged those of us who knew. Even among those that didn't, there was not a cop in the place who did not want to smash Rush's arrogant head open like a can of tomatoes. No one touched him though, at least none of the Feds. I couldn't speak for the actions of Cook County Investigators who would be the ones taking custody of Rush and carting him away in handcuffs. He was not arrested for possession of the cash. Though it was obvious the money had come from some illegal means and we all knew it was drug money, it is no crime to be in possession of large amounts of currency. Despite distinct clues Rush was breaking the law, no illegal contraband was found in the apartment. No drugs, guns or stolen property. Rush, by his own admission, was wanted for an outstanding traffic warrant because he failed to show up in Chicago for a court date after he had been caught driving with a suspended license. Rush, despite all the evidence of his dope dealing, was merely arrested on an outstanding traffic warrant. He would post bail and be released before the money was completely inventoried.

We were only permitted to seize the currency through the comprehensive powers granted by federal seizure laws. Unlike all other instances under our criminal justice system where the suspect is innocent until proven guilty beyond a reasonable doubt, an individual who has assets seized is considered guilty of obtaining them through illegal or illegitimate means until the individual can prove otherwise. The burden to protest seizures is solely on the individual to prove justifiable ownership by whatever medium possible. Using these statutes, the government and specifically, its agents, have the right to investigate and seize any and all assets which are believed to be derived from illegal or illegitimate means. Assets are defined as any amount of cash, conveyance or any other item of monetary value. The law worked well when it was followed conservatively. In this instance, Rush, who had no mechanism of support, such as steady employment, had obviously obtained his funds illegally. Rush would never be able to prove he procured his money legitimately and the seizure laws were designed to penalize people like Melvin Rush. Though the law was written with violators like Melvin Rush in mind, there were agents who abused the seizure laws, leaping at any opportunity to take things away from people who were not intended to be targets. This activity frequently came with the blessing of their supervisors because the confiscation of assets produced favorable statistics.

The search warrant executed against Rush had been obtained through the state system so Vreeswyck agreed the money should be seized by the Cook County Investigators. Rush could petition the State of Illinois for the return of his loot if he could prove the money had been acquired legitimately but, that would not happen. Two of the investigators scooped up the money, placing most of it in a sturdy Samsonite suitcase which had been secured from Rush's basement storage locker. The remainder of the cash was stuffed back into the black gym bag. Some additional money was placed into one of Rush's zebra pillowcases and hauled away for a final tally. The search lasted about an hour and a half during which time, I estimated Rush had been relieved of between $250,000 and $300,000.

Vreeswyck wanted to interview the apartment manager regarding any additional information she could furnish about Melvin Rush. She said he was a good tenant, promptly paid his rent and bills, occasionally hosted a party and dated numerous attractive women. She added he was friendly and courteous to other residents and no one had ever complained about him.

While Vreeswyck interviewed her, other investigators trickled out of the apartment. The two hour visit was over. I remained behind waiting for Vreeswyck to conclude his chat. Perez, still fuming over Rush's insulting remarks, decided to go back to the office to cool down. I roamed through the luxuriously furnished apartment contemplating how palatable indulgence really is. I wanted to take another look at his elaborate clothes closet where he harbored his beautiful garments. The clothes were all new with some still bearing visible sales tags from the exclusive department stores from which they were purchased. Rush hadn't even worn some of them. I decided the clothes were a bit too exotic for my tastes but, I reasoned that opinion was more reflective of my poor tastes in clothes rather than Rush's.

I opened a few drawers in the bedroom and recalled how the cash had been plucked like seagulls descending on a discarded fish carcass. I lifted the mattress. It had been searched. I pulled up the sheets and a blanket which had also been ransacked. I peeked in a small closet in the hallway. It looked undisturbed, so I tossed it finding only a vacuum, a basketball and some heavy winter coats but, nothing of value. The closet's order indicated it had been missed which can happen during some raids, especially when one takes a chaotic turn like the Rush raid had. Someone thinks the closet has been checked and in the excitement of finding contraband or in this particular case, money, the investigator assigned to check the closet gets sidetracked and forgets about it. That is the purpose of conducting multiple sweeps so, I searched the undisturbed closet and found nothing which interested me or Uncle Sam.

I entered the living room. I looked underneath the couch near the snarling, unhappy polar bear. I tossed a few cushions knowing full well the room had been thoroughly searched. By that time, Vreeswyck and the manager had eased into the living room and joined me. The manager curiously watched me as Phil Vreeswyck peppered her with questions. I was oblivious to Vreeswyck, who fastidiously took copious notes regarding everything the building manager said despite the fact none of it seemed relevant to me. I heard Vreeswyck ask her if she knew anything about "…other suspicious blacks occupying the building." I chuckled.

I probed the laundry room which I considered to be strangely barren given it contained no clothes or washing supplies, detergent or fabric softener. I reasoned Rush probably had to wash something in the machine at one time or another and my interest in the room was tweaked. For approximately fifteen minutes, I searched every nook and cranny of the six by six foot room. I was convinced Rush had something concealed in the laundry room but my search produced nothing. Meanwhile, I heard Vreeswyck's faint voice as he continued to offer inquiries tainted by his racist views.

I roamed into the kitchen and popped a few more drawers uncovering pots, pans, dishes and some scattered silverware. Rush had a pornographic magazine concealed in one of the utensil drawers. I briefly thumbed through it.

I opened the refrigerator. Rush dined well and appeared to be a big meat eater. The freezer contained about a dozen, frozen marbled steaks and chops. The refrigerator had a half full bucket of Popeye's chicken and three separate quart containers of their famous spicy beans. In addition, there were many condiments, cheeses, pickles, dairy products and plenty of soda pop. I reached down to the bottom and slid open the crisper drawer. It contained some tomatoes and curiously, a purple Crown Royal whiskey pouch. I knew immediately, by its unconventional presence, it contained money. The only thought in my head was to get that bag. I left the refrigerator open and ducked into the living room. Vreeswyck, whose back was to me, was attempting to convince the apartment manager to become a paid DEA informant. I returned quickly to the kitchen, almost leaping for the bottom drawer. I grabbed the purple pouch and stuffed it into my crotch. I yanked the adjoining crisper open and was disappointed to find it contained only two heads of rancid lettuce. I shut the refrigerator and walked hastily from the kitchen into the living room towards the hallway. It was the only way to get to a bathroom located at the end of the short corridor. I walked past the manager and Vreeswyck, neither of whom noticed the substantial bulge in my blue jeans. At least Vreeswyck hadn't but, the manger may have and attributed my apparent bewildering arousal to another indication of how bizarre the government agents were. I went for the bathroom like a retiree who had just located a rest stop after a four hour car ride. I locked the door behind me. I wanted to be sure I had not gone to this degree of trouble to pilfer tortilla shells so I slid my hand into the pouch to feel the chilly contents. Undeniably, it contained cold cash. Greed forced me to view the valuable contents. I pried apart the gold drawstring and saw three or four bundles of cash, each one about an inch and a half thick. Satisfied, I secreted the bag under the sink in a cabinet and covered it with a plush bath towel. I pushed the waste paper basket against the door on my way out so I would know if someone entered the room, it would be moved and I would hear the plastic bin be knocked over.

I excitedly returned to the living room and foolishly blurted out, "Are we almost finished here?" The abruptness of my interruption startled Vreeswyck. I knew my tone was aflame and not normal. He glanced at me and disapprovingly turned his back to continue his questioning. The manager looked uncomfortable. I sat down and considered what I had just done.

I stole evidence!

It was not trinkets, it was not pocket money. It was government evidence. I instinctively looked to the ceiling to see if any heads were popping out of previously unnoticed attics.

Oh God.

Had the manager seen my near robotic walk through the apartment and down the hallway. As I considered the possibilities, I realized inside the bathroom was a five foot wide mirror that I had just stood in front of while fondling the money. What a perfect place for a hidden camera. I had just participated in a state search warrant at an apartment I knew nothing about, where the owner had seemed suspiciously calm throughout the ordeal. I surmised he might as well have been an actor. I wondered if the whole god damn thing could have been some kind of a set up to grab a dirty state's investigator and instead, they caught a contemptible DEA agent. I jumped to my feet and walked quickly back to the bathroom. I did not enter. This time I wanted to see the adjoining wall the mirror pressed against. I realized it was the back wall of Rush's closet. I looked inside the bathroom without moving the door and setting off the crude plastic alarm I had set with the basket. The mirror did not seem to be flush against the wall. Certainly a person could not fit between the space but, a camera easily could. My head spun as I scrutinized the whole apartment as quickly as possible. I was not looking for money but instead, cables and wires which could be connected to cameras or video recorders. I was scared. As I searched, I prayed the little pouch did not contain dope. Just money. I paranoically figured the prosecutor's office would be more lenient if it was just money and not money and dope.

I could hear Vreeswyck and it sounded like he was finishing up his interview with the manager.

Why Now?

I frantically looked under rugs, behind cabinets. I tried to concentrate near the bathroom but I was forced out of desperation to probe in a frantic and disjointed manner covering as much ground as possible in the next few minutes. I went back to the closet and rummaged, clumsily knocking three expensive blazers on top of me.

"What the hell are you doing ?"

This time Vreeswyck surprised me.

"Huh ?" I stupidly asked as I pushed several coats off my head.

"You think we missed something in here?" Vreeswyck quizzed as his skeptical eyes drifted over the upper shelf which had contained cardboard boxes holding Melvin Rush's expensive shoes.

I tried to gain my composure, "You never know, we could have with those sloppy state's investigators." It was a pathetic statement expressed in a failing tone contrived to exonerate my awkward behavior. It sounded meaningless.

"I hope not but the way these guys went through here, in and out, we probably did. Anyway, I've got some work on this to get done, grab that portable radio." Vreeswyck stepped out of the closet, exposing the manager standing behind him who squinted at me with puzzled disdain. "Can you carry that water bottle with all that change. I want to take everything from this son of a bitch." Vreeswyck pointed to a five gallon water jug which was half full of assorted coins and a few scattered $1 bills.

We had just seized at least two hundred thousand dollars from Melvin Rush or I had just been nabbed in an internal affairs police sting and Phil Vreeswyck wanted me to lug a twenty-five pound jug filled with coins back to our office. Momentarily, the absurd request had caused me to forget my predicament and given me time to consider the prick Phil Vreeswyck really was.

"Yea, I'll get it." I walked over and picked it up. It was awkward and heavy. We started to leave then Vreeswyck suddenly stopped and fired another probing question at the manager.

"Do you know a Thaddeus Wesson?"

"Christ, Phil." I said, frustrated by my folly and perhaps the beginning of an embarrassing situation.

Vreeswyck ignored me and proceeded with the remainder of his inquiry directed at the matronly landlord who was beginning to grow noticeably perturbed. Meanwhile, my thoughts returned to the source of my consternation, the money. I had another opportunity. I calculated in my head there was probably about five thousand bucks in that bag. The bag under the sink with my fingerprints already on them. Though I had been interrupted during my impetuous search, I had seen no cables or evidence of any recording equipment. Instead of a quick $5,000 , I rationalized I was walking out of there with a ponderous jug of inconsequential nickels and dimes that Vreeswyck would probably request I count once we returned to the office. This was my take from Melvin Rush. I thought about the investigators and the circuitous route they would take back to their offices with the suitcase, and the pillow case and the nylon bag. I thought about that coffee table piling up with all that money and I thought about Rush's rude and insensitive remarks to Perez. I considered that purple bag and what I could do with five thousand dollars. I thought about that landlord getting it, having a free reign to go through the place after we left. She wouldn't though, I reasoned, she was too honest or dumb to look for anything we would have missed or worse, secreted away for ourselves. I briefly listened to Vreeswyck's rapid and inane questions while I considered the investigators with whom he associated. I decided they were all morons if they went straight to the office with all that cash and turned it over to the county sheriff so the State Representative could indulge himself, his wife and his mistress with three brand new luxury cars. I stood there holding that jug thinking about the hernia I might get lugging it back to Vreeswyck's automobile. I determined I would be better served implementing the awkward jug by placing it against my torso and stuffing the Crown Royal bag under my sweatshirt. No one would see it. The money would be mine. There was no sting operation. I convinced myself the notion was a product of paranoid thinking.

Fuck it, Mark. Go get it.

My conscience just had its ass kicked by the second of St. Gregory's list of the Seven Deadly Sins, Greed. I put the jug down near the bathroom door and went in, pushing the plastic bucket aside. I kept the light off hoping the camera, even if it existed, was not sensitive enough to see my actions, an additional safeguard though I hoped it was unnecessary. I kneeled down, beneath the sink and opened the drawer, shifting the towel away. Huddling over the loot, I pushed the bag into my waistband. It was still cold.

I heard Vreeswyck and the manager coming down the hallway, toward the bathroom, I shoved the door open and in the same motion, bent down for the jug. To Vreeswyck, if he had been paying any attention, I would have appeared like I was looking for a place to vomit. I picked up the jug.

"You fellas don't mess around, do you." The middle-aged manager smiled as she alluded to the trivial seizure of the jug.

Correctly sensing the manager was voicing an opinion about our pettiness in confiscating the jug of coins, Vreeswyck conceded, "Mark that looks heavy, why don't you just leave it here."

Committed to my theft, I declared, "No way, to hell with this...son-of-a bitch."

*

I had the pouch uncomfortably concealed against my waistband throughout the brief ride back to the office. I continued to safeguard the jug in my lap. My behavior was not suspicious because Vreeswyck had kept his trunk filled with a wide assortment of law enforcement gear. The rear seats of his Ford Mustang were so cramped with holsters, boots, bullet proof vests and raid attire, there was no place for me to keep the jug other than my lap. Fortunately, the apartment we raided was a short ride to our federal parking garage. When we arrived back at the facility, I waited for Vreeswyck to exit and then I cautiously stepped out of the passenger's side of the car. I told Vreeswyck, who was now fumbling near the trunk of the Mustang, removing even more raid gear, I wanted to get rid of my DEA raid hat. My excuse went unacknowledged but, it gave me the opportunity to hide the Crown Royal bag under the front seat of my car. Vreeswyck didn't notice as I dropped the jug onto the ground before hustling the fifty feet or so over to the parking stall where my car was. I pressed the lock release button on my keychain while simultaneously using my other hand to extricate the bag from my waistband. I heard the lock disengage and I swung the door open. Quickly, the bag was removed from underneath my sweatshirt and stuffed deep beneath the front driver's seat of my Mark VII, a new car I had been assigned to drive.

I did a double-step back to the office to get that jug to our group. It had served its purpose and I was obliged to transport it the rest of the way. Vreeswyck had been so eager to get back to the group and boast about his seizure, he hadn't waited for me. I walked about sixty feet behind him towing the unwieldy container which I wanted to simply drop in the street for vagrants to fight over and pigeons to shit in.

Back at the office, I was expected to prepare an initial report based on my observations about the raid. All that was on my mind however, was returning to my car. I entered the office and compiled a few notes about the raid. I made myself seen to a few people then I slipped out of the office and jogged back to my car, repeatedly warning myself to remain calm and act casual. The three minute jaunt gave me plenty of time to begin considering the ramifications of my theft. I figured if I had fallen into a trap, the internal affairs people would want to arrest me in possession of that wicked little pouch. As I entered the garage, I looked for questionable people. There was no one around so I continued to my car. I felt relieved when I was able to start the engine and drive out of the parking facility. I watched for other vehicles, expecting at any minute, a lumbering Crown Victoria to pull in front of me, two suits jump out and scream," Internal Affairs, you are under arrest." It did not happen so I continued, driving east on Jackson Boulevard, right on past our office in the Dirksen Federal Building. I accelerated and had to repeatedly caution myself to maintain my composure. After I made the light, I reached under the seat and felt for the pouch. The velvet cloth felt soft and I was thrilled it felt full too. I vowed not to pull it out until I was safely away from the vicinity of the office. I tried desperately but, I could not resist the temptation to extract it. As I reached Lake Shore Drive, only a half mile from our building, I reached down and attempted to retrieve the bag. Apparently, I had rammed it under the seat with such force when I had first concealed it, the bag had become stuck on the myriad of wires and metal parts which the manufacturer had installed to make moving the seat more convenient. I cursed the ingenuity of Ford's engineers as I tried to extricate the bag from its keep. I pulled several more times while I was still driving, periodically watching in my rearview mirror for suspicious followers. Growing more impatient, I violently yanked the bag from under the seat, freeing it but, hearing a piece of the flimsy cloth tear on something. I held the bag in my hand and immediately noticed the face of Andrew Jackson egregiously peering through the torn, purple cloth. I continued driving north on Lake Shore while fiddling with the drawstring which kept the bag shut. Finally, I pulled a bundle out and thumbed the pile, noticing it contained all twenties. There were a lot of twenties. I counted out five and estimated there was about fifty or so in that first pile. I multiplied fifty times twenty in my head while simultaneously grabbing another bundle. This bundle was mostly twenties, but, some fifties too. Suddenly, The blast of a horn jolted me enough to realize my car had begun to drift into the passing lane to my left.

"Relax, pay attention." I spoke the words out loud as if saying them would have more effect on me than simply thinking them. I returned the bag to its place of concealment. I reassessed its value and estimated maybe $6,000 or more was in that wonderful magenta sack. I also verified I was not being followed. As another precaution, I drove all the way up to Chicago's North Side from our downtown office. Of course, by this time, my behavior was the product of intense fear almost bordering on mental disorder but, I reasoned if I had come this far, I wasn't going to become careless. Ultra-conservatism was to be the plan. I decided to rent a room on Belmont Avenue, a Comfort Inn, that was often occupied by boisterous summer-time baseball fans when the Cubs were in town. I found a place to park right in front. I exited and placed the purple pouch into a gym bag I had in my trunk. I walked to the hotel and continued past it only to double back, just to make sure. Initially, I reached into the pouch and extracted four twenties to pay for the room. I thought again about a trap. I was being overly cautious but, I decided to go to an automatic teller machine and withdraw enough cash to rent the room. I did this just in case the money had been serialized. I figured it to be a small investment in maintaining my liberty. I rented the room in the name of Tommy Hutton, a former Philadelphia Phillies first baseman who was best known for his defensive abilities. I had six grand of Uncle Sam's money in my possession and it was me who had to play great defense now. With each passing moment of freedom, I came closer to the realization I had gotten away with it. I had pulled it off!

After I entered the room I planned to conceal the money and get my ass back to the office. I could not however, resist the fascinating captivation to ascertain exactly how much was there so I decided to count the money. I took the pouch into the bathroom. I locked the door and kept the light out because subconsciously, I think, I didn't want to see my own reflection in the mirror. I employed the crack of sunlight entering from under the door to count the money. I could barely see the denominations but, I was delighted to realize there were actually six piles of cash and I knew immediately I had more than my second estimate of $6,000. The first pile was all twenties and there was exactly 100. $2000 for me. The second pile also contained twenties and the person who had compiled it shortchanged me two. There were only 98. The third pile was twenties and fifties with a blissful small pile of $100 bills tucked into the middle. Piles four, five and six were random denominations of $10's,$20's,$50's and 100's. The final tally was $13,800. My stomach started to ebb with nausea with the full comprehension of what I had done. Though I was initially sickened and weak-kneed, I quietly thanked God and St. Gregory for imprecise investigators. I felt even better knowing I had just given myself more than a 25% pay raise, cash money. It was the equivalent of thirteen weeks pay and it was $13,763 more than I started the day with in my pocket. It was down payment on a condo or a car. Hell it was a car. Stereo systems, projection televisions, and other adult toys zipped through my daydreams before they were replaced in my imagination by a simple, unadorned piece of paper, a federal indictment. If I was arrested and convicted, I would go to jail for a minimum of ten years. The money then didn't seem like much at all when I considered it amounted to $1,300 bucks a year for ten years of my freedom. I pondered the vile consequences, briefly. I wrapped the money in a stiff and overly bleached hotel bath towel and exited the bathroom. I decided to leave the money in the hotel for safekeeping, with the option of picking it up anytime after work. I moved to the queen sized mattress and placed the money in the square base of the boxspring. I left it there for two minutes before I retrieved it. I thought about a variety of hiding places which included the bathroom, the toilet bowl, behind the curtains and in the drawers. I was confident that Internal

Affairs would not get me but, after having gone to this preposterous length, I wasn't going to let an underpaid Venezuelan maid rip me off either. I finally lifted the night table and placed the towel and money underneath in the hollow area of the table's base. The console rested unevenly so I had to redistribute the piles of cash in the towel so the table was level. Some strange feeling implored me to remove the Bible from the drawer, which I succumbed to and opened to the Old Testament before laying it on the bed. I don't know why. By my own admission, I was acting weird and paranoid, very much like a cocaine addict myself. I glanced at the section I had opened it to, the Book of Proverbs. I placed my finger down, randomly against the page. "He took his purse filled with money and will not be home until the full moon." I thought that picking that sentence was too eerie. I read on for inspiration or a foreboding prediction but was disappointed to learn the story was just about some horny guy picking up a prostitute. I closed it and attached a "Do Not Disturb" sign to the brass doorknob as I left. I walked down three flights of stairs, avoiding the elevator I had taken to get to my room. On the second floor, I rolled up the Crown Royal bag and buried it deep in pizza boxes and wax paper in the trash can. I returned to work where no one had realized I had been gone for over an hour and a half.

II

A quiet month elapsed without any internal investigations convened against me. There were no repercussions resulting from my bold theft of what turned out to be a trifling percentage of Melvin Rush's proceeds. Evidently there had been no cables, wires or cameras and my pilfered money was safely secured in my modest apartment. The official seizure had amounted to substantially more than I originally estimated, $424,755, which would be officially forfeited pending the submission of public notification of confiscation of the monies. The law required the seizure be made a matter of public record and that was accomplished by publication on three consecutive Wednesdays in the USA Today National Newspaper. A review would follow which was based on any petitions of protest filed by Melvin Rush, his attorneys or anyone else laying claim to the money. With no such appeal a probability, the money would be divvied up between the Drug Enforcement Administration and the Cook County State's Attorney's Office. Phil Vreeswyck had already been commended by our ASAC for his perseverance and dedication on the case. Hayes had nominated Vreeswyck for a performance award which included a cash bonus of $1,500. Vreeswyck, in turn, had acknowledged me and Perez for our help and had offered to buy us lunch though it never happened. I thanked

Vreeswyck for giving me the "opportunity" to accompany him on an exciting search warrant. Indeed, everyone was happy.

With the theft behind me, I was determined to lay low and remain cautious. The group's activity had slowed down considerably with many of the agents preparing cases for trial, including me. I had to prepare transcripts from a previous undercover case and I was expected to secure the continued cooperation of an informant who had traveled back to Mexico and couldn't be located. The informant was going to be needed as a witness despite my efforts to relieve him of the duty. I had pleaded my case to the Assistant U.S. Attorney handling the trial to proceed without the use of the informant, who feared testifying and fled to his homeland and abject poverty rather than face the dealer he had set up in Chicago. The prosecutor lent a deaf ear to the informant's predicament and insisted I find him, a difficult task from another country.

I didn't have much going on in the way of active investigations so, I was happy to accept a lead from another office. DEA Houston periodically developed information outside the purview of their own jurisdiction and would forward pertinent leads to us. The highways between Houston and Chicago were well traveled by drug traffickers, especially those transporting cocaine and marijuana. The DEA office there had received information that an apartment located in Bensenville, Illinois, was being used as a safe haven and rest area for drug transporting mules. "Mules" was a term police and some drug dealers used to describe poorly paid individuals, usually illegal aliens, who transported drugs or money to and from distribution points across the U.S. We had been informed DEA Houston had received intelligence gleaned during a wiretap investigation the apartment was in operation and was the domicile of several illegal aliens from Mexico. Some of the members of our group had been intermittently watching the place for about a week, usually when a few of us had nothing to do or just wanted to get out of the office. I was among them.

Members of my group had observed some routine pedestrian traffic going into the multi-unit building but, the specific apartment we were monitoring on the second floor, had seemingly remained unoccupied. We had been told by Houston if we could develop probable cause to search the apartment we should and that any actions we took would not jeopardize their investigation in Texas. We did not possess any information which would fulfill a judge's requirements to authorize us a search warrant so our game plan was to wait and hope we saw someone carrying bags into or from the apartment or other suspicious activity that might be behavior common to drug traffickers. We weren't planning to spend extensive time and effort researching the apartment. When we observed suspicious activity, we planned to knock on the door and influence any inhabitants of the apartment to grant us consent to search the place. We weren't going to resort to illegal means to obtain searches because we planned it wouldn't be necessary. It was usually very difficult for an individual to refuse entry to several daunting law officers when they were armed individuals determined to enter a residence. Intimidation was a great tool law enforcement officers, including DEA Agents, utilized and in this case, we intended to implement it. Sadly, from a law enforcement perspective, intimidation no longer works against hardened criminals so intimately familiar with the lenient criminal justice system, they possess no respect for the police and have absolutely no fear of enforcement action.

One evening, Brenda Xavier noticed a male standing on the balcony of the second floor apartment. Brian Sullivan had joined Xavier on surveillance and they had telephoned our office for assistance. Myself and Chad Jennings had been in the group at the time and we both agreed to help although I was the only one who joined them. Jennings never showed up and later said he had a dinner-date with his new in-laws which he could not break.

Three of us, myself, Xavier and Sullivan knocked on the door. The man who, only an hour earlier, had been enjoying a relaxing cigarette, was left seated at a disarrayed kitchen table explaining why he was at the residence with no identification other than a bogus Honduran passport. He had no answers for the rapid fire questions launched at him by Xavier and Sullivan who both possessed a working knowledge of the Spanish dialect Latin Americans spoke. I opted not to add to the confusion and was content to walk around the apartment making sure no one was hiding in other rooms or closets. The information from Houston was accurate. The place was a flop house and looked like a rest stop from which anonymous transients came and went. The apartment was stocked with bargain, second hand furniture which smelled of mold and moth balls. Clothes were scattered around the rooms, some drooping out of over-stuffed plastic trash bags and other items, mostly T-shirts, hanging off of a pressboard set of drawers and haphazardly tossed on closet floors and under the bed. There were clothes hangers but oddly enough only one item, a child's stuffed toy, was hanging on one. The animal, a tattered and filthy teddy bear, seemed to have been crudely executed, its head and neck wedged into the end of a hanger. As I formulated my opinions, I recognized how cynical I was becoming.

There was a makeshift altar in the corner of the small second bedroom. It was commonplace to find a platform for sacrifice in the residence of many Latinos and the existence of one did not surprise me. Many Hispanics believed in the power of Santeria, a religious cult originating in Cuba which had spread throughout the Caribbean and into the United States by the process of immigration and forced subjugation. Santeria developed out of the traditions of African peoples who from the 16th to the 19th century were transported to Cuba to work as slaves on sugar plantations. Santeria shared traits with other cults like voodoo but, it was grounded in its own philosophy and beliefs which combined blended elements of Christianity and native African beliefs. The adherents to Santeria placed a great abundance of their faith in saints or spirits known as Orishas. There was abounding evidence many Latinos, some of whom were drug dealers and couriers, worshipped and prayed to Orishas for the safe passage of their dope and money. I occasionally speculated about the decision Orishas made when faced with the conflicting requests of drug dealers faithfully praying for the bulwark of their drug shipments while anti-drug activists prayed incessantly to the same spirits for the tumultuous drug scourge in their community to subside. I examined the unpretentious altar and recognized the items placed on and around it for sacrifice included real and synthetic flowers, costume jewelry, alcohol, food, coins and even perfume, English Leather, the cheap stuff. It wasn't much of a contribution but, considering many of the people who had presented the gifts were indigent, it was a considerable financial burden to relinquish anything of value and the offerings were indeed a genuine sacrifice.

The search yielded no dope or money. No guns either and subsequently, there were no arrests. There were some telephone books and addresses as well as a few scattered notepads. The journals looked interesting and could possibly provide some leads for dope traffickers operating in the area so Brenda placed the items into an evidence bag. We decided to leave the complex, Sullivan and I for a local watering hole and Xavier back to the office to process the collected evidence. The resident of the apartment, at least that night, was thrilled he was not going to be arrested. He hoped we would not report him to the INS for immigration violations. We didn't. We encountered so many illegal aliens during our investigations it was not feasible to arrest and process them, bring them to jail only to have a federal judge release them pending the scheduling of a hearing they would never attend. We simply elected to let the scofflaws go and encourage them to stay out of trouble. The man was grateful and offered us budget rum on the way out. We declined. I looked at him and his gap-toothed grin and had no doubt he was a drug-running mule. Though I had no proof, my experience permitted me to make the assessment confidently. He probably transported a cache of coke or marijuana into the

Chicago area for which I reckoned he received no more than a $500 payment, a pittance compared to the value of the dope he had carried but, for him, the money was a windfall. A poor, unemployed man with no prospects and a wife and children to feed is willing to risk the gauntlet of U.S. drug interdiction efforts. Considering the mules' motivation, I briefly considered our own morality and the judiciousness of a system that condemned these foreigners to lengthy prison terms for delivering a product so many Americans demanded and craved.

On the other hand, I pondered how much cash the delivery would ultimately net the source. I considered the staggering amounts of money both ends of this transaction would reap. I recounted a case Carlos Perez had initiated where he was utilizing an informant who was an established and trusted member of a sophisticated network of Mexicans. The organization utilized mules to transport tons of marijuana through Texas to the Midwest and New England. Perez had the informant successfully set up two separate shipments of twelve hundred pounds of marijuana. With a value of $1,000 a pound in the United States, the cargo was worth $1.2 million each. Both were permitted by the DEA to pass through Texas and continue their journey through the United States to their final destination. The freight was continually monitored and then interdicted when it was determined it had reached its destination. The mules were arrested and prosecuted. Perez believed the informant had been burned and could not consummate any more deals with the group with whom he had been negotiating with in Mexico. The informant scoffed at this idea and produced a recorded telephone call with the source who stated, in essence, he inherently trusted the informant and the seizures made by the U.S. Police had made no impact on his bountiful warehouse of marijuana. He went on to boast he would run out of "mulos estupido," a Spanish term for incompetent mules, before he would run out of reefer. Unbelievably, Perez and the informant set up two more deals with the source that resulted in the seizure of 1,800 more pounds of marijuana and the arrest of five more mules. Finally realizing he was dealing with a snitch, the source went underground in Mexico while the majority of his couriers were sentenced to state prisons where they will remain for the preponderance of their lives.

Over our first beers that night, Sullivan and I concluded, the Honduran and his discount rum was evidence of another shipment missed.

*

Brian Sullivan had been a close friend of mine since I began my career at Chicago DEA. He had arrived in Chicago from New England two weeks prior to my assignment to the Midwest Division. He, like me, had been transferred to Chicago straight out of the DEA Academy. He was single, loved sports and also had no friends or relatives in the area when he was transferred to Chicago. I was glad he was in Group 5 when I started my career in the Windy City. Our collective circumstances led to an immediate friendship and one of our favorite pastimes was drinking.

We went out on the town together quite often after work and on weekends. Baseball, football or any other sport on television was a good excuse to go to a watering hole and toss a few beers down. When we both had free time, we went down to Chicago Stadium or Wrigley Field where we enjoyed the amenities of free admission because we knew so many of the police moonlighting as security personnel. There we would feel obligated to spend the money we would have expended on tickets to buy each other rounds of beer, debauchery which produced more than a few drunken incidents which served to bond us together as great friends.

One such occasion found us together at Wrigley Field to see the Cubs play a night game. Wrigley Field, the home of the Chicago Cubs is, in itself, a baseball icon. It is a revered baseball stadium full of tradition like its ivy-covered walls, monstrous green centerfield scoreboard and of course, Harry Caray, who entertained the crowd with a slurring and raucous rendition of "Take Me Out to the Ball Game'" during every seventh inning stretch. If the game happened to go fourteen innings, he'd do it again. Wrigley Field has also established itself in recent years as an acceptable meeting place for young professionals to converge and get sloppy drunk. Many of the Yuppies don't even pay attention to the ball game. The bleachers, where seating is general admission and the first who arrive get the best seats, is considered the place for the yuppies and anyone else whose intention was to get smashed. For Brian and I, inebriation was often our sole intention.

Brian had talked about going to the game all afternoon after work. We both had hoped we could drift out of the office unnoticed around four o'clock, have a beer and a bite to eat up north and then wander into the ball park and lay claim to some choice seats in left field. There we intended to heckle the Pittsburgh Pirates leftfielder, Barry Bonds. A late afternoon buy bust, set up by Brenda Xavier, ended our leisurely plans.

We ultimately arrested two white guys who delivered four kilograms of coke to Desmond Brokenborough, again acting as the U/C. The deal, which had been scheduled to go at three, finally was finished at 6:30 p.m. It had been a waiting game, as it almost always was, but two guys eventually showed up. They were arrested and relieved of their illegal contraband. I transported one of the suspects downtown for processing, fingerprinting and photographs. He had $1,900 in his pockets which I resisted a persuasive temptation to remove despite the relative ease with which it could have been accomplished. Uninterested in trivial matters like money, at least that day, I had processed the defendant alone, who had been forlornly consumed with his predicament. He babbled and cried like most people do after their arrest and he was so upset he did not know how much money he had in his possession. He would not miss the cash and in the confusion he would never remember who took what. Nevertheless, the thought of stealing a portion of it only flashed through my mind and I immediately dismissed it. My main objective was to get to Wrigley Field, inhale a few beers and enjoy the ambience of the "Friendly Confines." Once we had taken care of the paperwork chores, Sullivan and I hustled the prisoners off to the Metropolitan Correctional Center and headed to the game, albeit behind schedule.

We were relegated to standing in the last row of right-centerfield, a spot which is usually the only place left for late arrivals like us. There were no seats available but, still we were in the game, for free, and I had half a beer in me before I saw a pitch. We drank quickly and heavily. Though we were both avid fans of baseball, the game was consigned to mood music for the real parties in the stands and near the beer distribution kiosks. In the fifth inning, Brian and I drew the attention of two cuties who were walking outside the stadium along the fenceline which forms the perimeter of the bleachers. They were on Sheffield Street which runs the length of right field. They were the first ladies to respond to our catcalls which were mild compared to some of the remarks and requests made by a small group of intoxicated men occupying the last row of the centerfield bleachers.

From outside the stadium, the girls, who both claimed to live in one of the apartments across the street, invited us to join them. They said we were welcome on the rooftop if we would be inclined to leave the game. We were and exited the park, abandoning the contest in gleeful anticipation of our rooftop rendezvous.

The baseball faded as we drank to the point of utter inebriation. There were about forty people up on that rooftop, most of whom did not know each other. Our drunkenness had facilitated our obnoxiousness and I believe we had insulted at least half of them before the game ended. The two gals who had invited us on the roof had soon disappeared, probably ashamed they had propositioned us and hopeful the real tenants did not find out they did. As people trickled out, Sullivan and I continued to drink, Brian choosing to fix himself some potent whiskey-gingers and me, content with vodka and club sodas. I met one amorous brunette who I had carefully prodded into believing I was a member of the Ice Capades. I claimed I was worn out from a recent tour of Italy and Greece. She believed the whole tale even though I only spoke a few phrases in Italian, at her request. The phrases were not words but rather, the Italian last names of some high school buddies I remembered sprinkled with two words everybody knew, "Bertucci Rossi volare Tartaglione amore." She was smittenly amused when I told her that meant, "I would love to change her transmission fluid."

I ventured to her first floor bedroom where we wrestled and had clumsy, drunken sex. After she had fallen asleep, I returned to the rooftop to find Brian still drinking. He could handle his booze better than me but, whiskey made him a touch crazy. It was close to 4 a.m. when a liquor addled search through the vacant second floor apartment, foolishly left unlocked, yielded an unneeded six pack of beer, a bow and a box of two dozen arrows. We stealthily returned to the desolate rooftop, which had now been empty for two hours, except for us. Up until that point, we had both been relatively quiet and none of the tenants had the courage or the sense to ask us to leave. We were sloppy drunk but both possessed by a competitive nature which prompted us to employ the hazardous toys we had discovered. We engaged in a foolhardy challenge of archery skills of which neither of us possessed. We shot several arrows into the residential night air, destination unknown. Moronically, I shot one arrow straight above us and it came back towards the rooftop narrowly missing a beach umbrella and table before impaling itself into the weathered wooden deck on which we stood. Fortunately, the streets were dormant and nobody was speared by our errant and misguided sorties. We decided to fire several into Wrigley Field, giggling like little boys all the while. We attempted to hit the pitcher's mound which was about one hundred and fifty yards away. Brian came closest with an attempt that would have probably struck the second baseman had a game still been being played. As we laughed and staggered around, I came across some lighter fluid which had been left out from the game-time barbecue. We wrapped paper towels around the middle of the arrows but the paper burned too quickly and fell off the arrows before they were launched. Two more of the flaming arrows had dropped lamely into the street. We were not trying to damage anything but our minds were polluted with drink and this seemed the best way to appease our boredom. I ripped my T-shirt into strips and we finally succeeded in discharging four fiery arrows into Wrigley Field. It was a ludicrous and an irrational act and it was precisely the type of stupid and debauched stunts that land people in jail or worse, leave people injured or killed. The four burning arrows fizzled without damage but, we heard sirens shrill through the early morning air. Trucks poured from a firehouse on the opposite side of the stadium and at that point we knew our activity had been witnessed. We staggered down the rear stairway and fled. Though it was the act of utter idiots, it was also an incident which can serve as a catalyst for friendship forever.

The experience would remain in my memory along with many others of Brian Sullivan. In October of that year, which began the fifth of my service, there would be no more fun together. I accompanied Brian's body back to the small town in Vermont where he was raised. He had been murdered while on surveillance in a heavily populated black neighborhood on Chicago's West Side. Sitting in his car, a white man in a poor black neighborhood at night, they recognized him as a cop or possibly someone there to buy dope. Either way, his life meant nothing to the individuals who killed him. The motive was never concretely established but someone flippantly felt it was necessary to end Brian's life, even though the amoral exploit would not enhance their own. A manhunt, led by a task force of DEA Agents supervised by ASAC Caravan, Chicago Police Detectives and Agents from the FBI led to a jailhouse informant who fingered two young black teenagers, sworn members of the Black Gangster Disciple Nation Street Gang, as the trig-germen. Though both ardently denied involvement, they chose to plead for life sentences rather than face death penalties in a public trial. An FBI Expert on gang crime was prepared to testify the murder was the product of a bizarre gang initiation rite which required potential recruits of the BGDN's to assassinate a Caucasian chosen at random. An examination of Brian and his vehicle revealed twenty-two rounds of 9mm fire and eleven rounds of .45 bullets had been fired at him. Of the thirty-three rounds, twenty-one of them had hit Brian. The killers had meant what they had set out to accomplish.

∗

The Drug Enforcement Administration arranged to have one of its corporate jets, another product of a lucrative seizure, transport Brian's body back to his hometown. As Brian's closest friend in the Administration, our office had nominated me to escort his body home. Though I was honored to do so, the process disturbed me. Nevertheless, I accompanied several members of management on the trip. It was a solemn flight and I spent most of it thinking about Brian, whose body had been placed in a casket in the cargo hold with the ASAC's golf clubs. I knew Brian Sullivan did not deserve to be hauled back to his family like an overnight bag. The thought of him being tossed around in the luggage compartment infuriated and sickened me. I sincerely hoped his parents wouldn't know the heartless process by which their youngest son was returning home. Brian, who had been a confidant and a sincere friend, was reduced to being a piece of my property and I was to ensure his safe "delivery" to custodians from the Fleuhrer Funeral Home, whose hearse was waiting at the airport in Rutland, Vermont along with Brian's family.

The two-hour flight to Rutland went quickly as friendly recollections and humorous scenes flickered in my mind. However, when the pilot announced "prepare for landing" my stomach twisted and my throat weakened. What would I possibly say to his family? His parents? I had met both his brothers on several occasions when they had passed through Chicago on business trips or recently, when both had come to Chicago to visit Brian and attend a Bulls/Celtics basketball playoff game with him. Brian, his two brothers, both older, and I went together. His brothers were very impressed that we were admitted for free into jam-packed and sold out Chicago Stadium. I had also met his mother and father on two separate occasions when they had visited. The second time, his mother had brought me a half-gallon jug of maple syrup and a dozen coupons for free pints of Vermont based Ben and Jerry's Ice Cream. I was more than an acquaintance I supposed, but after all, I was only Brian's co-worker. I felt privileged I was entrusted the responsibility to escort him home but, when the wheels touched the runway I became nauseous and apprehensive. When his parents had last hugged him goodbye, he was a vibrant, friendly young man filled with enthusiasm and the promise of a bright future. Now I was accompanying his lifeless body home, his exuberance extinguished and his body reduced to a corpse whose last breath was taken on a glass-littered and graffitied street on Chicago's west side during a routine surveillance. His death was beyond tragedy because it was so pathetically senseless.

I had rehearsed what I would say before and during the flight but, the sentences all became mumbled phrases as the plane taxied to the terminal. "I'm sorry…He died heroically, on duty…He tried to make a difference." I considered other slogans which wouldn't do him or his memory justice. "He loved his job…He was a great person." Hoping to appeal to the deeply religious nature of his parents, I thought about offering, "He is in heaven now." I realized how ridiculous it sounded. If Brian was in heaven it was because he had brought love, laughter and joy to his family and friends during the course of his life. It had nothing to do with the lamentable fact he was riddled with bullets earning a pay check as a foot soldier for the wayward war on drugs. Selfishly, I thought, I must tell them I was not there. I did not want any blame for his death. I wondered if the family, when they laid their eyes on me, might consider that possibility. It didn't matter. Brian was a victim much like many other random and senselessly chosen victims of inexcusable street violence. I could not have changed the outcome and I hoped they would recognize it. I did not expect Brian's parents to understand the brutality of Chicago's streets. When they had visited, they had climbed the Sears Tower, strolled the dazzling extravagance of the magnificent mile and beheld the splendid lake front with its high-priced condominiums and their celebrity speckled addresses. I know they did not venture near the streets where Brian perished. They watched the news, they saw the numbing violence on television and knew Brian had a dangerous job but, I'm certain they never expected drama like the horror which had unfolded. Unfortunately, Brian's death was not theater but very real and I recognized his stark and unmerciful death would be indisputable when they finally felt the inert, cold hand of their youngest son.

I was the second person off the jet. I saw the family straight ahead as I walked across the concrete runway from the tarmac. Brian's mother was crying. She was guarded by Brian's father who was surrounded by three men and a woman who I reasoned from their stern and respectful pose were DEA Agents, probably out of the Boston Division. They had been dispatched to escort and support Brian's family through the grim process of recovering their son. The agents seemed like they did not belong and their presence was resented by Brian's family. I noticed an obvious distance between his parents and brothers and the agents. Brian's mother, her face pale and her eyes irritated and red from tears, ducked from her husband's embrace and rushed me. She hugged me tightly and wailed. I looked at Brian's father who placed his anguished hands to his face. I could not restrain my tears.

I rode with his parents and one brother back to the residence where Brian spent his childhood. The small talk about the flight and the unseasonably mild weather which had descended upon Vermont's

Lower Champlain Valley ended as we left the airport parking lot. Mr. Sullivan did not hesitate to ask the inevitable. "Mark, what happened to my son?"

I did my best to tell him. The city streets of Chicago, much like many urban areas in our country are proliferated with guns. The firearms are abundant and cheap and virtually every crook has one. Even more frightening are the teenagers and children who possess them. Kids, with impotent or non-existent value systems. Even the teenagers who are lucky enough to be reared in good homes often are dangerously afflicted with the ticklish plight of incessant boredom. They are fortuitous adolescents who benefit from a stable lifestyle and don't need to work or worry about subsistence but find themselves in constant search of gratification. They turn to guns to provide excitement. Some are protecting their illegal enterprises while others are simply doing it for fun. Robbery, assault, murder. Killing people. I told him the night his son was murdered, Brian had no chance. There was nothing that could be done because Brian was performing his job, a position that made him a target on Chicago's treacherous streets. I added the medical examiner stated Brian did not suffer. The consolation failed and the silence enveloped us all the way to the modest Colonial where Brian grew up. Anger welled in his parents' eyes and it was a sentiment I shared.

At the insistence of his mother, I examined pictures of Brian's childhood. I respectfully handled the plastic trophies he had won in little league baseball. A fourth grade spelling bee certificate honoring Brian as a runner-up to the school district champion still hung on his bedroom wall. His mother confessed she had placed it there when Brian had left for his freshman year at Northeastern. She said Brian would have been embarrassed but she had mounted it there because it appeared notably more acceptable than the torn poster of his favorite rock band, Aerosmith. His high-school flame, an Irish girl he had taken to both his junior and senior prom, paid a respectful visit to the house. She was now married to a plumber and the mother of a two-year-old daughter. Mrs. Sullivan showed me his varsity football jacket, insisting that I try it on. I accommodated. I realized I was a tangible link between them and Brian, a living, breathing reminder of what Brian had wanted to be. Brian must have told them how close we were and it was true, we were good friends. I was Brian's family in Chicago and as such they treated me well. I did my best to console the family, particularly the parents but, I could not help but feel it was an empty effort. I felt bad for them but, selfishly, I wanted the whole affair to be over. I wanted desperately to get away from the death, the agony and mourning. I wanted to return to Chicago without the burden of my property or my duty.

Brian's father approached me later, in the evening, after his drained wife had succumbed to fatigue and grief and had fallen asleep on the sofa. I remember his words. "Brian was so proud to become a member of your organization. We went to the graduation ceremony and he repeatedly showed us that gold badge. Back here, in Vermont, everyone wanted to see it. He was so proud that he had earned it. Brian was always good in school, better than my other ones with grades. We couldn't afford college but, Brian had his heart set on it so we applied for loans, grants, book stipends and anything we could get to offset the cost. Brian worked full time hours too, at a video store. We all sacrificed, Brian the most. He wanted to make something of himself. He said he wanted to leave a mark, maybe make the world a better place. You know, he just paid off the last of those college loans three months ago." His father's voice weakened. "His mother was so worried about his job. He used to joke about it, trying to cajole her fears. He told her he occasionally was asked to hide in mail boxes." Mr. Sullivan paused and reviewed the remark to make sure it was indeed a gag. A faint smile appeared, "Did he?"

"No." I thought about Brian's great sense of humor.

His father continued. "All he worked so hard to attain. All the efforts, the struggles, the triumphs. It doesn't mean anything now. Its gone... my boy is gone forever."

He was.

*

The funeral was respectful and serene. There were several representatives present from various local, state and federal law enforcement agencies. White Junction, Vermont, Brian's hometown, sent the bulk of their police force including its entire administration consisting of its Chief, Deputy and a majority of its thirty-five full and part-time auxiliary officers. I believed Brian probably had known most of them. I doubted he personally knew many of the members of the Vermont State Police, who escorted the funeral procession in polished squad cars whose lights ceremoniously flashed. There were also obligatory representatives from federal law enforcement agencies including the Federal Bureau of Investigation, the U.S. Marshals Service, Bureau of Alcohol, Tobacco and Firearms and of course, DEA agents who had been dispatched to attend from various offices under the jurisdiction of the Boston Field Division. By the level of its commotion, I reasoned the funeral was a big local event. It was a spectacle for the small town of 2,500 that rarely found itself the center of such attention. Many of the citizens, from my perspective, appeared excited by the regal ceremony and the infamous notoriety their community was receiving. I assumed Brian would have been extremely honored too but, I couldn't help cynically thinking the exalted cavalcade couldn't furnish a single additional breath for the corpse which led it through a town speckled with crafts shops, art galleries, antique vendors and bookstores.

Disgracefully, there were only nine representatives from the Chicago DEA office in attendance. Three of whom were front line mangers, Kenneth Starr, Special Agent in Charge of the Chicago Field Division, Associate Special Agent in Charge and number two man, Francis Black as well as my group's ASAC, Joseph Caravan. During the somber ceremony, Starr and Black each gave courteous and gratuitous speeches about Brian's work ethic and development as an agent. Black, who seemed to relish the opportunity to bestow a posthumous speech, glittered during his discourse. He spoke of Brian's honor, his valor and his determination to "fight the war on drugs." During the ten-minute speech he managed to insert his favorite saying, "Come back with your swords raised or carried on your shield." It referred to the practice of Roman soldiers who raised their swords in victory upon return to their city. Those who were killed in the fighting were honorably carried back on their shields as martyrs. Black was a man who commanded respect but, relished violence. While in the office, he often remarked about his gun battles on the streets of New York and Miami. During his eulogy, he had attempted to glorify Brian's death and make it seem worthwhile. To most, I'm sure it worked but, not to those who mattered most. I glanced toward Mr. and Mrs. Sullivan occasionally and determined they were neither proud nor honored. They were heartsick. Black's comments about the giving of one's own life seemed to be an exceptional message to the curious however, the true mourners, Brian's family and close friends, stood motionless, numbed by the tragedy and uncomforted by the remarks. While I examined the mesmerized faces of the inquisitive onlookers, I cynically wondered how many in the crowd had purchased illicit drugs the very day he was killed.

Starr, whose speech was written for him, was not eloquent. His diction and monotone was standard and uninspired and his message was diplomatic and run of the mill. He made a few personal references to his dealings with Brian during his career in Chicago. I knew they were erroneous because Brian and I often joked that Starr did not even know who we were. In fact, when Starr had asked me to return to Vermont with Brian's body, he addressed me as Mike. Nevertheless, Starr managed to attempt to express the condolences of the entire Chicago Law Enforcement community though he neglected to mention the failure of any of those offices to send a representative. I conceded the police departments did not maintain a budget for such expenses however, I was still disappointed none of the individuals whom Brian had closely worked made much of an effort to be present at the funeral. Starr, Black and Caravan had the cost of their trip paid out of the DEA's operational expenses. My trip was paid out of the fund as well, since I escorted Brian's body back home. However, I would have paid the money out of pocket had I been required. I seriously doubted members of management would have. Five other agents paid the cost of attending the funeral with their own monies, including three from my group, Brokenborough, Jennings and Sandy Foster. My boss, Bobby Hayes had attended as well. Fortunately, United Airlines provided reduced airfare and the agents who came additionally saved money by doubling up on hotel rooms. They were graciously granted one day's administrative leave to attend the funeral. However, all including me, were required to return to work via commercial airline in Chicago the day following his internment, on Friday. Starr, Black and Caravan, I subsequently learned, returned over the course of the weekend, at their leisure and the expense of the taxpayers.

I was disturbed only five field agents from Chicago attended the funeral. There were one hundred and thirty-five agents assigned to the Chicago Division, eighty-five of them served in the Chicago office itself. I suspected eighty of them knew Brian. At least 50% of those agents planned to attend the funeral until they were told the DEA would not absorb any cost of the trip. Then Brian's death became less significant, his friendship, less important. It distressed me to realize those who could meet the relatively modest financial obligation of the trip chose not to do so. The absence of my fellow agents at the funeral propelled me into a realization that there was a conspicuous lack of care, on the whole, throughout our office. When I returned to the division, to begin to perform my duties and endure the routine of my life, I could not help but wonder why it was Brian and not me with my hands clasped over my chest and a rosary intertwined in my fingers laying in that cherry-wood casket back in Vermont. Brian had been an honest and forthright person. He was a good man who observed and upheld every oath of his career. It was me who had begun to break mine.

The months following Brian's death was a catharsis for me and my career. I became introverted and bitter and his death permitted me to suitably rationalize my own deplorable behavior. I found his meaningless murder a convenient excuse to question the validity of DEA's mission and the accountability of its leaders. When I heard a remark by one notoriously lazy agent who asked if Brian's parking spot "had been assigned yet" I questioned the integrity and fortitude of the agents with whom I worked. I pondered the moral caliber of the "evil" drug dealers versus the "dedicated" agents who investigated them. I reasoned the expanse was in many cases, not great and in some instances, favored the dopers. I reflected inwardly for months while I compared my character to those of my fellow agents. I considered the common links I shared with the agents with whom I worked and the criminals whose behavior I had been slowly adopting. I reasoned there was not much difference other than the dope peddlers seemed significantly wealthier. Consequently, it was relatively easy to channel my energy more with the criminals than the cops and I found myself more interested in the lives of drug dealers. I began to find excuses to admire the enterprising Melvin Rush and the conniving Nunzio Maldonado. I fatefully decided I wanted to be more like them than the rigid, cynical and ignorant agents of the Drug Enforcement Administration.

It was a choice that catapulted me from random acts of pocket stuffing to a far more dangerous and exciting world of criminality, its route paved with bold and aggressive acts and careless decisions which jeopardized my career and ultimately, my life.

12

My new target was only twenty-one, according to the anonymous caller, whose motivation was fueled by jealousy and revenge. It seems the object of his frustration was the neighborhood supplier who utilized the person on the other end of the phone to deliver ounces of cocaine to his "clients." In exchange, the twenty-one year old dealer imparted my source of information with a few hundred bucks here and there. More importantly, he would also provide the anonymous voice an eight ball of coke a couple times a week. The cash was welcome but, the coke was the main reason he delivered the dope. The person supplying this information was unemployed and had lost his job as a roofer. He was unable to find work that paid nearly as well and allowed him to continue employment without fear of a drug test. He was thirty-two years old and had a wife and five-year-old child to support. He loved them both but, their needs were often secondary to his cocaine. The caller did not deny the cocaine addiction controlled his life. He also was not ignorant enough to attempt to blame his addiction on his supplier and I respected him for that. He readily admitted how much he enjoyed cocaine and his arrangement with the young dealer would have been fine, after all, he confided, he was getting his coke for free plus a couple hundred bucks a week to throw at his nagging wife. Supplemented with the unemployment checks coming regularly, the family was doing better financially than when he had been working. It was not his finances which brought him to the offices of the DEA and it wasn't his desire to break his habit. He came to our office because the twenty-one year old coke dealer, who was employing the former roofer as a runner, was also regularly fucking the potential informant's wife.

In this particular case, I was telephoned by a white male who described himself as a laborer of eight years who had gotten over his head in the coke business. He had called one evening while I was at the duty assignment desk. The duty desk responsibility required an agent to answer phone calls and requests from various law enforcement agencies and concerned citizens wishing to report drug dealers, crack houses, questionable neighbors, rumors or other suspicious activity. Most agents dreaded their duty which we were obliged to perform about once every three months. The duty only lasted one week, Monday through Friday. Most of the calls revolved around boring, uninspired official business but sometimes the assignment was fun because a call would come in from one of the crazies or the psychotics roaming the world. I was always amused by their fantastic tales. Stories about aliens transmitting their twisted orders through toaster ovens and stray cats seemed to be common complaints. Occasionally a lonely young woman would call who was more interested in speaking with a federal agent than turning in dope dealers. I often taped the calls and listened to them later with close friends who were greatly entertained by the wackiness and desperation of some of the "nut-callers."

I never considered the 32 year-old guy to be a wacko. I could immediately tell from the seriousness of his tone. I asked him some qualifying questions about his dealings with cocaine and he revealed himself to be an individual who knew what he was talking about. When an anonymous person calls our offices to report legitimate activity or information, the individual is only considered a source of information. They are designated as such only when their information is deemed intelligent and credible. If the material consists of intimate knowledge, the agent may be inclined to encourage the caller to become a cooperating individual however, the tipster is not considered an official "informant" until they demonstrate an interest in becoming one, a process which requires them to sign official paperwork and be formally debriefed. The goal, from a law enforcement perspective, when a source makes contact, is to encourage and maintain the interest of the individual to follow up on their desire to provide information. After receiving the telephone call, I requested the roofer come to our offices and, the next day, I was pleased to see the 32-year-old man arrive. I interviewed him extensively regarding his information about Mikey Brady, a young man he insolently referred to as his "twenty-one year old coke dealing, former mother-fucking friend."

The roofer readily signed the agreement to become a Cooperating Individual or a C.I. as we referred to our snitches. Cooperators did not like to be called snitches but, that is precisely what they were. The roofer even referred to himself over the telephone as a "stool pigeon." He admitted he never thought he would find himself in circumstances which would have him destined to the police for help but, Brady's decision to take advantage of the roofer's demoralized situation left him in a state where he could justify turning Brady into the police. He hated Brady more than he hated himself. The roofer's candidness was surprising but, the story had been the same as others I had heard before. He told a tale of woe about his gradual fall into the clutches of cocaine addiction. It cost him his job, many of his friends and his self-respect. It was a story told often but, I allowed the roofer to declare it because ultimately, he needed to get it off his chest. To him, during that initial meeting, I had been a sounding board but, all the while, I was writing copious notes about the information he divulged. If he wished to renege at any time, as he was at liberty to do, I would at least have the material he was initially willing to supply. While he broke down and confided, I listened and wrote.

Mikey Brady was two years removed from high school. He was a white kid from a middle class family. His Dad was a fireman, or did something along those lines, with the city. Maybe a paramedic, the informant wasn't sure. It had taken Brady six years to get through high school and for the last several years he had spent both winter and summer partying. Mikey was physically stunted, rail-thin and not quite 5' 5" with bad acne. He also had a new cherry red Corvette which he drove to a little cottage he had rented for the summer in Fox Lake. There, he kept a modest powerboat on which he took friends and love interests for spins around the tree-lined lake. The roofer answered all my questions thoroughly but, he seemed transfixed on Brady's appearance, his paltry physical stature. It tipped me off to his stifling insecurity but, I didn't allow it to interfere with the revelations he was making to me. The informant discussed precisely how he delivered cocaine for Mikey, sometimes as much as six ounces at a time to a single customer, carting around pounds of it through his neighborhood. He would drop the coke off and collect the money for the previous week's delivery. He said on one occasion, some two months prior to our meeting, he picked up ten grand from a customer who had been late. He was emphatic about the fact he ceded every dollar he picked up to Mikey. He never stole a dime. He did confess he hit a couple bags of coke now and then just to feed his habit but, he declared he was not a thief, just a coke addict. He seemed particularly proud he had never been on the crack pipe which he emphasized several times during our initial meeting. He gave me particulars regarding how often, how much and how easily he moved the cocaine for Brady but, he was reluctant to provide details about the customers. I realized some were probably friends whose confidentiality he sought to protect. There was no need to press him on the issue, after all, I wanted Mikey and he was going to be served up on a silver platter by his most trusted deliveryman. The roofer, who had failed in his attempts to keep it concealed, finally got around to acknowledging the basis for his motivation. Keep in mind it is very difficult for a person to come in off the street and tell a stranger, especially a stranger with a badge, that he is losing his wife because he is an unemployed coke user and can't compete with his wealthy friend who for fun, occasionally pokes his wife. I recognized his misery and felt sympathetic, but, I made it clear to the informant Mikey would do federal prison time if the information led to his arrest. The roofer affirmed he was prepared to see the case to its conclusion.

This investigation was easy. I directed the roofer to call me when Mikey had more than a half kilogram of cocaine at his house. The roofer had explained he had often seen a kilogram at the house and said occasionally, he had two. He revealed Mikey owned his own home, a small two-bedroom bungalow on Chicago's working class, Southeast Side. The only remarkable thing about Brady's home, noted the informant, was the floor safe installed in the basement underneath the washing machine. That was identified as the place where he probably kept larger quantities of coke and most of his money.

I authored an affidavit and had an Assistant U.S. Attorney on standby, waiting to provide me assistance to obtain a search warrant from a federal judge. The roofer stayed in touch, committed to the downfall of his nemesis, Mikey. One week after his initial phone call, we were on our way to raid Mikey's trite home armed with a federal search warrant.

There were six of us. The roofer had called around 4:30 p.m. and said Mikey had at least a kilogram and a half of coke at his house. It was more than enough for federal prosecution but, we didn't arrive until 7:45p.m. The delay had been due to unforeseen circumstances. First, I could not find the prosecutor. Then the judge was out to dinner even though we had requested he remain available. I feared our opportunity had been lost and Mikey would have already moved the dope. I received two frantic pages during the interim from the roofer who wondered where we were. He questioned my dedication to the effort and was not appeased by my explanations. Before we raided the house, we mobilized at the end of Mikey's block, at a convenience store. We put on our raid gear as several interested customers watched. We were one block away from the defendant's house and I hoped he would not be tipped. I watched the customers as I prepared for the raid. I hoped I would not see a scrawny pimple-faced twenty-one year old carrying chocolate candy bars and soda pop to a freshly detailed Chevy Corvette.

The raid was uneventful. We broke the front door off its frame but no one, including Brady, was injured. He had been playing with a Sega electronics game when we came through the front door. He let out a high-pitched scream as he was rudely bull rushed to the floor in the middle of an engrossing game of Mortal Kombat. I immediately despised him.

His home was well furnished, complete with creme colored leather furniture and a costly entertainment system. He liked to party as evidenced by the beer-meister installed in his kitchen which dispersed fresh cold draught beer from a tap adorned with a miniature Chicago Bears football helmet. He liked sports, one redeeming quality I found in him. He had several tattered posters of athletes hung throughout the house, which tastelessly contrasted his beautiful furniture.

His basement was furnished similar to a sports bar with several arcade games including pinball, and other plug-in units. He had even installed a small, hardwood dance floor. Pictures were scattered about which revealed he had hosted a particularly wild bachelor party. There were photos of young men in various stages of drunkenness coddling, pawing and eventually wrestling two naked strippers. The illicit photographs provided amusement to the raiding band. The basement had been ransacked and the floor safe had been easily found. I wanted to make that discovery discreetly but, Jimmy Walker had overzealously gone right for it. His decision would have burned our informant since he was one of the few friends of Mikey who had known about it. Fortunately, Mikey had been upstairs being interviewed by Chad Jennings and me. When I finally approached the safe, I was relieved to find it still locked. Walker, who boasted he was a master safe cracker, among other things, had failed to open it.

Mikey denied having any idea why federal agents would be raiding his home. The roofer had left at my suggestion hours ago and was not suspected. I liked the roofer and wanted to maintain his anonymity. I felt compassion for him. Mikey, on the other hand, I loathed. He was a dirty rat-faced little punk who was reaping lucrative monies selling coke. Of course, he denied everything and feigned astonishment at the suggestion he was dabbling in drug dealing. He claimed he worked for a living and was the beneficiary of a large inheritance. Of course, he could provide absolutely no proof for his ridiculous assertions. In fact, when pressed, he could not account for one job he had since he had given up his paper route at the age of fourteen. He was precisely the type of person who invoked my fury but, I professionally camouflaged my anger. Instead, I thought about the cash the little fucker might possess in that safe of his. As my interview progressed, I began looking forward to placing him in jail at the MCC, the Metropolitan Correctional Center, where we deposited all our prisoners. He would be scared shitless in there, I thought, with all those contemptible gangbangers who would love to intimidate the life juices out of the little bastard. Hopefully, I thought, maybe he ripped one of them off one time and now he would face the same swindled con locked in an encumbered jail cell.

Phil Vreeswyck discovered the dope. It was twenty-two one-ounce bags wrapped in clear plastic. The reserve was in a shoebox in his bedroom along with a money roll which consisted of about six thousand dollars. He had already moved half of the dope since the roofer had left. That fact annoyed me but, I was thankful we still had seized enough for federal prosecution. I was disappointed we couldn't find more but, what provoked me was his continued denial of his drug dealing. He claimed that one of us had planted the coke and the cash there. Planting evidence was a prevalent defense among individuals of Brady's ilk and they often made the same nonsensical claims in front of judges. But, alas, all magistrates recognize the motives of corrupt policeman and even the naivest of judges knew that dirty cops don't place $6,000.00 and 22 valuable ounces of coke on a guy just so they can enjoy the privilege of arresting him. Unethical cops have no interest in relinquishing cocaine and money to an evidence vault. Dopers never seemed to realize this and do not know how utterly incredulous they sound when they implement such a defense.

Mikey stubbornly refused to give us the combination of the safe. It forced us to call a locksmith who gladly came out and charged Uncle Sam $285.00 to drill the safe. It took him about fifteen minutes and the locksmith, aware we were federal agents, appeared as interested in the contents of the safe as we were. Unfortunately, there was no dope but, there was quite a tidy some of cash. It was transported back to the office by other agents and I never even had the chance to handle it, Truthfully, I did not consider taking any of it. The more contact I had with Mikey, the more interested I was in seeing the case build against him through good work and the thorough collection of evidence. I further detested Mikey when I saw a couple agents struggle to bring down a television box full of collecting cards, sports memorabilia and autographs.

Chad Jennings, the agent carrying the back end, dropped it. The box slammed against the third step from the bottom. I distinctly saw Mikey cringe with the notion a portion of his precious collection could have been damaged. The carton contained his treasure. He was young and ignorant and the loss of cash or dope did not bother him but, the memorabilia was his passion and his eyes teared as I walked over to inspect it. His immaturity was unveiled and he tried to conceal his anguish as Brenda Xavier, no sports fan by any imagination, picked out an autographed baseball with Nolan Ryan's signature on it.

She looked at it bemusedly then tossed it toward the box announcing "Never heard of him."

A look of horror washed across Mikey's face as the plastic cover encasing the ball struck the lip of the cardboard carton spitting the baseball out of its case. It dropped, then spun across the carpeted floor. At that point, I knew Brady's Achilles Heal had been exposed. I approached him and told him I would seize his cherished articles as proceeds from drug trafficking. He retorted by explaining "some of the stuff" had been his since childhood and "had nothing to do with anything else." To irritate him, I deliberately placed the box, full of his revered collection, next to him in the back seat of my car as he was transported to our offices for processing.

*

When I was young, I maintained a fervid interest in baseball cards. I had collected the cardboard portraits through my childhood and pre-adolescent years. The entire collection was sitting in the attic of my Mom's house in Philadelphia. My cards were primarily early 70's players including hundreds from my favorite baseball team, the Philadelphia Phillies but, the cards I possessed which carried the most value were bona fide stars like Pete Rose, Hank Aaron and Roberto Clemente. I had a few valuable rookie cards of players like Dave Winfield, Robin Yount and Mike Schmidt but, otherwise my collection was ordinary. If I was lucky, some of my cards would fetch a price of fifty or sixty dollars apiece though I would never consider selling them because they reminded me of so much of my childhood. The last time I even glanced at my own cards was some five years past and the day that I did brought back pleasant memories of ice cream trucks and wiffle ball games. When I was a boy I had a pretty good idea of player's abilities and I recall trading lousy utility players to the uninformed neighbors and my playmates for genuine superstars. I remember reasoning with the next-door neighbor and his little brother that players who appeared in action, photos taken during live game action, were more valuable than the guys just standing there posing for a picture. That philosophy enabled me one time to trade a '74 Willie Montanez, a flamboyant

Latino with modest career stats pictured sliding hard into third base, for future hall-of-famer Tom Seaver, who was, of course, just standing there. I remember the kids' father was so upset that I fleeced his son on that trade he forbade his children to bring out their baseball cards around me.

The loss of Brady's baseball cards should have been the furthest thing from our immature prisoner's mind. Mikey was fingerprinted, photographed and placed in his cell. He requested his one phone call which incidentally, only occurs on television. It didn't happen while in custody of the DEA unless a person wanted to cooperate. Otherwise, if a person wanted to make a call they weren't able to do so until they were transported to the MCC. Mikey pleaded he at least be permitted to call his Mom and tell her he had been arrested. Initially, he was quite proud of himself for being arrested by a renowned organization like the DEA but, his tumescent ego began to crumble under the mounting anxiety caused by the gravity of his situation. He slowly realized he was in serious trouble.

I looked into his beloved box and extracted some of the plastic binders he had kept on the bottom, underneath programs, pennants and a plastic bag full of ticket stubs. The jackets contained transparent pages of baseball cards which were filed neatly in groups of nine players per page. I expected to find contemporary player cards like Ken Griffey Jr., Barry Bonds and Frank Thomas. Those cards themselves are valuable, some being worth tens and occasionally hundreds of dollars. I was shocked when I opened the books. It appeared Mikey had been carefully investing in cards whose values were considerably higher. He possessed cards like Mickey Mantle, Jackie Robinson and Enos Slaughter. There were doubles of some and triples of others. Willie Mays, Roger Maris, even Ted Williams. Mikey had been investing considerable monies into the American Pastime's most prized memorabilia. I slipped some of the cards from their sleeves and was astonished to find, in most cases, there existed another duplicate card underneath. What I thought were three Willie Mays cards were actually six. I removed one, a 1952 Topps which had a price of $600.00 taped to the back. It was in near mint condition. So was a Sandy Koufax, 1957 Topps with a label indicating it was worth $150.00. A '56 Mantle, $350.00, '56 Duke Snider $100.00. Every card I examined was a well-known player from the 1940's, 50's and 60's era of baseball. He had a collection consisting of four binders with probably twenty-five transparent pages with each page virtually full of cards. With only a general knowledge of the cards, I appraised his set to be worth several thousand dollars. I went back to his holding cell, located in the south end of our fifth floor building. It was windowless and obviously afforded him no view, only a stale smell and a hard wooden bench to sit on and contemplate the grim future.

I knocked on the tall black-metal door of cell two and asked Mikey if he was alright.

"I'm O.K.. " The interruption from his solemn thoughts momentarily comforted him and he asked, "When am I getting out of here."

"You know you have some nice baseball cards out here. They are worth quite a bit, I'm sure you know." I delved into the area without really knowing just how much.

"It's a nice collection. It's taken me a while. Most of those cards are my Dad's though so leave them alone." He instructed, "He'll be here in the morning to pick them all up."

"Really?" I replied but, withheld my plans, "I bet those cards are worth a few thousand dollars, aren't they?"

He scoffed, "Put a zero behind it, asshole."

The remark detonated my blood pressure. I returned to my desk and contemplated the investigation. Vreeswyck told me that Mikey had $23,000 or so in the floor safe. That was now property of Uncle Sam. Based on the figures the roofer furnished, I reasoned Mikey made that in a bad month. I decided to do the best job I could to see that Mikey Brady would spend some time in jail. I returned to my desk and methodically completed every document associated with the case. I typed out the DEA-6 reports for the search warrant and the DEA-6 arrest reports. Any statements he made were documented in the form of typewritten pages. I finished the DEA 7 and the DEA 7A's for seizure of drug and non-drug related evidence. I systematically catalogued and labeled every exhibit which was seized. I dotted every "i" and crossed every "t." All activity in the case was recorded and every item procured as evidence was listed. Usually these formalities were taken care of in the morning but, Mikey's audacity so enraged me I spent the night completing the paperwork. Mikey had been transported to the MCC by other agents and the thought of him worrying about his naive little ass provided me the energy to continue through the night. Everything was reported and logged, including the seizure of the $23,000. Every item except his cherished cards.

At approximately 4:00 a.m., I leisurely perused his cards, looking at the baseball stars who had been heroes to me, my father and millions of others all memorialized in 2 ½" by 3 ½" little cardboard paper pictures. Campanella, Reese, Drysdale, Musial. He even had players whose glory years came during my childhood like Willie McCovey, Bob Gibson and Brooks Robinson. All the stars of a simpler time when drugs and guns were not fiddling with the lives of so much of America. I examined the players pictured, especially those of the fifties. Baggy uniforms, brush haircuts and flexed, sinewy muscles waiting to hit or throw an imaginary white ball. I began removing cards which were triplicates at first. I assumed those would be the least likely missed. Then I began removing cards because I liked the player or remembered him in a funny beer commercial. Before I was finished, I had selected about thirty-five cards from Mikey's collection. I placed the binders back into the box, on top of yellowed pennants, dusty programs and unrecognizable autographs on glossy photos. Only the cards appealed to me and the ones I had removed I placed in my top shirt pocket. I rationalized something so "American" as baseball cards should not be in the possession of someone so destructive. A drug dealer didn't know the true intrinsic value of such things and therefore shouldn't posses them. Baseball cards were something I collected and they shouldn't be tainted by their exaggerated values and exorbitant prices that only those with disposable money could afford to purchase. I became the judge and jury that evening and I arbitrarily fined Mikey for his arrogance, deciding his penalty should be three dozen baseball cards chosen at my discretion.

*

Several weeks later, I went to a sports card and memorabilia show in Rosemont, Illinois to dump some of my stolen loot. Certainly there were a few I kept but, the majority of them I decided to unload, just in case Mikey ever made an allegation.

Brady had been granted bail the day after his arrest and the long process of his criminal case would begin in the Northern District of Illinois. His release disgusted the informant, but I assured him Mikey was facing jail time. The roofer charged I had misled him to believe Brady would remain in jail, an assertion which I denied. I couldn't recall the swiftness or the degree of Brady's punishment being a topic of much discussion during the debriefing sessions, only that it would come. I told the informant that Mikey would go to jail unless he cooperated but, I could not guarantee when it would occur. The informant was not pleased and expected Mikey Brady to be out of his life. The informant elected not to return subsequent phone calls but, he was no longer needed for the prosecution of the case. The bitter informant elected to sever his relationship with me and since I had protected his anonymity, he was no longer needed for Brady's prosecution. My only obligation in the case was to prepare the file and wait for instructions from the prosecuting attorney. Brady, I was told, had not petitioned the U.S. Government for the return of his cocaine, the cash or the sports memorabilia collection.

I had purchased a Beckett's Official Baseball Card price guide which is considered the bible of sports card collecting. It contained a host of information about the world of card speculation. It also included general price quotes for every baseball card ever produced covering companies from Bowman, who manufactured some of the first collectible cards in the early 1900's to the leading contemporary companies like Upper Deck and Fleer. I really had no idea how many companies had jumped on the trading card bandwagon but, judging from the published information, the industry was not unlike any others. The demand must be met by supply and there was an abundance of manufacturers. I was delighted to discover many of the cards I had purloined had been priced accurately by Mikey. Of course, he had been the informed collector so I should not have anticipated otherwise. Some of the cards were even more valuable than he had documented. I was determined to sell a bunch of the cards and this time I would not be intimidated like I had been at the pawns. I casually observed the activity at the tables, adolescent kids walking around and negotiating sales of little cardboard placards. Some of the rustlers were as young as six and seven but, still possessed the business savvy of stock traders. They demanded considerations, discounts and better deals. Boxes of football, hockey, baseball and basketball cards were bought and sold as well as baseball figurines, autographed jerseys, framed photos, old ticket stubs and programs. Everything was for sale and people, mostly kids, frantically bargained and bartered to get the best deal. It appeared to me there were no prized possessions. Instead, everything had a price. I thought about professional athletes and their much publicized contract squabbles and I imagined them seeing their faces, names and statistics bought and sold. Was it wrong for athletes to ask for a piece of this fervid action? The process by which possession of the cards changed hands was certainly not the method I remember collecting baseball cards. Back in the early 70's, I plunked down twenty-five cents and hoped I received a few all-stars in a group of twenty cards, all smelling like the stale, processed bubble gum which came with every pack. This new, highly-calculated process of obtaining cards had relegated collecting to an industry with the kids buying and selling whomever they wished. Only the mega-stars were desired and carefully selected rookies who had never played a pro game but, were thought strong enough prospects to command high prices. The little boys and girls were like miniature speculators trading on the futures of a picture of a 19 year old country boy who could hit a batted ball 450 feet or throw one 98 miles per hour. I suppose it was, in a sense, gambling for children, a sad advertisement and another testament to our society's bankrupt morality.

I walked to a table which featured some of the same cards which I held in my pocket. They were glass encased with red labeled prices taped across their transparent wrappers. A sign boasted "Ask about bulk discounts." I removed my cards from my left shirt pocket and asked the vendor if he was interested.

He scrupulously examined them. He looked for creases and folds and dog-ears on the corners, all blemishes which decreased their value. He found none and he knew the cards I provided were in exceptional condition. He picked out one, a 1959 Topps Hank Aaron. He offered $50. I knew it was worth twice that but, instead of dismissing him, I decided to practice the charade. I countered with $100 and he laughed and rolled his bloodshot eyes. We went back and forth until I sold him the Aaron card plus two others of lesser value for a total of $150.00. Another customer listened to the haggling and made an offer for a Whitey Ford card I possessed. He said he was a longtime Yankee fan and had been trying to get the card for over a year. He was an older gentleman and I assumed he might not just be trying to turn a buck so I sold the card to him for the price of his initial offer. My quick concession to his first proposal prompted him to ask if the card was counterfeit. I said no but offered him his money back. He considered the rare card that he had negotiated into his possession. He probably assumed I didn't recognize its worth so, he artfully declined. I marched around many of the nearly one hundred tables that day. I sold half of the cards I entered with and left the show with a tidy $2,800. I know I had been fleeced on many of the sales but, I viewed the deals as a form of repentance for the underhanded dealings of my youth. I considered the affair my effort to exercise the ghosts of my trading card past when I routinely obtained superstars like Joe Morgan and Johnny Bench for team checklists, mediocre pitchers, .220 hitters and otherwise valueless utility players.

I left the financially beleaguered fathers and their prospecting sons to enjoy their shared "hobby" while I went to a bar and ate a nice leisurely lunch. I tipped the hard working barmaid whose service was excellent despite the bothersome locals who voraciously finished their draught beers while demanding she engage each one in flirting banter. I heard one tell her he had won $80 on a lottery ticket for the first time in his life. In celebration, he insisted on buying the house, which consisted of seven people, a round of drinks. It was a nice gesture which made me feel guilty I was sitting next to him with a wad of money secured with the sale of little cardboard figures filched from a drug dealer.

1 3

In the fourth and fifth decades of the nineteenth century, Joliet, Illinois developed with the promise of a secure future as a processing and manufacturing town reaping the vast resources and benefits of the Des Plaines River. Its geographic location, some twenty-five miles southwest of cramped and improvident Chicago, made it an attractive and inexpensive locale for new industry. With production beginning to bloom, its citizens dreamed of comfortable lifestyles and financial independence and few, if any, were concerned with the troubles of its much bigger northwest neighbor. The success however, was short lived.

The industrial abuse and pollution to the Des Plaines river, coupled with a dramatic decrease in the demand for the region's products, led to the closing of several large plants and the loss of thousands of industrial and steel mill jobs. By the early 1980's, the gritty town had been economically devastated. Its unemployment rate zoomed past 25% and was among the worst in the country. It seemed the city's most recognizable fixtures were its two maximum security prisons, institutions which housed some of Illinois' most deranged and despised criminals, serial murderers John Wayne Gacy and Richard Speck among them.

Understandably, the city focused its energies in resurrecting its image and saving its economy. When businesses did not respond, its politicians turned to the promise of casino riverboats to salvage the city's bleak economic outlook and rescue it from sinking into financial ruin and bankruptcy. The plan showed signs of injecting life into the biggest city in Will County. In addition to the riverboats, its revenue became tied to volume shopping centers featuring a conglomeration of retail stores with high profits and low paying jobs. The management staffs of these outlets, like the better paid employees of the riverboats, escaped Joliet and retreated to the satellite towns of Romeoville and Crest Hill to the north and New Lenox to the East to live their share of the American Dream. There, they built their homes in re-zoned subdivisions that were once corn and bean fields. The minorities, the blacks and Mexican immigrants of Joliet's East Side, many of whom were children of inmates of the prison system, were left to fend for themselves and did not enjoy any benefits of the modest windfall. Instead, they were ignored as authorities mistakenly believed their poverty and their problems would keep them confined and unnoticed on the East Side of Joliet.

I had visited Joliet for a fourth consecutive Sunday and it had not been for the purpose of calling on the lost town to try my luck against the riverboats' skewed one-armed bandits. Instead, I had adopted a plan to intercept a money courier. Lifting two grand worth of cardboard from Brady had been ridiculously easy. My appetite for more significant money had been wet by my heist from Rush. I realized the Rush opportunity had nothing to do with my preparation and I simply found myself standing in front of a crisper drawer with a bag of money in it. I knew I was better than that. I decided I would employ my own strategy to rob a drug trafficker and do it in fashion where the only representative from law enforcement around would be me.

I knew traffickers utilized a variety of conveyances to ship their drugs to Chicago and transfer their proceeds out. Among the cheaper and safer means of transportation were the use of trains. I played a hunch that Amtrak's Silver Eagle bound for El Paso, Texas, originating out of the Windy City, would be a primary route a courier from

Chicago would choose. I also knew that very few federal agencies worked on Sundays and that most state sponsored narcotics enforcement endeavors also did not take place over the weekend. I assumed narcotics traffickers might be aware of this as well, so I had been travelling to Joliet to meet the 5:55 a.m. Silver Eagle passenger train which went through Joliet's Union Station and ultimately, on to Texas.

Joliet's close proximity to Chicago made it a popular destination for drug traffickers who intended to move dope in the Chicagoland area. The traffickers often exploited naive or desperate people to do their bidding and Joliet, the County Seat, offered the perfect conditions to accomplish these goals. It was a relatively sparsely populated county compared to the heavily inhabited counties encompassing Chicago like Cook and its immediate neighbors, DuPage, Kane and Lake County. Consequently, Will County's police force was not large and most of its officers were not tenured. It was a common practice of Joliet Police to cut their teeth, gain experience and then travel north and eastward to better paying jobs near Chicago. Will County operated on a modest budget and was not well suited for spending money investigating sophisticated narcotic trafficking. Their money was spent and certainly understandably so, on protecting areas where taxpayers resided and insuring the safe and happy transit of gambling visitors who injected Joliet's deficient economy. Crime in the county was low except for the decaying county seat, which was gaining a deserved reputation as a sheltered haven for marijuana, cocaine and heroin traffickers. The Joliet Police Force, though dedicated, was spending its resources investigating an increasing number of gang related crimes of violence like robbery, aggravated assaults and murders. The escalating violent crime led Joliet to be labeled with an egregious designation as one of the most dangerous cities in Illinois.

Nevertheless, at 5:30 a.m. on Sunday, the town was quiet. The two riverboats, the Empress and Harrah's were dormant with their last sail having occurred at midnight. The ships were already docked by 3:30

a.m. with the next departure not slated until 8:00 that morning. There was sparse pedestrian traffic other than a haggard and filthy heroin addict I noticed roaming Cass Avenue looking, I presume, for his lost soul or most likely, his next fix. I disgustedly watched him scurry into an alley in a futile effort to escape the insatiable demons that possessed his bloodstream. Fortunately, for him and me, vehicular traffic was minimal as well. I took advantage of the relative tranquility by selecting a parking spot at the end of Jefferson Street. It was the same spot I had occupied the previous two weeks and it afforded me a perfect view of the refurbished train station, its parking lot and two of its three entrances. More importantly though, it was a private and inconspicuous place for me to quietly hide and observe.

I had come again, as I had for a month of Sundays, to watch passengers board the Silver Eagle. I enjoyed the advantage of closely scrutinizing each person who came to the station and waited for the train. It was coming from Chicago, its origination point, and a relatively short distance away for a passenger train. As expected, no one departed. I was there specifically looking for someone who would fit the profile of a money courier. I watched for particular indications, specifically someone who carried only a few pieces of luggage. Maybe a bag only large enough for toiletries and one change of clothes. Normal people travelling on a train going perhaps as far as El Paso would certainly carry luggage. My scheme was to identify a person who looked like a potential courier and decipher their destination and reason for travel. Ethnicity would play a significant factor in those decisions. I looked for someone who exhibited apprehensiveness and my objective was to find a nervous Hispanic, hopefully a woman carrying one bag as described and perhaps a second, smaller bag which would contain what I was after, money. I knew the tendency for a courier was to arrive late and probably be dropped off by an escort, who was most likely the rightful owner of the money.

During the first four Sundays, I had only observed one possible money courier. He was a Mexican man about thirty-five years old with a heavy mustache. He wore a bolero, an item few sported around Northeastern Illinois. What drew my attention to him was the small item he carried in his left hand, a bronze-plated crucifix, approximately three inches long. I had noticed it because he had nervously placed it on the counter top when he had paid cash for his ticket. I had gone inside the station to inventory the passengers and I noticed him wander in. I watched as he rubbed the cross incessantly while he fumbled with the money to pay for the ticket. He seemed to mutter to himself but, his behavior did not indicate insanity. Instead, I judged his actions to be that of a man who wanted wholeheartedly to be somewhere else, not travelling on the train for the purpose for which he had probably been chosen. I did not believe he was going to Texas, as I had heard him tell the ticket agent, to see old family members. I believed he was carrying contraband, money, and I surmised he was praying while waiting for the train to arrive. Religion is vital to so many traffickers who presume only by the grace of God they make their trips safely through the gauntlet of thieves and police who, sometimes, are the dangerous combination of one and the same.

This distinctive man had in his possession one overnight bag. The trip would take two full days and certainly a visit with family would require several changes of clothes. I hesitated but was sure he fit the profile of a money courier. I really was not quite certain what action to take, so I watched him and speculated how I could quietly and without commotion, interdict him. I was positive his trip to Texas was illegitimate. I wondered how much money his small black bag might contain. While I weighed my options, the train arrived. He was one of the last to board, opting to remain inside a small snack shop while others verified their luggage was loaded then boarded the train. I hoped I could approach him but, I wanted to be extremely cautious. I decided to wait. The conductor announced last call for boarding and he rose and walked onto the train. I let him go without obstruction but, his presence that Sunday inspired me to return. I intended to find another courier and in the meantime develop a concrete plan to intercept one without causing suspicion. My hopes were to approach a suspected courier, display my badge briefly enough to communicate I was a policeman and intimidate the suspect into moving to a discreet area where I could inspect the luggage. I believed I would know immediately by their reaction if the individual was attempting something illegal. After all, I had some experience at airports conducting profile stops and when someone had dope or money, they immediately became visibly anxious and often irritated when they were questioned. My goal was to examine the contents only if the individual appeared worried by my presence. Their was only one security guard at the station and on every Sunday I had observed him to be content to remain in his office drinking coffee and reading the Sunday Classifieds.

On the fifth Sunday, it drizzled. I arrived at Union Station a few minutes after five a.m. and was fortunate to once again be able to park close to the station. I felt excited and had a good feeling about the attempt. I considered the persistent rain to be an advantage providing additional cover for my activity. I once again studiously audited the security of the station. There appeared to be a couple video cameras mounted in the ceiling of the west end of the station with one fixed toward the main concourse. The second could not have been functioning since the cords which led from it dangled purposelessly from its base, indicating it was not connected to monitor or recording devices. Amtrak maintained a skeleton crew at the station at five o'clock in the morning. There was a ticketing agent at the counter and a second person who appeared to serve as a handyman, responsible for maintenance of the equipment and the station. I did not see the guard but, could see a light was turned on behind the closed blinds of the security sub station located inside the main concourse.

I returned to my car and waited for people to arrive. I cleared the beading windshield periodically. My strategy had not been to remain in my car but the precipitation's intensity had picked up. I decided to wait and observe from my car and avoid the drenching rain. I watched the first of several people begin to come to the station. I listened to the radio whose stations all seemed to be playing those horrible public service programs that are required by the FCC to be aired. The particular program which I found myself paying some attention to was a woman talking about her repressed memories and the profit motivated foundation she established to combat such indecencies. Lucrative donations from the financially secure solidified her place on the happier side of middle income. Disinterested, I reached to shut the radio off when I noticed a polished silver Blazer drive by me, going east on Jefferson. The utility vehicle came by a second time and its pass extended me ample time to view its occupants.

They were two Hispanics who I guessed to be in their late twenties. The proximity of their parking choice enabled me to make that assessment. The Chevy Blazer stopped across the street from me, a distance of no more than thirty yards. The driver exited the Blazer and retrieved a square blue suitcase from the rear of the truck. He walked to the passenger side of the Blazer, opened the door and placed the case behind the seat of the passenger. The activity was odd and I felt a surge of excitement. The driver walked back to his side and re-entered the automobile. The Blazer sat there with the brake lights occasionally glowing. The bust signal, I optimistically thought. I intently watched the vehicle for ten minutes as it sat there, wishing I could hear the occupants. I knew the activity was suspicious but, I wanted to get into the station. It was approaching 5:30. Without warning, the Blazer engaged and drove off with both its passengers. I was disappointed but, not discouraged. Though I was wrong, at least, I had not embarrassed myself.

Avarice beckoned me to abandon the warm comfort of my car. I walked through the sustained spatter of raindrops towards the station. The restored old clock outside the station read 5:31. I was surprised to see all four sides of the clock functioned properly. I thought its glass would make a good target for vandals, another cynical inspiration. I looked at the station square as I proceeded through it, noticing newly planted trees, when mature, would make the place a nice spot to eat lunch on a brilliant June day.

I bypassed the main entrance and routinely walked across the plaza to the east stairwell which led to the elongated platform. I figured there was no need to be seen by someone observant milling about in the main concourse. I did not believe anyone might remember my face from the previous Sundays but, I wore a baseball hat pulled low for disguise anyway. The existence of rain prohibited me from sensibly wearing sunglasses. Nevertheless, I assumed I looked like a cop and it was exactly the message I wanted to convey. I wore a blue windbreaker which concealed my gun, strategically placed in my waistband. I intended to let the jacket swing open when I questioned my subject so he could see that I was armed and was an officer. I would flash my badge but certainly prohibit the person to examine it. To make sure, I covered the gold-plated letters spelling D-E-A with electric tape. It looked hokey but, if my plan was going to succeed, the person who viewed it would never have the leisure to determine if it was legitimate. I would make no mention of the DEA or any other organization. My intent was to take charge, intimidate and view the contents of a bag.

I jogged up the stairwell to the concrete platform and was not surprised to see it vacant. A few puddles of rainwater twinkled in the splashing rain. I walked around a bank of payphones to the door leading to the concourse. I peered through the glass entrance and counted about eight people dawdling about inside, none of whom interested me. There was a Hispanic lady who was absorbed keeping her two playful children from running amok. The rambunctious kids appeared eager to embark on the train trip despite the gloomy weather. I saw two older men, both also Hispanic, wearing wrinkled cotton shirts and boots. They looked overburdened and broken as if they had not slept in a while. One had a liquor bottle concealed in a brown paper bag. I was not certain they were going to get on the train or had simply set out to rest in the drafty station. They might very well have been homeless so I dismissed them. An elderly African-American couple sipped coffee from Styrofoam cups and I suspected they were waiting to go south to visit a relative. The eighth person was a middle-aged Hispanic woman, probably Mexican. Her bronzed face bore more of the characteristics of the ancient Mayans than a Latin. She clutched three medium sized nylon bags which seemed to be stuffed with personal belongings though, of course, I had no way of knowing. I wished for x-ray vision. I chuckled to myself as I pictured those x-ray specks that were commonly advertised on the back pages of old comic books and I wondered if popular science would ever invent such an item. Ultimately, I disregarded her.

Ten more minutes elapsed and I was becoming despondent. No one else had arrived but, the train had. As expected, nobody departed the train because it had only just begun its extended journey some forty minutes prior in Chicago. A few of the people I had observed in the concourse had strolled toward the train, including the woman and her eager children who were scolded by the agitated conductor for playing too close to the resting locomotive.

Meanwhile, I returned to the concourse, out of the rain and out of view of other passengers. I dejectedly made the decision to leave. I walked down the main stairwell to avoid the rain, dancing across a gaping puddle from a leaking roof on the way. I contemplated my return the following Sunday and wondered if I had missed my only opportunity, allowing the man from the previous week to go without interference. I rounded the wooden stairwell and walked toward the exit doors. I could see through the glass doors and noticed parked outside the plaza was the silver Blazer which had returned. I noted the grey-white exhaust of the idling vehicle. I stopped to survey the activity. I glanced around the station and was stunned to see the driver of the vehicle now standing at the Amtrak counter. I hurried to get within earshot and I distinctly heard the ticket agent tell "Mr. Morales" to enjoy his trip to Dallas but, "hurry, the train was about to leave."

A polite Morales said "Thank you."

I watched him leave the counter and walk back toward the Blazer. Morales was dressed plainly and wore nothing that indicated he did or did not have money. He entered the vehicle. No more than thirty seconds elapsed when the passenger, a slight Hispanic man with a narrow face emerged. He wore jeans and a light sweatsuit jacket. He carried the blue squared suitcase which he clutched tensely under his right arm. The train ticket envelope which Morales had just purchased was clenched in between the man's teeth. I was transfixed on the case which I noted the passenger continued to grasp securely. I knew this was the man I would stop. He walked toward me in the station as that familiar swell of adrenaline spurted through my chest cavity. This opportunity was what I had hoped for and it was all materializing before my eyes. The last minute departure, the escort, the one way ticket paid for in cash. It was all classic activity by a dope or money courier.

The passenger reached the door and thoughts raced in my head. I could not confront the man with his escort in the Blazer sitting in front, monitoring his charge. Even if I could remove the bag and inspect it, the driver would see me from his view. If it contained money and I seized it, I would be forced to walk out with it right in front of its owner. That would be ugly. I wondered if the blue case contained money at all. I certainly did not want to cause a potential damaging scene so I could inspect torn and soiled underwear. I considered security and the potential for police and all the nasty ramifications if my activity was publicized. None of my anxious doubts hindered the progress of my subject who kept coming until he made his way into the concourse. I had to assume the Blazer's driver was armed. I felt secure with the abilities I possessed with my sidearm but, I didn't want to engage in a shoot-out on a Sunday morning in front of a train station. There would be no way I could "pull a Jackson" out of a disaster like that. I would fry. Meanwhile, the passenger looked confused and stood motionless with a look of bewildered amazement surfacing across his face. Then, the Blazer pulled away, confident his friend was safely on his way. The passenger stood with his suitcase and gym bag in hand and his ticket in mouth, assessing his next move while I considered mine. He saw the stairwell and went for it. I decided recklessly to pursue my plan.

I followed him right up the east stairwell. He was halfway up the first flight of creaking stairs.

"Hey," I yelled, startling myself with the loudness.

He wheeled around but, continued up the stairwell, his momentum propelling him up two more steps.

"Police." I instinctively grabbed my badge from my left rear pocket and flashed it. He looked befuddled but, not frightened. He shrugged.

I made my way to his step. "Police, I want to ask you a question or two."

He shook his head sideways. Not in defiance but, in misunderstanding. I looked him in the eyes hard, hoping to intimidate him and quickly discern his guilt. Instead, he remained calm.

"I am the police. Do you have any identification ?" I asked.

"No English. Me, no English."

I felt relief that he did not speak my language. My target wasn't reacting. I had picked a man who didn't recognize who I was and apparently didn't give a rat's ass. I thought about collecting myself and sheepishly walking away but, as he placed his hand to his chest in a gesture of innocence or ignorance, I noticed it quiver. It was a distinct sign of apprehension. It is what I had hoped to see and I intended to exploit the development. I knew then I would see the contents of that precious suitcase. Whether he possessed clothes, filthy skivvies, cookies for his abuela or money, I would know.

I said firmly, "Identification ?" I gestured not for his wallet but, the suitcase. I could see he wasn't armed with a gun as his jacket was stretched to tight against his thin frame. If he had a knife I could probably get away. Weapons, I knew, were not usually carried by couriers and this knowledge fostered confidence to pursue my plan. He stood with the train ticket, a billet to Dallas, he was not entrusted or permitted to purchase himself. My interpretation of the real purpose of his trip began to look favorable.

"The suitcase." I said as I grabbed for it with an instinctive demand exuding assured control. My heart pounded during this momentary encounter. He too, was scared. He pushed the blue case forward as I pulled it away from him. His wide chestnut eyes bulged from his face and I knew. So did he. I yanked it open right there on the stairwell, jerking the metal levers on the sides with sincere hopes they weren't locked. Fortunately, it was not and it fell open. The side closest to me dropped towards the floor. In my haste the lid opened upside down revealing a large turquoise bath towel which enveloped bundles of green paper. Money! I saw bundles of money!

"Get upstairs, policia." I motioned frantically pointing authoritatively up the steps." Policia, Policia! Go, go upstairs. Vomenos !" I yelled.

I did not know what else to do. I squatted trying desperately to keep the contents from falling out of the case and down the steps while still trying to maintain control of the situation. The courier was genuinely terrified and did not know what to do either. He knew he had been caught. I feared he would run but, in some sense I hoped he would, just not for the Blazer I prayed was gone. I grabbed his left shoulder and pushed him hard up two steps. Tears welled in his eyes.

"Now, vomenos." I screamed loudly. Others certainly must have heard.

He moved up the steps as I turned and walked down. The shot would come now if he had a gun. I instinctively winced as I moved down the steps waiting for the searing heat of a bullet to burn through my back but, it did not come. I walked faster, rounding the corner of the stairwell. I pulled the cap down over my eyes. My heart felt like it would explode. The Blazer, I thought.

Please be gone. Please.

I made it to the door imploring myself to remain calm. In essence, I was pulling off an armed robbery in broad daylight. I approached the main doors and the sight of the street without the Blazer parked on it provided an infinitesimal degree of relief. I still had to get to the car. I pushed the station's door with an unharnessed impetus which flung it open violently, causing the door to spin wildly on its hinges in a 180 degree turn that left it smashing hard against its adjacent partner. I managed two steps before moving into a full sprint.

Calm. Be calm, Goddamn it.

There was no way. I then noticed the suitcase had not been buckled shut. I held it closed tightly as I ran, knowing I was proceeding at a suspicious pace that looked like I was fleeing a crime.

What could the courier be doing?

As I raced the final few yards to my car I heard the blaring horn of the Amtrak train as it stood on the platform. I opened the door and threw the suitcase in like a desperate escaped con making his getaway. I did not fumble for the keys and I was proud later to have at least done that part right. I started the engine and slammed the transmission into drive. I pressed the accelerator and lurched forward. I checked the rear view mirror and fortunately, saw nothing including the grill of a silver Chevy Blazer. I was thankful I had the foresight to remove my license plate as I sped from Union Station and the neighborhood around it. I was at 60 miles an hour before I realized I was going to fast in the desolate city streets. I slowed down and was impelled to glance backward at the jostled contents of the suitcase. I almost climaxed as I saw two bundles with the handsome face of Ulysses S. Grant sticking out from under the sapphire towel. I enacted my getaway plan, now a bona fide armed robber.

✳

Suppressing the adrenaline was an extremely difficult task. Fortunately, the streets were still barren and my abrupt exit was not noticed by any pedestrians walking along sidewalks or more importantly, police patrolling the streets. I hadn't noticed signs of police activity during any of my visits to Joliet and that Sunday had proved to be no different. I knew I wasn't being tailed by the silver Blazer or any other vehicle and I was thankful the Silver Eagle did not pass through Joliet at 5:55 p.m.

I drove about a mile and a half north to a self-serve car wash, a brick building with six bays set off the main road out of the city's downtown section. I pulled around through the rear and entered one of the middle bays. I peered through my windshield out into the roadway through the open garage and observed nothing but a mongrel dog cautiously probing the trash of a nearby fast food restaurant. I sat for a few moments in the cinderblock bay and found it a perfect place to try to regain my composure. Resting may have been considered risky but, I had to allay my racing pulse and I did not want to rush through any more streets in Joliet with a suitcase of money lying in the rear seat. I pushed the automatic trunk opener and exited my car. I had planned to come back to this spot to safeguard my booty if I had ever succeeded in my plan. I really never expected to be here but, now that I had a reason to be, I was pleased I had the foresight to locate the secluded place prior to the execution of my robbery. I removed the license plate from the trunk. I had placed a magnet on the rear which easily affixed to the metal plate where the license should be mounted and it took no more than five seconds to secure it. I returned to the

rear of my vehicle. I leaned in and briefly examined the case and considered emptying the contents onto the floor and discarding the
moldy container right into the restaurant's dumpster. I reconsidered
and decided that act would be the behavior of an amateur purse-
snatcher. While bending in the rear seat, I looked out the windows of
the car to make sure no one was watching. Again, there wasn't. Even
the dog had moved on. I picked the whole case up, reeling in joy that
it felt somewhat heavy and I smiled with the possibility it was laden
with pretty green paper. I saw a few articles of clothing, the towel and
a few thick bundles of money. I resisted the near overwhelming captivation to count it there. I had to conceal the case in my trunk and
make my escape. I closed the cheap buckles on each side and placed
the case into the rear compartment, covering it with a polyester blanket I had stored in the trunk for late night surveillances in cold
weather. I examined the out-dated cover and concluded its purpose
was much more satisfying now. After the three minute respite, I
returned to the wheel and headed north out of Joliet, past closed deli-
catessens and second-rate auto body shops onto Route 53 and out of
Will County.

*

A relatively new highway transverses Chicago's far western suburbs,
running eighteen miles connecting two major highways, I-55 and I-290.
With Chicago's burgeoning suburban population, it was a much-needed
system. However, to pay for the cost of building it, the Department of
Highways inserted several toll crossings across its route, some of which
are only five miles apart. It was this highway which I chose to utilize to
access from Route 53 and flee with my spoils to my modest apartment. I
arrived at the first toll and fumbled for the correct change. I tossed two
dimes and two nickels into the basket and continued on my way. With
my loot on my mind, I did not want to run the risk of drawing even the

least bit of attention to myself. Of course, it was paranoia but, it was difficult to corral the fleeting thoughts of calculating exactly how much money I might have had in the trunk. I contemplated pulling over several times just to savor it. I wanted so much to know for sure what was there. The toll road was heavily patrolled by various suburban jurisdictions and is generally considered by most of those who travel it regularly to be a revenue-generating speed trap, so I did not take the chance. I must admit my greedy endorphins almost overpowered me but, I drove the stretch of highway as conservatively as possible. I knew there were clothes in the case and the more apparel there was, the less prized cash I would find. However, I reasoned the case contained at least $20,000 judging from the thickness of the bundles and one of the stacks which had a marvelous $50 bill on top. Hopefully the whole case was full of $50's and $100's and I wouldn't be bothered with the nuisance of having to count $1's and $5's. I thought the case might even contain $25,000 or more, maybe $50,000 but either way, at least twenty grand. As I considered the possibilities, I found myself anticipating disappointment if the suitcase held less than $20,000. A ridiculous notion, in retrospect but, directly attributable to greed. Either way, it wasn't bad for a little month's worth of Sundays' work.

I encountered the second and final toll I would pass through on my short ride on the I-355 Tollroad. I chose another correct change line and reached for the cup holder which held my loose change. It was usually full of silver but, as I reached for coins all I retrieved were copper pennies. I grabbed for a handful and recovered more pennies. The toll was fifty cents. I sat in the automatic change lines and frantically counted. I knew I did not have fifty pennies. I counted .34c. A horn blew from behind, flustering me and rendering me with a feeling of stupidity. I reached into the back pocket of my blue jeans and was vanquished with a sickening feeling. My wallet was gone. I patted my seat again with my left hand, then quickly placed my right hand to my other cheek. A falsetto horn sounded again, from one of those uncomfortable foreign jobs, as I began slapping wildly at my lap and my windbreaker.

"Where the fuck is my wallet?" I yelled audibly. "Fuck! Fuck!

I arched my back up as complete panic rocked my body. Not because of the toll but, the possibility my wallet had fallen from my jeans during the skirmish and robbery of the mule. "Please God, Don't let me have lost that wallet," I implored.

"Let's go asshole!" An irascible voice from behind echoed. It was the driver behind me. Behind him, I noticed a short parade of vehicles had formed. I had no choice but to pull through the tollbooth and explain to the booth operator I had no coins and had lost my wallet. I proceeded through the toll causing the loud bell to sound and a red flashing light to ignite. My only alternative was to drive to the shoulder of the road and park near the exposed phone booths reserved for stranded or confused drivers. I visually inspected the area for police hoping that none had stopped by to write a report or indulge himself with a powdered, creme-filled doughnut. I remained in the car and confirmed the doors were locked. I did not want anyone walking up and opening the door. The commotion subsided after I finally proceeded through the toll. I probably could have safely driven away since many tolls are ignored routinely but, there was no chance I was going to employ such a hazardous move. I did not want to give an officer or a state trooper any reason to pull me over even though presentation of my DEA badge would have been sufficient to vindicate me from any wrongdoing and certainly, save me the embarrassment of a moving violation. I lurched around in the car still looking for my wallet. I probed between the backrest and the seat feeling and hoping the wallet had slipped into the tight crack. It hadn't. I scanned my mind wondering how or where I could have lost it. Visualizing no resolution, I considered my best option was to resolve my first problem, the toll. I rummaged the change holder and found a hidden dime. I had 44 cents but, still not enough for the fifty-cent toll. Again, I verified no one was approaching me and exited the vehicle. I dropped to my knees and reached under the car seat for loose change. The area beneath the driver's seat was cluttered with rails and electronic wiring which serves to move the seat at the touch of a button. I saw a piece of the purple Crown Royal bag which had torn away during my last struggle with the driver's seat. I cursed it before stabbing myself on a discarded ball point pen. I continued to negotiate the tight squeeze. I felt a coin and pulled for it. It was another penny. Repeating my effort, I probed, this time feeling a short, brittle item which I extracted. It was a long since forgotten french fry which had grown so stale it had almost fossilized. Diving back again, I concentrated on the feel of round metal. I felt nothing but small, pointy, unidentifiable objects and I pulled my right arm violently from beneath the seat out of frustration. I scratched the top of my wrist drawing a trickle of blood in the process. I retreated and decided to ferret beneath the passenger's seat. I could have just flashed my badge to a toll employee and been done with all the trouble but, I didn't want to identify myself. I didn't believe I was composed enough to pull it off. I leaned in over the driver's chair to begin the search of the other seat. As I did so, I noticed the distinctive worn black leather resting between the passenger's seat and the console. My wallet! I plunged my hand toward it and gleefully extracted a crisp one-dollar bill. Indeed, it had been a ridiculous few minutes. I had been left frantically searching for stray coins and meanwhile had thousands of dollars in cash secreted in my trunk.

I walked toward the dull, weathered administration building to finally pay my toll. As I approached it, I heard a summons from one of the booths, "Hey."

I looked toward the collection of cubicles and saw a young man waving me away.

"Its Sunday. No one is in there." He yelled.

I walked toward his booth, the first one, which was about to be occupied by a large eighteen-wheeler, exhaling heavy black, polluted smoke. I started to ask for direction but, the tractor pulled alongside the enclosure, interrupting my progress. I waited for it to depart then I resumed my advance across the asphalt shoulder and onto the concrete roadway. When the attendant saw me again, he said, "No, don't come over here. Forget about it."

"What?" I responded.

"Go ahead. It's too dangerous for you to come over here. I'll get sued. Go, forget about it."

I continued walking toward him and then he held out his left arm, gesturing me to stop. Another vehicle approached, a mid-sized Winnebago.

"You can't walk over here, just go." He emphatically remarked, "forget the toll."

I acknowledged him and I returned to my car. As I walked a teenager felt implored to pay a snide tribute from his accelerating automobile, "Dickhead!" His adolescent wit prompted the overpacked car's occupants to howl with laughter. I began to raise my left arm to extend him the middle finger but, stopped. He was correct in his assessment. I entered my car and called myself every name I could associate with stupidity but the teenager's moniker seemed to fit best.

Mark, you dickhead.

I started the engine and drove the remainder of the way home, disgusted at my foolishness but, revitalized at the prospect of counting my cash.

∗

I arrived in the parking lot of my apartment complex located in Westmont, Illinois. It's a small town of about 22,000 situated twenty miles west of Chicago. The town deploys its own police and fire departments who capably handle the only significant incidents in town, traffic accidents and dumpster fires. The suburban commuter railroad line, METRA, maintains a station and one of Westmont's biggest employers, Rockwell Graphic Systems, a manufacturer of printing presses since

1885, raises funds for the annual "I Love Westmont" parade held on the town's main thoroughfare, a two-lane road known for nothing but asphalt. A few of the inhabitants are native but, most of the town's population is comprised of individuals who have moved from another suburb or like me, another state. Its transients are content but, always interested in opportunity.

It was 7:40 a.m., and my seven-story apartment complex, Westmont's tallest structure, hadn't begun to stir. I was forced to park my automobile in one of the last stalls since the parking lot was virtually full. Again, I ignored the temptation to examine the contents of the suitcase and chose to remove it from my trunk and proceed into my apartment, carrying the item as casually as I could and hoping I wouldn't run into one of my nosy neighbors. Once I reached the safety of my own premises, I locked and chained the door, unbuckled the case and poured the contents from it. A few pairs of socks rolled out along with a well-worn pair of blue jeans which was wrapped around a pint of tequila. I separated the debris from the bundles of cash that fell along with the bath towel. I ripped the cloth away from the bundles and tossed it aside. I started to gather up the cash when I noticed a bottle of Stetson cologne had been lying on its side, pouring its perfume onto my rug. The cap had popped off. I plucked the cheap perfume bottle and rushed it into my kitchen, leaving a musky vapor trail of heavy cologne. I walked back out and merrily collected the cash, ignoring the musky aroma and the other miscellaneous items which littered my floor.

I proceeded to my bedroom with my loot. I tossed the piles which filled my arms to the floor. There were large quantities of Franklins, Grants and Jacksons scattered on the neutral carpet of my bedroom. I could see the former presidents' stern faces despite the fact that I had pulled the shades closed tight. I picked up the bundles of cash and moved into my walk in closet to count it out. I preferred to place all the denominations in there own groups but, I could not help stopping to occasionally count a pile. Many of the rubber banded piles contained different denominations so I separated them. As I pulled the piles apart I estimated how much could be there. Twenty thousand had been inaccurate and I was happy to know I had underestimated my take again. It was much more! I separated the money and when I came to several consecutive hundred-dollar bills, I counted them out loud like a game show host giving money away to a giddy contestant.

"Twenty-six hundred, twenty-seven hundred, twenty-eight hundred..."

I felt almost dizzy with pleasure. It probably took me fifteen minutes just to separate the denominations. The twenties pile was twice as high as the hundreds but, the fifties pile was also three times the size of the twenties. I was elated. I counted the fifties first. There were roughly over 500 fifty-dollar bills. I say roughly because it's hard to count money. Flimsy bills throw your rhythm off. And new bills get stuck together. I counted again laying them in piles of 100. I had slightly more than five complete piles of fifty-dollar bills. That alone was over $25,000.00. I wanted to count again but, I was too eager to count the hundreds pile. That had 127. I counted it three times. 127, 127 and 126. Close enough, it was at least twelve thousand dollars. The twenties were anti-climactic. Almost bothersome to me, the nouveau rich. I muddled through it laying the twenties out in piles of $1,000 increments. Almost six piles. I counted again. I scrawled the rough tally on a napkin, before burning it . Over $43,000! I put the cash away, hiding the little presidents in the walk-in closet in a beat up second hand brief case that my brother lend me when I first joined the DEA. I threw a comforter over top and decided to treat myself to a hearty steak and egg breakfast.

I walked out of the bedroom and was hit by the overpowering smell of the cheap fragrance. I had not recapped the cologne when I had thrown it into the trash and the fluid had soaked my rubbish, filling the entire kitchen and living room areas with the cheap musk. I gathered the trash up and sent the whole thing down the garbage shoot at the end of the hall. I returned and examined the courier's scattered belongings on my floor. The clothes were tacky. A plaid button-down and those pathetic jeans. Most of it looked like stuff a thrift shop would be embarrassed to sell. Old and smelly. The stained blue-green towel was there too and it reeked of the unmistakable smell of rancid, moldy money. I reasoned the cash had been wrapped in that towel for some time. Maybe weeks. I put it all back in the case and bypassed the trash shoot. I didn't want to take a chance the luggage could become wedged in the trash duct and besides, I wanted all of the moldy things it contained out of my building. I carried the suitcase back to the car eager to dispose of the thing somewhere far away where it would never be seen again. I placed it in the trunk and drove to breakfast.

What I had hoped would be a leisurely, tasty breakfast turned into a meal left half-eaten. I thought about the money and the nefarious circumstances which had rendered it in my possession. I considered the fate of the man I had robbed. His loss of the money might bring grave repercussions and I had to admit he might end up murdered for what I had done. Selfishly, my compassion for him was drowned by thoughts of my own predicament as I considered my own fate if I were to be investigated for the robbery. I would go to jail for a long time. I recounted the whole episode in my head, trying to account for the whereabouts of everyone. The scene played again and again over my cold and tasteless eggs. The sub-station guard. The Blazer. The woman and her two children.

Did they ever board?

Were they waiting for him?

Was I seen in the car wash?

As I discounted one insane thought, another would eagerly emerge to replace it. Paranoia and fear had reared itself again

I never slept that night. I stopped counting how many times I had totaled the money when it fell into double digits. I had changed hiding places for the cash almost as much. I used to day dream about having fifteen or twenty thousand dollars to invest, now I wrestled with the methods I would employ to get rid of more than double the amount.

*

I spent several weeks considering what I was going to do with my acquired money. After my two big hits, I had now accumulated close to $60,000 in cash and all of it was sitting on a shelf in my bedroom closet. I contributed my assistance to a few other cases but, most of my time was spent thinking about the money. I was preoccupied with ideas about safeguarding the sum. Without mention of the incident, my paranoia had subsided but, I still occasionally wandered the halls listening for even the faintest glimpse of suspicious conversation. I spent a little extra time on the north end of the main floor where the ASAC's offices were located. I was hoping I might gain some inside information or glean a reason to be weary by the actions of the bosses towards me. I thought I might catch one looking at me strangely however, their mannerisms were routine and I continued to be disregarded in the same fashion I was before I had started my stealing spree.

As each day passed, my own suspicions waned and I concluded my thefts of Rush's money, the baseball card collection and my other ventures had gone undetected. I knew the courier hadn't reported the robbery and if he did, no Agent of the DEA was believed to be involved. Confident, my objective changed to finding a suitable place to hide the money. I reasoned I couldn't leave it sitting in a brief case in my closet. I would hate to have a curious apartment maintenance man stumble over it while replacing an HVAC filter. I deliberated about a safe deposit box, at the time, the accepted method of choice of most dope dealers for secreting large sums of cash. Renting it would leave a paper trail and I knew many of the IRS Agents in the Criminal Investigative Division had trusted connections with banks. I thought about concealing the money in my mother's house but, that would mean transporting the cash back to Philadelphia and leaving it there while I worked in Chicago, seven hundred and fifty miles away. I decided the safest thing to do was sit on it. Leave it right where it was, concealed in my closet with hopes an investigative party led by the Office of Inspection didn't raid my place.

When I got home that night, I was in possession of white paint and plaster. I used a hammer to break out a one foot by one-foot hole in the walk-in closet of my bedroom near the baseboard. I made too much noise in doing so but I continued carving until the hole was square. I combined the courier's funds with the bag from Melvin Rush and tallied the total. It was $57,540. I couldn't resist counting the money again before placing it inside its new cave. Just before sealing up the hole, I removed $7,500 which I decided to spend on myself. Since I had gone to the trouble of constructing the hole, I decided to put every item that I had purloined into it. I threw in the wristwatches and the Krugerrands. I had quite a little nest egg holed up in that closet. Including the value of the jewelry, it was the equivalent of one and a half-year's pay after taxes. I repainted the entire inside of the closet after patching the gaping hole. It was not the work of a professional but, I was convinced it was the safest place to hide my booty. Furthermore, I concluded, if an internal investigation had resulted in the approval of a search warrant at my home, the chances were my hide was already cooked.

I did not touch the money for two months. It remained hidden, collecting dust. During that time, I maintained a low profile and had been careful not to extend my expenditures beyond my income at all. If anything, I had even begun to spend more conservatively, careful not to elicit even the slightest suspicion. I continued to quietly go about my business, secure in the notion I would not be caught. I stayed out of Joliet and was weary of every Hispanic male I came in contact with during our work. Toward the end of my lease, I considered finding another apartment. I had grown tired of the hectic commute in and out of Chicago. The distance between my home and the office was not significant but the congested traffic was becoming unbearable. I weighed the convenience of logistics against the safety of my hidden assets. The traffic versus the sanctuary of my 60 grand nest egg. I decided to stay and renew my lease.

14

My efforts had slipped at work even though I knew my indolent attitude could lead to suspicions about me. It wasn't skepticism regarding whether I was corrupt but, questions about my intent on continuing my career with the Drug Enforcement Administration. Agents who were unhappy or looking for other avenues of employment frequently exhibited dissatisfaction with their jobs long before they made an announcement to leave. Of course, I had no intentions of resigning. I had a great job, a secure future and a supplemental income that had just put me over the six figure mark in annual earnings, lucrative figures and not bad for a person who only five years earlier was a floundering college graduate making $6.50 an hour peddling clock radios and cassette tapes.

My recent laziness had its origins in my drinking, which had increased. I wasn't an alcoholic but, I noticed I was paying much more interest in late-night carousing. I had always imbibed on the weekends but, I started taking advantage of Wednesday drink specials and Thursday ladies nights. The money lent me a sense of self-assurance which I had never before possessed. Admittedly, $60,000 wasn't a staggering amount but, to me, to have been capable of making it on my own and in complete control of the way in which I wanted to spend it was an achievement. Having access to it was a satisfying accomplishment and its existence in my apartment inflated my confidence.

Nevertheless, I remained cautious in my spending activities. It wasn't as if I was hanging out on the near-north side, in pricey nightclubs like Excalibur and the China Club. Instead, I was spending my money closer to home, in well-kept sports bars like Bleachers on 75th Street in Downers Grove, one of my favorites. It was there one evening I watched a local pour bills into a hungry video poker machine, doubling up on every one of his bets until he had effectively lost about $40. He mumbled something about getting his initial investment back and plugged another $20 note into its accommodating metal mouth. The slot accepted the bill despite its ragged and torn condition. I watched the affair and continued my amusement at the expense of the gambler's unfortunate luck.

The following day after work, having been inspired by the man's insatiable appetite to throw his hard-earned money away, I proceeded directly to a travel agent. I booked a round trip, non-stop flight for the weekend to Las Vegas. I paid cash for the ticket and the accommodations, choosing to make my reservations under the name of Ted Williams, the great Boston Red Sox Hall-of-Fame slugger whose card was one of those plucked from Mikey Brady.

★

I landed at Las Vegas' McCarron Airport in blue jeans, gym shoes and a modest button-down shirt. I achieved my goal of assuming the persona of an ordinary and typical tourist. I had boarded the plane in Chicago with $5,000.00 in my pocket and I was hoping no one had noticed me leaving O'Hare on a plane to Vegas. I wanted to avoid having to explain to anyone where I was going and fortunately, did not run into anyone that knew me, including any agents who worked the airports. I toted the money in a carry-on bag along with some magazines and a travel guide to Las Vegas. I usually consulted budget traveler's brochures while on vacation because they often provided humorous comments and suggestions about places off the beaten track which I loved to explore. However, my vacation to Las Vegas was not going to be bargain-minded. I intended to live luxuriously with the ridiculous limit of $5,000 to spend on the brief weekend furlough. I had made reservations at the classy, if not gaudy, Mirage Hotel. I cringed at the thought of paying $400 a night but that was the going rate for a suite. I could not, unfortunately, request the government employee rack rate. I sought a stylish trip so, I decided to fork over the money without regard for cost. I thought on the plane even though I had allotted myself five grand to piss away, my conservative nature would encounter difficulty, even in Las Vegas, to spend it on one weekend trip.

I took a short cab ride to the Mirage and its glitziness even exuded my expectations. I was instantly amazed by the fifty-five foot simulated volcano which erupted as I departed the taxi. While watching the spectacle, I couldn't help but notice the gaping mouths of passer-by who stood on the strip's sidewalk and marveled. After the eruption had subsided, I advanced into the entrance way which houses a natural habitat, a zoological display sheltering exotic animals including two remarkably beautiful, white Bengal tigers. I stopped to watch the stunning creatures and couldn't help but wonder if they knew how unimaginably displaced they had been. From there, and I can't remember how long I stood and watched the marvelous animals, I checked into the hotel where front desk personnel courteously provided information about my lodging all the while standing in front of a long aquarium containing assorted stingrays, cichlids, eels and sharks. As I went to my room, I hoped the weekend would be as compelling as the spectacular environment in which I would reside for the next two days.

It was three o'clock in the afternoon. I changed out of my middling outfit and into a pair of handsome Armani slacks and a silk print shirt which had cost the ridiculous price of $180.00. Before embarking on the Vegas' excursion, I indulged myself in a modest shopping spree at the costly Oak Brook Mall where I plunked down a small fortune on three pricey outfits for the holiday. Though I was somewhat disappointed with my suite and its very basic amenities, I was pleased with the charming presentation I made arrayed in fashionable attire. I ventured to the casino floor sporting clothes I had specifically purchased for this trip. There really was not many places I could wear them. They were too expensive to wear around the DEA Office with other moderately paid government employees. Stylish apparel like my outfit elicited suspicion. Consequently, my newfound wealth had become a perplexing sort of burden, with me constantly wondering how I could employ it without drawing attention to myself. On this trip though, I was determined to live the fantasy of a freewheeling spender even if it meant tossing the $5,000 around like it were cocktail napkins.

I hit the floor and was immediately offered a drink by a long-legged brunette who graciously if not down right seductively hawked drinks for tips. I complied and ordered an Absolut and tonic. I wandered around some of the blackjack tables. There were a few ten-dollar minimum tables available because it was midday and the real gambling had not yet kicked off into full gear. I did not intend to immediately sit down but the allure of the flashing lights, the clickety-click of plastic chips and the background chatter and excitement had me looking for a place to comfortably wager. With two thousand dollars in my pocket, the rest secreted away in a wall safe in my suite, I looked for a blackjack table. $2,000 is a conservative amount by Las Vegas standards, however to me, it was a lot of cash to be parading around with in my pocket. It was quite a bit more than I was accustomed to carrying and I found myself patting it constantly to verify its continued existence in my pants. I found a high backed wooden chair with a crushed velvet seat that looked very inviting. I sat down and almost on cue, the skilled waitress placed my drink into a round glass holder near my right wrist. I slipped her a five-dollar tip which I assumed would delight her. She accepted the five and without so much as a faint smile, departed. Still unable to escape my budget minded lifestyle, I though to myself I now had $4,995 left to spend.

My first deal soon followed and my ten-dollar wager was swept away with the other losers by the dealer who managed to deal himself two red, face cards. Two more wagers had me down thirty bucks before I came back to win twenty-five dollars on a single bet. I chased that with a blackjack. I increased the value of my bets gradually. My comforting victories seemed to fall sporadically among the frequent defeats. As I sat there I wondered how comical the concept of gambling amongst the uninitiated and unskilled really was. The idea of earning money for employing thought and strategy that was, in actuality, ultimately tied to luck was ludicrous. Still, the chance to make easy money appealed to millions as attested by the full gaming houses each and every day. When the chips were swept away by the dealer I could not help but feel the same emotion as everyone else, disappointment. Regardless, it was much easier to gamble with money that really was not my own. I suppose I sat at that table for nearly an hour and when I walked away I discovered I was only $350 in the hole, an acceptable deficit for a novice who was intent on masquerading as a high roller even though high rollers spend a lot more than $5,000 and assuredly would never be caught dead at a $10 blackjack table. Despite the psychology I was battling, I had to decide whether I was going to really pretend to be a high roller or just another dolt on a convention trip. Either way, I concluded, the idea was still to win money.

I found some five-dollar poker machines which were eager to trade my tokens for rotten deals. One pair then, nothing, nothing and a possible flush that amounted to nothing. Persistence rendered a full house and after fifteen minutes I had regained most of my initial investment. I slipped a few more $5 coins into various machines with negative results. I played the progressive slots for awhile and then reasoned I would encounter difficulty explaining hitting a jackpot on a solitary weekend trip to Las Vegas that if investigated, would show, I had spent lavishly in funding. I played the bandit anyway and after several more tries, conceded the enlarged photograph of the happy tourist posing with his over-sized check would not be me.

I decided to gauge the impact of my expensive outfit on strangers, I meandered around the casino floor, caressing my second cocktail. I am a decent looking man, sometimes feeling quite attractive and other days, not so much but generally, I consider myself fairly dogmatic and sure-footed. Wearing superb clothes, one of the expensive Movado wristwatches I had purloined and armed with the knowledge I had more cash on hand than most people, urged a cocksure swagger. Walking through the casino, even at 4:30 p.m. I sensed the intrigue I sparked.

I decided to retreat from the bells and whistles into the relative peaceful comfort of a lounge. I wanted to absorb the ambience and excitement of the activity around me over a cool drink. I watched for the occasional commotion of satisfied and successful gamblers. I was offered a Keno card and another cocktail. Unsure of the particulars of Keno, which I have since found out are quite simple, I chose the cocktail. I watched the methodical stream of eager citizens parade past. Most were people who appeared unable to afford the loss of significant monies. They ostensibly appeared to be on a leisurely vacation but, nevertheless were filled with the anticipation and hope of relieving the casino of some of its riches and returning home wealthy to Texas or Tennessee, Wisconsin or wherever. I observed some optimistic hopefuls throw their cash and coins at any machine or employee that would grant them the opportunity to do so. Though there were scattered winners, most of their investments served the sole purpose of ensuring the house's bills would all be paid and its owners would turn another profit by the end of the day. I was amused at the sight of some seniors who assertively jostled each other for space at a row of enticing one-armed bandits. I actually laughed out loud when I observed a blue-haired and tennis-shoed grey panther feed three slot machines at a time with a seemingly perfect rhythm between them, plugging in the maximum $1.25 into each slot, then pulling with vengeance. She moved systematically right to left and was so bent upon engaging the machines, she never stopped to see the results of her efforts. She continued the flurry of her bets, entranced by the allure of hitting a colossal jackpot. I noticed others at the machines and the envy each would exude when someone was fortunate to receive a decent payout. The bells rung and the siren wailed alerting other slot players in the area that somebody else had won again.

I noticed people ceaselessly shuffled around the floor searching for an obliging and lucky table. They clutched their modest bankroll of chips with significantly more care than the high-rolling foreigners who arrogantly sauntered about the casino, eager to display their handfuls of $500 markers.

The purpose of my trip was to masquerade as one of those wealthy folks. The more I considered the possibilities, the clearer the realization came to me that I was not capable of it. I was the son of a hard-working man and I too, despite my attempted charade, was still a working stiff. It became evident to me that I would be unable to uninhibitedly gamble away money even if it was unearned.

Two women soon sat down at the rounded glass cocktail table next to me. I assessed their age to be mid-twenties. Each were similarly attired, sporting khaki shorts and polo shirts and they appeared to be much more comfortably dressed than me. I decided to put to the test the image I had attempted to promote.

"Any luck, ladies?"

"We're not playing much. We decided to come down and just people watch."

"Its OK to look but, don't try feeding them." The remark drew smiles.

"I know, some old guy bumped into me and almost knocked me over. He didn't say excuse me or anything."

"Just almost." I sarcastically responded. "Hell, I made the mistake of throwing a quarter into some battle-axe's machine and her and her friend kicked my legs out from under me and stuffed a coin cup over my head."

They both chuckled.

"Security had to come and cut it off me with the jaws of life."

They laughed again and looked at each other in an effort to determine whether they could decipher if I was agreeable or just weird. I decided to determine whether or not they could see through my wealthy masquerade so I offered to buy them a drink. Normally, I would have approached and sat at their table but, I wanted to see if my facade could really work. I relied on the faith my counterfeit image would lure them to my table. It eventually did.

They each sat at opposite sides of me, the prettier of the two to my right. Neither had the appearance of local residents as their skin was not bronzed by the Nevada sun. I assumed, correctly, they were from out-of-state.

"How's your luck, win anything?" The red shirted one to my left asked. Her hair was frosted, a style that had passed but, she was still physically attractive. I immediately assumed from her demeanor she was anxious to assess my affluence. Her question was far from smooth and before I could answer, I watched her eyes descend along my left side, quickly and calculatingly assessing my income, my body and my intentions. Her eyes rested on my shoes, which seems to be important in forming a woman's judgment of a man. I had taken care in getting some advice from an experienced shoe salesman before my trip. The salesman had informed me the Prada leather loafers I was wearing were the current rage. At $375 a pair they better have been. Based on her extended review of the shoe's style and workmanship, I could sense she approved of the salesman's taste.

I interrupted her examination by answering her question. "Not so good but, I am enjoying myself. What would you like ?"

"A jackpot!" responded the one to my right.

"And a great suite." added the other who revealed her aspirations without divulging it. She was plain. Not in looks but, objectives. She wanted money, power and above all else, recognition. That fast, I had formulated an opinion of her. Of course, she desired the same abstract notions everyone else did, especially the inhabitants of the casino. I did too. My appraisement of her and her intent paralleled some of the agents I worked with in Chicago. They were often equally as obviously transparent in their motives. There was no difference between them and her and me, I supposed. I could sense she didn't judge me as critically since I was in expensive clothes and seemed tolerable. I was drinking premium vodka. My ensemble, the jewelry and clothes, were expensive and well maintained. My own personality, which is a good-natured one, was not an issue. Nothing about me was. It was about wealth and power. She could sense I had it, or at least was working toward obtaining it. What she did not know was my stature was the result of simple larceny. I was a thief. Even less, I was a policeman who was betraying the trust of his position. I was resorting to stealing, plain and simple. Sitting in that lounge, talking to people who would otherwise probably not care to know me, I recognized the veil was working.

I turned to my right and introduced myself. "My name is Mark."

She smiled again. It was a cute and coy grin. "I'm Terri." She extended her right hand, a gesture I liked. I hoped she wanted to stay a while.

"Terri with an 'I." Her friend proclaimed, seemingly attempting to expose Terri for pretending to be something she wasn't. Her hand came forward as well but, it was forced and inappropriate, offered only because Terri had done so. I politely touched it and they soon ordered their drinks.

My assessment of Terri began. Nice body, firm. Her legs were lean, her breasts small but, sensual. I calculated she was an athletic type who enjoyed the outdoors. She was healthy looking and did not rely on an overabundance of cosmetics to hide behind. She had an irresistible mole on her left cheek. Small, it was no larger than the dot of a medium brown marker but, it lent her character and I liked it. I examined her hands and observed an engagement ring, the diamond no more than a ½ carat, probably given to her by an enchanted and hard working guy who had spent the most he could afford. The ring complimented her smooth, artistic hands and the stone looked larger because of her sleek fingers. While the three of us engaged in small talk, I noticed she occasionally placed her hands between her thighs and tapped her knees together when she spoke. She was either uncomfortable or chilled. I asked.

"Cold?"

Yes, I'm freezing, they must have the A.C. going full tilt in here." She made no overture to depart and that made me happy.

"What do you do?" Chris asked.

I expected the inquiry eventually but, when it was finally asked, I did not have a reply. I planned to formulate an answer to this inevitable question while we talked but my interest in Terri had derailed my thoughts and consequently, I was left without a response. I thought about an old stand-by which I hoped would elicit a positive response.

"I jump barrels in the Ice Capades."

Terri, who had just began to sip her Long Island iced tea, coughed, laughed and dribbled a portion of her drink down her chin. She liked the little joke. I was delighted to see it entertained her and her friend. I knew I had ignited a flicker of interest and now I wanted to fuel it without losing the aloofness which maintained their curiosity. My response to the question was deceptive and, of course, they knew it was total bullshit. Nevertheless, the whimsical nature of the response put them at ease and also provided the notion they should not pursue the matter of my employment further. Still the remark was light enough to invoke a cloud of mystery around me which served to further entice them.

"Would you both be interested in going to a show later?" The question was bold but, I decided to ascertain my chances immediately.

"Which one?" Chris asked. I searched for another witty remark but failed. Chris, I predicted, probably wanted to see the most expensive show. My mind tried to scan the brochures I had perused on the America West flight. I could not think of the most extravagant one.

"How about Wayne Newton or Tom Jones. I mean we are in Las Vegas aren't we?"

Terri and Chris looked at each other. They seemed puzzled, hoping to gain a clue how to respond from the other.

"I mean it will be my treat but, just you two, not your boyfriends."

Chris quickly retorted, "We are here ourselves, with two other friends. Girls." She looked at Terri for approval but, without waiting to receive it, blurted, "Its a business trip" she giggled, then added "with very little business."

It was precisely the response I wanted to hear.

"I wouldn't mind going if you don't." Terri quizzed Chris. I considered chiming in to encourage them to say yes but, I allowed them the time to hash it out.

"If he's buying let's go." Chris said, reassuring herself and reiterating to me I would be expected to pay.

"Ok. How about we meet here later. Give me your hotel and room and I'll call." I asked.

They both trusted me and Chris did not hesitate to announce, "We are staying here, room 712. If we are not there try 714, that's our friends room."

"Alright. I'll call." I excused myself without letting them know I was at the hotel too, in a significantly nicer room that was, in fact, a suite.

*

I returned to the casino floor at eight o'clock. Again I roamed the tables, eager to succumb to the alluring inducement of the wheel of fortune. I ventured to a craps table and bet a few rolls. Its not customary or wise to play like that I suppose but, the players at this particular table gave me bad vibes. They all seemed prepared to lose. A few were drunk and obnoxiously rowdy, the kind of regular folk I normally would be comfortable around however, on this occasion, I wasn't satisfied to be amongst their ribald company. My clothes, the money in my pocket and my sobriety made me feel like they were beneath me in a peculiar way. I left determined to impersonate an opulent and refined individual, someone I knew I was not.

I waltzed over to a $25 minimum bet roulette table. Although I have visited a few casinos while on vacation in the Bahamas and Atlantic City, I am by no means a proficient bettor. Roulette, like all casino games, possesses subtle intricacies that are only fully understood and capitalized on by accomplished and professional gamblers. I plopped down a $25 red and white chip on black and promptly hit with a 26. Confidently, I placed two large wagers on my lucky number five. Each was a bet of $50 and had I won at thirty-five to one, I would have received $1,750. I didn't come close. My betting was representative of the uninitiated but again, certainly more palatable with someone else's money.

I returned to the lounge and had a beer. While waiting for Terri and Chris to arrive, I asked a buxom and scantily clad waitress to explain Keno. She started to define the basis of the game which is made up of marks and hits, chance and odds. I half-heartedly listened to her explanation and then requested her permission to observe a while. She gave me a quizzical look and walked away.

It required arduous effort but, I had managed to acquire three tickets on a Friday evening for Tom Jones at Bally's Celebrity Showroom. It was particularly difficult to find three seated together but, I was able to pull it off. It had required several phone calls and eventually I had to hail a cab to visit a ticket broker. I could not put the charge on my credit card so I had to see him in person and pay cash. I was careful not to leave any record of me having been on this trip. I had used bogus names for the plane trip and the hotel booking and I planned to continue my esoteric anonymity with Terri and Chris. The unyielding broker wanted two hundred a piece for the tickets. I suppose he relied on charging exorbitant prices to desperate people willing to pay through the nose to see the classic Las Vegas entertainer. If I didn't plunk down the money, someone else would, he assured me. I begrudgingly handed him $600 for the tickets. When I received them, I noted their face value was $65 but, they were good seats. I was told the "$600 would be worth it." The "it" of course, being relative. After I had them in my possession, I was delighted with the notion the excessive price had not really been an object of consideration. It was a wonderful feeling knowing I could pay the amount simply because I wanted to go. I thought living a charmed life with unlimited financial wherewithal, albeit just for a weekend, certainly enhanced life's quality and made it a helluva lot more fun.

Terri and Chris were fashionably late but, looked very appealing when they finally arrived. Terri wore a two piece white skirt and top that complimented her slim waist and great figure. Her long legs were accentuated by a classy pair of white pumps which elevated her to a height of 5'10". She had placed a loose wave in her otherwise straight silky, sandy hair which looked natural and alluring. I assessed her choice of clothing and attempted to interpret the message she was sending. I wondered what adventure she anticipated the night might bring. She looked sexy but, classy and elegant. I decided to let the events of the evening play out but, in the back of my mind, I would press to spend the night with her.

Chris, on the other hand, had absolutely succeeded in revealing her intentions. If not me, she certainly was interested in attracting the attention of others. She wore a tight red dress and stiletto heels which were probably too high. It appeared she had invested time in distinctly exposing her cleavage which rivaled the endowments of any Vegas showgirl. I admitted to myself she looked pretty sexy herself. I toyed with the egotistical idea of bedding them both. I had never enjoyed such luck before but, I could always hope, after all, I was in Sin City. I had already spent more than $600 dollars with tickets and drinks and I did not think it was brash to believe I wanted something in return. They must expect that too but they could be taking me for a ride like every man's been taken before. I caught my own reflection in a mirrored column descending from floor to ceiling and was pleased by my appearance. I had changed into a silk black Perry Ellis blazer with stylish coordinated pants, distinctive clothes which furnished me the aplomb to continue my charade.

We had a couple drinks and engaged in trivial but enjoyable conversation about the casinos, the heat and of course, all the extravagance around us. Finally, we taxied to the show. The entertainment was what I expected, ostentatious and stereotypically Vegas complete with smoke-filled air, the timbre of cocktail glasses clanging in the dimly lit cabaret and inane entertainer/ audience banter. The music included a medley of horrible covers of eighties pop songs. I think Prince might have been vilified had he heard Jones' version of Little Red Corvette. The girls had a great time though. They laughed and drank and even sung along to the recognizable melodies. We had a nice time and I never once considered the ridiculous expenditure on the seats. I was slightly disappointed I was not able to gauge Terri's feelings for me. The vociferous music and the rapid pace of the show prohibited me from starting any significant conversation with Terri with an "i". Jones closed his set with his trademark "Its Not Unusual" and a very forgettable and rushed Huey Lewis number. I wanted to assess the returns of my investment and suggested we hit another casino and play some more games. The ladies excused themselves to the rest rooms where I hoped they would evaluate their position and provide a clue to their expectations. They returned to the gaudy, over-lit lobby and said they were eager to go to a casino and try their luck. Chris surprised me with a request to get some coke along the way and also asked if I knew where we could get it.

The request intrigued me. I wondered if cocaine was a normal progression at this stage of an evening. My recent dates usually knew I was some sort of a policeman and would avoid making any statements about the use of drugs. However, these two girls knew nothing about my career in law enforcement. Now I was able to see the use of drugs first hand. Her request spurred me to wonder how prevalent and casual the use of cocaine was. Was it an accepted routine to find a guy peddling a couple grams and snort coke to keep the night flowing smoothly? As a narcotics agent, I knew the general routine and manner of traffickers. I was knowledgeable regarding the methods of smuggling and selling cocaine from the jungles of the South American Andes Mountains to the corner distribution markets of inner city Chicago. However, faced with a simple request to obtain some coke, I was unsure how to respond or how to accommodate. I decided it would best, in this instance, to be myself.

"I don't use coke."

Terri examined me. "I don't either." I was relieved at her response then, Chris chimed in.

"Yea, me either." Her tone was sarcastic and I wondered if my decision had blown the whole evening. I contemplated exploring it further but, yielded in the same fashion they had about my employment.

We casually walked along Las Vegas Boulevard, passing garish neon lights and the consecutive, inviting parlors of Harrah's Imperial, the Sands and the Desert Inn. I mentioned Circus Circus because I had wanted to go there before I left. I couldn't imagine trapeze acts in a casino. I was happy the girls agreed with my suggestion and I hoped the twenty-minute walk would present me the opportunity to let Terri know I was interested in her.

We found the casino to be loud and frenzied with a wild carnival atmosphere supported by the furious activity of jugglers, magicians and clowns. The assault of bright colors throughout the casino further served to scintillate the senses. The three of us canvassed the place and found it amusing and friendly but, I perceived Chris quickly became bored and interested in more lurid discoveries. We eventually went to the craps tables and that's where I was able to garner Terri's sole attention. They both observed me place wagers that ranged from fifty to an occasional two hundred-dollar play. They were impressed with the size of my bets and knowledge of a sophisticated game that intimidated them. Once again, I relied on a topical comprehension of the game but fortunately possessed the sporadic luck of the rolls to continue playing. I courteously asked Terri's advice occasionally and my requests granted Chris a hint as to whom I was most interested in. Chris took the cue and decided to roam the floor. I'm sure she would not be lonely long and would have little difficulty finding someone to talk too.

I played until I had dropped about twenty-five hundred bucks. During the games, I noticed Terri became excited when I won but, seemed even more intrigued at my happy-go-lucky attitude when I lost. I know she wasn't hoping I would lose but she seemed quite interested at my carefree response when I did, particularly on a big roll. We stayed a while longer and then decided to get a quick snack at one of the prominent casino cafes. There, I learned her story.

She was twenty-six from Sandusky, Ohio. She was attending seminars and a convention sponsored by her company with three co-workers, two of whom were married, including Chris. Terri was engaged to be married later that summer to a guy named Philip, a union painter. Terri confided Philip was loving, hard-working and would make a good husband. She worked at a software firm and was generally content with her life. Terri worked out at a health club when she could and played softball and volleyball for the local bar team. She had earned an associate's degree from a junior college in computer programming.

I found her very appealing. I was enamored with her amicable smile and found I could elicit it with many of my silly remarks. She seemed quite comfortable with her life though the liquor in her had prompted her to admit something was missing in it. Some form of excitement or interest. I hoped it was raunchy, anonymous sex but, conceded it was probably a child or two of her own.

What I found most interesting was her unpretentiousness. She was open about her feelings, her hopes and desires. She freely discussed her successes and failures in a manner which was honest and appropriate despite our abridged acquaintance. She was comfortable with herself and her candidness embarrassed me.

I had told her I was a divorced financial planner who had reaped a small windfall in mutual funds. I realized money didn't excite her and then tried to downfall my fiscal successes. I wanted to find out more about her and discovered myself genuinely interested in her life. After the snack, I requested she come to my suite and I was delighted she blushingly accepted.

There, we talked for over an hour. It was probably close to three in the morning but, I felt refreshed. We discussed simple, even silly things like TV shows and bad movies. It all flowed freely and soon I was caressing and kissing her. Her style was warm, the kisses sweet and passionate. I graciously unbuttoned her top and felt the soft skin which encased her ribcage. I lifted her top from her flanks and over her shoulders and head. I removed her bra and began aggressively kissing her breasts and licking her aroused nipples. I held her in my arms and pressed her back to my bed.

She squirmed from my embrace and said, "I can't."

I was completely disappointed. I wanted her. In the few hours I had spent with her I had become smitten with her. She was intelligent and beautiful and completely real. Her personality was genuine. She had hid nothing, electing to rely on confident honesty. I, on the other hand, was a phony. A complete liar and a forgery. A fraud who didn't belong in her company. I did not pressure her to give in to my lustful desires though I think she might have if I had persisted. I didn't because I believed she didn't want to betray the trust and love she had with her fiancée and I recognized I didn't have the right to soil her admirable covenant. The human sense of adventure had enticed her to dance between the Scylla and Charybdis but, her integrity had prompted her to gain control. She rose from the bed and placed her bra on. I recognized the activity was not part of a game but a valid request to honor her rectitude. She could have done anything and no one but us would have known but, she didn't. I admired her for her behavior. I knew that I had presented a counterfeit image and now I had deeply regretted it.

We talked a while longer, then I escorted her to her room. It was generic and cheaper with certainly less amenities than my expensive suite but, nevertheless, it was her room. The smaller bed she would eventually rest on would permit comfortable sleep enhanced by the soothing comfort of a clear conscience.

15

The DEA personnel manual requires an evaluation by a group supervisor be completed for each agent every six months. The evaluation is supposed to be based on the agent's ability to initiate and develop high quality investigations, their skill to recruit and develop informants and overall capability to interact, assist and cooperate with fellow agents. The ratings are categorized as Outstanding (O), Excellent (E), Fully Successful (FS), the dreaded Minimally Successful (MS) and Unsatisfactory. A (U) on a rating was virtually unheard of within the ranks of the DEA even though there were certainly some agents who deserved such a poor appraisal for their continuous demonstrations of complete incompetence or even more deplorably, a lack of effort. However, during my years with the DEA, I never knew of one agent who was given an Unsatisfactory rating primarily because a (U) would prevent an agent from receiving an annual raise and it would seriously jeopardize his or her future potential for promotion. Since virtually no one was ever fired from the DEA for lack of productivity, supervisors were hesitant to bestow a rating which would cost an individual money. Consequently the most frequent method supervisors employed to handle an unproductive agent was to transfer him or her out of the group, effectively rendering the agent someone else's problem.

Though efficiency does play an important role in the rating process, agents who cooperated with and to even more an extent, socialized with supervisors, were more likely to gain favorable evaluations. Sometimes ratings were based primarily on the supervisor's personal opinion of the agent rather than his or her work productivity. Common interests would greatly affect an agent's review, especially if the agent shared the interests of the supervisor. If the supervisor enjoyed drinking, either after work or during, it would behoove the agents to drink with him. If the supervisor was partial to working on home improvements, it would be very wise for an agent to offer assistance toward the projects. Paint a room, dig a garden, whatever. One summer I must have spent thirty working hours helping build an outdoor deck on my first boss' house. Later that summer, I spent many more hours, some working and leisure, at his house drinking beer, playing pinochle and barbecuing. In many working environments, it is considered acceptable and wise to adopt the interests of the boss. However, in the DEA, where promotion potential and movement was often based on opinion rather than achievement, "brown-nosing" was an essential technique to enhancing one's career growth.

Fortunately for me, I was able to establish sound relationships with the three supervisors I had during my career in Chicago. I enjoyed what they liked so it was no great effort on my part to develop common bonds with my superiors. I had been a responsible agent. I worked well with others, developed decent cases and I believed I had the respect of most of my fellow agents in the office. I had never received a rating of less than Excellent though at times, at many times, I really did not believe I was doing excellent work. However, there existed other agents who were accomplishing virtually nothing; making no arrests or seizures but nevertheless, enjoying ratings of Outstanding. One agent in particular, Larry Mitchell, who worked in Group 3, the heroin interdiction group, was recognized as quite the ladies man. He probably had not made an arrest in three years but, he had an ability to invite his supervisor to parties and get him laid on occasion. Since the supervisor had sex virtually every time he went out with Mitchell, I wondered whether Mitchell was using paid escorts to pleasure his boss. It would have been a small investment to make every other month or so, since Mitchell's continued financial success relied on his ratings. Either way, the supervisor rewarded Mitchell for his "admirable" ability and bestowed him with ratings of Outstanding for three successive years. With this type of blatant favoritism being conducted in the office, I did not hesitate to accept my ratings of excellent every six months.

Bobby Hayes, my supervisor during the time my pilfering activity started, had developed a bad drinking problem after returning to the Chicago Field Division. The boozing stemmed from his failing marriage and his estranged relationship with his two children, both teenagers. He was distressed with the path his life had taken and at age 51, he possessed very little interest in the politics of our office. He wanted agents to do their job and expected their behavior to be professional. At one time, I was told, he was one of the most dedicated and finest agents in the New York Field Division. That was circa 1974, when narcotics investigations were adaptable because no one in law enforcement really knew how to conduct them on a grand scale. President Nixon had created the Drug Enforcement Administration in 1973, and the members of the fledgling agency, supplied with a new and inflated budget, were able to conduct their investigations autonomously. The agents employed various methods of investigation and relied on their own personal techniques to infiltrate drug trafficking organizations. Expenditures were of little importance and most agents spent money without caution. If an item was needed to further an investigation, it was purchased.

Undercover buys were made liberally, ensuring the agents much greater knowledge and trust with the dealers they were investigating. Covert agents were able to invest time and money in developing relationships with suspects. From what I learned from the "old timers" as we called them, an undercover could take a suspect out to dinner. He could have a few drinks with him. He could get to know the violator. By doing so, the investigations produced detailed and intimate understanding of entire organizations. Though it was an effective method, the existence of a close relationship proved too dangerously tempting for some agents. A few crossed the line and became too friendly with their suspects electing to engage in criminal recreation themselves but, for the most part, the protracted undercover operations led to the development of a precise knowledge of the dope dealer's activity and the network in which he functioned. Whole organizations were often indicted and arrested rather than just one individual, as was taking place in the DEA of the present.

Informants, I was told, were rewarded for their efforts. Traffic tickets were fixed, jobs were secured and their controlling agents were generally interested in helping the cooperators. The informants were paid, usually on time. Informant relationships were encouraged and nurtured. Most significantly, informants viewed working for the DEA to be a worthwhile experience. The informants of the 1970's and 80's were interested in providing information and possessed a keen desire to see suspects arrested. Of course, their primary motivation was financial compensation but, at least they received it, for work well done. There was a large contingent of voluntary informants who were supplying reliable and valuable information simply because they wanted too. Conversely the DEA I worked for discouraged the establishment of relationships with informants. We were told to use them for whatever information we could. We were encouraged to lie to them. Present them with an enticing proposition that they could expect to make twenty-five percent off all seized cash, property and related assets. We knew they would never get that kind of money and in the rare instances they received approval for large sums in rewards, it usually took over two years to pay them. Voluntary informants had the potential to develop good cases but could see they were being used and often reneged on their agreements to provide information. Consequently, the contemporary DEA was relying principally on defendant informants who would do anything to remain out of prison. Many of these individuals would resort to any formula to gain freedom including setting up the innocent or even blood-relatives in order to escape stiff prison sentences.

During the early years of the DEA, operational expenses, like hotel rooms for dope negotiations, rental houses for surveillance perches, high tech electronic equipment for exceptionally difficult cases and even jet planes and power boats for sublime undercover facades were freely furnished for an agent's utilization to develop evidence against large scale drug traffickers. Travel to other countries and offices was routinely conducted to further develop essential information against whole organizations. The travel was necessary in order to organize and coordinate efforts of other DEA Agents as well as those of additional cooperating law enforcement agencies on national and international levels.

The Administration I worked for was primarily concerned with statistics. Upper management was obsessed with numbers and produced quarterly publications charting each group's arrests, confiscation of dope in pounds and seizure of cash and related assets in dollars. Their emphasis was on constantly improving the numbers. The pressured tactics produced aggregates which continued to increase but, the numbers did not accurately reflect progress or success in stemming the tide of drugs. Certainly, the DEA was seizing more cocaine, heroin, marijuana and other drugs in 1990 than they were in 1980 but, there was proportionally more drugs being distributed as a whole. With more dope on the streets, the potential was apparent to seize more. The rush to arrest and seize produced numbers but, failed to infiltrate organizations. Consequently the Administration was settling for the apprehension of low-level members who were easily replaced and the capture of small percentages of the financial windfall being reaped by sophisticated networks.

"It ain't what it used to be" was a frequent expression used by Bobby Hayes. He utilized the term to describe most everything, the new generation of agents which included me, the management and direction of our agency, its high ranking officials and the United States' Attorney's Office which prosecuted our cases. For the boss, the only item that had remained constant was the booze, which had become an increasingly integral part of his life.

People talked about Bobby, my boss, like he was two different people. The first Bobby, the respected agent, was an incredible case-maker. He worked international cases, frequently travelling to Central America and the Caribbean to apprehend cocaine and marijuana sources for defendants he had arrested in Chicago and New York. It seemed to me, based on what I heard, he conducted investigations in the ideal fashion we were supposed to be completing them.

Bobby Hayes was also known for treating defendants fairly, if he liked them. If he was not fond of them, their personality traits or their lifestyle, Bobby was eager to administer his own form of justice. Usually in a cramped holding cell, or the back of a surveillance van. I was told he once handcuffed a known and twice convicted child molester to a telephone pole and peppered his ribcage with a rapid barrage of vigorous uppercuts until the guy was puking blood. I had heard other stories about Hayes, the funniest of which was related to me by a secretary who had been with the agency when Hayes started his career.

Apparently, Bobby had roughed up a defendant pretty good during an arrest. The suspect had sold Hayes a quarter pound of coke on two separate occasions. A half pound of cocaine was a significant buy in the mid-seventies. The secretary recalled Hayes had the foresight to envision cocaine would be on the crest of the dope wave of the future and concentrated many of his investigative efforts towards cocaine dealers. He wanted to be on the cutting edge. Anyway, Hayes had taken a particular disliking to the certain guy on the second purchase when the suspect had mentioned he was supplying coke to his step-daughter's high school friends. The suspect had bragged he had taken one of the girls on a cocaine whirlwind which had turned "a chaste sophomore into a street whore." Evidently, the defendant, who was a career petty thief, had also told Hayes he had "knocked one of the girls up and was trying to talk her into getting a cheap abortion." Bobby Hayes despised the guy and had made it known that he couldn't wait to get his hands on him when it came time to arrest him.

The day of the arrest, Hayes' prudent supervisor sensed trouble and specifically directed Bobby not to participate in the arrest. Hayes had been the undercover agent and would be closest to the defendant when the opportunity to arrest him was presented so these orders were going to be difficult to execute. Nevertheless, Hayes agreed to comply with the request. The day of the suspect's arrest, Hayes was equipped with a large, bulky transmitter which was wrapped around his waist, affixed with a beige ace bandage. Fortunately, technology has since relieved agents of the need to wear such easily discernible equipment however, the use of unwieldy devices was an example of the hindrances with which Hayes' generation worked. The recording apparatus made it feasible for agents to monitor Hayes' negotiations for signs of problems or distress and thanks to the piqued interest of jury's and judges, the use of the equipment became obligatory fixtures for most narcotics investigations.

As the story goes, Hayes met the defendant in a fast food restaurant. The negotiations went well and Bobby had the guy ready to deliver two kilograms of coke to him. Hayes told the defendant to go into the men's room where they would consummate the deal. The agents, monitoring the conversation, were perplexed but allowed Hayes the latitude to conduct the deal in his own way even though the plan had not called for the delivery to take place in the bathroom. The agents had hoped Hayes and the suspect would come outside where the defendant could be easily and quietly arrested. Bobby Hayes had something else in mind. As the two walked toward the bathroom, the transmitter cut out. The monitoring agents allowed a few tense moments to pass, hoping the transmitter's reception which often faded in and out, would return. It did not, so one of the senior surveillance agents decided to walk into the restaurant and decipher what was happening. The agent casually went in and after only a few seconds came running outside frantically waving for other agents to join him. The other surveillance agents leaped from their cars and went running in, guns drawn. The unannounced appearance of armed men frightened many of the patrons who had no idea what was taking place.

The semi-conscious defendant was found laying prone on his stomach. He was already handcuffed and was bleeding profusely from the nose and mouth. Two teeth were laying scattered on the floor near his head. There was a small path of blood which led into a stall. In the cubicle, the toilet had a collection of blood in the bowl and on the seat. Apparently, Hayes had beaten the guy and in the process, had literally attempted to stuff him into the toilet. After viewing the condition of the suspect, one of the concerned agents rushed into the dining area only to find Hayes seated in a booth happily enjoying the last few bites of his quarter pounder with cheese.

The battered defendant was transported to the office for processing. No bones had been broken but, I was told, he looked unsightly. Both his eye sockets were swollen with coagulated blood and his upper lip was fattened like a breakfast sausage. His grin, if he were capable of smiling, would reveal a gaping hole which once was occupied by his front teeth. Nobody wanted to explain to the boss what had happened, including Hayes, who had given his word something like that would not occur. More significantly, the defendant was expected to be taken to see the magistrate for a probable cause hearing and no one was anxious to place the guy in front of the judge in the condition he was in.

The quick thinking Bobby Hayes came up with a plan. At this time, Hayes' partner was an accomplished agent in his own right, Mattsori Tokaiyami. He was an American Asian who was affectionately and more conveniently known as Matty T. Hayes solution was to have Matty T completely disrobe. Hayes then provided Matt with a purple feather which had been plucked from a defendant's old hat left lying around the office. Hayes instructed Matty T, who was completely naked, except for the feather, to enter the defendant's holding cell and attempt to tickle the defendant. Matt was extremely reluctant to do so but eventually agreed with the understanding Hayes would owe Matt several large and considerable favors some where down the road. I was told the scene was absolutely hilarious as the bruised suspect wailed with confused horror trying to escape the advances of the naked, diminutive Asian. To further the chaos, Matt chanted "Toro, toro" as he chased the suspect in the small holding cell, lunging toward him with the feather. The suspect was left with no recourse other than to cower in the corner as Matt tried to tickle him with the impotent plume.

Only an hour after his ordeal had begun, the defendant was escorted to federal court and placed in front of the judge for his preliminary hearing as required by federal law. The judge could clearly see the condition of the defendant and asked Hayes what had happened. Bobby Hayes told the judge the defendant had resisted arrest and had been bruised in the scuffle. The judge looked wearily at Hayes with understandable disdain. The defendant screamed in protest, claiming truthfully he had been injured before he had been arrested. The defendant's words raced almost incoherently from his mouth as he tried to explain that he had been savagely attacked before he had been informed Hayes was a police officer. Excitedly, the defendant began to tell the judge how he had not only been thrashed and beaten but also been placed into a holding cell where "a tiny, naked Jap" had chased him around with a purple feather.

Upon hearing this unbelievable revelation, the astonished judge approved charges against the defendant and ordered him held without bail pending a complete psychiatric evaluation. In rendering his opinion, the judge cited the unstable defendant was a danger to himself and the community.

Hayes would occasionally tell this story but, only after he had polished off several scotch and sodas. He had done his best for the most part of his career but, now had been reduced to a recurrent ritual of getting drunk and reliving past comical adventures. The drinking served to cloud the loneliness. He had done a great job for the DEA but, unfortunately in doing so, he sacrificed the relationship with his wife and children. He was reduced to living in a modest apartment and after twenty-three years on the job was left with only a few funny stories to tell.

Upon my return from Las Vegas, Hayes informed me it was time for my review. I had not been thinking about my position much over the course of the last couple months and I thought my lazy behavior had went unnoticed. I had counted on Hayes drinking to impede his perception. I realized after the evaluation had begun, I had either overestimated the frequency and volume of Hayes' drinking or underestimated his capacity to recognize the degree of effort exerted by his subordinates.

"Connors, you been acting differently." He said abruptly.

I had attempted to go about my business as routinely as possible. I believed my assistance with other agent's cases obscured what had become an unproductive quarter as far as DEA supervision was concerned. I had believed no one had noticed. I was wrong.

"You're not even married, Connors. You should be out making cases, kicking down doors and staying out all night."

"Well, its not that easy, boss."

Hayes scoffed, "Shit."

I looked about Hayes office, noting the many photographs on the walls. Most contained pictures of Hayes posing with fellow agents and law enforcement officers from other cities and countries. I could tell the pictures were dated, making my assessment based on the outfits some of the agents wore. Men with large bushy sideburns sporting wide lapeled Qiana shirts and bell bottoms. They often were photographed standing behind their seizures. Men smiling, occasionally embracing, while they posed behind burlap bundles of marijuana, cardboard boxes and wooden crates of cocaine. A few featured Hayes standing in front of cartons of U.S. Currency.

"When you gonna get some pictures of yourself?"

I had been drifting and Hayes reeled me back.

"I don't know, Bobby, soon I hope."

"See that one on the far right." Hayes pointed toward his east wall. I looked and saw several pictures, one stacked below the other.

"On top?" I asked.

"No. Just beneath it. See that boat in the background?"

I squinted to see the photograph. I rose from my chair and walked over toward the wall. The top picture was directly in front of my nose. I partially squatted to see the framed photograph mounted below it. The photo was taken of three men, one of which was Hayes, who stood in the middle, his arms around each man beside him.

"Nice beads, boss. Are those puka beads?"

"Those beads got me laid, brother. From what I hear around here, you could use a couple pair."

I chuckled.

"That boat behind us, that was the bad guy's, a forty-two foot Bayliner. Nice, real nice."

I examined the craft behind the men, a large fishing boat with trolling lines pointing at forty-five degree upward angles.

"You know, I got laid on that boat with the bad guy. He brought a couple broads out with us one afternoon. Right out on Lake Michigan. Shit right in front of the North Pier. I don't know how many people saw us."

I laughed again, envisioning Hayes screwing some woman while surveillance agents squinted through binoculars, sweating in the blinding glare caused by Lake Michigan.

"Who are the other two guys?"

"Leroy Wilson, on the left…he retired. I think he's in St. Louis now, but I really don't know."

"And the other guy?"

"The white son of a bitch?" Hayes asked.

"Yea, I guess so."

"That prick is dead, I hope."

The man had a large beer gut which was magnified by his tight and ill fitting button down shirt. The buttons seemed to strain from the task of retaining his ample belly.

"Is he the bad guy?"

"Shit no. He was my supervisor." Hayes revelation surprised me. "That mother-fucker was always on me. Seems he didn't care for brothers too much. Always telling me to make more arrests, do better cases. He was a real prick." Hayes paused, then asked, "Do you think I am a prick, Connor."

"No way, Mr. Hayes." and I didn't.

"I don't think so either but, I'll tell you what. You don't starting making your own cases, and I don't man these chicken shit kilo rips, I'm talking conspiracy, long term work, then I'm gonna become a prick. You know what I mean."

I did.

Hayes warned, "You better watch your ass too. You ain't acting right."

Hayes removed a single sheet of paper from his middle desk drawer. It was the evaluation. "Now sign this and get to work." He tossed the paper toward the end of the desk. I stopped the page from slipping to the floor as it slid across his varnished desk top. I sat down as I looked toward the bottom of the page, the space where the boxes containing the rating categories were found. The box containing the word "Excellent" had been checked off with a black inked "X." I examined it briefly and then signed the form, above Hayes own flamboyant signature.

Admittedly, my work had suffered. Instead of developing informants, initiating cases and conducting investigations, my productivity had slipped. I had believed my inconspicuous ventures had not had a visible effect on me however, Hayes had been incisive enough to see that some form of change was going on inside my head. I wrestled with the degree of suspicion Hayes might have had and concluded Hayes was making a general determination and couldn't be aware of any specific behavior I had undertaken. All considered, he was right. My efforts had subsided along with the quality and caliber of my case work. I determined there was no way however, Hayes could have been insinuating he knew about my extra curricular activities. I was determined to prohibit paranoid thinking from assuming control of me.

I had been reflecting on the ease with which my thefts were completed. I had over $55,000 left, plus an additional $1,500 which hadn't been squandered in Las Vegas on gambling, clothes or cocktails. I had enjoyed myself spending the money and the thought of the remainder of the cash dry-walled into my apartment wall, disturbed me. I had fun papering Las Vegas even though by the desert town's extravagant standards I had only spent peanuts. To me though, it was a lot of money. I weighed the existence of the hidden money in my apartment and concluded the only purpose it was serving was as a crude form of insulation. I realized the more times I resorted to grabbing $10,000 or $20,000 the more likely I was to be caught. After weeks of deliberations, I decided I would bide my time before stealing anything else. I would wait and calculate, analyzing the drug dealers I was investigating with the sole objective being to take one down in possession of a very large sum of money. I reconciled it might take months or perhaps even a year or two but, with the fifty-five grand safe-guarded in my place, I would be continually motivated. I planned to proceed at a premeditated and cautious pace. I would strike at precisely the right time and sit on the spoils, finishing out my career, perhaps in Intelligence or Technical Operations, enjoying leisurely lunches and waiting for retirement.

16

Three agents, Jim Walker, Barney Sharkey and Rasheed McKey, comprised one of the teams in my group and worked cases together. Of the three, Walker was clearly the most dedicated. He often spent hours tediously sifting through records which he had subpoenaed including telephone and pager subscriber lists, utility checks, credit card expenditure reports and other data provided by Intelligence. His most recent efforts were directed toward infiltrating and investigating a Colombian network of cocaine dealers who he had painstakingly identified.

Walker was known to tirelessly debrief informants who he cultivated and encouraged by presenting a convincing facade of concern and interest in the their personal lives. Walker accomplished this by granting the informants favors whenever he could but, only if it came without much effort. Typically he used his professional contacts to facilitate the dismissal of pending court cases against them. Whenever possible, he tried to pay them lucratively, sometimes supplementing their payments with his own money, a flagrant violation of DEA policy. He further broke rules by occasionally inviting informants to his home, to eat and enjoy the amenities a federal salary could bring. He drank with them, socialized and sometimes even went on holiday with them. Walker treated his informants respectfully but, in reality, he absolutely loathed them. He viewed informants as necessary evils to be utilized in furtherance of his investigative cases and ultimately, his career. Though it seemed he sympathized and wanted as much to help informants as they helped him, his use of cooperating individuals was in actuality, reckless and self-indulgent. He did not hesitate to jeopardize the confidentiality of an informant if it meant his own investigation would prosper.

I recalled one instance when Walker was utilizing an informant's assistance to ascertain the whereabouts of a high profile Mexican cocaine dealer who was also a DEA fugitive. The informant provided very reliable and credible information which eventually led to the capture of the evasive outlaw who was wanted on charges of international drug smuggling and murder. When Walker eventually arrested his suspect he demanded the fugitive's cooperation. Jim Walker knew this defendant had substantial information which could help Walker as he developed an investigation against a large Central American smuggling ring. Walker astutely recognized the informant who had helped him capture the fugitive could not match the potential intelligence the fugitive could provide. Pressured and facing a lengthy prison sentence, the fugitive agreed to cooperate but not before addressing his own egotistical request. He made it a condition of his cooperation that Walker disclose the identity of the individual who had provided the information which led to his arrest. The fugitive said that he would have to be told so that his efforts to arrange future drug deals would not be wasted on an individual who was already cooperating with the government. Walker knew the fugitive's assertions were ridiculous but, selfishly agreed and gave up the informant's identity. He relied on a bogus promise nothing would be done to the informant in retribution. Only one month later, the initial informant in the case turned up slaughtered. His decomposing carcass had been discovered in a $28 a month storage locker in Palatine, Illinois. Walker made a half-hearted effort to question the fugitive about his role in the slaying. The new informant denied it and his productivity and potential permitted Walker to accept the fugitive's passive denial of responsibility. Other agents in the office, including myself, found it particularly distasteful that Walker, himself, was convinced the fugitive was responsible however, refused to pursue evidence of his guilt. Walker casually accepted no responsibility for contributing to the death of his former informant. Walker believed his relationship with the new informant was tantamount to the meaningless death of another snitch. He rationalized the death of the informant as "the price of business" in the drug trade and postulated his own career was of much greater significance than the death of one, two or any other number of "stoolies," a term Walker often used to describe informants.

Sharkey and McKey were content to let Walker make those decisions. Walker was solely responsible for the development and success of their cases, while Sharkey and McKey's role consisted of performing gopher duties and submitting reports, paperwork chores which Walker did not like to complete. As Walker's partners, they received equal credit for the development of the cases but, in reality, Sharkey and McKey were more concerned with their own personal interests. Sharkey preferred working out in the gym. He spent at least two hours per day lifting weights and another two hours attending to unknown personal business. His daily routine consisted of no more than three hours a day devoted to narcotics cases. Sharkey would perform sporadic surveillances and author an occasional compulsory three or four page report but, only when those endeavors could be squeezed into his personal schedule. Walker would seldom complain but, the relationship continued because Walker hated to attend to the record keeping rigors of the job and Sharkey seemed to despise real narcotics work.

Rasheed McKey, similarly, accomplished nothing. And when I assert he did nothing, I mean less than Sharkey. He did not submit reports, he made no effort to develop cases and had no legitimate informants. He rarely spent more than three hours in the building and when he was in the office it usually was because he needed to make long distance phone calls utilizing the federal telephone system. We often joked in the office that McKey probably did not even have a long distance phone company at his home phone because all his personal long distance calls were made from the office, all at the expense of taxpayer monies.

McKey had the intrinsic ability to be a superior agent. His four and a half years of experience as a patrolman in Harvey, Illinois, a rough south-side Chicago suburb with its share of crime including narcotics traffickers, should have given him a wealth of information to begin his career. McKey knew the streets having been raised there and could have developed any number of informants from his personal and professional contacts. Perhaps his close contact with many of the people that lived in the community was a contributing factor in his decision to avoid the area. I could understand that. However, there was no excuse for McKey's lack of effort in focusing on other areas of Chicagoland. Instead he shirked responsibilities and brilliantly maintained a low profile. I believed his motivations were based on his interest in taking advantage of the DEA's Policy and the Federal Government for that matter, on eliminating racism at the workplace. There had been several racial harassment suits filed over the past years in the DEA and, as a result, it became a common policy of management to keep off the case of black employees and other minorities even though some of them were guilty of negligence, misconduct or incompetence. Though McKey wasn't a heedless agent, he always seemed prepared to exercise the racial trump card if he was ever challenged about his productivity. With that reputation established, McKey's laziness continued.

Virtually all of the black employees in our office earned their pay, completing their job tasks with dedication and sincere effort. They worked as hard as everyone else. In fact, there were quite a few more white agents who slacked than there were black and other minorities. However, McKey shrewdly recognized he could exploit the racial issues and did. I wondered if Hayes would address the issue. However, as Hayes' tenure developed as our boss, I recognized Hayes wasn't interested in starting fires where none existed. There were too many infernos blazing within our group as it was.

Both Sharkey and McKey were quite content to play second fiddle choosing to enjoy the status and recognition as Walker's co-case agents while continuing to reap yearly pay increases and satisfactory evaluations. Because Walker's cases were generally focused investigations on high-profile traffickers, the front office accepted the arrangement and concluded, I suppose, the triumvirate of Walker, Sharkey and McKey was a good team.

*

Racism is a consideration which continues to influence and affect the peoples of our nation. It is apparent in law enforcement as well. Its existence does tamper with decision, judgments and conduct. Its biases penetrate behavior by officers in the same negative way it affects members of the public. I believe it seems more obvious in law enforcement because officers on the street are always forced to deal with racially charged issues anytime the police respond to a situation involving individuals who are of a different color than themselves. The police don't have the same luxury of being able to ignore a situation the way the general public can. Civilians can walk away from a hostile situation whereas the police can not. Conflicts can be anything from traffic altercations to business disputes to employment considerations. The members of the general public can overlook these problems or let them adjust themselves. Conversely, a law enforcement officer must make his or her decision immediately, occasionally with only seconds to review a developing skirmish. The job description requires them to protect and serve which means intervention. Their simple presence can often escalate tension, especially in neighborhoods where they are not trusted. A good officer, regardless of race, is constantly accused as a racial persecutor and racial harassment and intimidation is an overly used defense to acquit portions of the guilty. Though every officer has opinions shaped by insight, education and learned experience, most officers, at least the ones I came in contact with, treated people regardless of race with the same respect which was extended them. I believed when racist views or opinions were evident, the police were more often the victim rather than the aggressor. Still there is no question, the actions of a few officers can influence the public's opinion of the whole lot.

*

As part of a multi-group effort, I had been assigned to participate in a surveillance with Chicago Task Force Detective Hank Bradley. Bradley was one of those people who adhered only to his own ignorance to dictate his opinions and dominate his beliefs. He sought no other outside influences, like books, facts, perspectives or views. He didn't extend anyone the benefit of a doubt and even though I had only known him for less than two hours, he had managed to slip the phrase, "better to be hung by twelve than carried by six," twice into our conversation. It was an old police adage which generally meant when in doubt, kill before being killed and empower the courts to figure it out. I can't say I disagreed with the philosophy but I was fortunate enough to never had been compelled to the rationale. Bradley hadn't either but, I could tell he was looking for the opportunity.

Detective Bradley, or Brads as everyone knew him in the Chicago Police, was a bitter, balding son of a son of a Chicago Cop. His Grandfather "cut his teet," as he put it, soaked with the entrenched slang of a fourth generation Chicagoan, busting up the Capone gangs and their prohibition-era, illegal alcohol manufacturing enterprises.

"Dat's when a crook was a stand-up guy, not like these mother-fucking niggers and spics dat run around shootin' people over drugs. Shooting fucks out da sides of their Lexusesees and Mercedeeses Benzes."

I privately snickered at his mis-pronunciation of the automobiles.

"You see Capone respected da men in blue, Everyone did den. You did your shit den when you were caught, you paid your dues." He said, reminiscing about an era which precluded his first birthday by at least twenty-five years.

I estimated the age of his grandfather and believed if he was a Chicago "copper," as Bradley claimed, he probably would have been around to arrest Capone. Bradley was in his mid-forties, built more stockily than he probably had been in his twenties. I presumed he was in pretty good shape most of his life but, the last few years had registered, especially around the midriff. He contributed his girth to his zest for beer, specifically Old Style, Chicago's classic working man's beer. He also confessed he had a particular weakness for pizza which he liked to have delivered uncut. He described the process in which he preferred to roll the pie like a submarine and eat the thing like a giant sandwich. I chuckled when he told me but, picturing it, gave me the impression of a gluttonous slob sucking in sauce, dough and cheese while sausage shot out the opposite end like miniature cannon balls.

"My Pop worked the riots. Dat's when we lost control of dese fuckers." He nodded in self-affirmation, "The sixties."

I recognized who he was referring to but I humored myself and asked, "The African-Americans?"

Bradley didn't appreciate my stab at political correctness, not at all. He looked over and glared. I didn't look at him. Just sat there staring at the apartment building off of 45th street, where we were supposed to be watching for a wiry black male who drove the Ford Escort parked in front. The building was one of three possible residences for a suspect named Wes and Wes had been seen behind the wheel of the Escort we were assigned to tail. According to the information we had received, Wes was a trusted deliveryman operating on the South Side. He was a member of the Black Gangster Disciples as everyone else was who happened to be involved in the dope trade on Chicago's gritty South Side. A BGD at least, if he wanted to stay alive.

"What, you go to college?" Brads asked sardonically.

It was a question to which Brads knew the answer but asked anyway. All of the agents in the DEA were college graduates. It was a requirement to be considered for hire and I assumed it was also a subject for many of his disparaging remarks about the DEA, its agents, and its policies. I probably would have agreed with some of his contentions if we ever had the opportunity to sit down and logically discuss them but, I didn't want to be at the deal, he didn't want to be in my car, taking direction from me or any other fed and neither one of us wanted to be friends.

"Yes, I went to Temple."

"Temple? You don't look dat Jewish to me." He said, quizzically.

"I'm not." I laughed and begun to inform him that the school was founded in honor of its patron, ordained Pastor Russell Conwell, who started the institution to prepare and tutor young men for a life of Christian ministry. I hesitated then decided it wouldn't be worth the effort. Bradley didn't notice and I broke the transitory silence by offering, "Nope, not Jewish at all but, I wouldn't mind having some of their money." It was a remark that gained some temporary favor with Brads and his prejudiced and frustrated sentiments.

"Where's that school, " he paused, "look at this pathetic fuck." He pointed behind me and I followed his direction over my left shoulder.

There was a tall, lanky black man, poorly dressed in a haggard t-shirt and grimy, grease-covered corduroy jeans that I suspected were once tan. His long arms were curved 90 degrees at the elbows as he carried two items. One was a child of about two that he grasped at the waste, awkwardly. The lack of balance between his grip and the child's inability to coordinate his own equilibrium left him precariously teetering back and forth, his head occasionally drifting down toward the adult's knees. The man collected the child by jerking his right knee upward causing the child's rear end to rock backwards followed by it's shoulders and head until he was again level. In his left hand the man held a car battery, which he caressed and held tightly, apparently with much more attention. He approached us.

Bradley warned, "Don't even roll de window down."

It was advice I did not need but, I fully intended on heeding. To engage the panhandler in conversation of any length would require us to give him some money, just to make him leave. I rationalized he wouldn't settle for any coins either. His peculiar collection of child and car battery combined with his appearance gave me the impression he was a skilled moocher, one who couldn't be easily dissuaded. It would require paper money to dispatch him.

He knocked on the left side of my car with his fingertips. I ignored him. He gained a little more confidence and rapped lightly on the window with his knuckles. I gestured with my right hand, waving across my face, clearly expressing no interest.

"Would you look at dat cock-sucker. Dat kid is filty dirty." Bradley remarked.

The vagrant was not easily thwarted and drew upon the talent of any successful panhandler, persistence. He knocked again on my window, this time with his balled fist.

I cracked the window less than a quarter inch, cautiously, preventing him a target to which he could spit through, if inclined.

"Go away, we're not interested."

"Man, don't tell me you can't use a brand new car battery." He offered through a missing front tooth.

I rolled the window back up but undaunted, he continued his pitch.

"Do you believe dese fucking animals. Look, he looks like a chimp. Look at dose lips and dat smashed up nose."

I refused, knowing full well any eye contact with the man would motivate him to continue his hard sell. He knocked again, less forcefully than the previous rap and the effort sounded as if he was finally ready to concede. He moved further into my peripheral vision and I could see he was on his way, child and car battery in arms.

Bradley began to roll his window down.

"Don't!" I blurted as he cocked his head out the half-opened window. "Yo homey."

The man turned, rejuvenated at the possibility we had reconsidered.

"How much for dat little monkey?" Bradley said, applauding his own quick wit.

"Fuck you, mother fucker! Fuck you and your fucking mother."

The man stood cursing as Bradley rolled up his window, content he had caused a commotion we did not need. I couldn't decipher his entire monologue but, could clearly see the man was enraged. I expected his vehemence to subside after a few moments but it did not. He placed the child down, onto his own feet but, the boy unprepared or unable to stand, collapsed under the weight of his unsupported body.

Bradley laughed harder and the man responded by stepping toward the car. He raised the battery as if to throw it. Bradley responded by reaching for his Beretta 9mm. He removed it from its holster. He rested the weapon against his knee, the barrel fortunately facing the door. An impasse ensued with the vagrant contemplating the logic of engaging in a battle with a bulky projectile while his adversary possessed a loaded firearm. The child began to wail, sensing impending catastrophe, more or perhaps less than he had already experienced in his short life.

"Go ahead, make my day." Bradley uttered, gutturally, as he pulled the automatic weapon's hammer back making it even more ready for fire. The expression was a staple of many policeman's vocabulary ever since Clint Eastwood's most recognizable character, Dirty Harry Callahan, had first uttered it.

The tramp wisely withdrew the battery to his waist. He stooped to pick up the child as he screamed at the innocent boy, "Shut the fuck up." He turned and resumed his path down the block.

"Easy there, Callahan." I said, referring to the character Eastwood had made a hero to many gung-ho members of law enforcement.

There was no response as Bradley's adrenaline dissolved into his bloodstream. He uncocked his weapon and holstered it, giving me a great sense of relief.

"Would you have shot him ?" I asked.

"Fucking damn straight." He replied.

"How the hell do you think I would have explained that, Brads." I asked. "A shattered windshield, I wouldn't be able to justify that."

"You only would have to if I hit de fucker."

"And if you didn't?"

He frowned and answered in a condescending tone which indicated I should have already known, "We just drive away. It ain't like we're in a marked car."

Silence followed as we both watched the hobo shuffle down the street. He approached two guys sitting on porch steps. They were only about twenty yards away and easily witnessed our confrontation though neither bothered to interrupt their conversation to look at us. I wondered what possessed a man to allow himself to plunge to the depths of begging on the street. If he really was a toasted junkie he probably would have sold the kid to Bradley despite the disparaging remarks. Junkies will do anything to get money for dope, absolutely anything. Steal, rob, murder. They will have sex with men, women or both or even animals if it will help buy the next fix. Whatever the mind could fathom. Any act whatsoever that nets money, even selling one's own child, can be done. It is done. Probably daily someplace, somewhere.

"You're a big fucking fed, right." Bradley announced, turning his agitation toward me, perhaps embarrassed at what he had goaded the man into. "How come you didn't go for your gat," slang, for a gun.

I could have replied honestly. I could have made a remark that would have festered in his crawl for days until he eventually slapped his kid or kicked his dog but, I figured there was no sense.

"I didn't think you would miss." I said.

Bradley laughed and liked me, for awhile.

The panhandler found no interest in the two young men he spoke to on the stoop. Nevertheless, he spent several minutes with them, longer than he would have needed to find out they had no desire to purchase the car battery. They probably spoke about us and he sought their allegiance. In a community where death didn't always need a reason, they elected to remain neutral. They dismissed the vagrant as well as us. They respected neither, us or the bum, status which made me feel very uncomfortable. I didn't like being associated with cops like Bradley but, I was resigned to the fact that I was a cop and cops were respected much less than vagrants here, in this neighborhood.

"You married?" Bradley inquired.

"No."

"Good. Stay that way." Bradley offered. "No reason to unless you want kids and I got two of dose. Always need something. Eighty dollar shoes, computer games, school clothes. It never fuckin' stops."

I interjected, "We were the same way, only the games were cheaper then."

"Yea, but I never got de shit. Our family didn't have money."

"And neither did ours." I shot back, quickly and annoyed. Bradley sensed he had succeeded in irritating me with his observation and kept quiet, happy he had been able to fire a volley back at the big fed.

I continued to watch the door of the apartment and the little car parked outside. There was no movement. I monitored the sluggish neighborhood around me, a street of single homes past their prime. A few were kept up, recently painted with their fences intact and their small grass patch yards landscaped. Most though were slowly falling apart inhabited with residents, I assumed, uninterested in maintaining roots in the neighborhood. If a chance came along to live somewhere else, a better place, they would seize it and regret nothing. While scanning the neighborhood, I noticed the panhandler further down the block still in possession of the battery and the child. He continued to walk down the street and was very close to the apartment building we were surveilling.

"I can't even play wit' myself anymore, with dis prostrate shit going on."

It was a revelation that was not part of my business and I felt was inappropriate. Nevertheless the frankness of it amused me and I chuckled.

"Jesus, that sucks, Brads." I wondered why he would make a remark like that to me. Maybe he didn't think I was so bad after all. Or maybe he had a sense of humor and just wanted to lighten the moment. Either way, I considered it an attempt to make the situation more amicable.

Before I could respond with a witty assertion of my own, I noticed the panhandler suddenly bolt across the street toward a variety store located on the opposite corner of the apartment building.

Bradley noticed too and asked me, "What de fuck is he doin' ?"

I shrugged my shoulders but his swift movement across the street had definitely intrigued me. His sling was slightly hindered by the battery and the unbalanced child but, his guileful movement reminded me of a cat stalking an unfortunate starling. The object of his pursuit had been a bicycle which had been left leaning against the a store's wall. From our distance I determined it was a mountain bike, some of which are very expensive. He crept up to it, placing the battery on the sidewalk. He straddled the bike, the child still under his left arm.

"Is he going to steal dat thing?" Bradley asked.

"I think he is."

The man mounted it and began to peddle. He had obviously not been on a bike in a while and his lack of coordination was glaringly evident as his feet and legs pumped faster than the pedals. The uncoordinated effort caused his feet to slip off several times. The child's presence did not support his balance either. He had clumsily progressed about thirty yards from the store when he finally had achieved some momentum. Then, the owner of the bike, at least that day, exited the store and discovered the bike missing. Immediately his head shot up and he detected the source of the theft. He chased the suspect as he biked toward us, the thief some forty yards ahead of the bike's owner, who looked to be about fourteen or so.

Bradley started laughing and so did I. It could be considered our obligation to intervene but, I was entertained and wanted to see how the circumstances unfolded. Bradley, I suppose, was similarly inclined as he made no effort to intercede. The man, unaccustomed to the bike's sophisticated gears, could not get it going and as he passed us the teenager had closed the gap to within ten yards. As they approached the top of the block, the determined teenager had corralled the fleeing man with a right hand that gripped the man's ragged t-shirt. The effort slowed the man and as he came to a stop, the teenager's momentum propelled him past the vagrant, his handhold so tight, the shabby t-shirt tore in half across the thief's torso. They both yelled, the younger louder and at first, with more authority. The man dismantled the bike and lunged toward the teenager, the child still held beneath his left arm. He swung wildly with a right hand that missed its target but, succeeded in surprising and scaring the teenager. The owner of the bike vaulted backward as the man swung a second time. The youth was not quick enough in his retreat and the punch grazed the boy's face.

"Maybe we should stop this, Brads." I offered.

"Are you fucking nuts, dis is great." Bradley replied, howling. "It's de SSCC!"

"What's that?"

Brads momentarily repressed his laughter, "Hell, its de South Side comedy channel."

None of the other neighbors, at least five who clearly were watching, elected to intervene either. The second punch had failed to injure the target but, it had succeeded in terrorizing and intimidating the teenager who retreated. The man placed the screaming child down, where he stood, in the middle of the street. The man returned to the bike, which had fallen as he had dismantled it. He righted the expensive bicycle and mounted it. He pushed ahead calmly with his left foot striking the ground twice as he coordinated his right foot with the pedal. In five seconds or so, he was moving in sync, the pedals powered by the coordinated efforts of his legs and feet. He pedaled away assuredly, leaving the crestfallen teenager and his forsaken child crying in the street.

I7

Jim Walker was a former city police officer born and bred in the hometown which he once served, Waukegan. He had spent three years on the force before he had been accepted to the DEA Agent Academy. He was three years older than me but had only one more year of experience with the agency. He had developed several investigations which had been praised by upper management for their merit. One of the cases he had worked involved the arrest and conviction of a state senator's son. The case had received significant media attention, something the DEA's officials always relished. In developing some of his investigations, Walker had relied on established law enforcement connections in the modest towns and anonymous hamlets north of Chicago with which he was familiar. The seasoned investigators aided Walker in initiating and expanding many of his first cases with the DEA. Wisely, he continued to cultivate relationships with other local law enforcement agencies in the same communities and always sought to capitalize on oversights and neglect by other federal agents operating in the area.

Waukegan is a commercial and residential city built on and beyond a bluff forty feet above Lake Michigan. Its the County Seat of Lake County, a northeast section of Illinois whose many homes are over-sized Colonials, sprawling Prairie Styles and gargantuan Victorians with grand bay windows. Most of the homes, especially those in the pristine and affluent towns along the lakefront such as Lake Forest and Bannockburn boast old money inhabitants who love to frolic and picnic on their vast and park like lawns. Waukegan, blue collar and recessed, does not enjoy similar luxury. Its residents are mostly low income, a minority population whose problems of gang violence and urban crime are overlooked by its wealthy county neighbors who rely on the buffer zone created by the mostly closed Great Lakes Naval Training Base to confine Waukegan's failures.

In the beginning, the region was strictly inhabited by Indians, the sedate Potawatomies who flourished amongst rich woodlands and the benevolent lake. The region's natural wealth eventually enticed explorers, tradesman and trappers, farmers and merchants. The new settlers, who called themselves "a civilized people," gradually assumed control of the area and by 1841, accepted the area as a place they called Little Fort. Lured by the promise of work, immigrants poured into the village. Though initial attempts to industrialize the area failed, the geographical advantages of the large lake propelled the fledgling town to become a city whose name was changed to Waukegan, the Indian equivalent to Little Fort. It was the only recognition the new inhabitants extended to the former tribal populace.

These folks intermingled with the successful people exploiting the land between Chicago and Milwaukee and soon many people were prospering in Lake County. As Chicago expanded, its wealthy sought residences outside the burgeoning metropolis. Doctors, lawyers and merchants gobbled up land and built wonderful, stately homes. It's a trend which continues today for most of its voters. Of course, the county had experienced fluctuations between growth and economic slump which mirrored other counties in the state. In the 80's, the region suffered a mild recession but, the next decade brought new development, especially in the realm of commercial and residential real estate.

Most of Lake County enjoyed a comfortable position in the growing economic pecking order in Illinois. The only area which did not reap comparative success was Waukegan. Its most prolific manufacturer, Outboard Marine Corporation, a major producer of outboard motors and fiberglass boats employing a work force of as much as five thousand, was forced to lay workers off and move a portion of its operation to the sunbelt. Part of the failure was caused by the company's own executives who ignorantly dumped mass amounts of polychlorinated biphenyl, a toxic carcinogen and a waste product of the company's manufacturing plant, into the very lake which supported its existence. The cleanup, requested and assisted by the Environmental Protection Agency, continues at a creeping pace. Other manufacturers, like the Manville Corporation and U.S. Steel, simply shut down while other companies fought a prodigious battle just to remain in business. To say that Waukegan did not share in the amenities of Lake County gentility would be an understatement but, it would also be equally inaccurate to believe Waukegan completely failed to experience any benefits from a surge in its economy. The only difference was the rest of Lake County's rise was attributable to a revived and legitimate system where Waukegan's was connected to drug trafficking.

Waukegan was a place where renown comedian Jack Benny attended high school. He went to the same public secondary school which produced football legend Otto Graham. It was a community whose residents could trace their roots back to one of its most founding fathers, Dr. Vincent Price, grandfather of the Hollywood Actor of the same name. It was not thought of as a town, though it had become over the period of the early 90's as a haven for high ranking Colombian Cocaine dealers. Several theories developed why this modest town had become a nesting ground for Colombian traffickers. The theories, and everyone who had any stake in the region proposed one, were as sublime as they were far-fetched. Nevertheless, they were all intriguing. Some espoused the Lake County Prosecutor's Office and many of its publicly elected officials and judges had been bought. Many pointed to recent developments which left many of the staunch, old political guard replaced by vibrant, young professionals who seized control of the seat of Lake County by neutralizing their lack of experience by exploiting bottomless war chests to fund their expensive campaigns. Walker subscribed to this theory, having lived his entire life in the Waukegan area. He cited the acute changes in the county's leadership, its politics and its economy as glaring examples of a town, as he believed, who had sold its soul to drug traffickers. Others with slightly skewed superstitious persuasions believed the name of the airport situated nearby, the Palwaukee Airport, translated to some safe and secure meaning in Potawatomi Indian rites and the habitually religious Colombians had adopted the area as a place where God had directed them from which to distribute. Like everyone else, I formulated a theory but mine had a foundation based in simplicity. I believed there was no tangible police presence in the area and Waukegan was geographically far enough from metropolitan Chicago that it did not draw much, if any, federal or state law enforcement attention. That is, attention in terms of dedicated manpower or dollars. Regardless of the reasons, many of the cocaine cases that developed in DEA Chicago could trace ties back to the small maritime town of Waukegan.

This fact gave Walker quite an advantage over other agents in the office. Since he had been raised in the town, he knew the nooks and crannies of it. He had observed first hand the subtle changes in the community as well as the drastic ones. He was fully aware of those families who had owned profitable stores, generation to generation, and he could compare their success with the new businesses which had just sprung up from vacant lots and abandoned buildings. Narcotics creates money and Waukegan, which had otherwise been a sleepy community struggling with a failing economy and lack of services, was experiencing an influx of money and business. Simultaneously, a rise in economic activity supported by its growing dope trade, brought the vehement scourge of the gangs. As they began to form, relying on the recruitment of teenagers and adults alike, communities began to segregate and tree-lined streets once free from violence became dangerous and deadly. Unlike the often slow decay of neighborhoods, drugs furiously expedites erosion and some of the once serene neighborhoods of low key Waukegan had deteriorated in a short period of only five years, barely covering a single term of the mayor who had literally watched it happen before his eyes.

On the other hand, stores were reopening in places which had remained dormant. Though they were pizza shops and budget electronic boutiques instead of fine furniture stores, the injection of money was welcome by the politicians, the same legislators who refused to believe their town and their lives were being taken over by drugs. Used car dealerships, fast food restaurants, video stores, all opening in downtown shops that had been deserted for years, some as much as ten. All this activity for a town which had not seen one major manufacturer open or even expand its operations in fifteen previous years from 1974 through 1989. A parsimonious community that had not received one significant government subsidy, contract or loan. A municipality which had systematically been built on the production of boats and pleasure craft and which had not witnessed the expansion of any watercraft manufacturer operating within its boundaries found itself the unexpected focal point of a rise in economic activity, a financial verve directly and absolutely attributable to the drug trade.

Unfortunately, the municipality had been completely caught off guard and its services soon foundered. Law enforcement, the judicial system, hospitals and social service workers were not prepared for the chaos that international drug peddlers would bring. Violence escalated and by the last decade of the twentieth century, Waukegan had become a discreet but, bloody playground. The drug peddlers flourished and so would Walker who fully intended to build his career studying, infiltrating and dismantling their lucrative enterprises.

Walker and his fledglings had made modest progress in their investigation of the Waukegan peddlers. They had begun to piece together a skeleton of a Colombian organization which had quietly organized. Walker and his partners decided to be very selective in the violators they would pursue. A few low level traffickers had been arrested and via their eager cooperation and Walker's persistent efforts with the Waukegan Police, he developed an initial target, Jesus Santilles. Walker had discovered Santilles, who maintained a permanent home on Florida's Gulf Coast, had been making frequent and very suspicious trips to Waukegan.

Santilles was described as a 51 year old single man, no taller than 5'7" with a relatively thin build except for the slight paunch which drooped from his midriff. He was balding and preferred cheap K-Mart clothes, usually opting for polyester pants, cheap synthetic leather loafers and rayon shirts. He didn't work and a review of his financial information revealed he had failed to maintain steady, gainful employment since he was 22 years of age. He kept a Social Security card, immaculately preserved in a laminated folder as told to Walker by one of his informants. The informant did not know if Santilles was a naturalized U.S. Citizen but, he recalled Santilles had once told him he was born in Barranquila, a city of less than 1,000,000 in Northwest Columbia, fifteen miles from the Caribbean Sea. He told us Santilles boasted he had never been the target of police scrutiny and often bragged he had never been issued so much as a traffic ticket. We were told he owned a small bungalow in Naples, Florida where he lived with a female companion half his age. Santilles had few acquaintances in Waukegan but made frequent visits to those he did know.

The informant revealed Santilles made semi-monthly visits to several Waukegan residents but, only during full moons. Santilles was profoundly influenced by astrology and inherently believed activity around and during a full moon produced his best chance for good fortune. The disclosure was credible because we had encountered similar odd convictions among traffickers during other investigations. The informant said Santilles habitually wore white clothes and arrived via airline, frequently paying cash for his tickets at the gate, just prior to departure. He preferred to fly into Chicago's O'Hare Airport because, he confessed to friends, hated Chicago's alternate airport, Midway, because he deemed it unsafe and dirty. Apparently he feared a bomb could easily be transported through Midway's incompetent security personnel. Occasionally, Santilles would fly to Indianapolis International or Milwaukee's Mitchell Airport, decisions based solely on unusual hunches. In any case, he would rent a car, preferring low profile mid-size cars, and drive to Waukegan. There, we were told, he would briefly visit his "friends", staying no more than two to three nights before leaving. It was alleged Santilles was a trusted money collector for the Cali Cartel.

A hand picked cash courier chosen exclusively by the cartel was a significant position and one which carried earnest and perilous responsibility. A money courier working for the cartel could only be accepted through nomination. The courier typically would be recommended by a trusted member of the cartel who would often vouch for the selectee using his own money or family members to act as collateral. In the instance of arrest or the seizure of contraband by a law enforcement agency, eminent members of the cartel in the United States, usually located in Miami or New York, would review the actions of the courier and determine if he or she had acted carelessly and their behavior had led to the loss of the product or currency. If the cartel concluded the loss had been contributed to by the reckless behavior of the courier, the courier would be killed. If the courier was guilty of being robbed or worse, skimming, the courier and often another person, typically a close relative of the courier would be slain as punishment. Occasionally, even the person who recommended the courier would also be assassinated. The dire penalty was enforced because of the momentous stakes the cartels placed in their most trusted runners and it motivated the couriers to do whatever they could to ensure the cartel's precious commodities would be transported into the United States, distributed and most importantly, the revenues would be collected and returned.

In compiling his intelligence on Santilles and members of his organization, Walker fundamentally relied on the information of three informants, none of whom knew about the existence of each other. When one made a statement Walker corroborated it with the independent confirmation of another. CI's often boasted about their information and often fabricated or embellished it to enhance their value and their rewards. Walker skeptically debriefed his informants and meticulously cross-referenced one statement and name with another. Through this process, Walker discovered the Cali Cartel had been successful in the Waukegan area because they had begun to employ the use of autonomous units known by law enforcement terms as "cells."

The Cali Cartel, one of the most highly skilled and organized crime syndicates in the world often utilized these cells which consisted of individuals who each performed distinct roles within their respective group. For instance, one individual would be responsible for transporting narcotics, and in the case of the cartel, it was almost always cocaine but, sometimes heroin and sporadically marijuana. The person or persons would be responsible to transport the dope to the U.S. border and hand it off to another courier who brought the dope to a specific destination in the United States. Once there, another person would warehouse the dope in a home or business, providing security for the shipment which could conceivably consist of anywhere from five to eight hundred and sometimes even one thousand or more kilos of coke. The amount would always depend upon the credibility and past performance of the cell and the trustworthiness of the individuals working within it. Another person or perhaps several others would negotiate for the distribution of the coke. Those people would move divided quantities of the shipment for distribution to another individual or group. As the shipment was allocated, the cocaine would be dispersed throughout the region which could encompass a city, a portion of a state or, depending on the size of the payload, an entire region of the country. Each time portions of the haul were being handled by more and more people but, individuals with less and less knowledge of where its fountainhead had been. The people who ended up distributing and delivering the smallest fractions of the shipment usually were the maladroit souls who were the offenders caught by the police during sting operations. These people often delivered the cocaine for stipends which paled in value when compared to the staggering profits reaped by those managing and directing the large loads. Some might receive as little as $100 for the delivery of a kilo of coke which had been purchased for as much as $25,000. If they were not captured by the police and had avoided the greater danger of robbery and or murder, they would return the monies collected to a house or apartment to obtain their petty indemnity. All of these people usually functioned with no idea, or at best, a cursory understanding of what others within the cell were doing. This covert yet extremely successful business was facilitated by the anonymous and ambiguous industry of cellular telephone and beeper communication.

The great advantage of the cells was their independence, both within and without. Many people functioning within the cell were not aware of the existence of the others. For security reasons, some did not want to know, fearing the wrath of the cartel for "knowing too much." The courier who brought the dope did not necessarily know the person who negotiated for its delivery. The person who safeguarded the product often was placed there at the direction of a faceless voice on the phone, long after the dope had been delivered. All of this behavior was designed to promote anonymity. It also served the purpose of restricting information to the members of the cell who might be savvy enough to attempt to start their own business. If the people didn't know where the dope was going or to whom the money was coming from, they certainly would be less inclined to rip people off in favor of initiating their own pursuits. Furthermore, there always existed the fear of violent reprisals which was a constant caveat for the transporters, distributors and sales associates. On occasional instances when one individual would branch out in his own venture, he would inevitably find the poisonous tentacles of the cartel were swift, sure and far-reaching. The whole idea was extremely simple in concept yet incredibly difficult to infiltrate by law enforcement personnel who essentially relied on insiders to outline the organizations, identify its players and detail its methods. If a potential informant didn't know these vital particulars, he served little purpose. Certainly the possibility existed law enforcement efforts could apprehend and cultivate more than one person from a cell but, by that time, a cell had already broken down and the cartel had the acumen and capacity to replace it. The philosophy of the cartel in employing cells paralleled an assembly line used to manufacture products with a series of replaceable parts. When one part, in the cells' case, a human being, broke down, was arrested or killed, the cartel substituted the eliminated confederate with another. When more than one part was corrupted, they threw the whole unit away and built another.

The only disadvantage for the Cartel in utilizing the cell network was the abundant amount of people on its payroll. A vast amount of people were subsidized with nominal monies considering the significance of their tasks and the importance of them. So many people performing a variety of assignments sometimes actually facilitated its existence. The sheer number of people relying on the progress of the dope dealing ventures motivated people to do their best to maintain the secrecy and success of the drug dealing enterprises. Even those who had no involvement in the use, sale or distribution of illicit drugs maintained businesses which often flourished in drug dealing neighborhoods. Whole economies have been enhanced and supported by narcotics monies. The restaurants, video stores, ice cream parlors and especially the proliferation of the electronic media , businesses like cellular phone stores, beeper places and check cashing and money-order exchanges all had their stakes in the success of the dope trade. All would suffer if the main business, the drug business, crumbled. By 1991, this concept was glaringly evident in the once quiet trading post on the spot of Waukegan, Illinois.

As Walker meticulously pieced together the information he shared it with those in the group who were curious enough to express an interest. Most agents were not, alternately consumed by the appeal of their own cases and the egotistical and ignorant belief their cases were superior. I, on the other hand, was very interested in the information. I admired Walker for his ability and patience to analyze, decipher and penetrate the sophisticated networks he was investigating. It was tedious work and I watched him tirelessly mull over phone records and credit card receipts for hours trying to interpret possible associations and confederacies. The work was an attempt to identify people who often had multiple identities or simply none at all. Despite his efforts and the significance of the developing case, Walker received little help from his partners, McKey and Sharkey. I decided I would offer my assistance. I knew Walker was formulating the beginning of a notable case and I assumed, if developed correctly, it would also help my career.

The most fascinating discovery resulting from Walker's investigation was evidence that more than one cell was operating in the Waukegan area. The mere notion one cell was effectively working in the area lent credence to the existence of another. However, when Jim Walker began debriefing credible informants and others with intimate knowledge of trafficking in the region, he postulated perhaps ten and as many as fifteen different and highly organized cells were flourishing in the small city of Waukegan, and the surrounding towns of North Chicago, Gurnee and Kenosha, Wisconsin. He estimated each cell was conservatively importing about ten kilograms of coke per month. At a minimum, a bare minimum, the existence of ten cells importing and distributing ten kilos a month, at a wholesale price of approximately $23,000 per kilo, were moving 1,200 kilos per year, a figure which generated $26,000,000 in gross, non-taxed receipts per year. The estimate was a staggering amount and was one-seventh the annual budget of the entire Lake County Public Administration. Despite the seemingly incomprehensible number, it was an excessively conservative calculation. The figure could even be considered preposterously low if one were inclined to believe one of Walker's informants who claimed shortly before his arrest, he was aware of a routine shipment of two hundred kilograms of cocaine delivered to a Waukegan grocery store. A haul that had been unceremoniously secreted in the bed of a fruit and produce truck.

As the information was compiled, I considered the potential of investigating such a large and relatively unknown organization. Aware that my own productivity had slipped, I offered to join Walker's team. My niche would be debriefing informants, conducting surveillances and offering other assistance which included support McKey and Sharkey seemed unwilling to extend. However, as I learned more about the financial scope of the investigation, my motivation discreetly shifted from career enhancement to nefarious greed.

18

After a painstaking two month investigation, Walker had compiled enough information to warrant the request of a dedicated surveillance of Santilles. Walker requisitioned the approval of Bobby Hayes to utilize our entire group to maintain three consecutive twenty-four hour surveillances for the purpose of identifying and tracking Santilles' movements and activity. Hayes was hesitant to commit all the agents to such an endeavor but, it wasn't because he didn't think the plans had merit. The main basis for Hayes' reservation was the apathy and unwillingness of other agents to participate. Every agent in the group had his or her own cases and subsequent agenda and a devoted twenty-four hour surveillance covering a period of three days would require the cooperation of the entire group. It would mean every agent would be asked to put their own cases aside and assist without personal benefit or gain.

Hayes called a meeting on a Tuesday morning to discuss the surveillance and schedule personnel. Immediately, the idea of a designated surveillance was met with resistance. Two agents, notorious for their inability to cooperate, flatly refused to be involved. One was my partner, Chad Jennings, who was mildly incensed I had even volunteered to help Walker. Jennings didn't balk when I initiated and developed my own investigations because, as my partner, he always stood at least something to gain. However, my association with Walker wouldn't provide anything of value for him and he rejected the notion I help him in any way. My partnership with Jennings had not been productive in recent months. I had been taking into consideration Hayes remarks during my evaluation and I sensed I needed to work on a good case. The idea of assisting Walker, to Jennings, was ludicrous. In addition to Jennings and his indifference, Carlos Perez had problems developing at home with his disenchanted wife who had discovered some of his late nights were not always spent on surveillance. Though their job description required them to assist other agents, Hayes didn't press the two and their lack of discipline and apparent disinterest prompted Hayes to accept their refusal to participate. Hayes simply removed their names from Walker's proposed schedule. It was a development I found deplorable but, after five years dealing with the egos and selfishness of some DEA Agents, I found sadly predictable.

Two other agents, Phil Vreeswyck and Brenda Xavier, said they could only devote a few hours a day to the surveillance. Both claimed their current investigations required day to day communication with the U.S. Attorney's Office. Their assertions were absurd. Both of these agents had been working together on a gang case which had failed to produce a single arrest in over eight months. Yet, their "special investigation," required constant attention and Vreeswyck and Xavier requested they only be scheduled between 10:00 am and 2:00 p.m. Travel to Waukegan required at least an hour so their request, if approved, effectively removed them from the schedule as well. Hayes weary of confrontation, shrugged his shoulders, begrudgingly accepted their petition and excused them from the assignment.

Then, late in the meeting, Rasheed McKey, a case agent on the investigation and one who stood to gain direct benefits for its success, stated he had weekend plans with his daughter. He revealed he had intended to take her to an amusement park for her birthday, a promise he could not break. He said he would not be able to work Saturday and for some reason, added most of Sunday as well. Immediately this disclosure sent reverberations around the room. Here was a case agent requesting the help of others and then conceding he would not be able to provide the same amount of assistance. I observed a brume of disgust and resentment drift over the room. In all, only about half the agents in the group were willing to participate in the surveillance. Since two of them were case agents, Walker and Sharkey, that left me and two others, Sandy Foster and Desmond Brokenborough as the only ones willing to lend a hand. The lack of cooperation and commitment by people who were commissioned to "fight the war on drugs" and were compensated quite fairly to do so, was in practice, an absolute disgrace.

The surveillance was scheduled to begin on Thursday of that same week. Friday evening was to be a full moon.

*

On Thursday morning, I met Walker, McKey and Barney Sharkey at the Waukegan Police Department. There, Walker proposed making me a case agent. The status would permit me to make recommendations on how to develop the case and what specific methods to employ to investigate it. The designation would also mean my name would appear prominently on all the reports, arrests and seizures. I would be given full credit toward the development and success of the case and it would be taken into account during my next evaluation period as well as for purposes of future promotion. Of course, I believed any credit I would earn would be deserved, based on McKey's and Sharkey's past contributions toward Walker's cases. By offering me case agent status, Walker was officially requesting my assistance and confirming he would need more help than McKey and Sharkey appeared ready to provide. He knew that I had a deserved reputation for being a cooperative agent and as far as he knew, I was responsible and earnest. He also recognized I should be rewarded for my assistance and making me a case agent would probably satisfy my desire to obtain credit for my efforts. I accepted his offer and became the fourth case agent assigned to the investigation.

The focus of our surveillance, Santilles, was expected to arrive in Waukegan on Friday, the following day. We did not know how or when he would arrive but a CI had promised Santilles traveled to the area strictly on or around periods coinciding with full moons. The informants we used on this case, two of which were on the street and not incarcerated, submitted lists of individuals and addresses that were relevant to the investigation. Some of the locations were residences or businesses Santilles was known to frequent. The most reliable informant, a thirtyish Colombian-born male named Jorge Carrasco, had given us a dated picture of Santilles standing with other men and a woman. Carrasco had identified every one in the photograph including Santilles. We had not divulged to Carrasco who we were specifically interested in although, if Carrasco had any degree of sense, he could certainly figure it out. The pitfall for us would be if Carrasco determined we were focusing principally on Santilles. Then instead of providing credible, verifiable information, Carrasco could be motivated to provide stale, embellished or completely fabricated information in an effort to reap larger payments. At this stage of the investigation, we believed none of the CI's knew Santilles was our initial target.

Armed with the addresses, the photos and a little common sense, we established surveillance on various locations in and around Waukegan, hoping Santilles would show up. Walker had observed the same resentment I had sensed at the scheduling meeting and wisely had not requested further assistance from other members of the group until Santilles was actually observed walking along on the sidewalks of Waukegan.

I agreed to sit on La Paella Tio Pepe, a restaurant Santilles frequented for dinner and cocktails. It was known as a Colombian hang-out by those who kept track of such things. It was a place where the Colombians felt comfortable. I was there for several hours and with each passing one, I tended to lose concentration, no matter how dedicated I hoped to remain. I was looking for a man I had never viewed in person. I had a description and a photograph that was as much as ten years old. I did not know what he would be driving or whether he would be alone or in a group. His description, obtained from the aged photo and Carrasco's dull recollection, might fit any number of people I had already observed enter and depart. The day had turned to nightfall and the faces I watched pass in and out were not easily decipherable. Still, my intuition told me that Santilles had not arrived. Nevertheless, I continued to do my best to remain stoic and observant, watching for a short, balding man outfitted in cheap white clothes.

I ended up stationed on the restaurant close to thirteen hours. The surveillance had begun during bright daylight and had eventually yielded to heavy blackness and cool night. The dim lights of La Paella Tio Pepe failed to illuminate most of the parking lot. I had placed my eyeglasses on to better see the license plates of vehicles coming and going. I had collected over forty plates jotting down a varied combination of numbers and letters on loose leaf paper which covered two full pages. I had noted several vanity plates, one of which, 6ULDV8, I observed on the rear of a Fiero operated by an attractive brunette. I had made a notation on the second page to investigate that further. I listened to the radio to pass the time. I had left for a while to get a greasy hamburger and fries which I ate uncomfortably in the car. It was after nine o' clock in the evening and as I battled indigestion, I assumed none of the men I had watched had been Santilles.

I was in contact with Walker. Both of us had DEA supplied mobile phones. We talked occasionally and less often as the surveillance wore on. Walker had been watching an apartment complex and had advised us Santilles had not been spotted there either. We talked in codes utilizing cellular phones because the DEA did not have the use of enhanced radio communication capabilities in Waukegan. The DEA had not established a base station or antennae located far enough north of Chicago so any contact over a distance greater than a mile had to be done via telephone. Cryptic words were used because we didn't want any inquisitive neighbors armed with portable scanners curiously joining our surveillance. We considered utilizing Waukegan P.D. radio but since they operated on only two bands we elected not to use their communication equipment. In addition to meddlesome neighbors, we also were concerned about intrusive police eavesdropping on our activity. Consequently, I was not in contact with McKey or Sharkey. They did not possess mobile phones and our car to car communication wouldn't work since they were too far away. If they had observed Santilles they were expected to find a pay phone and call Walker or me with the information and location. I had received no communiqué from either and assumed they were as bored as I was. At 11:45 p.m., after over thirteen hours of surveillance and armed with the knowledge Santilles was probably not even coming until the following day, we terminated surveillance. When I left La Paella, the staff was beginning to clean up and making preparations to close.

It took me an hour to get home. I sped the whole way with the windows down hoping the chilled air would relieve my throbbing headache. I was nauseous from the grease-logged burger and stopped for antacid on the way.

*

We returned to Waukegan at eight o'clock the next morning. I again went to the restaurant, which was not yet open. Walker had made an intelligent effort to check the passenger manifests for United and American Airlines for flights from Tampa, Naples and Fort Myers, Florida to Chicago. There had been no one aboard listed as Jesus Santilles for any of those airline flights. Of course, the information did not preclude Santilles from coming. There were twelve other carriers which conceivably serviced the gulf coast of Florida and Chicago, most of which would not divulge passenger information, even to federal law enforcement personnel. Even if they did, Santilles could fly under an assumed name, like I had flying roundtrip to Las Vegas.

La Paella opened at 11:00 a.m. I gradually began to see the same cars I had observed the prior day. Employees, a few loyal patrons and many with nothing else to do but talk and drink the day away began to arrive. I observed these activities from an excellent vantage point set up across the street where I sat in the parking lot of a twenty-four hour supermarket. I sat there with sparse notice from anybody. Occasionally, a housewife would catch me utilizing a pair of binoculars. Of those, some would stare at me trying desperately to figure out what I was doing and who I was watching. They would squint and strain, at me and towards the direction in which I was pointing the binoculars. They would examine my car trying to determine if I was a cop. I might have been but, most cops didn't drive Lincoln Mark VII's. Accordingly, most probably dismissed me as a private investigator following a wayward husband. Others probably just assumed I was one of any number of local weirdos. Two people were bold enough to approach my car and ask me what I was doing. These are the kind of people surveillance agents despise. I thought to myself what business is it of theirs who I am watching or what I am doing. Most people don't approach other people in parking lots and ask them what they are doing but, if someone senses you are the police, they think its perfectly acceptable to saunter up and demand to know what is happening. One time, while I sat in a public parking lot, a middle aged lady marched up to my car window and demanded, "Let me see your identification."

Feigning bewilderment, I asked her, "What identification?"

Unamused, she stated, "I want to know your business because I've called the police on a number of occasions about dogs defecating on the lawns around here."

I stifled my laugh as she proceeded to elaborate on the health hazards of unattended excrement. She further suggested if I was investigating the failure of people to curb their dogs and clean up their feces, I would be better served monitoring the Millard Fillmore Middle School where, as she said, the school grounds had become "a toxic shitland." She was stunned when I told her, after she had bored me with a ten minute diatribe about the perils of doggie poo, I wasn't a cop but had a little fetish for masturbating in my car while looking at old ladies. As I began to unbuckle my belt, she shrieked in horror and sprinted away.

Boredom on surveillance is inevitable. The act requires patience, diligence and self-control. Some agents couldn't sit still for thirty minutes. They would talk on the radio, fidget in their seats and move their vehicles from place to place all the while claiming they were trying to find better surveillance positions. In truth, they were restless. I was not afflicted with the impatience which motivated such behavior. I could amuse myself and was generally content sitting on places for hours, as long as the possibility existed something interesting would happen. Adjusted to the routine, I sat content waiting for Santilles or, at least, word of his arrival. I considered the potential and benefits this case might bring and I began passing the time daydreaming about robbing Santilles and the riches the Colombian might yield. I was willing, even eager, to wait all weekend for Santilles to arrive. At about 5:30 p.m., Walker telephoned me on the cellular phone. He explained the informant, Carrasco, had spotted several Colombians at a Gurnee bar, the Windjammer, and he believed one of one of them had been Santilles. Gurnee was an unassuming town best known for its large outlet mall. It was situated just west of Waukegan. McKey had been assigned to watch the Windjammer and when we assembled near the place, the unwitting CI stated Santilles had been inside for over two hours. McKey was embarrassed and begged forgiveness for not realizing it. We all recognized Santilles could have slipped by anyone of us and I think we all felt relieved that it had happened to someone else.

None of us knew specifically who we were really watching. But now, thanks to the informant's description, our meaningful work was about to begin. We sat and waited for him to come out.

Walker called Bobby Hayes and told him Santilles had arrived. Walker requested five agents be sent out to assist in the surveillance. It was 6:30 p.m. on a Friday night and the metropolitan rush hour was at its zenith. Most agents had already left for the day and this meant notifying them via pager. Agents were notorious for ignoring their pagers on the weekend and by 8:15 p.m., only one other agent, surprisingly Chad Jennings, had arrived to help follow Santilles.

Santilles had already exited the Windjammer by then. He had been travelling alone. He was poorly dressed and looked absurd in his white windbreaker and ivory colored canvas loafers. It was no more than forty degrees and he resembled a typical Floridian who had been unexpectedly plucked by aliens and dropped into the frosty Upper Midwest. He drove a Chevrolet Lumina which bore distinctive rental plates from the Avis Company. The sun had fallen and the full moon could be clearly observed in the vast, clear sky. The CI's information had been precise and Santilles had indeed, arrived as scheduled.

Santilles first stop while under surveillance was a humble bungalow badly in need of paint. Aluminum siding dangled from the side of the house and a rusting Chevy Nova sat idle, dilapidating in the driveway. It had been an address we hadn't identified. We were not aware whose house it was or who may be inside. Santilles, wearing the light windbreaker, entered carrying and concealing nothing. He stayed about fifteen minutes. We had hoped it would be a short visit and were delighted when he exited but, disappointed when he left without anything. He drove to another small, inconspicuous house, this one in Waukegan. He stayed briefly then moved to another anonymous residence. We followed him the rest of the night as he continued his roving campaign through Eastern Lake County.

Santilles methodically drove the Lumina through the Waukegan area. He made two stops in North Chicago, the small low-income suburb to the south. There he visited another bar and then, a beeper store. He returned to Waukegan and visited three single homes, two apartment complexes, one of which Walker had identified as a trafficker's flat and two closed businesses. He drove cautiously, obeying all traffic lights and signals. He did not drive fast but more in a methodical, deliberate style. If a light turned yellow as he approached it, he would stop. He signaled for every turn, even signaling once to make an abrupt U-turn, a move which alarmed Walker. The sudden run prompted Walker to consider abandoning our tail for fear Santilles might be feeling the heat of the surveillance. I did not believe Santilles was cognizant of us following him and I persuaded Walker to continue the surveillance. Everyone agreed but Jennings, who had grown disinterested and after only three hours, informed Walker he had to leave. Walker knew he was not being asked permission and did not respond, knowing Jennings had probably already started home when he had made the announcement.

The most interesting stop along Santilles' journey was his final visit, to an auto garage near the lakefront intersection of Sheridan and Clayton streets. By the time Santilles arrived there, it was close to 12:45 a.m. Most people know there are very few mechanics who will perform work after midnight, a fact which substantially piqued our interest. Even more significantly, when Santilles arrived, the business was vacant and no one was there to meet him. To us, this development probably indicated Santilles was not travelling around making random social calls but, was purposely visiting specific places for particular reasons. It was apparent Santilles was maintaining pre-arranged appointments. He sat in his Lumina contentedly pulled up to a closed bay door waiting for someone to arrive. The undistinguished garage was tucked only one hundred yards from the historic Genessee movie theater which once hosted national premieres but now sat, idle and abandoned. No more than ten minutes elapsed when both McKey and I observed a newer model black Camaro pull up and park next to the Lumina. The driver exited and without acknowledging Santilles, entered the business. Immediately, lights went on inside the garage, the bay door opened and Santilles drove into the garage. The door closed and we could see through a small window that only after getting inside, did the two acknowledge each other. Strangely, a small curtain was drawn over the rectangular bay door window eliminating any chance for us to observe what was occurring. Our imaginations ran wild. I thought about the possibility of money being loaded into Santilles vehicle. Walker radioed me and asked if I thought it was a dope related transaction. Of course, something was happening and we all could agree to that. Walker mentioned he would like to walk into the office on Monday and be congratulated by Bobby Hayes and members of upper management for the success of his dedicated efforts. Sharkey and McKey envisioned the same adulation though everyone else knew that their effort had not been comparable to Jim Walker's. I did not care about the success of the case from an enforcement standpoint. Instead, I thought about all the cash Santilles might be accepting. I considered the pernicious methods I might employ of separating myself from my partners and interdicting his booty. I also considered the driver of the Camaro. He looked Hispanic but, he could have been a Caucasian. There were no plates on his car, only a licensed-applied-for sticker. I watched him enter the garage but, he had carried nothing. Whatever they were exchanging had to be already in place when Santilles arrived. I discounted the possibility Santilles had brought anything to the location. We had a surveillance of Santilles throughout and had not observed Santilles carrying anything to or from the vehicle. Furthermore, we believed Santilles was in Waukegan to pick up money and return to Florida with it. Whatever reason Santilles came to Waukegan, we were all convinced it was rooted in drug trafficking.

I sat in my car considering the variety of possibilities. My mind seemed consumed with the auto garage and the covetous visions of all the bags of money being placed into the vehicle. I examined the deteriorated exterior of the garage, casing it like a petty criminal. I theorized where I might break into it in the future. The bay doors seemed solid and the windows were too small for me to crawl into but, the office door was glass and could be easily shattered with a hammer. I hoped this was the place where the money would be exchanged because I felt confident in the future it would be an easy target for me to hit. But where was the money stored? Was it in a false wall? or a car? A secret compartment built into a wall or the floor opened only with the garage's hydraulic lifts. Again, I found myself wishing for the superhuman, comic book fantasy power of x-ray vision.

Only fifteen minutes after entering, the bay door opened and Santilles exited. He drove out and onto Sheridan Road in the same calm manner he had driven all night. At this stage, surveillance had to be outstanding. The early morning hours had rendered the street abandoned and vehicles driving through town were scarce. Walker immediately directed me to follow the Camaro with McKey, a request which I instantaneously resented. I wanted to follow Santilles to see where he went next and know exactly what he removed from his vehicle. Instead, Walker and Sharkey would follow him and I was left with the unknown and probably less important confederate. Though I was unhappy, I accepted the assignment without complaint. I allowed the Camaro to travel a block and a half in front of me to decrease the potential for the driver to recognize he was being followed from the garage. In the trafficless road, I monitored him easily for several minutes. I notified McKey over the car to car radio the automobile had made two, consecutive right hand turns. I had to let him go after the second and if he made a third it meant he was looking for surveillance. Rasheed picked him up and announced the Camaro had gained significant speed and had just blown a light on Belvedere Road. I encouraged McKey to discreetly attempt to close the distance between himself and the Camaro but he responded by saying it would be too suspicious. Further surveillance of the Camaro on the desolate street was impossible and we had to let it go. I heard the banter between Walker and Sharkey as they followed Santilles who continued to drive cautiously and consequently, was easier to monitor. I telephoned Walker and told him we were not able to remain with the Camaro and subsequently he "was out of pocket," a phrase we used to convey we had lost the suspect. Walker confirmed my transmission but, sounded disappointed in doing so. We attempted to join the surveillance of Santilles, who had taken a route in a parallel direction, west on Grand Avenue.

Walker called out that Santilles was heading in the direction of Elmwood Avenue. It was an address Walker had identified but, gave no further information about, perhaps due to the possibility our radio traffic was being monitored by outside sources. Walker explained it was the home of a possible love interest of Santilles. The mere knowledge of the place lent even more credence to the information the informants had given us about Santilles. Walker was elated when he was able to report Santilles had made a right hand northbound turn onto the 100 block of Elmwood. Walker wisely allowed Santilles to make the turn without being followed and shouted over the radio instructions for no one to "dare go up that street." Sharkey acknowledged he was exiting the car to obtain a position on foot. It was a dangerous act, especially if he planned to traverse people's yards in the middle of the night and a curious neighbor elected to release a watchdog to investigate.

It turned out Sharkey's decision was a brilliant tactical move. Santilles decided to square his block and came back onto Grand Avenue. Walker's car was parked among other cars on the same street but, he had alertly doused his lights before Santilles had noticed it. Santilles apparently paid no attention to it. Meanwhile, Sharkey had exited his vehicle with a portable radio and obtained a position hiding behind a tree. It was a stroke of luck that McKey and I were not in the immediate area where we could be observed by Santilles who surely would have been skittish if he had seen a strange conglomeration of idling vehicles around his house at this time of night.

Sharkey reported Santilles had turned back onto Elmwood Avenue. He said he would be forced to turn his radio down to avoid Santilles hearing its static. I stopped my car several blocks away and waited to hear what happened next. There was no need to go into the area and I hoped Sharkey would be able to observe something though I couldn't imagine him close enough to know if Santilles was carting money around. That would have to be left to our imaginations.

Several minutes passed before any information was reported. Walker said he had just driven down Grand Avenue and looked up Elmwood Street and related he did not see Santilles car. He alluded to the possibility Santilles may very well have driven away. It was a prospect which disappointed us yet one we could not discount. We had done our best to monitor Santilles and if he had eluded us it would not have been through lack of effort. I started wondering about the meeting at the garage. I thought about the complexes that Santilles had visited, the bungalows, the apartments and the other places.

"This is oh-nine. This is oh-nine." It was Sharkey.

"Go ahead, nine." Walker implored.

"I'm still hiding....up in this tree," the words came in gasps as Sharkey tried to catch his breath, "I was behind it and Santill....the bad guy came back up the 'E' street." He paused as anyone with a lengthy transmission should do. "I hid behind a tree and when I saw him, I climbed up into it."

I smiled at the thought of Sharkey perched in a tree.

"The guy parked in a driveway, the car is right here, in front of me." Sharkey's excitement ebbed as he gained more composure. "He took two small suitcases out of the trunk and took 'em into a house. I got the address." He paused again, "A woman was holding the door open for him, she didn't look bad either."

Sharkey had seen the suitcases and there was no doubt the CI's information was true. We had maintained a seven hour surveillance of Santilles in which he had not been to his trunk the whole time. There was not much question he picked up the cases at the garage but, what was in them?

*

Having mutually decided Santilles was home for the evening we debated whether we should terminate surveillance for a few hours so we could all go home and obtain some much needed rest. There are very few domestic flights which leave O'Hare Airport before 6:00 a.m. so we expected Santilles would remain bedded down for at least a few hours. It would have taken me another hour to get home and Sharkey, who lived in Northwest Indiana, twice as long. Walker lived in the area in a desolate section of Lake County and invited us to spend the night at his house but, with two children, one an infant son, and a cranky wife waiting for him to come home, we declined. Instead we opted to request Hayes permission to secure hotel rooms to rest for a few hours. McKey elected to go home to Chicago's South Side and I doubted whether I would see him back early the next day. After all, he had a date at an amusement park. Hayes authorized us to book the rooms and I welcomed the recess even though I probably would have stayed out all night, sparked by the recent developments.

I laid down in a dingy, cheap hotel room with a lumpy double bed and thought about the lucrative drug trade and what I had witnessed that evening. I considered the leisurely pace by which Santilles went about his business, visiting people with the repose of a priest collecting offertories from delinquent parishioners. I was convinced money made up the contents of those suitcases and I tried to estimate how much Santilles had collected. Though I hadn't seen them, I judged the take based on Sharkey's description of their size and the amount I had pilfered from the courier at the train station. Jorge Carrasco was correct, Santilles was a money courier for the cartel and I found myself wondering what method Walker would employ to seize the monies. The DEA conducted a variety of methods by which the money could be interdicted. If Santilles went through the airport, the most logical manner would be a profile stop by which a potential narcotics or money courier is interrupted at the airport and questioned by the police. Federal courts have upheld the right of law enforcement officers to conduct such stops based on the "profile" of a courier. The term "profile" is very indiscriminately defined by design and grants law enforcement officers or agents an enormous degree of latitude when deciding whom should be stopped. During the mid-to-late eighties, virtually everyone who was stopped was an African American or Hispanic. One might assume those statistics bear racist mentalities however, the truth was many of the blacks and Hispanics who were interdicted were caught because they looked and acted like the stereotypical dope dealer. Not necessarily due to the color of their skin but more attributable to their style and behavior. The men and even the women who were captured almost always wore large amounts of expensive jewelry and dressed themselves in silk designer-named jogging suits. They purchased one way tickets with cash and never checked luggage. The flights from Los Angeles to New York, Houston to Chicago, Miami to New York and San Francisco to Detroit were frequent airline routes taken by drug couriers. In reverse, they often were apprehended transporting money. They were picked off by observant agents who would simply stand by the gates and watch passengers deplane. In the late 80's, tens of thousands of pounds of drugs were being transported via domestic airline flights. The DEA believes only about 5% of this traffic was interdicted via profile stops. Conveniently, the DEA didn't maintain figures regarding the number of people who were guilty of nothing more than being black and flying domestically from one metropolis to another. Into the 90's, less was seized via profile stops as drug barons began utilizing other means of transportation to convey their product. Some were as simple as mailing drugs via overnight shipping companies and transporting drugs through automobiles with custom-built secret compartments. Certain operations were highly sophisticated including one cartel which had actually purchased a small submarine surplused by the navy of the former USSR in an attempt to smuggle mass amounts of cocaine via clandestine midnight deliveries into US ports. The only reason the precocious scheme failed was the submarine was found to be unseaworthy and the parts needed to repair it couldn't be procured through the defunct Soviet navy.

The law provides specific rules of engagement regarding profile stops. The law enforcement official is restricted in the type and style of questioning he can pursue. For instance, the officer is not permitted to obstruct a suspected courier's movement but, is only allowed to request the individual's cooperation. By law, the person must voluntarily submit their person and belongings to be searched and if the individual refuses, the suspect is supposed to be left alone. The individual can not be touched, impeded, detained or denied the right to proceed to their destination. The individual may decline at any time to submit identification and also refuse to allow his bags and personal belonging to be searched. In all cases, the individual is supposed to be permitted to proceed in any way to their destination without harassment from the police unless probable cause can be developed to request a search warrant on the luggage or the arrest of the individual. Of course, this is how the law is written. In the real world of drug interdiction, it is virtually impossible to develop enough probable cause to obtain a warrant during a brief encounter unless you know the specific contents of the bag. Judges do not maintain offices at any airport or train station and even if they did, no practical judge is going to sign a search warrant on a piece of luggage because an agent says the person fits the profile of a narcotics courier. So, when a suspected courier makes his way through an airport, the officer must rely on cunning, skill and most of all, the ability to intimidate the individual into cooperation. The suspect must be made to feel he has no choice but to submit valid identification, answer all the questions posed by the agent and submit his belongings for inspection if asked. An experienced officer can ascertain almost immediately if his suspicions are correct. If the person is cooperative and only exhibits slight nervousness, he or she is always dismissed without the request of a search. It is a rare occasion when an experienced officer requests to see the contents of luggage and doesn't find some type of contraband. Certainly it is not unreasonable to anticipate someone would become unruffled and demonstrate confusion and even apprehensiveness if they were unexpectedly stopped and questioned by a police officer. Nervous behavior is normal. On the other hand, the courier always exhibits considerable more worry and the person who is guilty of transporting contraband usually exposes him or herself by nervous gestures often accompanied by stuttering and sweat from the upper lip and brow. The longer the questioning lasts, the more excited and worried the courier becomes whereas the person who is guilty of nothing often expresses relief, knowing they have nothing to fear. The most calm, cool and collected courier is going to become nervous if approached by the police. And every year, the Drug Enforcement Administration seizes hundreds of thousand of dollars in drugs and monies through the utilization of profile stops.

I thought about the possibility of a profile stop in Santilles' case. There would be no opportunity for me to steal money if we were to consider such a stop. We would be required to conduct the stop through our airport detail, who would manage the interdiction and take custody of the booty. I would never handle the cash and my chance to steal any of it would be vanquished. As the night wore on, I slept little and found myself consumed with the thought of getting an opportunity to steal some of Santilles' cash. I planned to propose to Walker in the morning he consider a plan utilizing me and someone else portraying ourselves as bad cops.

I had assumed the role before in a case where myself and Chad Jennings dressed ourselves in the attire of two Chicago cops. We had hoped to make a small time ounce dealer an informant by striking fear in him and by robbing him of his drug proceeds. We intended to terrorize him a couple of times in an effort to make him realize he would have no choice but to cooperate with our investigation. We proposed our plan to the U.S. Attorney's Office who surprisingly granted us authorization to utilize the aggressive but, dangerous technique. As law enforcement officers, we had the right and the duty to seize illegal contraband which included monies acquired from the suspected sale of narcotics. The U.S. Attorney's Office sanctioned us to snatch anything illegal we might find during the stop with the intention of indicting the suspect at a later date. With surprising permission to seize without arresting anyone, we enacted our scheme. The dealer we were targeting made daily runs on Chicago's West Side delivering ounces of cocaine and picking up cash. We suspected he might have as much as twenty thousand on him at a given time. The incident was early in my career when I had no thoughts of theft or corruption. At that time, everything I seized, every piece of evidence was properly and meticulously processed, documented and inventoried. We were very pleased we had received permission from the U.S. Attorney's Office to relieve this drug dealer of his property though the office had no idea how forcefully we had planned to do it.

One evening, Jennings and I borrowed some old Chicago Police shirts from of one of our co-workers and fellow task force agents. We both wore our own dark colored pants which upon close inspection were not police issued but were simply plain black "Dockers" brand slacks. We did not possess Chicago Police badges or hats. We really did not look much like policeman at all except for the one prop which we planned to rely on most if our ruse was to be effective, our weapons.

It was nearing 8:30 p.m. on a frigid, cold February evening. We were driving together in an '84 Ford Crown Victoria, the type of automobile some of Chicago's tactical officers were driving at the time. We had to obtain permission to retrieve the car from our moth-balled surplus fleet to make the bogus police stop more effective. Armed with a portable red light that I had purchased with government furnished funds from a novelty shop, we made our stop. I placed the red light's adapter into the lighter jack and put the flashing strobe on the dashboard. To obtain the effect of flashing headlights, I kept the normal driving lights on but flashed the high beams intermittently. Before resorting to the lights, we had followed the suspect for about twelve blocks, making several abrupt turns with him. We were certain he suspected we were following, and it was a suspicion we wanted to create. When we ignited the lights, he immediately pulled his rusted Buick Century to the side of the road. I pulled in behind him, leaving the headlights on, but removing the "red ball' from the dashboard. He was nervously fidgeting when we walked up.

Instantaneously, Jennings assumed control. He did not ask for identification, as required by normal police procedure. Instead, he referred to the fidgety suspect with a moniker randomly selected, "Clyde." Jennings ordered him out of the car. A pale of fear seemed to pass over the driver's face as he quickly recognized this was not going to be a routine traffic stop. As he stepped out, my partner spun him by his shoulders and then slammed his body toward the automobile. The air spewed from his chest cavity as his sternum was slammed against the roof of the car. Jennings dragged him by the collar back to our bogus tactical car and searched him. I never said anything during the altercation but, relinquished authority of the precarious situation to my seasoned partner. In the back seat, with his face now buried into the moldy vinyl upholstery by the strong grip of Jennings' right hand, my partner demanded his drugs and his money.

"Where's your fucking money?"

"No man, please. I don't know…" He appealed through a muffled voice, his mouth pressed against the seat.

"Where's the money you mother-fucker?" interrupted my partner's demand whose over-dramatic rage was even scaring me. He took to the role like a duck to water which, in retrospect, induced later suspicion. He gripped a large hand full of the black guy's unruly hair. "Look here Clyde, you see this" he twisted the scalp to allow the man, whose actual name was Warren Cheeseboro, to view the muzzle of the silver-plated .45 Smith and Wesson, "this is the nasty end of a forty five. This is the side your about to become very acquainted with if you don't tell me where your shit is."

It was a concise but effective remark. Cheeseboro immediately confessed his money and a few ounces of cocaine were hidden under the middle console, in a brown paper bag. The information was beseechingly disclosed in between pleas for my partner to spare him. I hustled back to the Century to find the sack precisely where Cheeseboro directed. I reached for the console and upon my touch, the whole unit collapsed against the driver's seat. The console was not mounted but was left to rest between the two seats. I lifted the grey plastic to find a medium-sized greasy, tan paper bag. I quickly peered into it and saw bands of twenties and fifties wrapped together along with three transparent baggies containing the all too familiar white powder. I grabbed the bag and pushed it into my coat. I sauntered back to the car to find Cheeseboro bleeding from a fresh cut over his left eye. I easily determined the source of the injury after my partner backhanded the side of his weapon into the terrified man's skull a second time. Casually, I informed my partner that I had the money.

"How much?" He asked.

Before I could answer, Cheeseboro confessed that it was at least fifteen thousand. Again he made a plea for his life. My partner leaned forward and pushed the handle, opening the right rear door.

"Run, Clyde and don't ever stop running!"

Cheeseboro correctly recognized the remark as an invitation to flee. He lunged for the door. He landed halfway out, with his torso dropping against the asphalt street but, his lower limbs still inside the car. He spun his legs wildly in an attempt to find a position which would allow his legs the foundation with which to get way. His flailing recoil led to a glancing kick to my partner's face, an assault I know Cheeseboro would have regretted had he known he did it. Before Jennings could react adversely however, Cheeseboro had gained his feet. He stumbled forward some ten yards before he achieved a full stride. The bleeding Cheeseboro fled into the night, abandoning his car which was left with its engine running.

I was out of breath. I was not sure what my partner had planned and for a few fleeting seconds I thought he might kill the man he referred to as Clyde.

"Let's go." Jennings directed as his inflamed demeanor easily subsided. Chad Jennings seemed happy, content and his manner returned quickly to his normal and easy-going personality. He examined his weapon as he began to holster it.

"I hope his thick skull didn't break my gun." He quipped.

We relinquished custody of the cocaine and the money, which turned out to be $19,650 to the U.S. Government. The whole affair had taken less than three minutes to pull off. Cheeseboro would never be inclined to identify us, judging from the fear in his eyes that night. We never had the opportunity to rob him again because later that month Cheeseboro was found with a .357 round in his head. His body was discovered under a littered I-94 exit ramp. I didn't ponder the circumstances of Cheeseboro's death for more than a few minutes but, I never forgot how easy it had been to steal his money.

19

We had assembled at 6:30 a.m. near Elmwood Street to begin the day's surveillance. I did not enjoy a restful sleep but, I was excited about the previous evening's developments and the opportunities the case had presented. As I traveled to the meet spot while the morning broke, I had reached the conclusion robbing Santilles and getting to keep any of his money was probably not going to be possible. The realization left me slightly discouraged. There would be no profit from this day.

I had considered the methods by which Santilles would be relieved of his cache and they all would include efforts with other agents. I determined Walker would be content to seize the money and he and his fellow ride-a-longs, McKey and Sharkey, would be thrilled to accept the congratulatory remarks by our superiors. I, on the other hand, would have been equally happy to report we had failed in our efforts and had been victims of lying informants who greatly exaggerated Santilles' importance. The brief castigation by Bobby Hayes would be infinitesimal compared to the joy of counting all the stolen cash.

Jim Walker did not share my blunted enthusiasm. He was walking on cloud nine when I arrived for the surveillance. He delightfully predicted Santilles was in possession of a large sum of money. He based his assertion on information supplied by Carrasco, who told him

Santilles typically made cash pick ups in the range of $300,000 to 400,000 per trip. The thought of Walker turning in all that cash to Uncle Sam rendered me physically nauseous. Probably anticipating some excitement, our team was joined by three more agents including one of the two who had promised to show up for the previous evening's surveillance, Sandy Foster. Carlos Perez and Desmond Brokenborough also joined us. Perez approached Walker with a lame excuse about his absence the night before with an explanation about a daughter with colitis and Foster simply chose to justify her absence by ignoring the issue. Walker did not care, he was too happy about the favorable developments to ponder the nonsensical excuses. We had six agents, including myself. At that point, I figured there was no way I was ever going to enjoy the opportunity to steal any loot from Santilles. I conceded the best thing for me to do was to observe and learn the tactical idiosyncrasies and conduct of a large scale money courier.

At precisely 8:30 a.m., Santilles departed the residence. The home was an inconspicuous place with the exception of its garishly painted kelly green steps. Nevertheless, the home, even with the loud stoop and its conspicuous lavender blinds, did not look much different than some of the other houses which were similarly adorned with superficial accessories. Flamingos, flags and even a chipped and dismembered lawn jockey guarded one lawn. Carrasco described Santilles' past demeanor on prior visits as diligent and professional, a man who approached his money collecting duties as work. Therefore, it was not surprising when Santilles departed early, dressed in the same catchpenny attire he wore the previous evening, the cheap white clothes which he donned for good luck. However, the clothes looked freshly laundered. His pants had been pressed and his jacket had been washed. Foster, who occasionally drove a van, had been asked to utilize it to sit near the house and report activities. She had monitored the house from a location near the base of the street and was in excellent position to report Santilles had reloaded the two suspicious suitcases into the trunk. Additionally, she reported he kissed a woman goodbye. I wondered about the contents again and felt almost a sense of disgust. If the suitcases did indeed contain money, I couldn't believe he carried it with so little regard. I considered how careful I was when carrying $2,000 in Las Vegas and here was a man who was going to drive around with $300,000 or more in his car. The thought was so preposterous, so unfathomable, I concluded Santilles wasn't carrying money after all. Or, if he did have money, it was still in the safe house and the suitcases contained something else of little or inconsequential value. I rationalized Santilles had perhaps sensed sur-veillance and was safeguarding the money in the home while he made a dry run out and around Waukegan to determine once and for all if he really was being tailed. I had been thinking for hours and spent the time considering every option Santilles might contemplate.

Santilles started the Lumina and we followed him cautiously. He drove to a convenience store where he filled his tank and was observed purchasing two packs of Marlboros. He had bought nothing else. Santilles then drove west along commercial Belvedere Avenue. The thoroughfare was considerably more busy than it had been seven hours earlier and the activity made surveillance easier. Belvedere Avenue was typical of any main drag through a suburban town. Businesses like used car dealerships, discount clothes stores and restaurant chains teased budget-minded patrons with rebates, special offers and all-u-can-eat extravaganzas. Jesus Santilles just bobbed on past it all, I thought, with as much money in his trunk as some of these businesses would gross in a fiscal year. The rhythm of people shuffling in and traffic pulling out of these shops made surveillance easier, distractions which prohibited Santilles from concentrating on what exactly was happening behind him. He continued for several miles passing main north-south routes like Green Bay Road and Skokie Highway. His orderly progress gave us the impression he was travelling again with a specific destination in mind. Ten minutes after departing, he approached the I-294 tri-state

state tollway connecting Wisconsin with Indiana via Illinois. He entered the southbound lanes heading in the general direction of Chicago.

The Lumina cruised along at a conservative speed of 55 miles per hour for close to ten minutes. It was difficult for us to remain behind Santilles because most of the impatient drivers were exceeding his speed by ten miles an hour. I elected to pass Santilles while remaining close but, in front of him. I was employing an accepted technique of a moving surveillance as long as there were enough vehicles behind Santilles to monitor his course. I did not want to be included in the parade of five vehicles which were scattered over a quarter mile behind him. Sharkey soon took my lead and also passed Santilles, reporting the driver did not appear to be interested in his vehicle as he advanced. We passed several exits along the four lane highway which increasingly grew heavily congested with people heading into Chicago. Dense traffic on highways usually makes surveillance conducive and since we had been following Santilles pretty closely over portions of the last two days, we welcomed the congestion as enhanced camouflage for our surveillance. We continued for ten more minutes, passing through two separate .45 tolls on the way. Santilles went through the exact change line on both occasions and I consciously acknowledged he had the wisdom which I did not possess when I had bumbled through a toll with no coins to deposit. I decided to attempt to slow my vehicle so I could manage to get back behind Santilles but, his restricted speed and the increasing flow of accelerating traffic made it impossible. I decided to get a little closer to the city then exit and re-enter the highway.

My plans were dashed when Santilles unexpectedly pulled toward interstate 90 westbound exit. I-90 led west out of the city and continued on to the dairy lands of Wisconsin then, the woods and lakes of Minnesota. Desmond Brokenborough, who was a competent surveillance agent, called out the sudden move and was in position to take the exit as well. As Santilles made the smooth transition onto westbound I-90, an outraged

Walker screamed over the radio. He chastised Sandy Foster for making an obvious turn from the far left lane onto the exit. To other drivers, Foster's move was inconsiderate at least but, to an inherently suspicious and skeptical money courier like Santilles, it could have been a clear indication he was being followed. Walker emphasized we had adequate surveillance and she should not have made the bold move across four lanes of traffic. Foster fired back and a brief but volatile argument via radio ensued. Fortunately, as we had approached Chicago, we had remained on a car-to-car frequency and the heated exchange had not taken place over our repeater channels subjecting the confrontation to the monitor of any DEA employee who had been in tune. The verbal fray went on almost long enough to prohibit Brokenborough from relaying more significant information. Apparently, Santilles had indeed seen something he did not like, perhaps Foster's well-intentioned but irrational surveillance move. His vehicle had pulled off the exit ramp onto the road's shoulder rendering it implausible for anyone to stop moving along the ramp. I heard the agents call out as they passed him on the ramp. Only Perez had been left behind and he had been silent during the surveillance. Sharkey and I frantically looked for a spot that would allow a U-turn. I realized I had probably waited too long to exit and now it would be extremely difficult to get back into surveillance. We both had no choice but to proceed almost two more miles to the Irving Park Avenue exit which was heavily congested with coffee-guzzling motorists.

Walker frantically pleaded for someone to obtain a position at the entrance to I-90 near the ramp. He specifically directed Sandy Foster not do it, a request which Foster obliged by leaving the surveillance altogether, as I was to learn later. Carlos Perez had the foresight to have already pulled over and observed Santilles from behind with binoculars. He explained Santilles had cut back across the exit ramp and was travelling again on I-90. He no sooner had reported that development when he relayed Santilles was exiting the highway again, at the I-190 exit for O'Hare Airport. Perez fired back into traffic after speeding along for more than a quarter mile on the cinder paved shoulder. The daring move was risky but the only chance we had to maintain a tail of Santilles. Driving along the shoulder is not considered courteous behavior and Perez confirmed he was being honked at by several uncivil and irate drivers. At one point, while simultaneously trying to describe Santilles progress, a virulent motorist swerved deliberately into his path and refused to yield. Perez was in the middle of a radio transmission at the time and inadvertently shouted at the driver to "get the fuck out of the way." He then referred to the stubborn individual as a "fucking stupid bendeco," a Spanish term which I know is not an endearment.

We did not have time to verify whether Santilles had rented the vehicle from O'Hare but it now became apparent the airport was his destination. Walker attempted to communicate with our base operator who was asked to notify the DEA O'Hare detail we were in the vicinity and needed their assistance. A few minutes later, Walker became enraged when the base operator reported the O'Hare office was unoccupied.

There was no question where Santilles intended to go when he exited on I-190, the direct access road to O'Hare Airport. Santilles was headed home and there was no doubt in my mind the suitcases contained cash. He passed Bessie Coleman Drive, a road which takes drivers to the international terminal. A twinge of invigorated anticipation crossed my mind as I considered one more fleeting possibility I could somehow intercept Santilles. There was no viable way but, greed often negates rationale. I was far behind the surveillance, thanks to the heavy traffic. I figured Santilles would be in the terminal before I was even on the access road. Nevertheless, I sped toward O'Hare, weaving in and out of traffic, racing northbound on Route 45, a four lane road which paralleled Santilles. I listened to the radio chatter of Perez and fellow agents as Santilles moves were announced. Perez believed Santilles behavior indicated he was cautious and suspicious.

Santilles chose to bypass the rental car return entrance and continued driving on I-190, essentially an oval highway which serves as a loop around O'Hare Airport. It serves no purpose other than accessing the airport from the main interstate that runs next to it. There is no reason to use the road other than business with the airport. Unless of course, one is looking for surveillance. Then, it is a perfect road to watch for vehicles stopped behind or circling more than once. Santilles decision to bypass the terminals, the parking exits and the rental car return was an unequivocal sign he was skeptical about something. Perez wisely had not followed Santilles too closely as he made his second loop of the airport. Santilles circuitous driving had Walker very concerned. Perez tried desperately to remain behind Santilles while directing everyone else to find a stationary position. Meanwhile, Walker begged Sharkey and me to get back into the surveillance and provide two fresh cars which Santilles hopefully would not remember having seen. As we frantically drove toward the airport, I listened as Perez called out and related Santilles again bypassed the rental car return and was on his way out of the airport loop a third time. Before doing so, Santilles slowed down near the parking facilities and Terminal 5, reserved primarily for cargo shippers, which Walker reported was mostly dormant. Perez related he had no choice but to continue past Santilles and enter the ramp back towards the highway and into the city. Perez could not risk being seen driving around the airport loop again. Perez added Santilles had watched his car pass, his head swiveling with eyes masked behind cut-rate, oversized sunglasses. I was finally able to reach I-190 and decided to pull into the first terminal and wait for Santilles to make up his mind. By this time, Walker had been able to locate Santilles and said Santilles was now coming around a fourth time through the airport. Walker directed Brokenborough to follow him with the arduous request to avoid being seen, a tall order with a suspicious man driving in this manner. Brokenborough was finally able to locate Santilles and saw him driving his Lumina into the rental car return lot. Walker should have made the decision right then to stop Santilles. It was obvious he was carrying something in those suitcases and he was taking whatever it was with him on an airplane. If my intentions were strictly case related, I would have demanded an interdiction be the course of action we pursue. However, since I was still hoping for some opportunity. I elected to remain quiet and let Walker screw the whole thing up anyway he pleased.

Walker again attempted to reach the still unoccupied office of the O'Hare detail. Meanwhile, Brokenborough and Perez parked and followed Santilles through the process of returning the rental car from the Avis structure while my mind raced with incomprehensible circumstances which would separate Santilles from the contents of the suitcases. Sharkey joined me and we were forced to wait outside to see if Santilles would be dropped off by a courtesy van. Neither Brokenborough or Perez had the forethought to bring a mobile radio and consequently, we were not kept appraised of their activity inside. In the confusion that ensued, the surveillance, which had been fairly well coordinated and successful, began to unravel, a fortunate development in which I hoped I might capitalize.

I suggested Sharkey and I separate, find our partners and specifically, Santilles. Sharkey obliged willingly and his departure granted me my wish for the ability to accost Santilles alone, if I could find him. It was outrageous thinking, in retrospect. I ludicrously considered grabbing his cases and simply running. This would require the two of us being alone, an impossibility in perpetually crowded O'Hare Airport. Then I considered walking up to him and putting my gun in his ribs. I could threaten to kill him and even march him, carrying the bags, directly to my car. The logic was absurd, of course, but, I had been so consumed with the idea of getting my paws on the riches in his bags my thought processes were beginning to border on insanity. I knew stealing the money would require quick and effective decision making and there would be no way to accomplish it as easy as I had done at the train station. I looked around to see if I was being joined by any of my partners.

Aware I was not, I scanned the building for the medium sized Colombian.

I was in Terminal 2, the terminal for Northwest, Continental and TWA Airlines. I remained there for several minutes and, after a swift but thorough search, I was convinced Santilles was not there. I embarked toward the terminal of United Airlines, Terminal 1, and the largest terminal at O'Hare. I made a cursory glance back through Terminal 2 and confirmed none of the passengers who stood in line was my slick target.

A quarter mile separated the terminals and I was out of breath when I reached Terminal 1. My sinister plans dwindled when I saw Brokenborough, Walker and Perez at the ticket counter. I slowed my walk as to not draw attention but, I was quite anxious to learn the whereabouts of our South American friend. Sharkey was talking on the counter phone to someone. Perez then told me Santilles had just purchased a one way fare back to Fort Myers for a whopping $795.00. His flight was scheduled to depart in twenty-two minutes. He floored me when he stated Santilles was carrying one medium sized suitcase which he had refused to check. Santilles elected to check the other case which had already been accepted into baggage despite the lateness of his arrival. I asked where Santilles was and Perez said Sharkey had gone to the gate in an effort to monitor him until the last possible minute. Meanwhile Walker was in a frantic discussion with United Airlines Management to determine how he could get access to the baggage handlers and inspect the luggage. He covered the mouthpiece and complained to me that he still had not been able to contact any agents from the airport detail. He chastised himself for not contacting anyone the previous night, a rationalization I said was foolish due to the late time we had concluded surveillance. Believing there might still exist a slim possibility I could steal a portion of the cash, I suggested Walker and I conduct a profile stop and determine once and for all the contents of the bag. It was a proposal I thought to be quite reasonable under the circumstances and I was fully prepared to conduct the questioning. I had some experience doing it while working occasional weekend support duty with the airport team at Midway and I felt comfortable with the task. Before replying, Walker was summoned to the gate desk by a pretty young attendant while I watched Santilles as he carried his precious suitcase into the men's room. I followed him in and attempted to monitor his activities in there but, he entered a stall. At O'Hare Airport the bathroom stalls are very private with large aluminum doors standing seven feet high from the floor. Whoever had designed the bathrooms at O'Hare had privacy in mind. I thought about the farcical notion of bursting into the stall and taking the bag. As debased as my thoughts had been even I knew that an act like that would be deranged. I couldn't exactly race out of the bathroom and expect Santilles to remain sitting on the commode after he had been robbed of three hundred grand. The hapless circumstances left me no choice but to see how the affair played out. I dejectedly left the bathroom and met Walker who had returned to my location and stated that he had gained permission to access the baggage handler areas. He said the manager was going to retrieve Santilles bag which had been fraudulently registered in the name of Jose Velez.

I again offered to approach Santilles when he exited the restroom but, Walker surprised me with his request to allow him to board the plane. Walker had cold feet about conducting the stop. Not so much from a legal standpoint but, incredulously, Walker said he couldn't be sure money was actually in the carry-on case. He said if anything, the money was in the checked luggage. I believed the opposite to be true. If Santilles was carrying cash, the cash was in the case with him where he could safeguard it. Walker argued if we tipped our hand now and came up with nothing, all of our intelligence and efforts regarding Santilles had been for naught. My contention was that we were certain he had money, and probably most of it, if not all, was in the bag he refused to check. I implored Walker to attempt the stop for the sake of the investigation, though, realistically, I hoped the deed would enhance my portfolio. A United Airlines baggage handler approached us. Walker directed Sharkey to follow the handler who would escort him to the bag. Walker turned his attention to me and emphatically warned me to leave Santilles alone and allow Santilles to board the plane.

Santilles eventually emerged from the restroom, moving in a slow, methodical pace. He clutched the bag routinely and did not overtly look like a man carrying what some labor as much as fifteen years to make. He walked towards the jetway. I looked at Brokenborough and Perez who had joined me. I asked Brokenborough if we should interdict Santilles and he correctly advised, "You're the case agent, you decide." Santilles briefly glanced at me but, without recognition or emotion. I looked back toward Walker who nodded vertically like a father denying permission to his son. I disappointedly yielded to Walker's desires and Santilles shuffled onto the plane carrying one medium sized black canvass suitcase.

A few minutes later, after the jetway had been closed, Sharkey telephoned Walker using the gate phone. He had found the other black suitcase and against the protests of the baggage handlers, had opened it. He verified it had contained several packets of currency but, Sharkey had allowed the bag to be placed on board the plane. Sharkey had not seized the bag. Apparently, as I was to learn outside the airport, Sharkey had been advised by Walker to simply inspect the bag and confirm its contents. I had been right. Santilles has money and I reasoned almost all of it was in the carry-on, probably at 33,000 feet over the naked cornfields of Indiana. Walker was determined to allow Santilles to return home content that Santilles would return at another time and that the informants would be able to tell us when he would be back in Waukegan. In allowing Santilles to return with his booty, Walker and the rest of us had served as little more than federal escorts for the Colombian dope dealer. It was inexcusable conduct which Hayes reamed us for when we returned to the office. The affair also cost me

$95 when I was forced to travel to the impound lot to retrieve my car which had been towed for being parked illegally outside Terminal 2. I was not reimbursed since the administrative director decided it was negligent behavior to have left the vehicle unattended at O'Hare.

After I retrieved my car, I resolved vacillation would never cost me money again.

20

I had the remainder of the weekend along with everybody else to interpret what had occurred. I was disappointed I didn't have a chance to
grab any of the money for myself but, I was at least encouraged there
would be future prospects. I concluded Walker's decision to let the
money go would facilitate Santilles' continued financial ventures in
Waukegan and hopefully, an opportunity for me.

We reported to the DEA offices the following Monday and were met
by an exasperated supervisor, Bobby Hayes. Apparently Sandy Foster,
after she had abandoned the surveillance, telephoned Hayes to inform
him she resented the condescending treatment she was given by Walker
during the Santilles surveillance. While complaining, she evidently had
also revealed to Hayes we were certain Santilles was in possession of a
large sum of cash. Certainly we had intended to keep Hayes appraised
of developments but, it wasn't wise to assume anything in the drug
business therefore, neither Walker or me had told Hayes that Santilles
had been definitely carrying money. Foster had made it sound as if we
were convinced and consequently, Hayes expected us to return to the
office with a suitcase full of seized currency. When Hayes came into the
office Monday morning, Walker told him we had seized nothing. Hayes
hadn't had time to immediately address the issue but, after the supervisor's weekly meeting, he directed Walker into his office. I noticed

Sharkey and McKey were not eager to follow Walker inside, especially after the screaming started. Walker began telling Hayes about the lengthy surveillance and his decision to permit Santilles to return to Florida unimpeded. Walker conceded we had intercepted one of Santilles' pieces of luggage in the airport and confirmed that money was indeed inside. The revelation sent Hayes into a histrionic diatribe laced with profanity, the words heard clearly through the closed door of his office.

"Do you know what your job is, Walker. You're a federal fucking drug agent. You get paid to make seizures of drugs and related fucking assets." Hayes continued, "You been putting this case together for months and asking for help but, when the time comes to do something on your own, you drop the ball."

Walker wisely remained quite and allowed Hayes to vent.

"You have got to seize that money, son." Hayes paused briefly and then asked the inevitable, "How much was there anyway?"

We couldn't hear Walker's response but, whatever his estimate had been, it should have been lower.

"Are you kidding me Walker? And you just let it walk. Shit, God-almighty."

Walker was getting blistered and although he was the lead case agent, I thought he shouldn't be taking it alone. I glanced at McKey and Sharkey. Both had their heads down, content to remain at their desks while Walker absorbed the full force of Hayes' verbal assault. I walked toward the threshold of the door and knocked on the metal frame. I opened it and immediately saw Hayes' facial muscles were strained with anger. He looked up long enough to change the direction of his tirade toward me.

"Connor, you're an experienced God-damn agent, why didn't you do something?"

I hedged my answer hoping for words that would exonerate all of us. "Well Bobby, we really weren't sure..."

"Not sure. You been doing this for five fucking years and you were not sure?" His words were sharp and peppered with truths but, there was no sense in fixating on them because any assertions he made regarding our stupidity were all accurate and justified. We verified Santilles had the cash. At least Sharkey had. We confirmed it and the money should have been seized for the benefit of the case, and at least, for Uncle Sam." For the first time, I thought about the money as what I should have considered it all along, evidence. Hayes words came back into audible focus, "I mean what the hell does it take?"

Sharkey and McKey slinked into the room. They had observed I was willing to take some of the heat for Walker and they prudently decided they should do the same. I'm sure their hesitant entrance was also motivated by their interest in maintaining credit for the case even though, at this point, the investigation had not yielded any seized contraband and therefore, no accolades. The importance of the case was supported by the activity and despite our ineptitude even Hayes could not discount that certitude. Seeking justification for failing to seize the money, Sharkey boldly suggested doing so would have been illegal. He mentioned we had no right to inspect Santilles luggage without his consent.

"Are you for real Sharkey? Do you do everything through that lily white tight ass of yours?" He followed with another poignant question, "Are you a cop or a lawyer because if you want to practice law you're on the wrong floor!" Without a reply, Hayes angrily added, "Do you think that friggin dope dealer is going to hire a lawyer and sue the government to get his drug money back."

Sharkey wisely relented but then McKey added, "If it was me, I would have seized it boss."

The remark re-ignited Hayes angered embers. "I heard you weren't even there, McKey. You were jacking off on a Ferris wheel, weren't you?"

Hayes was not about backstabbing and the purpose of McKey's remark, to equivocate blame, was apparent to everyone in the room. Hayes rose from his desk, side-stepped it and closed the office door which McKey and Sharkey had strategically left open, to encourage Hayes to quell the volatile offensive which they hoped to avoid. Since Hayes was still in the room we all knew we were in for a continued dressing down, which we received for the next several minutes. Individually and as a group, Hayes identified and elaborated on our professional shortcomings. My work had been respectable and Hayes had not spent significant time embarrassing me but, he emphatically demanded I become more of a leader especially, if I expected to some-day move into a management position. He reiterated about the improper determination to let the money walk and added if it was rep-resentative of future decisions one could expect from me then, I should reconsider whether I had the ability to truly lead people. He chastised me and Walker for making a terrible tactical judgment.

He attacked Walker for being too conservative and he questioned his desire to really do his job. I felt it was more of a motivational address than it was criticism. Most of the office recognized Walker to be a very dedi-cated agent although he spent excessive energy researching categorically meaningless data and records but, positively no one ever questioned his effort. I observed Walker' reaction to the caviling and sensed it caused him great distress. Respectfully, Walker sat there and listened and made no attempt to defend himself.

Hayes then turned toward Sharkey and McKey. I expected more of the same but, I was shocked to hear Hayes' poignant review of their work. He spoke to them together as they so often were, at the gym, at lunch and on the phone. Apparently, Hayes was not quite as out of touch as they had mistakenly assumed. He reamed them both, calling them lazy and scheming. He also asked them, "How long do you plan riding other people's cases through your evaluations?" Before he was finished, Hayes had made it abundantly clear that individuals in upper management also recognized Sharkey and McKey's indolence.

My respect for Hayes grew as a result of his bombast. Though it was insulting, the harangue was directed to catapult our careers. Hayes often recounted the methods once employed by a proud agency which he had admitted seemed to deteriorate to an organization where everyone was out for themselves and devoid of those willing to take a chance for the sake of an investigation. Sharkey foolishly attempted to interrupt Hayes and said something about the lack of zeal on the part of the U.S. Attorney's Office. It was a smoke screen which some of us, including me, relied on when we were not producing cases. We would typically blame the criminal prosecutors alleging our investigative strategies were being ridiculed in the AUSA's Offices. Hayes saw right through it. I'm sure he had used similar excuses years earlier when he was a street agent.

"Sharkey, that's all so much bullshit. The attorney's have nothing to do with your arrests. They get the case after the arrest, remember? You know what is really wrong with this agency. There is no cooperation. No one wants to work together but, everyone wants the praise. You have to stick up for each other when things get rough. And they do. You guys made the wrong decision out there. All of you. It was stupid and dumb and it was the work of inexperienced or afraid agents." Hayes shrugged, "Maybe a little of both. But don't come in here and tell me that you did not make the decision together. Don't dare come in here and tell me one wanted to do this and someone else wanted to do that. Anyone could have made the wrong choice, that happens all the time on this job. Sometimes it can cost you a life. But don't come back here and be afraid to take responsibility for your actions. That is called being a coward." He looked directly at Sharkey and asked him, "Are you a coward? Before he could respond, Hayes remarked, "This is a whole city full of cowards, Shit, there is a whole fucking building full of them right here. Now, get the hell out of here and do your jobs."

It was the first time I had ever heard a DEA manager speak with candor without fear of reprisal. Bobby Hayes told us exactly what he thought of us and our efforts. In doing so, he revealed his ability to keenly perceive the activity and behavior he observed around him. I always suspected Hayes was an intelligent man however, I did not extend him the efficacy to determine what I privately believed. The agency consisted of many people out for themselves who only wanted to advance their own career. They didn't care about the community, the drugs or each other. Only their own precious advancement and their own bi-monthly paychecks. Some of those people's behavior was obvious and could easily be detected. In others, motivations were not as easily discerned. I wondered what assessments Hayes had made of me and how accurate they had been. I wondered what I knew about Hayes and I realized it was virtually nothing, only what had been told to me by others.

The rest of the day progressed calmly with all the agents of Group 5 remaining diffident, especially the members of Walker's team. It was the first day I could remember Sharkey and McKey remaining in the office past 6 o'clock. I hadn't said much to any of my group mates and sat silently preparing a surveillance report regarding the weekend's activities. I had waited until Hayes had left for the evening and telephoned Kevin Jensen, an agent who lived only two short blocks from the office in a highly over-priced one bedroom apartment. I desperately wanted to have a couple cold beers and Jensen had been one of the guys who Brian Sullivan and I had frequently accompanied on the town. Jensen and I had mutual tastes which included our enjoyment of sports, dry jokes, beat authors and our shared fascination with slim women with counterfeit breasts. Typically we met at Cavanaugh's where we played on our rapport with the cute waitresses. Most of the girls tolerated our sexual innuendo and dirty jokes because we were friendly and good tippers. Jensen had agreed to meet me there, after work.

I left the office and walked into the remodeled bar alone. I discreetly canvassed the tables looking for Jensen who I knew always preferred to sit near the pool tables and dart boards. There, he could casually engage female customers who were bored or lonely enough to play one of the bar games.

I could see through the dormant haze of cigarette smoke that Kevin had not yet arrived. I decided I would pick out a table that would suit both his flirtatious interests and my desire for a cold beer and quick service. I walked through the mixed crowd, excusing myself and trying to appear like I belonged. Suddenly, I felt a stiff hand grip my left shoulder, strong enough to whirl me and twist me slightly off balance. I spun counter-clockwise to see Mike Kamenski, the BATF Agent, retaining me with his right hand. I had not given much consideration to Kamenski or his thieving actions since the raid we had worked together. Occasionally, I thought about the maelstrom his conscience had dunked him into however, for the most part, I had my own personal and professional worries to consider.

He smiled, then unsuitably roared, "Hi Mark, how the hell are you?"

It was a loud and obnoxious introduction and inappropriate because we were not friends, let alone the sort of good friends who would typically exchange such a boisterous greeting. It was the type of salutation that should be reserved for a companion who hasn't been seen or heard from in years then, unexpectedly, you're face to face with him and before you can think of what to say, the great memories have flooded back and drowned calculating decorum.

Mike Kamenski was drunk. His face was flushed but, in a far different way than when I had seen him steal the three ounces of coke. His eyes were bloodshot and glassy and his lids hung drowsily over his eyes. My immediate inclination was to pull away, even push him away but, I sensed an obvious brush-off might be observed and later questioned. My impression of him was that he needed reassurance. He wanted me to tell him he would not be in trouble for what he had done.

"How are you?" I asked, reservedly.

"Great, Mark…really. That was a great raid, a great warrant. It was a pleasure working with you." He emphasized the you. It had not been a great warrant or even a great raid. It had been a routine enforcement action except for his blatant and foolish attempted theft of three ounces of cocaine from a defendant and exacerbated by his botched effort to conceal it.

"It was a ..."

"Mark, let me buy you," Kamenski interrupted, "what are you having, what would you like?" He summoned the bartender, "Janet, Janet, give Mark here something from the top shelf, whatever he wants."

I knew Janet. She worked hard four nights a week and listened to the ravings, complaints, solicitations and miseries of all the broken down customers. Most were stressed out brokers from the Chicago Board of Trade however, some were federal agents who fraternized unnoticed in the crowd. There had been a time or two when she had comforted me after a harrowing day with her service. She was a good bartender, friendly and dependable.

"A Budweiser, Mark?" She knew. I always felt a degree of welcome there especially when the employees knew your name and what you drank, albeit I did not think I visited enough to be considered a "regular." I affirmatively nodded as she glanced at Mike. She gave me a slight roll of the eyes cognizably warning me Mike was beginning to be a pest because of his inebriation.

"Who you here with?"

Before I could reply, he continued, uninterested in my response, "Can we sit down a minute, you know, just a little while?"

Mike knew I had hovered above him, watching as he stole the coke and my pretext in the ceiling had not worked. I was sure he had been planning this meeting since the incident and wished it would be an offhanded and light encounter. He undoubtedly had spent weeks daydreaming of the method he would employ to finally broach the subject but, now he was drunk and had lost the cunning to coyly bring up the delicate matter which concerned him so much.

"Mark, we have to talk." His arm had made its way around my left shoulder blade and enveloped me in an embrace of sorts. Janet brought back my beer and before I could reach for it, he placed his drink on the wooden bar. Judging from his malted breath, it was whiskey. He retrieved my beverage in an overly subservient manner. He forced the brown bottle into my hand.

"What I want to say is thanks…"

I interrupted him with a gesture. What he had done that morning was of his own volition. I did not want him and anyone else who had cared to notice think I was a confederate. His uncomfortable clasp led me to try to duck from under it.

"Mike, let's go sit down." We were not friends and I wanted him to know we were especially not co-conspirators. He followed me to the table, staggering slightly but fortunately, not obviously drunk. As we sat down at the oaken table I stated, "Mike, I know what you want. I'm not going to pretend, you aren't…"

"Mark, Mark, Mark" he interjected. He was determined to plead his case. His behavior became more belligerent. He reached for his wallet, opening the black leather to show me a photograph of two very cute preschool children. A playful blonde haired boy of about five in a navy blue sailor suit and a spunky girl slightly his junior smiling despite her unabashedly broken and gap-toothed grin. "These are mine. I would do anything for them. I love them so much, anything." He pushed the wallet toward me, the photos still inside their laminated holder. When I failed to immediately reach for the billfold, he placed the photo directly in front of my face leaving me no choice but to look into the eyes of the faultless children. I hoped to convince him the impending guilt-ridden soliloquy he was about to deliver was unnecessary and I had absolutely no plans to pursue any action. I tried to talk.

"Mike, I have no …"

"Mark, look at those kids. They are so beautiful. I love them like they are my life."

I detected the same failure in the voice I had heard several weeks prior when I had discovered him stuffing his crotch with another man's cocaine. Nevertheless, intoxicated with booze, he gained confidence and spoke in a louder volume. I wanted to get out of the crowding bar before we were overheard.

"Mike, listen. Let's go somewhere else where its quieter."

"No, Mark. Look at me. These kids of mine mean the world to me and…"

He was too loud. "Mike, shut your fucking mouth. Let's go right now. Collect your money. I won't sit here anymore. We will go for a walk or we won't talk at all." I stood up and left and he obediently followed. Kamenski wanted desperately to be in control of the situation and he knew he was not. He understood he must follow my direction. My friend Kevin had not yet arrived, a circumstance which relieved me. I had no alternative but to leave with Mike before his drunkenness had him confessing his transgressions to the entire bar and coupling me with many of them.

We walked out and turned south on Dearborn Street toward the federal garage. I thanked God he remained silent. Evidently, he understood he had become a nuisance and was too boisterous. We entered the garage together as I swiped my card through the access slot.

"My car is right here. Let's get in and we'll drive out of here and talk where no one can hear us."

We entered my Mark VII. Still thankfully silent, I drove out of the garage with Mike seated beside me. I glanced at him and noticed he appeared to be sulking, blankly staring straight ahead. I thought maybe he was just beginning to feel the effects of his alcohol but when I spoke his reaction proved he was brooding.

"Mike, there is no need to tell me about your family. There is no problem on my end. Nothing is going to happen." There could have been no doubt about the subject we were speaking about because neither of us had yet made any specific reference to it.

He responded, "I have a family. There is nothing in the world that means more to me than that family. I will not let anything happen to them."

"Mike, nothing is…"

Again, he refused to let me finish, "I mean no one is going to take them away. No man, no group of men and certainly not you."

The tone had become threatening and I was not about to allow Kamenski to intimidate me. I wanted to find a place to stop and park so I could impress upon him I intended to forget I had seen him do anything. I had hoped I could reason with him after we left the crowded bar. I signaled for a left in an attempt to cross the far left lane as we made our way southbound on the one way thoroughfare which was Clark Street. I swiveled my head to see if any fast approaching cars were coming from my left.

An explosion shattered the early evening. Twinkling shards of glass collided into the dashboard, the steering wheel and onto my face, arms and hands. The window, which I had been peering through disintegrated. I instinctively let go of the wheel and covered my face trying to comprehend what had happened. An instant passed before I looked toward Mike who sat slack-jawed, looking at me with his heavy lidded eyes. He held his. 357 magnum in his right hand and I could see clearly, despite my chaotic state of confusion, that its muzzle was pointing right at my rib cage. I couldn't react, there was no time and if he wanted me dead he would have already pulled the trigger. In an instant my mood had gone from irritation to terror.

"Do you fucking understand?"

I was too shocked to answer. I didn't feel much other than numbness as I waited for death. My whole body seemed paralyzed. He took his left hand and still pointing the gun at me, opened the passenger door, fumbling briefly with the handle. This was my opportunity to lunge for the weapon but, I just couldn't move. He opened the door and indifferently stepped out onto Congress Parkway, a six-laned, heavily used feeder to the Eisenhower Expressway. As he slid out I concentrated on the gun's muzzle which slowly turned away from my torso. He backed from the car, looking at me. He fumbled to place the gun into his belt. He staggered and almost tripped as he slowly moved backwards. Horns blared as he spun and vacillated through the pattern of traffic, back in the direction of Cavanaugh's which was only two blocks away.

I lowered my arms from my face and tried to collect myself. I sat looking around and noticed a few people on the sidewalk staring, some at Kamenski's unsteady form as he walked away. I looked toward my left trying to decipher if anyone had been hit by the ricocheting bullet. No one laid prostrate or otherwise seemed to be shot. I felt relief but scarcely enough to quell the adrenaline which purged my chest. It was a far different dose than my stealing endeavors had produced. I placed my right foot instinctively on the brake when the shot had been fired but, I was forced to precisely but quickly decide my next move. I realized my vehicle sat awkwardly angled in the street, abruptly stopped from my reflexive braking. A car or two had passed me and I remember seeing one of the astonished faces of a driver gaping at me as he rolled past. A black man observed from the corner of my left eye approached from the sidewalk. I glanced briefly at him, then released the brake. I pressed the accelerator hard. My thoughts were to escape even though I had committed no offense. I think he yelled to me but the noise of the engine responding to the emphatic demand of my foot rendered the words inaudible. The car lurched forward causing shards of glass to spin and careen wildly off the dashboard as shattered pieces of the window collapsed onto my lap. I sped down the street and detected my ears were ringing loudly. I smelled the gunpowder as my senses began to assimilate the surrounding environment. I felt no pain. I looked into the rear view mirror and inspected the right side of my face, the side closest to Mike. It was intact. I turned to examine the left side of my head and immediately saw a narrow stream of blood slithering down my left cheek. I felt the air whistle through the gaping hole where my left window had previously occupied. I moved my eyes in the rear view mirror to focus on the people whose reflection stood watching me. There was a few but their expressions dulled as my distance from the bizarre scene increased. I felt warm and it was several more seconds before I felt the sensation of dampness. I glanced down and observed, through the twinkling glass crystals, I had wet my pants.

That fear took a long time to subside.

2 1

Kamenski's debased and reckless conduct had frightened me enough to believe I was in real danger. There were several people who witnessed the incident and we were so close to the federal parking facility when it happened, I had to consider the possibility someone who worked with me or Kamenski or perhaps a federal employee who might have known us both, had reported it. I had a shattered window to explain and if I did not proffer an excuse for its existence, I would be subject to any conclusions people would make. I considered getting the window repaired myself but, I wasn't guilty of anything. Kamenski had shot it out and I couldn't agree to begin concealing his activity not knowing what additional steps he was planning to clear his own name. I returned to work the following day with the intent of seeking the advice of the only DEA Agent I trusted, my Supervisor, Bobby Hayes.

I understood if I approached Hayes, I would be required to tell him the whole truth about my dealings with Mike Kamenski. My intention was not to expose him but, protect myself from any accusations he might make against me. It was called C.Y.A., an acronym for "Cover Your Ass." I hoped Hayes would provide a rational solution and I also trusted Hayes would direct me to proceed with a settlement which would have the least serious implications for Kamenski.

Before I had the opportunity to speak to Hayes, Sandy Foster surprised the group by announcing she had planned a deal for later that afternoon, a deal which would utilize Alexander Carstaphian, a machismo North Side informant who claimed he hailed from the islands of Greece. It was not known to any of us and probably not even to Foster whether Carstaphian was living legally in the United States as a naturalized citizen or staying in the US illegally, as many of the informants who worked for the DEA. Regardless, Alexander or Alexi as Foster called him, was on the payroll of the US Government as a paid Confidential Informant.

Alexi had not been able to arrange any deals with any substantial targets. There were rumblings among the group he never would either. Most of us, including me, believed he possessed entrenched and valid drug dealing connections however, he maintained his status as an informant as a contingency in case he was ever arrested during a drug deal. His status as an informant confirmed, he would claim he was setting up a deal for the DEA.

It was a very common scenario. Our informants, the reliable and successful ones anyway, all maintained active criminal enterprises. Every one of the successful snitches had extensive criminal histories and the best usually had spent some time in prison, serving time for trafficking, or the usual crimes associated with narcotics like weapons, counterfeiting and tax evasion. A few had murder arrests but, usually no convictions. A murderer, a convicted one, is a dangerous informant. Not because of his prevalence toward violence, most of them possessed that trait. It was the blemish of a murder rap that was recognized on the street as a stigma, an infamous badge of treachery which usually prevented that person from doing work with any others except those who were comfortable dealing with murderers. A person who is known to have killed is feared and often avoided. Those people willing to maintain an association with those that have murdered have probably committed the act as well. Both are willing and able to kill again.

Many agents, including me, were uninterested in seeking out violent subjects for investigation when there were so many easier, non-violent targets from which to choose. It simply wasn't worth the risk. Informants with criminal pasts were likely to remain involved in crime. Dope dealers continue to deal dope, burglars keep stealing and a murderer has even less remorse, if any at all, the second time.

It is no secret informants often put deals together against individuals they do not like. Some of them are competitors who the informant is seeking to eliminate by setting up. Alexi was an individual who fell into this category. We believed any persons he was attempting to entice into deals were dealers whose existence was reducing his profits. He relied on the blanket protection of being a DEA informant in case he got caught by a police agency, all the while promising Foster " The Big One," a deal I believe he never intended to deliver.

I begrudgingly volunteered to assist Foster and requested Hayes let me ride with him so I would have the opportunity to present my predicament with Kamenski. I expected to have ample time to make my presentation to Hayes since none of Carstaphian's deals had worked in the past.

Carstaphian was smooth and cunning. He often showed up at the DEA offices late on Friday afternoons promising Foster he had spent the whole day putting together an intricate deal. Through his self-proclaimed finesse, he had been able to make complicated details seem very simple. He typically claimed the individuals he was working on were high profile couriers and members of heroin and cocaine cartels from all over the world. His assertions were ridiculous but, they succeeded in duping Foster, who believed someday, Alexander Carstaphian would be her ticket to a big promotion.

"This is the Son-of-a-Bitch's last chance." Bobby Hayes announced as he was coming through our office door. He didn't appear in a very good mood and his disposition made me re-assess whether or not I wanted to discuss my delicate issue with him. It was a Tuesday afternoon and he had been out of the office all day. I was not sure where but, his demeanor suggested it was not a place he wanted to spend it. Hayes had received word from Foster she had hoped to consummate a deal with Carstaphian. Hayes had probably not intended to even return to the office however, I knew Hayes was inclined to monitor Foster's work because she had a propensity for immersing herself in situations which placed her and others in jeopardy. Hayes particularly disliked Carstaphian and I think Hayes was sincere when he told us the deal would be Carstaphian's last if it did not produce dope.

"You coppers ready to do a deal tonight?" Carstaphian boasted as he was escorted into our offices. CI's were not supposed to be in our office areas and instead had their own rooms where they were supposed to be debriefed. There was confidential and investigative information as well as personal effects scattered on top of most of the agent's desks. Carstaphian could see by happenstance or deliberate effort information he should not have been privy to. Nevertheless, Foster often disregarded the rule and brought her informants into our office area. None of the agents cared for it and I was surprised Hayes had never addressed the issue. I thought on that occasion, Hayes might but, he chose not.

I walked into Hayes' office and found myself in the middle of a phone call which seemed significantly more important.

"What is it, Connors?"

I hesitated. "I just thought we could ride together, tonight. I want to talk."

"Yea, yea. Whatever." He retorted and then waved me out of the office. "Yes, I can't believe this is the way its turned out…" I heard him say as I closed his office door.

An hour later, we were sitting together on surveillance outside a near-North Side restaurant waiting for Carstaphian's guy to show up with three kilos of coke. Carstaphian had set up about six deals and none of them had gone and I didn't think this would either. Every time, his supplier was someone else. First an Iranian, then a Nigerian, then a white kid from the Gold Coast, the wealthy community on the near north side. The list of his accomplices was growing preposterously long and Hayes seemed to think so as well. Hayes had been very sedate during the ride out and his unusual silence did not seem to present the ideal situation for me to bring up my dilemma with Kamenski. Fortunately, Hayes had volunteered to drive and we did not use my automobile. I elected to wait, feeling like the hesitant son trying to find the courage to ask to borrow the family car.

Carstaphian had been about to go inside the restaurant, a low-priced, aluminum sided diner specializing in budget Italian dishes. The individuals who had entered and exited did not bear any resemblance to the person Carstaphian claimed he would meet who, this time, was a white male with long pony-tailed dark hair, a man who referred to himself as "the Doctor." None of us had ever heard of the Doctor. We watched the restaurant and its patrons, most of whom were seniors trickling in and out seeking some of the daily specials whose less than appetizing descriptions were printed in ink on paper plates and loose leaf paper taped to the windows.

"You think this one will go?" I asked Hayes rhetorically, hoping to elicit some conversation.

"Shit no but, this time we are going to find out if he is really trying." Hayes fiddled with his portable radio, changing the knobs on the top. "I got this thing from Tech Ops," he announced as he activated the radio.

Hayes informed me he had obtained a special transmitter which our Technical Department had developed. Hayes explained the radio operated on a stronger signal and could receive transmissions from the kel unit given to Carstaphian. Carstaphian always wore recording equipment, something all the CI's were required to do however, Carstaphian did not know the unit he had been given, a small pager device, could not be deactivated. Alexander's recordings were prone to be interrupted by his frequent decision to disable the devices when he engaged in conversations which "had nothing to do with drugs" as he put it. Informants were required to keep the devices on but many, especially Carstaphian, preferred to turn them off from time to time. It was an issue which caused concern among most of us but, particularly the US Attorney's Office whose staff collectively cast disparaging suspicions at all our informants. This time, according to Hayes, we would hear everything Carstaphian was saying whether he wanted us to or not.

"Lets see what this guy is up to." Hayes stated as Carstaphian departed his vehicle and entered the diner.

We heard the bustle of a semi-crowded room, glasses jingling and a waitress yelling about a spill. The transmission was surprisingly clear.

"Is Frank here?" It was Alexander's deep, distinctive voice.

We could not here the reply, perhaps because there wasn't one.

"I'll sit over here and wait. Hey, give me a cup of coffee."

"This is one. Eight are you monitoring this." Hayes asked Foster over the car-to-car radio to verify the transmissions were being heard, at least on the inferior kel unit.

"Ten-four one." Foster replied.

We heard music. Hayes and I reasoned Carstaphian had elected to deposit some coins into one of those old metal jukeboxes which sit on many tables in those cheap, greasy-spoon diners. It sounded like Carstaphian's first selection was Patsy Cline's "Crazy." His behavior angered Hayes who felt Carstaphian should have known the music would disrupt the transmission and hinder the kel unit.

"Eight, did you tell the Charlie Indian he shouldn't sit near a music source."

"Yes, one. He knows that's a no-no."

Hayes shrugged. "Yea, I bet he does." Hayes turned the monitoring device down to lessen Miss Cline's vocals.

Hayes quickly announced, "This deal is going to be a nut," a phrase we used to indicate a deal was probably not going to be consummated and was a waste of time.

We sat quietly. Hayes periodically adjusted the volume on the receiving device and we heard muffled words but, mostly the continued pattern of music which had now become an unrecognizable song. The sound continued for a little while longer. I still didn't feel the time was right to further agitate Hayes with my problem regarding Mike Kamenski.

"Eight, you monitoring the kel."

"That's a negative, boss. It must be off. I haven't heard anything lately."

Carstaphian, like he had so many times before, had probably turned off the kel transmitter. This time, thanks to the Tech Ops device, the wily informant would continue to be monitored by us. "Well, we're hearing it." Hayes confidentially reiterated as he manipulated the volume on the portable radio which allowed us to continue monitoring the activity inside which appeared to have little, if anything, to do with drug trafficking. Carstaphian wasn't talking to anybody. Occasionally, we heard the clang of ice against a glass. Someone seemed to be laughing. This went on for twenty minutes. Then we heard the sound of the jukebox fading and Carstaphian appeared outside. He walked down three short steps and entered his car. He started the engine and departed. Hayes informed Foster and the rest of surveillance, which only consisted of two other cars.

"This is eight, Charlie is out of the diner, I'm gonna meet him and see what he says." Foster offered.

She drove to a spot near us while we listened to Carstaphian whistling in his car. His transmission was very clear even though he had pulled out of the lot. We watched as he drove up the block and parked close to Foster to update her.

We heard Foster meet with him and we observed Carstaphian jump into her car.

"He said he'll be here in an hour." Carstaphian stated even though we had heard nothing that sounded like negotiations while monitoring the special device.

"Eight to one. The bad guy said he'll be here in an hour," Foster relayed the information to us not knowing we were monitoring his conversation with her.

Hayes looked perplexed and asked me if I had heard anything that sounded like conversation about a deal while the informant was in the restaurant. I told him I had not. "How's he know that, eight?" Hayes inquired.

We could hear Hayes question reverb from Foster's car radio via Carstaphian's transmitter. The echo was confusing but we could understand the informant's response. "I just talked to him on the phone," Carstaphian answered, directing his response to Foster who relayed it back to us. Carstaphian then added, "Don't that dumb nigger boss of yours know how dope deals work?"

The remark was heard by both of us and its transmission was crystal clear. Hayes handed both the portable radio and the car-to-car radio transmitter to me. He calmly unbuckled his seat belt and loosened his tie.

Foster announced, "We are going ten-eight momentarily." Ten-eight meant off the air. "The Charlie India is going to move his car and I'm going to follow him." There was no need to shut her radio off to do so, a fact which did not escape Hayes consideration.

"Tell her to stay right where she is." Hayes stated as he rose and exited the vehicle.

"Negative eight, stay on the air and stay put." I directed but, I saw the tail lights of her Monte Carlo glow and observed her place the car in gear. Hayes had already began walking toward the car. Eager to see Hayes' response to Carstaphian's audacious insult, I requested Foster remain stationary a second time.

"Five-o-eight, stay where you are."

My plea was either ignored or Foster had already had shut her radio off. I exited the passenger's seat and yelled to Hayes who could also clearly see Foster and Carstaphian in her vehicle, pull away. Hayes turned to me. "I thought I told you to tell her to stay where she was."

"I did. She must have already turned her radio off."

Hayes walked back toward the car and I could see anger and rage building in him. I tried to assuage his building frenzy. "Bobby, don't do…"

He cut me off. "Connors, who's the fourteen around here?" referring to his GS pay rating, a fourteen rating denoting he was a supervisor.

"You are, boss," I acknowledged and decided whatever Carstaphian had coming to him he deserved. I just hoped Hayes wouldn't shoot him. Meanwhile, the portable radio I was holding was receiving nothing but intermittent static.

Hayes grabbed the car to car, "Eight you up, where are you?" There was no response. Hayes demanded I maneuver the antennae and hold the radio up until we began hearing their conversation.

"Stick that fucking thing out the window."

"Wiggle it around a little!"

The commands came is rapid succession and each was tendered before the results of the previous one could be determined. "I'm going to find them," he promised.

We began driving around the area, looking for Foster's Monte Carlo. As the minutes elapsed, Hayes frustration mounted. He had been unable to promptly reply to Carstaphian's indignity and he was further vexed by the fact we could not find him even though the snitch had been sitting in a car in front of us only moments before.

"Hold it higher!" Hayes head swiveled wildly as he probed the scene around our speeding car. He was hunched over the wheel like a deter- mined jockey over the mane of his charging second place horse. Suddenly, the portable picked up sporadic transmissions of Carstaphian and Foster's voices. As we approached a traffic signal, their voices became clearer.

"Move around to the side." It was Foster.

"I like when you do it that way." Carstaphian replied.

Hayes looked at me as I him but, neither spoke. Hayes furled his brow in a concerted effort to concentrate on the broken dialogue and decipher exactly what was happening. To do so, Hayes pulled the car over.

"Um…yea. That's it Sandy, baby."

Hayes glared at me and for an instant, I thought he was going to strike me. His fury was boiling and I noticed his grip tightening on the steering wheel.

"Yea…When you going to let me fuck you Sandy. I can't go for this all the time."

"Do you believe this shit?" Hayes asked. I nodded my head and stifled a chuckle. It sounded like Foster was performing fellatio on her inform- ant.

We moved through the intersection and the voices faded into inter- ference. "Find these two, Connor!" Hayes demanded.

"I'm looking." I said but, secretly I hoped we would only get close enough to hear the climactic conclusion of their interlude before it was interrupted.

Hayes accelerated the vehicle. "They must have been down that street we just went through. I'm gonna kill both of them."

We made a right and then another right and the transmission returned to an audible focus.

It was Carstaphian directing Foster, his controlling agent, to lick his balls.

"Mother of Sweet Jesus" Hayes said and I couldn't help but laugh out loud. "Don't Connors or you'll be joining them in a grave." His head pivoted faster from side to side as he searched frantically for the Monte Carlo. The lucid quality of the broadcast indicated we were in close proximity to their location but, we could still not locate Foster's vehicle.

"Do you see them, Connors?"

"No, I don't."

"Well, find them, God-damn it." He ordered again.

Carstaphian proudly announced, "you keep that up and I'm going to come." to which Foster responded, "Not in my mouth this time."

"I was wondering why none of his deals ever go down but at least I know why this bastard is always pretending to set one up."

It was a comedic statement but Hayes did not laugh. We continued down the street, slowly, looking for the libidinous pair. Hayes frustratingly called out over the radio, "Five Oh-Eight."

Carlos Perez responded, "She's ten-eight, one." Perez and the other agent, Desmond Brokenborough had no idea what we were listening to and I tried to figure out how I was going to describe the circumstances to them when we met later.

The transmission was lost again as we continued to circle the block looking for the missing paramours. We drove around the populated neighborhood several times with no luck. I did not offer any snide remarks though hundreds were flowing through my mind. Suddenly, Foster came back on the air.

"We're heading back to the restaurant, one."

"Where are you, eight?" Hayes demanded.

"I had to get fuel, I'm at a gas station at Racine and North."

The station was only a two blocks from our location. "Don't move, Foster. Don't move!" Hayes made a wild U-turn at an intersection and suddenly we were heading south on a one-way northbound street. "Is that...is Carstaphian with you?" Hayes was so irate he mentioned both their last names over the air, a breach of DEA Policy, especially regarding informants though I think, at that point, Carstaphian was no longer considered a DEA informant.

"Yes, the Charlie India is with me." She paused then added, "Don't use the name, boss, he's upset because some of this stuff is monitored."

You have no idea, Foster. I thought.

A car travelling northbound veered quickly into a parking space to avoid a collision with our illegally moving vehicle. The old woman driving her automobile blew her horn and raised a crooked hand to her nose, a gesture which I hadn't seen in years. Hayes was so determined he did not notice. We reached North Avenue and I could see Foster's Monte Carlo backed in next to a small garage. Hayes zoomed toward the vehicle, disregarding a light which had turned red a moment before we proceeded through the crosswalk. Another horn wailed. Our vehicle awkwardly jumped the curb under Hayes' angered control. A hubcap flew off the right rear wheel but its jettison did not concern Hayes who immediately pulled parallel to the Monte Carlo. Carstaphian was sitting in the passenger's seat, grinning.

"What's up Bobby H.?" He asked through his cheesy smile.

Hayes exited the vehicle and proceeded right to the passenger door. "You are," he said as he grabbed a handful of Alexander's neck. He pulled the informant halfway through the open window before realizing the Greek's corpulent waste prohibited him from being extricated through the half-opened window.

Foster shouted, "What are you doing, Bob?"

Hayes opened the door and pulled Carstaphian out, still relying on his overpowering grip to yank the former informant from the passenger's seat. He cocked his left leg and kicked Carstaphian in his buttocks.

"Ow. Why are you doing…Ow" He said as Hayes kicked him a second time. The velocity Hayes' conjured and the subsequent miss of a third kick freed Carstaphian from Hayes' grasp. The impetus of Hayes attempted boot launched his left shoe high into the air. It lazily dropped to the asphalt surface as Carstaphian screamed, "Jesus, are you a crazy man?"

Hayes reached inside his blazer and Carstaphian instinctively yelled "Ow!" I suppose expecting a bullet to sear through the flesh of his fat ass. Carstaphian wisely began running.

Foster knew somehow Hayes was privy to their rendezvous. After her initial objection, she remained silent. Hayes calmly retrieved his shoe and walked back to our car. He entered the vehicle and started the engine. He addressed Foster.

"Don't come back to work until I call you."

Hayes adjusted his tie, returned his glasses to his face and picked up the car to car radio head.

"Group fifteen units. The deal is a nut."

22

I took the next day off and secretly had the window fixed at a car dealership. I considered my options and decided I would remain quiet. The repair cost me $200. I elected to wait and see if Kamenski would contact me with at least an apology. He didn't.

Meanwhile, the Santilles investigation continued with little progress. Jorge Carrasco disclosed Santilles had mentioned he was suspicious about "things." The informant had no idea what we had done and to what extent we were investigating Santilles but, the fact that Santilles had commented on anything at all to his associates indicated skepticism and it worried me. I questioned Walker but, he seemed nonchalant and unconcerned. None of the confidential informants we were utilizing were sure what Santilles' next move would be but, we reasoned he would continue to collect the money. Certainly the lucrative dope trade would not cease because one money courier had slight misgivings. In what turned out to be a futile attempt, we had continued surveillance of the modest homes and businesses that Santilles had visited during the two days he had been in Waukegan. Over the course of the next three months we watched the locations before, during and after each full moon. The surveillances did not prove fruitful and Santilles failed to return to Illinois. Walker had tidbits of information regarding people in the Waukegan area but, not enough intelligence had been accumulated to determine who was delivering the drugs and where it was being stored. We only knew the cells were functioning and they were continuing to supply vast portions of the Upper Midwest with cocaine using Waukegan and tranquil Lake County, Illinois as a base for distribution.

Walker was hesitant to tell the informants anything we learned. He was perpetually concerned he might inadvertently tip off an informant that we were targeting certain people. Walker frequently kept the information he gleaned concealed and at times, didn't even inform fellow case agents about some of his discoveries. In an effort to identify people we didn't know, we began taking photographs but, since most of the activity at these locations occurred at night, the quality of the photos was poor. Though considered a prominent worldwide investigative agency, the Drug Enforcement Administration continued to utilize archaic surveillance equipment. The night vision photography equipment we were using was dated and inadequate and did not help us catalogue or identify anyone. Walker's extreme caution regarding information he disclosed about this case also prevented him from exploiting the FBI or another agency, like U.S. Customs, who were notorious for their use of sophisticated, technical accouterments which would have vastly improved our investigation. To utilize their equipment, Walker would have to share his information and he had no interest in doing that. Consequently, we made no queries to other agencies for help. His peculiar stubbornness expanded to include fellow DEA personnel as well as his old mates at the Waukegan Police Department. The narcotics detectives appealed to Walker to permit them to help but, Walker was content to exploit their equipment, their intelligence and even their informants without reciprocation. I wondered how long the one-sided relationship would last. Privately, I was elated Walker was so discreet because the confidentiality of the information we learned, which had been minimal of late, presented all the more opportunity for me.

I had volunteered to sit on the auto garage because I was very sure that Santilles had picked up his money there. I was extremely interested to learn what transpired there in the evenings so I sat and watched, diligently focusing on the facility. Although the garage had frequent visitors, I observed very little being conducted in the way of automobile repairs. Unfortunately, I didn't notice activity which typically would constitute narcotics trafficking either. I didn't observe packages or bags trading hands and even though the bay doors, as the cool air of fall enveloped the Midwest, usually remained opened, I never saw cars being placed on the hydraulic lift or so much as even a tire being changed. Instead the visitors to the garage seemed to be gathering for social visits. I noticed on a daily basis around 8:30 p.m., the doors would shut and everyone would leave. I knew the evening Santilles had arrived it had been close to midnight. Over the course of several weeks, I spent many evenings watching the auto garage. I disappointingly noted no activity which paralleled what I had observed when Jesus Santilles had visited.

Walker was pleased I had expressed an interest in conducting the surveillances. He had also privately expressed his dismay to me that Sharkey and McKey, his partners and co-case agents, seemed to have no desire to come out and help. One planned surveillance fell in the middle of a three-day weekend. We were, of course, salaried employees, so we received no extra pay for working holidays. Since we set up our own schedules, virtually no one ever worked over three day holidays, including me. However, I saw the personal financial potential of this case and zealously volunteered to assist Walker. Sharkey and McKey did not even show up for the surveillance leaving Walker and I to conduct them ourselves. Although Walker was disgusted, I was delighted. I calculated the less agents involved the better. My onerous motivation was to learn as much as I could about the movements of an individual like Santilles. The more I knew the more robust my chances were of success. Since my interests had incorporated a significantly more sophisticated target in Santilles, I believed it was imperative to my success that if any opportunity arose, I be completely prepared to act.

Grievously, my intent did nothing to develop the case for Walker who incorrectly believed I was participating to assist the progress of the investigation. I felt derelict knowing he trusted me when in truth, I did not intend to tell Walker anything about what I learned other than cursory information which would provide little leads. Actually, the individuals which I observed and had suspected being involved in narcotics trafficking, their descriptions, their vehicles and their activities, I copiously noted but intended to keep to myself. Tragically, if I did by happenstance see Santilles, I was prepared to monitor his activities and deliberately not report his sighting to Walker. Unfortunately, over the course of the nineteen days in three months time I had been on the dedicated surveillances, I had not observed Santilles. The information provided by the CI's had corroborated the theory Santilles had been hesitant to return to Waukegan.

Walker had become increasingly perturbed about the lack of concern or effort his partners were providing. The effect of the tirade unleashed on us by Hayes had waned and McKey and Sharkey had slipped back into their former listless routines. McKey was content to sit at his desk for a few hours talking to his many lady friends, while Sharkey fine tuned his body at our gym and found new places to dine on low-fat salads. Meanwhile, Jim Walker studiously analyzed the growing mound of telephone records he had been subpoenaing from Illinois Bell. It was an effort which I did not advocate. By then, I had been an agent for close to six years, and had spent significant time during my early years analyzing data including telephone records. Like Walker, I had precisely compiled the attenuated records, learning who was telephoning whom, where bad guys lived, their girlfriends addresses and so forth. The information was vital to filling out lengthy DEA reports which served to aggrandize the case file and make supervisors happy. However, I realized that very little investigative leads were produced by the time-consuming analysis. Actually, the records we obtained from Illinois Bell were often delayed by two to three months. Smart traffickers frequently changed their addresses, their phone numbers, their cellular phones and their beepers which constantly rendered the information we obtained stale and basically, useless. What we would end up with would have been great intelligence if we had known the facts as they occurred. Instead, we were at least sixty days behind the paper trail of the traffickers and it was extremely frustrating. Still, the record analysis would provide agents something to do when nothing was happening. And in the Santilles case, nothing was happening.

I noticed Sharkey was spending less and less time in the office. I had wondered why he seemed content to expend so little energy assisting Walker. After all, Sharkey had no other pending cases and since he had not participated in an arrest of an individual he had investigated since his last evaluation, I found his malaise a point of curiosity. After I had began paying closer attention to his behavior, I noticed he had begun to upgrade his wardrobe. Sharkey was usually concerned about his appearance so he customarily wore nice clothes, usually a button-down shirt and freshly pressed slacks but, since I had taken the time to notice, I observed he had purchased a new leather jacket and several fashionable designer sportcoats. I also noticed what appeared to be a Rolex steel and gold Submariner on his wrist, a watch I knew retailed for more than $3,000. Though Sharkey was making a salary over $45,000 I knew he did not have the surplus cash to afford that kind of an expensive accessory. He also was the proud father of a new baby boy and I was sure his wife would never have permitted such an extravagant purchase. I found it to be a queer idea Sharkey was also considering the purchase of a new automobile, something along the lines of an Acura. The more I listened to his conversations, the more inclined I had come to believe he had made his own similar advances into my entrepreneurialships.

I considered the possibilities when he might have had the opportunity to steal cash. Sharkey had not been assigned to any of the warrants that I had worked in the past few months. I knew he had no distinguished cases where he was close to identifying a major trafficker. Of course, one never needed a major trafficker to make a hit. Sharkey could have seized an opportunity working on someone else's case but, I had never known him to be inclined to offer to assist anyone. He could have been renegading on the street, shaking down dopers but that method did not seem to be his style and frankly, I couldn't imagine him pulling it off without the assistance of someone more experienced. Anything was surely possible and the more time I invested trying to figure him out the more frustration I encountered. Admittedly, the notion was absurd but, I found a sense of jealousy pervading my thoughts, as I realized the existence of Sharkey's trinkets was evidence he was succeeding.

I squandered more than a few rides home wondering when and how Sharkey had struck. Then a minor development occurred in the Santilles case. I was astonished to learn that Sharkey had been intrepid enough to make his move right in front of me.

*

Jorge Carrasco called Walker and berated him for blowing a surveillance and fool-heartedly making a small seizure when the possibility existed they could have gotten Santilles with much more. Walker was confounded to learn, after three months, Santilles had been ripped off at O'Hare. According to the CI, Santilles believed he had been robbed at the airport, though he conceded he did not believe it was accomplished by the police. Santilles had confided in someone who had subsequently disclosed to Carrasco that Santilles believed he had been the victim of a burglary at the airport by bumbling thugs. Walker called a meeting of the case agents to reveal the details of what he had learned.

Santilles had placed as much money into his carry on luggage as he could fit, just as I had predicted. In the remaining suitcase, which was larger, he placed the scant supply of underwear and toiletries he had brought with him. In addition, Santilles placed the remainder of the money which would not fit in his carry-on case. Santilles, according to the CI, had picked up more money than he had anticipated and thus had to utilize the second suitcase. The cooperator revealed Santilles had returned to Florida with about $400,000. I felt my greed meter escalate while quietly my blood boiled. Walker went on to say Santilles was almost humored by the ineptitude and misfortune of the thieves. Apparently, Santilles could not find room for some $80,000 and elected to hide it in the larger suitcase, concealed in bath towels and sweat pants within the soft-sided container. When Santilles arrived in Fort Myers, he retrieved his luggage, which he had immediately noticed had been opened. As Walker recounted the tale told by the CI, I noticed an unmistakable paleness manifest itself across Sharkey's face. Apparently, Carrasco said Santilles believed only about $15,000 had been taken from the suitcase while the rest had been left unnoticed and untouched. Santilles, according to the CI, was pleased he had placed the significantly larger amount in his carry-on luggage and the thieves had found only a small portion of his booty. The CI said Santilles regarded the loss lightly and considered it the cost of doing business. Nevertheless, Santilles believed one of the luggage handlers was responsible and vowed not to use Chicago's O'Hare Airport again. Carrasco said he believed Santilles would return to Waukegan in the future to collect receipts but, not until the weather had warmed. Apparently, Santilles dismissed the vehicles he had observed following him near the airport or, at least, did not make the connection between our cars and his loss of a portion of the money. We also learned Santilles had not delegated anyone else to collect the drug receipts and, we hypothesized, Santilles next visit would be for the purposes of collecting an accumulated and substantial quantity.

I waited for Walker to query Barney Sharkey about the suitcase and his inspection of it. Instead, Walker announced he believed Santilles was unaware of how much money he was carrying. It may sound incredulous to the average man but, it certainly is possible to miscalculate a figure as large as $15,000 when varying denominations are collected, counted and transported in such a capricious manner. However, I wholeheartedly trusted Santilles' judgment and experience as a skilled courier. I also believed the information we were receiving from the CI. Santilles knew precisely how much money he was returning to Florida with and his assessment of what had happened had been correct. A baggage handler had stolen his money but, he was not an employee of an airline. He was a DEA Agent and he was also the proud father of a new baby boy.

23

It was getting close to Christmas and things were usually slow. We worked cases when we wanted too and nobody wanted to be bogged down around Christmas time. Everybody preferred to run errands, shop and work a light schedule, so nothing was going on in the way of productive investigations. I never felt particularly guilty about that. I couldn't remember a job I had where the employees didn't slow down at Christmas. The only exception was when I worked behind the audio counter of a retail department store while in my freshman year of college. The holiday season assured a steady flow of family members shopping for cheap gifts, teenagers buying inexpensive clock radios for their parents while the same parents wasted money on over-priced car stereos which they new nothing about. Retail employment can leave someone detesting the holiday season, especially with the bogus Christmas songs playing repeatedly at the insistence of bedraggled store managers desperate to make their numbers.

The Christmas season at DEA meant socializing, fostered by a wide variety of parties sponsored by various government agencies. Some of the DEA personnel, particularly agents, prided themselves on their ability to attend all the major Christmas parties sponsored by each agency in the weeks prior to the holidays. I considered the fetes excellent opportunities to develop new contacts and enhance established ones. In the years I worked for DEA, I regarded the U.S. Marshals Christmas Party to be the best. It always featured plenty of liquor and usually a delectable buffet consisting of wings, ribs and seafood. Their affair was always free and consistently attracted an abundance of good-looking women, none of whom were federal employees but, mostly friends of friends. I joked to a few colleagues they were probably wives and girl-friends of federal prisoners.

It was also a tradition to have a Christmas dinner among members of our own group. We would go out together with the intention of leaving the job behind, concentrating on remodeling old relationships or attempting to develop new ones. Much like other corporate settings, my group mates did not completely cooperate with each other and in some cases there even existed perceptible animosity and contempt fueled mostly be jealousy or egotistical insidiousness. I suppose it was a prod-uct of an environment which forced a bunch of people, each with dis-tinct habits and interests, to work together for a common goal, the eradication of drugs. Unfortunately, each was evaluated on individual success. A cooperative team player, though vitally important, was often overlooked. The concept of the team was left on the shelf at the basic academy's dormitories. Though success was occasionally determined by the agent producing the best results it more often was governed by whom the boss liked most. It was an unusual setting but nevertheless, one in which I attempted to flourish. I worked at establishing cordial relationships with most people in the group however, there were a cou-ple I just didn't like. The Christmas party was designed to reduce those feelings of ill-will and celebrate the season. Hayes acknowledged the existence of egos but, despised the fact some people refused to get along with each other. Though Hayes was capable of grasping the concept he elected to reject the existence of feuds and competition. He was a good manager who really wanted his people to be happy. He considered a Christmas dinner party an excellent prescription for establishing friendship and trust. I agreed with his assumption but some, of course, did not. Hayes liked his drink and expected others to as well. There were teetotalers in our group who viewed the affair as little more than an extended drinking session. I have to admit, they were right. However, Hayes believed liquor facilitated the socialization process. Again, I concurred and looked forward to the party while a few thought it was in their best interest to ignore it. Hayes invited members of other groups to come in their place and the party usually turned into a drinking orgy.

Hayes took great pride in making dinner arrangements and setting up economical deals. He boasted about the feasts he could arrange and how little they would cost. When analyzed, Hayes' parties never featured any spectacular savings of money but in assuming control, we decided, Hayes main objective was to insure the party would not be held in a Mexican restaurant. Hayes detested fare with origins south of the border.

It was a week before Christmas and Hayes had announced we were going to a popular Greek restaurant on Halsted. It was in Chicago's Old Greek town and I had no objections because it was within easy walking distance of one of my favorite local bars, McDugan's. Hayes insisted everyone in the group attend but, some chose against it. Sandy Foster was still embarrassed by the discovery of her episode with Alexi Carstaphian. Hayes had not pursued disciplinary action against her and had demanded my secrecy regarding the incident. It was an impossible request for me to honor since the story was so hilarious. I had told a few trusted people who had also confided in some of their friends and after a week or so the whole story had made its rounds through our office. By the time it had gotten back to me, Foster was suspended and contrived rumors had spread about how she had been screwing all her informants, was pregnant by one and had appeared in two pornographic movies. I recognized I was not completely to blame for the scandal when Hayes confessed he had told at least two people himself. In addition to our indiscreet lover, Brenda Xavier and Phil Vreeswyck also neglected to attend for reasons known only to themselves. It was so simple to go along with the program but for dogmatic or petty reasons a small minority reaped great satisfaction refusing to do so.

Hayes knew the owner of the restaurant, a Greek immigrant who had only been in the United States for seven years. On the occasion of that particular Christmas party, Hayes had not been exaggerating. We were treated royally. The proprietor, Christos Theosopolous, was quite proud to have a large contingent of federal agents and support personnel dining in his establishment and elected to showcase us by seating us in the middle of his elaborately adorned dining room. He pulled three large tables together to accommodate our party of seventeen. We were treated to an assortment of appetizers which included specialty dishes like taramasalada and fassoli. We chomped down the native goodies with blissful shouts of "Opa!" while Theosopolous did more than a capable job of keeping us in our cups with an ample supply of subtly potent Greek wine.

We had begun our lunch at 1:00 p.m. and had remained at the establishment drinking late into the afternoon and long after the meal was consumed. I would estimate of those who had begun indulging in the wine, and I was among them, each found themselves falling under the trance of its inebriating properties. One of the agents who was particularly rollicking was Wendell Mack, a gangly agent from Group 6, the heroin group. Mack always meant well but, occasionally came up short. He was by no means a drinker but admirably, he attempted to keep pace with our boss and the seasoned others. He recognized the importance of consorting with management and acutely observed his boss, Frank Willis, was one of Hayes' close office associates. When Willis accepted Hayes' invitation to join our luncheon, Mack saw it as an opportunity to be included as well. Hayes extended an invitation to Wendell and he eagerly accepted.

I could clearly see Mack was intoxicated. He had started speaking loudly at 3:00 p.m. and by 4 o'clock he had made several improper and slurred toasts. His superior, Willis, should have cut him off but it was the holidays and the overwhelming theme was to "have another." Besides, I think Willis was surreptitiously entertained by Mack's folly.

Wendell was one of those guys who constantly wanted to demonstrate to everyone how intelligent he was. He would quote the Holy Bible, Shakespeare, Socrates and other notorious written works and their respected authors. Not being particularly well-read myself, I could never discern whether he was making items up or simply misquoting words but, whatever he said, the message always seemed slightly erroneous. Once he had wished an agent, who was planning an investigative trip to Bogota, a safe journey by stating he would say a prayer to Job, who he incorrectly announced was the patron saint of travel. His remarks, though certainly well meaning, often elicited snickers. Admittedly though, he was harmless and was generally viewed as a decent person to have around.

Greek wine may not have a robust flavor but, it vigorously assaults conventionality when it is consumed in large quantities. I had noticed we had emptied approximately twenty-one quart bottles. The restaurant and some of its patrons had no doubt had their meals ruined by our boisterous behavior which had approached levels of obnoxiousness early in the afternoon. I personally heard Christos explaining to one large table that our conduct should be excused because our assembly consisted of very overworked policeman who had spent our entire year working in dangerous and life-threatening situations. I remember Theosopolous' distorted explanation drew a reaction of noticeable disdain from the unimpressed table.

As the hour approached six p.m., after almost five hours of assiduous drinking, Mack decided he wanted to tell a Greek joke he had remembered from college. Again, I thought it would be inappropriate and I recalled the only Greek jokes I could remember all involved anal intercourse or some reference to it. As Mack began to tell the joke, he seized the urgency to rise from his chair and climb atop it. The effect served little purpose other than adding to the potential for the disaster which soon followed. Mack wobbled and mis-stated the joke by telling the punchline too soon. He said the joke was so funny he at least, be granted the opportunity to re-tell it.

Mack was interrupted by Desmond Brokenborough, who constantly did his best to monitor and check Wendell's behavior. Desmond was a well respected agent in the office and Mack emulated him. Wendell Mack usually listened to him but under these conditions, the wine racing through Mack's head, drowning any degrees of decorum, he refused to heed Brokenborough's sagacious advice.

"Wendell, at least conceal your gun. Man, your gun is sticking out." Brokenborough warned.

And indeed it was. Mack's posture atop the chair and the appearance of the weapon gave the impression Mack was planning to announce a hold-up. Mack responded by grasping the gun, whose handle stuck precariously out from under his wool sweater. Instead of slipping the hem over the protruding plastic and metal grip, Mack removed the gun from his waistband. I heard a scream and the outcry startled Mack from his perch. He slipped backwards, clasping the gun as he dropped. The firearm discharged and before Mack's back hit the carpeted floor, he had wounded the mount of an expensive chandelier. Brokenborough jumped from his chair and disarmed Wendell Mack before he could accidentally shoot anything or anyone else. I had the wherewithal to duck under the table when I observed the gun's barrel rise toward the ceiling. I didn't see the felling of the chandelier but, I heard a second scream and the crash of a table of glass and metal.

"Its O.K. It's an accident. We are cops. We're the police." Brokenborough yelled. He secured Mack's weapon and held his own credentials in the air. The gold badge still managed to glint in the dim light of the restaurant despite the tarnish of Wendell Mack's actions. The announcement was of no comfort to an older couple who leaped from the seats and hustled out the rear door through the kitchen. Christos came running through the doors by which they exited, screaming. He thought his place was being robbed and admirably came out wielding an iron skillet to ward off the armed felon. Hayes jumped up toward Christos and reassured him. Mack collected himself and sat with his head in his hands, his drunken revelry displaced by the quick realization he had seriously jeopardized his career, not to mention all the patrons. I could not help but look at the astonished faces of my fellow coworkers. Though the mistake was serious, most tried to conceal their uncontrollable laughter.

After order was restored, a middle-aged and determined lady approached our table and sternly requested to see Brokenborough's badge. She demanded to know what unit of the Chicago Police Department for whom we worked. Someone deceivingly mentioned juvenile crimes before Bobby Hayes intervened.

"Maam, I am extremely sorry for what has happened. Are you alright?"

She realized she had the attention and sympathy of Bobby Hayes, who by his demeanor and age, she correctly assumed was in charge of our pathetic group of rag-tag drunken diners. Peculiarly but, of no surprise to me, Mack's boss, Frank Willis, remained seated and silent and allowed Hayes to assimilate the woman's scorn.

"Sir, I have been in here for approximately an hour and I have never witnessed such a disgusting and slovenly display."

Christos, who had been talking to Hayes, attempted to subdue the women's anger by offering her and her companion a complimentary dinner.

Instead Hayes commendably assumed responsibility for our conduct. "Miss, you are absolutely right. We have been drinking and…"

"No! That is no excuse. I demand to see your identification. An apology is not quite good enough. Some of you should be arrested."

Chad Jennings shouted, "Go ahead lady, call the police. We are the police."

"No Jennings, shut it down." Hayes responded. There was no way to cover this one up and Hayes begrudgingly removed his credentials from his rear pocket.

"Maam, we are with the Drug Enforcement Administration." Hayes held out his identification for the complete review of the overwrought woman. The photo of his face taken ten years earlier looked significantly more dignified than it had at that instant.

"Mr. Hayes, if these hooligans are your men, you should be ashamed."

"Don't say a thing about him, lady, It was my fault." Wendell Mack stood up, angered by the bashing that Hayes was undertaking because of his unbecoming actions.

"Mack, shut your mouth." Willis declared.

"Not before I get his name," the woman sneered. "Give me his name and every name at this table, Mr. Hayes. I intend to complain to the city."

The woman had failed to realize we were federal workers, not employees of the city or state. It did not matter. The woman would find out who we were and file a complaint. Hayes offered to comply but, only agreed to supply his own name.

"Everyone's name won't be necessary. I am the supervisor of these people and I'll take responsibility for their actions." Hayes relinquished his business card to the irate woman and then requested we all leave. Temporarily satiated, the woman stammered back to her table where her nervous and chagrined husband timidly awaited her.

We collected our jackets, paid our bill and left. Brokenborough took Mack home and Hayes hailed a cab. I walked down to McDugan's and looked for someone to tell.

24

With the Santilles investigation stalled, I found myself volunteering for other assignments to help fellow agents make cases both in my group and outside it. I generally was available and never turned anyone down if they needed a helping hand in a surveillance or an arrest. I enjoyed going out and doing the work. It continued to be exciting despite my alternative interests in lining my own pockets. There still existed a burning desire within me to put bad people in jail even though I was objective enough to admit I myself, had joined the ranks of the criminal element. I had rationalized no persons were getting hurt by my actions, and believed I simply had the guts, the intelligence and the guile to carefully identify opportunities and relieve my targets of part of their ill-gained booty. In helping other agents, I hoped that every arrest would yield a successful dope dealer, who in turn, would create financial probability for myself.

As I volunteered for more assignments, I found I yearned to steal more money. I was at the point where the first thoughts that entered my mind were how I take money even though I was thrilled to enter homes and apartments to conduct arrests.

Ideally, narcotics and most law enforcement operations involving undercover agents attempt to conduct negotiations and deliveries in public places to lessen the risk of gunfire and robberies. This principle was based on the simple theory a bad guy was less likely to resort to violence if his actions might be witnessed by several if not dozens of people. Unfortunately, bad guys began to realize negotiating deals in public places was a common tactic of law enforcement. Dealers, the astute ones, began changing their methods of delivery. The greedy dopers still would do virtually anything to turn a profit and they were often investigated and easily apprehended. The intelligent traffickers began backing off from deals in public places to the point if an under-cover agent suggested a public spot, dealers sensed a sting operation and would cease negotiations with undercover agents. Dealers moved their transactions from parking lots, restaurants and malls and trans-ferred their operations inside, often renting apartments, houses or utilizing small businesses where they were familiar with the owner and the clientele. For a stipend, people were very happy to perform duties which hindered law enforcement. Lookouts were paid a few dollars to stand guard while dealers negotiated hundred thousand dollar deals in back rooms and kitchens. This technique created a dan-gerous situation for law enforcement personnel, who often waited outside locations as many as four blocks away to lessen the chances of being observed. When a deal would go down, the arrest team would rush to the scene as quickly as possible but the distance between them and the target's location often included pedestrians and traffic, required precious seconds to transverse. Drug deals involving tens of thousands and often hundreds of thousands of dollars are very tense situations. No one trusts anybody. With all that money around, people become very greedy and act in ways they normally would not. Sometimes rational thinking goes out the window, even faster than the crooks alluding the police.

When undercover arrests were conducted in this manner, chaos was often the result. People would be running in all directions. Crooks, spot-ters and even uninvolved pedestrians would find themselves in a confused scene. It was easy to become disoriented, especially with cars speeding and screeching and unidentified people in street clothes racing around carrying shotguns, machine guns and battering rams. Spirited public chases would often ensue and people would be tackled, punched, kicked and sometimes shot. Both good guys and bad guys were subject. The arrest team usually was in the midst of the commotion and it was the position I most enjoyed. I always wanted to participate in the arrest. It was dangerous but I believed in my training and abilities besides, the adrenaline rush was fantastic and taking somebody's liberty was an ego trip as well. As soon as the signal went down, I gave it my all to protect the undercover and my fellow agents. I had to because I needed to believe they were doing the same for me. As my stealing endeavors persisted, I continued to relish the opportunity to be on the arrest team. However, after a successful arrest was executed and everybody was secured, my focus did not become the acquisition of evidence. It had became the acquisition of cash money for myself.

In Chicago, bad guys began utilizing separate apartments to conduct deals. The apartments were usually flop houses but, occasionally, an amateurish dealer would use his own place. Even unskilled dealers by nature of the lucrative business often made considerable money despite their incompetence. A dealer who used his own residence was easily identified. Doltish dealers who risked their own apartments and residences were easy targets for my endeavors. They always had the drugs and their money in the same place. After arresting the guy, we would search the residence. I found myself separating from other agents, looking in rooms where no one was. I was looking for places where money was concealed, not drugs. The quantities of drugs we often were looking for could not have been found in wallets, strongboxes or purses. But that is where I searched. Always interested in picking up a few hundred or thousand dollars. It was pocket change compared to the big heist I had planned to pull off but, it was too enticing to pass up. I had become addicted to robbing cash.

I wondered if anyone ever noticed. I suspected they hadn't but, I as my experience expanded, I periodically noticed similar conduct by others. I saw other agents behaving in the same manner, searching spots they would not expect to find guns or drugs. They were not always DEA Agents. In fact, they were from a variety of law enforcement agencies. I even observed an FBI Agent acting strangely on one arrest. There were instances of county sheriffs, detectives, uniformed police, IRS Agents, and others who I identified as possible thieves like me. Though the ATF Agent, Mike Kamenski, had been the only one up until that point I had visually observed, I knew there were others, including my own group mate, Barney Sharkey. I remained mindful of other strange behavior and was certain that others were doing exactly as I was. I did not know to what extent until February of the new year.

I had been asked by Bobby Hayes to assist another group in the execution of a series of arrest and search warrants. Several agents had been working on a Hispanic dope dealer who had ties to a brutal street gang known, rather auspiciously, as the "Imperial Gangsters." Like all the street gangs functioning in Chicago, the Imperial Gangsters derived substantial income from illegal activity which included robbery, gun peddling and, of course, narcotics sales. Each gang also had established "trademarks" which differentiated particular gangs from one another. The Vice Lords, an organized black gang operating on Chicago's West Side, relied on behavior they called "violations" to keep members obedient and non-members intimidated. The violations were beatings, murders and arsons that were requested and sanctioned by the hierarchy of the gang. They could be authorized against members of the gang who did something the established leaders did not like or they could be utilized against individuals outside the gang who posed a threat to the activities or profits of the Vice Lords. Violations could be endorsed against members of law enforcement, civil, political or judicial leaders but, usually violations were only carried out against individuals who had little means to fight back, like merchants, neighborhood folks and weak gang members.

The Latin Eagles, a North Side gang primarily comprised of Hispanic individuals with a small mixture of white and black youth were known for their perverse initiation rights which included, for females, a rite called "dice." The dice referred to the requirement by females wishing to gain admission to the gang to take a pair of die and roll it. The number that would be rolled, anywhere from two to twelve, would be the number of men in the gang the female would be required to sexually satisfy in order to gain acceptance into the gang. It was a strange and bizarre initiation rite but, oddly, I found during interrogations of female members of the Latin Eagles, it was a mandate women were proud to complete. I was told some of the girls were often fourteen or younger when they performed this ritual of passage.

At this time, authorities estimated there were approximately thirty seven thousand gang members in Chicagoland with ties to as many as forty-one different gangs. The Imperial Gangsters, like most of their Chicago gang counterparts, were violent. However, the Imperials were known for their extreme viciousness and the extravagant manner in which they carried it out. I was told by Chicago's Gang Crime Detectives of an incident involving a suspected police snitch who had been brutally murdered by the Imperials. The gang's trademark in carrying out murders was adopted from the Cali Cartel in Columbia which utilized armed men on motorcycles to carry out hits. A motorcyclist and a passenger sitting with his back to the driver of the cycle would speed by a mark leaving the passenger in position to open fire on the target, often in a publicly crowded street or park. The Imperials employed the same technique however, they glamorized it one step further. Both the cyclist and the shooter, who would be armed with a heavy assault weapon, like an AK-47 or a Mac 10 capable of emptying an entire clip of thirty rounds in less than two seconds, would outfit themselves in black ninja clothes to carry out an assassination. In the instance of the snitch who had been shot, two units of ninjas on motor-cycles had been used to carry out the murder. The individual, who had in fact been a Chicago informant for less than two weeks, was riddled with sixteen bullets while he stood on a corner purchasing a shaved water ice from a street vendor. During the altercation, the vendor, who was an innocuous but revered and harmless old man in the neighbor-hood was also shot and killed as well as an eight year old girl who had the misfortune of innocently indulging herself in a flavored ice that day. I was told the Imperials paid a large cash stipend to both families of the vendor and the girl to ease the loss of their loved ones. However, no one was prosecuted and witnesses who understandably, feared for their own lives, stated all they saw were individuals, race unknown, dressed in black pajamas.

What was particularly horrifying and sadistic, in addition to the deaths of the three people, was the actions the Imperials undertook during the suspected snitch's funeral services. His viewing was held at a North Side funeral home at approximately 2:30 in the afternoon. Though the home was not particularly crowded with mourners, the intersection where the parlor existed was active. There was a busy, fast food restaurant and a gas station at opposite corners. I was told by C.P.D. gang crime units during the viewing, two motorcycles pulled up with four individuals wearing the familiar ninja costumes aboard. It was unknown then as it remains to this day if these were the same indi-viduals who had carried out the murders or volunteers also eager to demonstrate their loyalty to the Imperials. The ninjas stormed into the funeral home and rushed the casket containing the body of the slain snitch. To the horror of the mourners, which included the man's wife, 5 year-old daughter and mother, the ninjas yanked the body from the cas-ket while simultaneously waving guns in the air to effectively intimidate and deter interference. The ninjas dragged the lifeless corpse through the home past screaming friends, horrified relatives and felled chairs and into the busy intersection where the four of them stood over the body and pumped automatic weapon rounds into the corpse. The agonizing mother attempted to intervene and rushed the assailants. She was rebuffed with a swipe of a pistol's butt across her face, a strike which opened a large wound across her forehead. The assailants returned to their motorcycles casually leaving both the bleeding mother and the son's ravaged carcass prone in the street. Again, there were no willing witnesses and with a gang as violent, there was no doubt in my mind why anyone would be hesitant to testify against the members of such a feared group. Without witnesses or a confession, it was difficult if not impossible to prosecute the individuals responsible for such heinous acts. A detective once told me "You might have all the evidence in the world but, if you don't have a witness or a confession, most juries won't convict. They want all their murder trials to be wrapped up, start to finish, in an hour, just like they see on TV" He added, as a commentary on his opinion about most victims of crime, "These people bring it on themselves" and he left it up to my imagination to figure out who "these people" were.

It was the members of the Imperials in which my counterparts in another group had been so vigorously pursuing. After the investigation, which had lasted some ten months and involved multiple undercover purchases, wire-taps, and long surveillances, the case agents had produced enough information to gain indictments and search warrants against some of the high ranking members of the Imperials. I had been asked to provide assistance to one of the members of that group, Sonny Jenkins, who had been given a minor task, search a storage locker rented by one of the Imperials.

Storage lockers in the germane world are used to store things which can't be placed anywhere else. Usually these items are of little monetary value but, are of enough importance, they are not considered rubbish. People store old furniture, books, clothes and knick-knacks they want to preserve. Businesses often utilize storage lockers to house promotional and seasonal items they do not have room to warehouse. In the narcotics trafficking world, storage lockers safeguard contraband and assets that dealers don't want to be associated or found to be in possession. That list could include drugs, drug manufacturing equipment, automobiles, guns and other related assets. I had not encountered it, but some agents were discovering dealers were using storage facilities to warehouse large amounts of monies. I had not participated in many search warrants which had yielded anything of interest or value at a storage facility but, I hoped the particular Imperial to whom I was assigned the task of executing a search warrant might have stored something significant if not at least interesting, though I doubted it would be money. I just couldn't imagine salting thousands of dollars away in such a publicly accessible place. I couldn't fathom having access to such a large sum of money and leaving it in a place as uncontrolled and unadorned as a cinderblock storage locker for safekeeping. Instead, I thought maybe the locker would contain dope or maybe even another corpse.

I met Sonny Jenkins, the agent from group three, at the predetermined location. He seemed perturbed that I had actually showed up, though at the time, I was not sure why. In passing, he told me we were also scheduled to meet two other detectives from the Chicago Gang Crimes unit. I thought it was peculiar we were going to use four people to serve a search warrant on an unoccupied storage locker. I asked Sonny and he told me the locker was as big as a one car garage and he had no idea what or how much of it the locker might contain. He requested I drive my own car to the location so that if a large amount of items were seized, we could utilize two cars to transport it back to our offices. Having been on fruitless search warrants before, I was glad to accommodate him, knowing full well that the location of the locker facility was closer to my residence than the meet spot. I anticipated conducting the search and going home early. When the two Chicago detectives arrived, I was introduced and the four of us proceeded to the storage facility. I noticed the two detectives, who were very friendly with Sonny, both drove in his car, rendering little room in his mid-size vehicle to transport evidence. My initial inclination was to protest because I supposed Sonny was planning to let me be responsible for the transportation and processing of any evidence found while he went merrily about his business after the warrant was concluded. Before making my concern an issue, I decided to wait to see what the warrant produced before I would protest.

We were irritated to find the management offices closed when we arrived at the facility. It was midday and we fully expected the facility and its offices to be open. The storage place was large with over 700 garages of varying rectangular sizes. We could not get into the storage area without a digitized keyboard code whose perimeter was guarded by a chain link gate and fence. The boundary security was easy enough to circumvent. Another person came to the facility and entered and we thought about following him in but, Sonny conceded we were not sure exactly which storage locker was the suspect's and we needed verification from the custodian and his records. I asked Sonny how the case agents had obtained a search warrant if they weren't sure which container was his. Sonny smiled and shrugged. I found an alarm company's sticker on the deserted office's window and called hoping to find an owner or manager. The alarm company said they would notify the proprietor and he would telephone me on my cellular phone. After a half-hour's wait, a manager finally called and disclosed he was over an hour away but, would come as quickly as possible. By the background noise over the phone, I surmised he was in a tavern.

I entered Sonny's vehicle and notified him about the manager and the longer delay. When I entered the car, I noticed my abrupt appearance disturbed one of the detectives who had been sitting in the front seat conversing with Jenkins. The detective apparently had not expected me back and seemed irritated I had unexpectedly opened the car door. I stifled my own annoyance and walked away with the perception I was not wanted. Sonny beeped the horn and gestured for me to return. I walked back to the car and entered the front seat as the detectives exited the car. When I was satisfied they were out of earshot, I asked Sonny if they had any problems with me personally. He assured me they did not. He admitted he had known them a long time and they had an impression of "Feds" that was not favorable. I told Sonny I had already noticed. After a few minutes, the detectives returned to the car and both entered the rear seat bringing with them a noticeable air of uneasiness. The detectives did not address me directly but, spoke to Sonny. Immediately, I sensed something sinister.

"Sonny, this is bullshit, we should just open up the locker. If it ain't his we'll just close it up. Fuck, I'll buy a two dollar lock for it." The detective spoke right behind me, talking to Sonny but, scattering my hair with his close and agitated breath. I sensed he thought it was my fault we were waiting. I elected to remain silent, as did Sonny.

A few moments passed with no one speaking. The angry detective, a white man with a pot belly, prematurely graying hair and an unshaven face, started again, "Sonny, let's just fucking do it."

"I would Frank, but I'm really not sure which one it is. I mean the guy changed his locker a couple times and we have to hit the right one."

The other detective inquired, "Well how many are there? Two, three or what?"

Sonny replied, "The records said he just changed last week. He rented it the summer of last year and changed in October. Now he just changed it again."

'Man, I am sure tired of waiting on these mothers!" Frank proclaimed.

I heard the second detective speak and before I could consider what the reason for their impatience was, he spoke again.

"What did the CI say, he kept all his money over here or what ?"

Now I knew, the money. The detectives had their designs on cash and before I could formulate Sonny's motivation, I noticed him glance into the rear view mirror and raise his eyebrows, a gesture intended to evince displeasure at the detective's obtrusive announcement. There was no doubt why I was not welcome but, as circumstances stood, now I was sitting in the car and probably was going to be part of it, willing or not. There was silence, this time a little longer than before.

I sat looking out the passenger's window, waiting for the manager who I knew to still be at least forty-five minutes away. As I stared out through the window I realized I was at another precarious point in my life, a setting where a decision could significantly change my direction, for the better or for the much worse. I considered the last few months and people like Maldonado, Kamenski. I resolved they had made the crucial mistake of donating their control to the whims of others.

Sonny, I suppose, felt compelled to say something, for he knew as did everyone else what the intentions of the occupants of our vehicle were. "The CI said this guy keeps his dope and his money here."

"That's cool." I replied, hoping to deflect the tension and appear like I had not sensed their illegal intentions. "I guess it will be worthwhile."

"It fucking better be." The detective known as Frank replied and added without hesitation. "I didn't work this case with these scum sucking jag-offs to come up empty. These guys are killing people and getting rich doing it. They got everybody scared. They took over my old neighborhood. Shit, my mother is still there and these fucking jag-offs have broke in twice."

Detective Frank, I supposed, had taken my expression as an agreement to enter into whatever conspiracy he planned. I had no desire to be a confederate with these guys whom I did not know and certainly did not trust, Sonny included. While I mulled my predicament, the detective elected to expound his position.

"These gangbangers, they don't know work. They sleep all day and gang-bang all night, ripping cars, shooting and fucking. What a life, don't do a fucking thing. Just dirty up this city."

The second detective was better dressed, fit and more polished but, only slightly. He was younger than Frank but, still some fifteen years older than me. He chimed in, "Whatever we find in here, we find together, right Sonny."

I glanced at Sonny and he was visibly uncomfortable. He looked straight ahead and did not immediately reply. He probably thought the same thing I thought, these guys are absolutely reckless. They had not known me for more than an hour and they were proposing an alliance that would place us all behind bars for the better part of our remaining years if we were ever caught. I had tried to think fast and suddenly found myself hoping the manager would forget about us and sit in the bar all day, drinking gin and tonics until he passed out.

The second detective spoke again, "I'm saying we are all cops and when it comes down to it, that's what we got to remain, a fraternity. We are in this together against them, against everybody. We got to stick together and if we don't we all will lose in the end" He paused, then explained, "I mean we are all just cops! No one is better in here than the other. There ain't no fucking Feds in here and their ain't no city dicks, all of us just cops with badges that say we got to stick together. You know what I mean, us against these jag-offs, Sonny?"

There was no reply.

I waited for Sonny's answer for some indication as to what my response should be. Surely Sonny knew these guys and I surmised he probably had done similar things in the past but, now these guys had boldly announced to another agent, one they had never met, what their ambitions were to be. They were that defiantly injudicious.

"Hey, I said something and I expect an answer."

The second detective had addressed Sonny but, now I could feel his eyes on me. I slowly turned my head toward him. He was seated behind Sonny but, he was looking directly at me with an obvious disgusted sneer on his face.

Fuck you, was my first thought but, I didn't say it.

"Like I said, there are no fucking holier-than-though Feds in here, just fucking cops, right." As he made his last remark he raised his service revolver in his right hand. He cocked the weapon and placed it to the head of his partner, Frank, who was seated to his right. "If someone thinks about giving it up, this is what they get."

Instead of fear, I felt fury. These detectives held such little regard for me they felt they could bully and threaten me like they did the petty criminals they worked over in the street. I no longer felt intimidated and instead of yielding to their threats, I assumed a stance of rectitude that surprised me when I thought about it afterward.

"You can do what you want." I turned toward Sonny and addressed him. "Sonny, I hope you know I am cool. Whatever happens here will happen with out me. I got things to take care of and I got better things to do than sit here and wait for some fat, grease-ball manager to open up an empty locker with nothing but dusty old, dirty magazines." I exited Sonny's car and entered my own, leaving the three of them to do as they wished.

As I drove home, I was confident I had identified at least three more colleagues who were in the same racket as me. I wondered how many more there could be and if any could dare be more reckless.

25

Throughout the chilly Illinois winter, Walker continued to scour the ponderous information piling up on his desk, most of which had been acquired through the use of administrative subpoenas. The growing mound of paperwork included subscriber and telephone toll records, hotel logs, rental car registries, airline manifests, property deeds, automobile title histories and daily reports of mail covers being conducted by the United States Postal Service. U.S. Postal Inspectors offer a service which entails logging every piece of mail delivered to a particular address. They will notate to whom it was addressed, from where it was sent and the post mark. It is a tedious process if several pieces of mail are being delivered to a location. Walker did not endear himself to the inspectors when he provided them with a subpoena for 21 different mail covers. Two or three were usually sufficient but Walker was a fanatical data collector. The majority of records contained identifying information which was of little use to our investigative efforts. It was common knowledge only trustworthy and honest people submitted legitimate names and addresses. The criminal element, especially the sophisticated ones, maintained a host of aliases which insulated and protected their true identities and I found the most skilled of these were foreign born persons who had no real identity in the United States anyway. The colossal pile of papers did contain information relating to the cells operating in and around Waukegan but, because there was simply so much undeciphered and obscure material, finding it would more likely be attributable to fortune than good detective work. Nevertheless, I half-heartedly assisted Walker in compiling a rudimentary chart of the cells which included the aliases of possible warehousers, distributors and revenue collectors. The flowchart we conceived was based primarily on conjecture and speculation, with one exception, Jesus Santilles. He was the one person positively identified as a known and confirmed money courier.

The case, which had yet to prove its worthiness in the front office, still offered great potential. However, McKey and especially Sharkey, seemed quite content to go about other activities, none of which had much to do with narcotics enforcement. I remained curious about Sharkey's activity and I was certain he had stolen money out Jesus Santilles' luggage. I watched his movements and paid specific attention to his behavior. He had not made mention of the purchase of an Acura since the informant's report of the theft from Santilles but, I couldn't resist the temptation to bring it up during an informal group bullshit session. I asked Sharkey when he was going to purchase that car he had talked so much about but, he dismissed the question by telling me and everyone else who cared to listen he realized the car's price was "way out of his league." I chuckled while noticing Sharkey had also ceased wearing his $3,000 watch, replaced by the moderately priced Seiko he had been accustomed to wearing. In fact, Sharkey had made no more extravagant purchases since Carrasco's revelation and his new conservative charade had me convinced he had managed to grab at least fifteen grand for himself.

Jorge Carrasco, our most reliable informant, contacted Walker and revealed he believed Santilles was planning to return to Waukegan. He wasn't certain when but, the next full moon would be visible at the end of the week. I expected Walker to request another dedicated surveillance by our team. I noticed McKey and Sharkey paid no attention to the lunar calendar and had been given only slightly more attention to the case. I had assumed Sharkey would probably be content never to see Santilles again for fear somehow his thieving efforts might come to light. Rasheed McKey did not appear as if he cared one way or the other. Meanwhile, I had spent days considering excuses and advice I would furnish Walker regarding surveillance of Santilles. I planned to tell Walker I would not be available due to personal plans and following him might not be a good idea unless we had the full commitment of the entire group. I intended to advise Walker that Santilles would be extremely cautious in his activity and a poor surveillance would destroy any opportunities to interdict his contraband in the future. My intention in attempting to derail the surveillance was completely self-serving. I had planned to follow Santilles myself without the interference of my groupmates.

I hoped Walker's partners' lack of interest and my hints would encourage Walker to leave Santilles alone, though I never imagined Walker would consider anything but a dedicated and committed surveillance of Santilles. If the case needed a break, it would come through Santilles since he was the only validated high ranking member who had been identified. I was astonished when Walker decided on his own he did not want to tail Santilles for fear the Colombian would make the surveillance. Walker elaborated and said he believed Santilles was coming to Waukegan to make a dry run and the sole purpose of his mission would be to determine if he was being tailed. In deciding against the surveillance, Walker elected to rely on the competence of his able bodied informants who, he believed, would be in position to relate the distinct purposes of Santilles trip.

I concluded Walker's decision was ludicrous. In my opinion, a man like Santilles did not come to Waukegan to test the waters. He came for a specific reason and that was to collect the cell's receipts. Our intelligence had established monies had not been collected by Santilles for over three months. It was a possibility the cell had authorized someone else to collect the money and if that were true, our informants had not known who the person was. However, if so, there was no reason for Santilles, who apparently did not like Chicago, to return to the area. I decided if Santilles was going to come back to Waukegan, I was going to be there to observe what he did. I salivated while I enacted my own strategy to follow Santilles.

*

It was the last day of the work-week, Friday, which also fell on the third of the month and the first visible full moon in two. I had a meeting with an Assistant U.S. Attorney earlier in the day regarding a case I had worked, a three kilo buy-bust which had happened over nine months ago. The case was finally coming around for trial and the AUSA wanted to make sure I had prepared all the transcripts regarding the undercover negotiations between the undercover agent, the CI and the bad guy. I told him I had but, I had not completed them. The US Attorney's Office was full of some of the most anal retentive people I had ever met. They were terrified at the prospect they might end up in court without having turned something meaningless over to the defense for discovery purposes. Many of the prosecutors were so determined to present every shred of information compiled by investigators their sincere efforts served only to help otherwise overwhelmed attorneys formulate a defense. While the defendant's counselors never submitted information to the prosecution, so much information was disseminated by the prosecutor, investigators and attorneys lost track of insignificant details which were turned over. Consequently, a shrewd defense attorney might focus on one document containing notes which had no bearing in the case and turn it around to make the investigator appear incompetent on the witness stand during testimony. On one occasion, I had mentioned to a prosecutor I had written a defendant's license plate on a fast food napkin during a quick-moving surveillance. When I couldn't produce the napkin because it had been thrown out after the arrest, along with the greasy chicken nuggets they had been served with, the prosecutor nearly telephoned the defense attorney to arrange for a desperate plea. I subsequently rescued the case by lying and telling the attorney I had also jotted down the number on my car seat. Believe it or not, the prosecutor immediately informed the defense attorney and later, for court purposes, I was required to remove the front seat of my car and bring it to court, all to "prove" the car's plate I had initially written was the same one the defendant had secured on his vehicle when we arrested him, two hours later. It was ridiculous and the charade cost the taxpayers $850 to dismantle the old seat and install another. As a recourse against such farcical adventures, many investigators simply discarded frivolous information rather than turn it over to the defense to be subject to pointless and confusing cross-examination later.

Instead of focusing on the transcripts, I prepared a few short reports and left the office. I had taken a walk on State Street to think but my mind was restless. I thought about the possibilities of going to Waukegan. What if I actually saw Santilles and I observed him picking up bags and suitcases. What would I do? Would it even be worth it? I was sick of the fifty minute ride to Waukegan which, in heavy traffic, was an hour and a half from my apartment. I thought about the ramifications and the possibilities of the trip all afternoon. I decided after work I would have a beer, wait out the congested evening commute and decide whether I should make the journey.

I walked north on Dearborn Avenue speculating how I could possibly rob Jesus Santilles. I envisioned how I might go about pulling him over with my flashing red light placed in the dashboard only long enough to get his attention. I did not want anyone else, especially local police, to see it. Stopped, I would approach him and intimidate him. I had to get into his car and hold him at gunpoint. I would handcuff his left wrist through the steering wheel to his right forearm so he could not escape or reach for a weapon, if he had one. I hoped he would not entertain thoughts of going for a gun when I approached the vehicle. I assumed he would not be armed, hardly any couriers ever were. They just didn't need the hassle of being pulled over by local police and arrested for carrying a weapon. Besides these guys were ranking members of the cartel and they were so feared they did not need a weapon. Nevertheless, I had to at least consider the possibility he would be armed. I had to avoid a gun battle at all cost. Of course, if he chose to defend himself with a weapon, I had to be prepared to protect myself. I really didn't believe I was evil enough to kill a man for money but, if it meant my life or his, I had to be ready to do it.

I decided I would douse his lights to avoid notice and then I anticipated removing his keys from the ignition and casually proceeding to the trunk. There, I would grab the treasure and return to my car, placing the bag and whatever it contained onto the rear seat. I would back away and make a U-turn, leaving Santilles stranded and handcuffed inside his vehicle. I would wipe down the handcuffs removing them of fingerprints before I placed them on him. I must be careful not to touch anything and I must hold on to his car keys. I could stop my car on the interstate which would be dark enough to allow me to transfer the suitcase to the trunk. There I would toss Santilles keys into a field. Finally, I would cover the case with my raid gear and my DEA raid jacket. If a trooper was bold enough to pull me over and brazen enough to request a federal agent open his trunk, he would see the raid gear and DEA emblazoned clothing. If this did not deter the trooper from a continued search than the hell with it, I would be caught. But, of course that would not happen. No trooper is going to risk professional embarrassment harassing a properly identified, cooperative DEA Agent simply going home after a night of stressful work. The scheme was simple and when I decided that it was the plan I would adopt, I realized I was standing in front of Harry Caray's Restaurant, a glorified bar which is little more than an overpriced tourist trap. I was a mile and a half from my office. I decided to forego the beer and retrieve my car. I wanted to be thoroughly sober and alert when, and if, I found Santilles.

*

Night had fallen by the time I had battled the suburban traffic and arrived in Waukegan. I decided to eat a decent, well-cooked meal instead of the greasy fast food time constraints forced me to often consume. I ordered a salad and roast beef platter with mashed potatoes and apple sauce but, before I had finished the first course, I had become anxious and restless. I was concerned the few minutes I spent in the restaurant could be valuable time Santilles would spend in Waukegan. Besides, I realized the less people who saw me here, the better I would fare. I left twelve bucks on the table, gulped down a glass of skim milk and headed toward surveillance of the auto garage.

I sat there for hours diligently watching the garage, a red brick building which had been hastily and sloppily whitewashed. It had a five foot rim of aluminum siding around its top, some of which had cancered from the moist lake winds. Foreboding Lake Michigan was only a quarter mile east, separated by a narrow park, a four lane roadway and a barren marina. I thumbed a magazine blindly in the dark, picking my nose and listening to the radio. I enjoy rock music but as I became older I had begun favoring jazz and new age. The smooth melodies seemed more soothing, especially when passing time looking at an unoccupied and depressing building. I did not want to fall asleep however, so I alternated between guitar and horn riffs to obnoxious sports talk radio shows. I considered myself an avid fan of sports but, I honestly could never understand why people would wait on the phone for twenty-five minutes so they could express a vague opinion about the town's professional football coach. Usually the call would be terminated before the guy who called in ever completed two sentences. I gloated thinking about some of those fat bastards filling themselves with beer and pizza, wiping mustard stains off their shirts while I sat waiting for a man who might bring me a quarter million dollars. Admittedly, I didn't think it would happen but even if I failed, at least my efforts were spent more wisely there than on the end of a phone waiting to make a fool of myself. Nevertheless, the inane banter between illiterate ex-jock and the frustrated weekend warriors kept me alert and interested in the activities or lack thereof at the auto garage.

While I sat watching the generic establishment, I noticed a familiar car drive through the area. It was a Buick Regal, the type of car Walker drove and as it moved closer I could see the distinctive black radio aerial that rose from the rear window. It was Walker! I could not allow him to see me but, there was no opportunity to leave. My car was wedged in between an abandoned station wagon and a large metal trailer which had sat unattended on Sheridan Road for several weeks. I had a perfect spot from which to watch the garage but, if Walker drove down the avenue, his experienced eye would easily recognize my vehicle. I was trapped. All I could do was slouch in the front seat as I watched him cruise through the vacant auto garage's concrete lot. Perhaps Walker's curiosity had taken hold and he wanted too see for himself if Santilles was going to visit the garage. Worse, maybe he was here for the same purpose I was. Either way, there was no plausible explanation for me to be in Waukegan and there certainly was no sagacious reason for me to be on surveillance. I was some sixty miles from home and it was Friday, 10:30 in the evening. I had not notified Walker that I would be out there and he was the lead case agent. He would be disturbed if he knew I was conducting a surveillance on my own and even though I thought Walker was naive, I don't think he would have difficulty crafting a motive for what I was trying to accomplish. As excuses raced through my head, I watched Walker's car veer north and proceed up Sheridan Road. I knew he lived a few miles north, in secluded Winthrop Harbor but, he might come back. I watched the tail-lights fade over a darkened and distant hill then I started the car and made a U-turn south on Sheridan. Relieved I had not been observed, I conceded my scheme to rob Santilles was absurd. I started the engine and turned south, aiming for home.

The streets were mostly desolate again. The lakefront district was primarily reserved for small businesses and a few municipal government occupied buildings. There were a few scattered low rent apartments but, for the most part, only storefront businesses and antediluvian county buildings dotting the area along Sheridan Road. The gas station that Santilles came to that night sat only two blocks from the county's criminal court building. The Lake County Jail sat adjacent to that.

I abandoned the entrance to the quicker Amstutz Expressway and continued south driving along placid Sheridan Road, out of the downtown area, past the corrupted stores that once thrived with honest commerce. Further south, some remained vacant while others housed hokey second hand shops and bargain clothes stores. The shadowy lake was off to the left, ever vigilant but still polluted.

I speculated whether Walker had seen me though, I knew he hadn't. I was well concealed. I glanced at the illuminated digital clock and calculated I had been on surveillance in Waukegan for more than five hours. It was close to eleven. Santilles had come to the garage shortly after midnight the night we had seen him. If I waited an hour more, I might see Santilles. I pulled to the side of the empty road and watched approaching headlights. Again, I slouched down in the seat. The car was not Walker's and of course, it couldn't have been since we had proceeded in opposite directions. I reconsidered options and ultimately decided to retreat would have been a bashful and unqualified waste of planning, energy and time. Audaciously, I gripped the wheel and spun back towards the auto garage gambling the courier would eventually show up and Walker, my fellow agent, would not.

I drove back to the strategic spot where I originally established my vantage point. I pulled in and maneuvered my vehicle so that the front was again facing the garage. I was preoccupied with parking the vehicle before I realized the auto garage's office light was on. I grabbed for the binoculars which lay in the back seat. The garage was over one hundred yards away and I had to utilize visual aids to determine the faces of those that might be inside. I could see a man moving around in the office area but, the posters on the window prohibited me from seeing more than his legs and waist. I searched the lot and didn't notice any cars that hadn't been parked outside before I had left. I watched diligently for another vehicle to arrive. None came. I attempted to see through the fusty windows of the garage door but could not determine whether the lights were turned out in the garage or the curtains had again been pulled over the windows. I was excited and my interest encouraged me to get a closer look. I decided to approach the garage. I placed my gun in my waistband and exited the vehicle running across the street, using storefronts for cover. Halfway there, I considered the outrageous possibility of creeping right into the garage. I dismissed the notion. If Walker decided to come by again I would be easily identified walking on the deserted avenue. I walked back to the car, disgusted with my lack of foresight and disenchanted because I hoped to be prepared but, in actuality, I really had no plan at all. As I made my way across the street, a short distance to the car, the bay door moved open. Immediately, a vehicle began to back out. I ran behind my own car and watched. I did not want to draw any attention by opening my door and igniting the light. The car moved out swiftly and drove quickly onto Grand Avenue, heading west. There was no way to see the driver or any possible occupants of the vehicle in the darkness.

I lunged for my door and yanked it open. I started my car and immediately engaged the transmission. I could feel the adrenaline spurt. I recklessly maneuvered my vehicle out of the tight space I was in, hitting the sidewalk's curb with my rear wheels and banging against the abandoned wagon with the front bumper. I had finally extracted myself but not before backing up onto the sidewalk. I bounced the vehicle off the curb and the awkward departure tapped the top of my head against the roof.

Get control, Mark.

I saw the red tails of the vehicle which had pulled from the garage. The car looked like a domestic job. It was about two blocks in front of me but, with the lack of traffic, I easily closed some of the distance. There was no way to know who was inside or how many there were. The car continued west on Grand Avenue passing the few Victorian gingerbread and Queen Anne homes which survived the flurry of rebuilding which occurred after the turn of the century. I wasn't thinking about the maritime town's history though. My thoughts were consumed with the method by which I would enact my plan. There were no other vehicles behind me or in front of me other than the one I was following. There wasn't much traffic at all. I observed only one car sitting perpendicular at a stoplight as we passed through an intersection, first my suspect and then me, some fifteen seconds later. There was no sign of Walker. I decided to close the gap and attempt to determine who was inside. I increased my speed considerably until I was only thirty feet behind the Ford, which I now determined was a Thunderbird bearing Wisconsin plates. The Avis Car Rental Company used distinctive plates on their vehicles and I immediately recognized the license to be that of a rental car. My senses were heightened as I observed there was only one occupant, the driver. I had to determine if it was Santilles. The T-bird continued west and I realized we were along the same route Santilles had taken to get to his girlfriend's house. If this car made a right onto Elmwood Street, which we were fast approaching, I might have Santilles. I glanced at the moon, which was completely visible in the cloudless sky. It was brilliant, sweet and full. Elmwood Street was only two blocks ahead but, the circumstances were not developing as I planned. I had expected time to carefully chart my moves and these circumstances presented me none.

The right rear light of the T-bird flashed indicating a right hand turn, a deviation which would place the vehicle on Elmwood Street.

Its now or never.

I slowed, almost stopping in the street while the car made its right.

Fuck it. Go for it. Go for it. Its him. Get it, get the fucking money!

I kicked the accelerator and zoomed toward the car, following it around the corner. The tires strained loudly to maintain their traction. I tossed the red light onto the dashboard which I had made readily accessible. It was the only item that had served its pre-planned function. I flashed the headlight beams from normal to high simulating the flashing wig-wag lights of a police car. After all, I was in a Mark VII, not a clearly demarcated police car. The driver pulled immediately to the right side of the street, like an obedient motorist would. I wasn't thinking clearly and trepidation encumbered my judgment. Instead of pulling behind the car, I pulled alongside it. In doing so, I thought I would immediately determine if this was Santilles.

I pulled the car parallel to the Thunderbird and I could see Santilles' tanned and cleft face. It was indeed him but he looked calm, an unruffled gaze which frightened me. Before determining the significance of his reaction, I jumped out of the car, leaving the engine running. I drew my weapon and pointed the barrel right at Santilles' face. He saw it and his eyes suddenly grew wide with alarm. If he had a gun and was inclined, he would attempt to defend himself and I knew that but, I was out of control. However, I wasn't conducting a standard traffic stop. My activities could be best described as a form of carjacking or at least, armed robbery. I approached the door and opened it. I grabbed the startled old man by the throat through the opened door. I pointed the barrel against his nose.

"Shut it off, shut the car off!" I screamed.

"Ugh." He mumbled undiscernibly.

He reached for the ignition but not quickly enough. With my left hand I released my grip of his neck and reached in to turn the key. I kept the gun's metal pressed to his face, an act which could have enabled Santilles to disarm me. We were taught in the academy how to neutralize someone with a gun that close to your head. However, those guns were plastic. There was no fear factor. Now, I was as scared as Santilles but, I had the gun. I could see Santilles was terrified. I pulled the keys out with my left hand and fingered them. There were two keys and I recognized the larger of the two to be the one most likely to be the trunk key. I leaned backwards against the driver's door and pushed against it. I bit down on the keys so I could maintain control of my hostage. I grabbed a secure handhold of his thinning hair and yanked him from his seated position.

"Por que?" He moaned loudly but I didn't understand.

The door swung open and struck my own car as I hauled out the considerably smaller Santilles. The old man felt frail in my grasp as I shook him violently to assure him and myself I was in control.

"El dolor." He screamed.

I smashed him across the left side of his head with the handle of my weapon. He instantly fell limply to the ground.

I jumped over him and went to the trunk. I clumsily fumbled for the larger key in my mouth to open the trunk. My hands were shaking violently but, I managed to get the rounded key into the trunk. I twisted the key with too much strength, heightened by the adrenaline surging through my torso. The key bent but, not before the trunk popped open. A large black suitcase illuminated in the dim light of the trunk. I grabbed it with my left hand and pulled it from the trunk. I ran to the driver's side of my vehicle and attempted to stuff the case into the door. It resisted, as the case caught the driver's console. I pushed it anyway and still it would not go. I stuffed harder and felt the soft sided case remain rigid, refusing to bend. I pushed harder with only partial use of my right hand which was burdened with my weapon. The barrel wriggled unsafely as I wrestled the case. I used my groin and then my leg to jam the case into my car. I jumped into the idling vehicle and ripped at the transmission. The car lurched forward with the driver's door still open. I pulled it closed with my left hand. I floored the accelerator and sped up the street.

I panted frantically. My head felt like it was on a swivel as I searched in all directions looking for police, accomplices, hit men, witnesses and monsters. I don't remember how I escaped only, that I had driven too fast, zooming around corners to flee the crime on Waukegan's secluded streets. I exceeded the speed limit in a mad rush to abandon the area. As much as I demanded, I could not calm down. All the way, the whole route out of Waukegan and along the interstate, I drove with the case stuffed awkwardly between the seat console and the dashboard. I drove along the highway and through several small towns policed by skeleton departments. I could have been stopped but, thank God, I wasn't. I wondered if Santilles was dead. I thought about his capacity to remember my face if he wasn't. The more I thought about him the more I hoped he was dead. My heart continued to pound. I repeatedly checked my side and rear view mirrors for vehicles, flashing lights and more demons. I examined my hands and clothes for blood, either mine or Santilles. I felt my crotch for warm dampness. I opened the two power windows hoping the frosty night air would fill my lungs and pacify my racing heart.

I drove for forty-five minutes, paranoically searching the night. Finally, I arrived at the parking lot of my apartment complex. I was still shaking and my stomach was churning like a college dorm's lone washing machine. I instinctively grabbed for my waistband to push my gun aside as I customarily did while exiting a car. It wasn't there and an immediate cold sweat surged through my pores as if my body was a sink sponge which had just been squeezed. My heart felt like it stopped. The gun would surely identify me. The detectives would find it and contact the manufacturer who would query their records and find the gun to have been purchased by the Drug Enforcement Administration. The DEA would be contacted and they would find the Sig Sauer model P226 was issued to Agent Mark Connors in December 1988 upon his successful graduation from Basic Agent Class 63. The same gun found next to the assassinated and bludgeoned South American dope dealer in

Waukegan. I was done, my life and career ruined by a murder fervently motivated by greed.

The thoughts dashed through my mind and then I remembered throwing my gun to the floor when I tried futilely to stuff the normally pliable suitcase into the car. I felt the floorboard and found the gun was there, its barrel resting along the raised carpeted floor leaving its muzzle pointing straight at its owner. I slowly eased the gun until its target was no longer me. I breathed deeply and felt for my wallet and credentials. I had everything. No identification had been lost at the scene with my name and address on it.

I looked around trying desperately to gain my composure. I picked up the suitcase and felt relief the lot was dark. Though it had been over an hour since the incident, I still quaked with anxiety. I exited my car and yanked the case from its wedged position. I walked toward my apartment looking for someone to jump from the shadows. As I approached the building's entrance, I recognized for the first time how heavy the suitcase was.

*

I placed the canvas case on the floor. I drew the shades and turned on the kitchen light to add feint background light. Subconsciously again, I supposed, I hoped the swarthiness might conceal my evil malfeasance. Whereas with other thefts I could not wait to see what I had stolen, the existence of that case resting in my living room filled me with dread. I stepped back and dropped to my knees letting my back rest against the wall as I debated the sanity of opening it. I considered the ridiculous possibility it had been booby-trapped with an explosive. I wondered if it had anything of value at all or had I just beaten a man, maybe to death, for his cheap clothes. I rose and went to the kitchen and retrieved a cold beer.

I guzzled it seeking the courage to open the case. When it didn't come, I finished a second and gulped a mouthful of scotch whiskey to ease my tension. The bottle had been given to me at Christmas but, I never had any intention of opening it. I swallowed another mouthful of the biting malt in an effort to soothe my guilt. The remedy only served to water my eyes. I returned to the case and sat down in front of it. I had already committed the act which rendered it in my possession, so I figured I might as well determine precisely what I had acquired. I unfastened the two buckled straps which further secured its contents and slowly unzipped it. The case was now accessible but instead of pulling it open, I laid close to it and listened. For exactly what, I didn't know.

I slowly opened it but didn't immediately recognize the unmistakable moldy emanation of drug money. My first thought was sheer disappointment but the dejection was fleeting. As I pried open the case, I saw clear plastic wrap pulled tightly over the contents of the suitcase. It was the type of heat wrap which is used to seal meat at a grocery store but when I reached inside I knew I had more than hamburger. I ripped apart the taut wrap, tearing it off like a ravenous wildman. I instantaneously saw fifties and hundreds banded in thick piles some two, others three inches thick. There was so much I felt my stomach constrict. I had seen more money, many times, during multi-million dollar reverses but none of it had ever belonged to me. Then, the cash was little more than a valueless prop. This money was mine and I had never been in possession of so much. For some strange reason the notion of the board game Monopoly popped into my head. I thought about those orange $500 bills and how much they were supposed to be worth. The treasure before me was now far more than I ever dreamed of holding and the mass of money far exceeded any amount I had ever possessed, even during Monopoly. The money, large denominations, filled the entire two by three foot case. I reached into its inviting depth and pushed the notes. The case was so tightly packed they did not budge. The second time, I plunged into it like a starving man. I removed a packet, then another.

The money had been packed so tightly, it was difficult to remove. I had extracted five bundles before reaching the case's canvas bottom. I flicked through the bundles and saw no one but the dignified faces of Ulysses Grant and Benjamin Franklin. I freed several more banded packs amazed a man could nonchalantly drive around with such a staggering stockpile of riches. The case was completely full of money and there wasn't room for anything else. I continued extricating thick bundles and then gasped when I saw two heavily taped packages. I recognized immediately what the duct taped sheaths contained. Cocaine.

I sat and stared at them, losing track of time.

I had been involved in arrests for two kilos of coke. I had been a witness for the prosecution in cases where the defendant had been arrested with less than even one kilo of coke. They had been possession, not necessarily even delivery cases, and those defendants had all received sentences of over five years in federal prison.

I was sitting in my own living room with two kilograms of cocaine, my cocaine.

Cautiously, I picked one up and felt a strange sense of power, very unlike I had felt before when handling the substance as evidence. Some agents were spending months in the office trying to set up deals and seize just one kilo and I had easily just stolen two. I held one in each hand, sitting there with those things which I had taken an oath to purge from the country during the last six years of my life. Instead of abhorrence though, I felt a feeling of dominion. It was such an inexplicable and sinister sense of defiance. There was enough money sitting in front of me to change the lives of my yet unborn children and the commodity I was most fascinated with were these two two-pound packages of cocaine- hydrochloride. Powder derived from coca leaves.

There was no question what to do with them. Destroy them both, immediately.

I carried one in each hand to the toilet. I tried to break the first open by smashing it against the rim of the bowl but, the abundance of tape and plastic wrapping prevented the casing from coming undone. I was forced to remove several layers of the grey tape, uncovering a word, "Malo" drawn in black marker. It was common practice for cartel members to identify and label their kilograms. Once our group had seized four kilos with stickers of Mickey Mouse on them. Another kilo we had once seized had emblazoned the name "Babe Ruth" on it. I tore the last remaining protective layers off the package and exposed its last containment, transparent plastic wrap. I smacked the compacted block against the toilet rim and it broke apart. I flushed several times. The package burst letting its contents fall harmlessly into the water. I reckoned with each pull of the metal handle, I washed away the potential for thousands of dollars.

I opened the second and followed the same routine. I came near the end of the contents and another peculiar feeling passed through me.

I examined the chunky white pieces which looked remarkably ordinary and no more appealing than hardened baking soda. An apparently insignificant by-product of ground leaves and ether yet powerful enough to threaten the fabric of societies around the world. For some it was more seductive than sex, more destructive than fire, more ruinous to nations' peoples than any bomb or bullet. Stronger for some than basic needs of sustenance like food, water and shelter and I had a whole handful of it in my hand. Nature's kryptonite.

I drew my right hand close to my nose. I thought about the consequences. Certainly, I wouldn't die. How many informants had told me they used this stuff all the time. Hell, some friends from high school were regular users and they were no worse for wear than me. I never knew what all the excitement was about. I really had never had any desire to use it and now I scrambled against the provocation to ingest it. I could not buffet the incredible lure.

Once won't hurt.

I leaned toward the stuff and sniffed hard drawing the substance into my right nostril. I detected the surge of a burning sensation percolate through my sinus followed by a dull numbness in my nose and throat. It remained for a few moments and gradually subsided. I felt little else. Certainly no feelings of happiness, ecstasy or joy.

I decided to package the remainder which I had not flushed. I don't know why other than to continue to savor a perverse sense of supremacy. Maybe I would later share it with some bimbo I had picked up at a bar. There were several times I knew I could have used a little to get some girl to pull down her pants.

I put about two ounces into a plastic lunch baggie I had never envisioned myself utilizing for something other than a sandwich. I hid the portion up in a drop ceiling which was in my walk-in closet. It was only a few feet away from the wall where I had secreted my previous heist. I figured I might be back at that wall again, opening up a bigger place to hide my new hoard though I was certain the space would never be large enough to cloak the new fortune.

I returned to the pile of pretty green paper. I counted in the same manner I was accustomed but, I did not feel the same sense of excitement. The vision of Santilles crumpled on the asphalt flashed in my head and it caused me to lose count several times. I thought he should have survived my strike to his head but, I never did see him move after I had thumped him. In retrospect, the blow wasn't even necessary but, I had to demonstrate my superiority. It was an uninvited thought but, I was glad I had done it even though, I hoped he had not died. Then again, if there was a chance he would remember me when he did regain consciousness, I hoped he was dead. I rationalized he was just a dope dealer and if he had perished, no one would truly would miss him. The defective excuse did not appease my conscience. I yielded to the money presuming the counting would emancipate my swelling guilt or at least, displace it.

When I was finished placing the money in piles of like denominations, I utilized a calculator to tally my booty. I had spent an hour placing the bills in groups of hundreds and fifties. I discovered I had approximately $575,000 in cash. I rose to place the money back into the suitcase before I realized I had actually neglected to count seven more piles of hundred dollar bills which I had placed behind me when I had begun sorting the denominations. I computed the additional funds which brought my new aggregate to $710, 000 from the old man's case.

I didn't sleep that night. I laid until well past dawn debating with my memory whether I had killed Santilles. I recounted the sequence of events in my head over and over. I tried to recall traffic, neighbors and familiar vehicles like Walker's Regal. I reviewed in my mind's eye the force of the blow I placed to the old man's head and the intensity changed with each strained recollection. I admitted I wasn't sure if the ferocity I used was just enough to knock him to the ground or so powerful that it caved in his aging skull. I hoped he was alive. No one should ever die over money. Either way, I didn't know the true results of the blow. I was too busy grabbing for that precious suitcase which was now my property.

I had dumped the money into two satin pillowcases, each filled to the top. I had left the apartment with the intent of hiding them but, of course, there was no safe place to conceal two containers of close to three-quarters of a million dollars. I immediately returned. I unloaded the money back into the suitcase in an unacceptably haphazard manner which prevented all the bundles from fitting snugly back into the case. They had been placed into the case in a methodical and orderly manner with the wrap serving to pull the money tightly together, compacting it so more could fit into the case. The person who had prepared the money completed the task at a careful and leisurely pace. Conversely, I was frenzied and mildly hysterical trying to think of a safe place to camouflage the stolen money. I didn't have the energy or the supplies to dismantle and reconstruct the closet space where the other monies had been hidden and since it was still early in the morning, I recognized it was too soon to begin a reconstruction project. The noise would unequivocally indicate strange behavior in my apartment. So, I just laid in bed with the money sitting on the floor next to me. Most of it inside the suitcase and the other dozen or so bundles laying at the foot of my bed. All of my senses were sharp. I listened for burglars, scrutinized shadows and smelled for the burning embers which would indicate fire. The odor would have to be that strong to transcend the inexorable stench of the moldy money which surfaced once I had extricated it from the wrap. I considered my options. I thought about the safe deposit boxes and concluded there might not be many boxes large enough to hold all the money I had accumulated. I considered putting the cash in a rental car and heading home, back to Mom's to bury or hide it in her dusty attic but, I didn't want to involve her. She would be crushed if a search warrant was ever executed at her home. I dozed off twice but, both times my reprehensible subconscious zapped me into attentiveness. I had nearly one million dollars within reach and I was completely sick with worry.

By dawn I had decided to temporarily conceal the suitcase in a rented storage facility just like the gangbanger had done. Before doing so, I had to obtain one. I took the suitcase and all the money I could stuff into it and placed it in the storage area of the building complex, the same location where I had previously secreted obtained contraband. I placed the black case under an old comforter given to me before my move to Chicago by my mother, who said after giving it to me that the item would protect me from the shivering winds of Chicago's winters. When I had packed it I never dreamed I would be utilizing it to conceal proceeds possibly obtained through murder. I was ashamed to think about it. I left the suitcase in the wooden and chicken wire covered cage secured only by a frivolous $2 padlock. It was absurd to entrust all that money to a cheap restraint like a small padlock. Also inside the locker was some of the jewelry I had purloined. Though the items were valuable they seemed trifling and insignificant compared to the staggering amount of cash which sat next to them. Taking the jewelry now seemed to have been a waste of time. In a way, I supposed my poor effort to safeguard the large sum of money was subliminal evidence of a despicable man hoping to be caught. Again, for the thousandth time since my acquisition of the money, I wondered if I had actually killed a man. I considered the cocaine I had snorted and the handful of powder I had hidden in my closet. I thought about the closet wall containing the other monies. I contemplated all my actions over the last several months and admitted, I had embraced evil. Then, I thought about how many men were roaming the streets of America. One hundred and twenty-five million or so. Of those, how many had used cocaine and of that group what percentage had stole. Of those how many had killed. I considered the numbers and felt comfortable knowing I was only one of a thousand. The only principle exception was I was one who had displayed the ability to acquire close to one million dollars. Decisively, I set out to find a storage locker.

2 6

I couldn't wait to get back to work. I knew if something had happened, if Santilles was dead and it had been witnessed that I killed him, investigators from headquarters in Washington would be at the office waiting to interview me. Internal Affairs Administrators with brief cases, legal pads and mini-cassette recorders. Looks of consternation and disgust would abound and word would spread quickly about another dumb agent taking the fall.

If it was going to happen, I wanted to get it over with quickly. I rose before dawn, showered and went to work. I was unaccustomedly early, arriving by 7:45 a.m., a fact which did not escape Bobby Hayes' attention. Even though he was our supervisor, he regularly was the first member of our group in the office. I examined him for any indication of skepticism.

"Connors, what are you doing here so early, your wife throw you out?"

His casually indifferent remark calmed my frazzled nerves and I assumed, at least at the time, I had not become the subject of an investigation. In analyzing his remark, I had forgotten to respond.

"Connors, lay off that stuff. Its starting to turn you into a zombie."

"Huh?"

"Forget it."

Immediately, I thought about the cocaine. Preoccupied all weekend long with the safeguarding of the money I had forgotten about snorting the stuff. I reflexively wiped my nose and upper lip as if to disperse remnants of the powder though I knew, after two days, there couldn't be anything on my face.

I glanced at my hand and fingers and confirmed there was no residue on them. The thought of a urine test crossed my mind. The subjects were chosen randomly and tests were sporadically conducted. I tried to remember when the last time I had been requested to pee into a plastic container. I recalled it had to be over three years, maybe even four. In fact, I had only been given one urine test since I had been hired by the DEA and it was, after thinking about it, four years since my last one.

When I had worked at the nuclear plant I remembered having three drug tests in the period of fourteen months. With the DEA, I had only one since passing the initial screening given during pre-employment examinations. I suppose the management of the nuke plant was more concerned with drug usage by its employees than the Drug Enforcement Administration.

I went to my desk and began an unproductive work day. Agents filtered into the office all morning but, I paid little attention to their activities or banter. I anxiously waited for Walker, who never arrived. If something strange had occurred in Waukegan, he would be the first DEA employee to know about it. Agonizingly, I speculated about reasons he had not reported for work. Finally, I questioned the secretary and she related Walker had not telephoned in his itinerary and consequently, had no idea where he was or what he was doing. Unbridled, paranoid thoughts popped in my mind like the bursts of fireworks on a patriotic holiday; interrogations, accusations, a homicide investigation. I continued examining the eyes of my co-workers in a nugatory attempt to extract information they were hiding about me. Later in the afternoon, the suspense was to much to endure. I paged Walker.

Thirty agonizing minutes passed before the faded beige phone at my desk rang.

"Hello, group 5, Connors." I answered.

"Yea, Mark. Did you page me." It was Walker.

"Yes." There was a brief moment of silence during which I hoped Walker would say something about Santilles but, he remained quiet. I tendered a meaningless question, "You up there, in Waukegan ?"

"Yea. I figured I'd meet with a couple of the gang dicks up here and see if they had anything new. Why, what's up?"

Was Walker being coy or was he genuinely wondering why I had paged him ?

"Uh…its just dead in the office, I thought if you needed some help I would come up there."

Walker did not immediately respond. He seemed as if he was contemplating. The delay in his reply was torturous.

"Tell you what, Mark. How about working on some of those telephone records on my desk. I have fallen way behind on those."

His blase demeanor indicated nothing had actually been discovered in Waukegan. Santilles wasn't dead. He had not even reported the incident to the police. He took his beating and dismissed it or at most, chose not to report it to the police. Santilles must have accepted the robbery as the price of doing business in the narcotics game. There was no body and there was no murder and apparently no one else had witnessed it either. Only Santilles and I knew. My confidence was restored. I really had pulled it off.

"Phone records," I said sarcastically, "Walker, I'm not that bored."

I hung up and approached Hayes with a lame excuse about needing to leave the office to check an address. He knew it was bullshit, the same weak excuse he had no doubt utilized to sneak out of the office when he was an agent my age.

"Go ahead Connors, you check that address but, wear a condom. Remember what Sammy Safe-Sex says…Slip it on before you slip it in."

I chuckled and added, "I wish."

"Oh Connors," He added, "can I expect a good case out of you before I retire?"

"Yes sir, very soon."

I left the office and walked hastily to my automobile. I resisted the desire to skip and sing. I think if I started running I might have lifted off the ground and flown. After all, at the other end of my forty-minute ride, secreted in a small, indistinguishable Westmont apartment building was a fortune approaching $800,000.

*

I purchased a cheap vinyl recliner from a used furniture dealer on the way home. I tied it into the trunk and lugged it back to the apartment. I carefully pulled apart the seam and sewed Santilles money from the suitcase into the lining. I ignored the other $57,000 holed up in the wall, content to view it as sort of an insurance policy. I moved the piece myself and worked via flashlight inside the grey cinderblock unit I had rented for $24 a month. It took me about three and a half hours to do but, I kept telling myself it was the best job I ever had. I laughed when I calculated my salary as a little less than $200,000 an hour. I surrounded the recliner with cardboard boxes filled with soaking wet newspapers. I thought if they were damp there would be less chance of a fire. I resigned myself to believing this was the safest place I could keep my money. If catastrophe like flood, fire or earthquake struck and the money was lost or stolen, I would have to live with it. If an investigation ensued and I was snared I reasoned I had at least been caught stealing a worthwhile amount. I decided I would leave the money in the storage facility for a couple months until I determined the safest plan to secure it. Before closing the hem, I elected to remove $10,000 with the intention I would throw myself a celebration party. After all, I felt like Chicagoland's newest young mogul.

As the days passed with no unexpected revelations from Walker, I grew more comfortable with my nouveau rich status. Walker spent more time in Waukegan while I spent less time volunteering to help him. I began daydreaming about how I would spend the cash. I purchased some financial magazines in an attempt to learn where I might hide the money for the long term. I went to the library and researched information about off-shore bank accounts in Europe, the Caribbean and New Zealand. I even found a real estate trade rag which featured high priced homes in the exclusive Barringtons and Fox Lake regions. For the hell of it one day, I drove by some of the smaller estates and reveled in the satisfaction I could plunk down $500,000 or $600,000 and buy one of the sedate mansions if I so pleased. Of course, the home would be on the servile end of gentility but, that standing is a helluva lot more cozy than the upper end of mediocrity. My sense of being independently wealthy transcended the thoughts of the considerable consequences I faced if my means of obtaining my affluence were ever discovered.

The work-week concluded and another two more followed with no news from Waukegan so, I resolved to treat myself with a $10,000 spending spree. I rented a suite at the Chicago Hilton and Towers, one of the most exceptional hotels in Chicago. The suite ran me several hundred bucks for one evening which I spent without regret or hesitation. I rented a limousine for the night and made reservations for four at the 95th Floor, the restaurant which sat atop the Hancock Building, the world's third tallest free standing structure. It was a classy restaurant frequented mostly by tourists. Many Chicagoans escorted visitors to the lounge to satisfy their guest's requests to enjoy the best view of Chicago's magnificent skyline in all its illuminated splendor. I chose the eatery because it was somewhat elegant but, since it was considered a tourist trap by the natives, my chances of encountering someone I knew were greatly reduced.

I arranged to have three paid escorts come to my suite at the hotel and I called several services to procure exactly what I wanted. My requirements were querulous and were designed to encompass a medley of fantasies. I specifically requested a beautiful Caucasian with blonde hair and large, fake breasts. I wanted a Hispanic girl with deep, dark eyes and very long, well maintained curly hair and I also requested an African American woman with a body as tight as a snare drum. I informed the manager of the escort service I would not be happy unless I received exactly what I had specified. I insisted I had the financial wherewithal to accommodate my lavish and precise request and as a token sign of my financial resources, I had a bell boy employ a taxi driver to deliver a manila envelope containing a gratuity of $500 to locate and deliver the women I wanted. I instructed the manager to keep the money if he fulfilled my abstract demands, return only half of it if he failed.

I had the limousine pick me up at Midway Airport. I had worn my own best suit and driven my car to a parking lot there. I did not want to have the limo driver retrieve me at a spot where he might later remember me personally but, I had hoped the events of the evening would leave an indelible imprint on at least one stranger. My goal was to shock and entice the imagination and leave a memory for all who had witnessed my extravagant behavior. My other goal was to assure Mark Connors was not identified as a participant.

The driver showed up on time in a classic black stretch limousine. He commented about my lack of luggage which did not disturb or worry me. I could see by his expression he was delighted to carry out my request to be taken to the Chicago Hilton for he undoubtedly knew the hotel catered to wealthy and exclusive clients. I informed him of my plans to dine with three very attractive ladies and advised him of the possibility things might get a little out of hand. He laughed and assured me the limousine was not his and I could feel free to utilize the vehicle as I wished. In doing so, he appeared to salivate at the thought of the generous tip he hoped to receive.

I checked into the elegant hotel and immediately ordered a bottle of fine champagne. I wanted to have a few drinks before the ladies arrived. Although I wanted to appear smooth, I felt nervous. I had never resorted to the use of a professional escort service and really had no idea how the night would proceed.

I hadn't finished my second glass when the front desk informed me Monique, a guest, had already arrived. I apprised the front desk I was expecting two other visitors and when they appeared they should be permitted to come right up. I waited and wondered what flavor Monique would be.

She was the black girl. She entered and I was mildly irritated she did not appear the least impressed with me or my lodging. She introduced herself then walked in and probed the rooms, eerily casing the suite, looking in closets and behind doors. I was taken aback by her rudeness but, her looks were stunning. The three escorts cost me a whopping $2,700 and I assumed I would obtain a little degree of graciousness with the price. After her mindful inspection, she returned from my bedroom and placed a right hand on her curvy hip. She informed me she was not into "group thangs." I offered her a glass of champagne which she refused. I asked her if she had been told what the night would entail and she replied that she had been told to spend three hours with me to "do the usual." She also said she was aware there might be another girl but, she emphatically stated she would not have sex with her.

It appeared the woman before me was prepared to have three hours of sex. I told her instead I planned an evening that would fulfill a fantasy of mine and she would be expected to play a part. She rolled her eyes. I told her I intended to take her to an exquisite restaurant in Chicago in the company of two other women. I added I did not necessarily expect her to have sex with them and depending on how the night progressed, we might not even have sex.

My statement prompted her to ask, "You can't get it up, can you?"

I started to become a little agitated. I felt for the money I was spending, I didn't deserve this type of antagonism.

"Look, Monique. I came into some money and this is something I always wanted to do. I plan to see and be seen with three gorgeous women. Looking at you, I have one third of my wish. Now, if you would feel more comfortable pulling down my pants and sucking my cock, then go ahead. I certainly will not stop you."

She smiled briefly, then stopped. "About the money, I get $900. That's not for me. That is for my employer."

"And how much of that do you get?" I asked.

"Zero."

"Bullshit."

"Well, I get some but, I make my money on tips."

I smiled and responded, "Well, most people get tipped on their service, if its good."

She assumed her patronizing pose again and said," Honey, you going to be real happy with what I do. Your eyes are going to pop out when I slide this dress off."

Of that, I had no doubt. The short gold macrame gown was gaudy for my tastes but, what was inside was exactly what I had ordered. Her skin was caramel and as sleek as a snake's. The dress seemed to have been designed for her body and the heels she had on complemented the whole package. Her hair was long and soft and the black curls swung seductively around the nape of her neck and along her collarbone.

I went to the bedroom and returned with $1,500. I handed it to her.

She looked at the money and appeared satisfied but greedily added, "This is a start."

"Now how about that champagne?"

Willingly, she accepted my offer.

The doorbell rang and I walked to the door. I opened it and found the blonde and the Latino together. Neither could have been more than twenty-three and my first impression was they were both high. Their eyes were glassy and they stumbled clumsily into the suite. The Hispanic was enchanting. She had a red dress which was so tight if she had a quarter tucked in her panties, I could tell if it rested on heads or tails. Her face was classic Latino and the cherry red lip gloss she wore could only look provocative on a woman of her ethnicity. Her eyes were deep and tactile and were accentuated by her thick eyebrows. I suspected she was Cuban and she easily assumed a position as my favorite of the three. The blonde was overdone. She was attractive but her appearance was overblown with makeup and preparation. Her hair stood tall, molded by mousses and sprays. She removed her pretentious sunglasses to expose the brown eyes whose color was modified by blue tinted contacts. The counterfeit lenses made her pupils seem cloudy and dull. Her skirt was black and was also tight. By design, the hem fell short of covering her garters which held up her sheer silk nylons. The look was certainly sexual but, not what I had hoped for. Briefly, I considered canceling my plans to take them to the restaurant but, then I reconsidered. My purpose was to be seen and what better commotion could be caused than walking into some stuffy upper crust restaurant with these three divergent vixens.

The two entered the room and seemed surprised to find another woman. The curious blonde fanned out through the suite just like Monique had. Her excursion gave me the opportunity to ask the beautiful Hispanic her name.

"Spice."

"Was that your given name?" I playfully queried.

"No, but I like it better. Besides it goes with hers." She acknowledged the presence of the blonde, who had wandered back out of the bedroom with a freshly lit cigarette. She giggled, dumbly.

Spice nodded her head and proclaimed, "That's my girl Sugar. Everything is funny to her."

I introduced Sugar and Spice to Monique, who appeared uneasy with the arrangement. I immediately addressed any concerns they appeared to have including the most pressing, how many other men were going to show up. They all seemed skeptical when I explained that it was only going to be me and no one else.

"You must have quite a bit of stamina," joked Spice as she looked at the assembled group. She made the statement matter-of-factly and her presence struck me as that of an intelligent person, someone without the sensorial apparel and make up might have been a studious under-graduate or a young corporate employee.

She turned to Monique and asked, "What agency are you with?"

Monique answered and the three began to engage in a brief and superficial conversation about managers, services and nightclubs. The respite allowed me to pour myself another glass of champagne and col-lect my thoughts. I was able to examine my investments and concluded just fucking Spice would be a gratifying and fitful conclusion to the evening, though I certainly intended to indulge myself with the other two as well. I poured a glass for both Sugar and Spice and returned to the sofa.

"You got any coke?" Sugar requested.

"No, just champagne." I briefly visualized the two ounces of coke that lay hidden in my apartment before telling her, "The money I'm paying, you can get your own."

Sugar apologetically added, "I thought we were going to party, that's all."

"Oh, I intend to party, I just don't do that anymore." I replied. I quickly reconsidered my response and decided I did not have to portray myself as a coke user. After all, I was capable of paying these girls what they wanted and the money, of course, was the only reason they came. "I hope you two don't expect me to supply coke as well."

Spice gestured by shaking her head sideways as Monique offered, "Its your money and your time, if you just want to sit around talking and drinking that's fine with me but, you only got two hours and forty more minutes with me, honey."

"Wow, I guess we better get moving then."

I called the front desk and ordered the driver. The ladies stood and prepared to leave. Sugar went to the bathroom a second time. She left the door open and I heard the sound of her inhaling quickly. She evidently had her own coke and my initial impression of her was correct. She was intoxicated. I was pleased that Spice did not indulge.

The three of us left the lavish suite and proceeded through the lobby. I was disappointed my entourage only drew mild interest in the scattered foyer. However, I was delighted to see my limo driver's reaction when I exited with the three women. He leaped from the car and raced to the passenger door facing the curb. Opening it, he allowed himself to lustfully inspect each lady as they approached the car. He seemed particularly enchanted by the blonde, who further piqued his excited frenzy by patting his buttocks as she entered. His eyes then met mine and he shamefully cast them to the sidewalk as if he had just realized he forfeited any hopes of acquiring a decent tip.

Reassuringly and without aggravation I asked, "Dave, how they look?"

"You're a lucky man, Mr. Goulet."

I had told him that was my name. For some reason, I had always wanted to pretend I was French. I claimed my name was Michel Goulet, who was in reality, a retired professional hockey player whose skills I had always admired. But admittedly, I looked no more like a Frenchman than a freshly barbered poodle. The champagne had served to further expose my Irish heritage by adding to the flushness of my face. It was my whimsical drama however, and I decided it would play out the way I wanted.

We made the brisk trip to the restaurant in less than ten minutes. The short ride did not prevent Sugar from consuming nearly a quarter of a fifth of blackberry brandy from the limousine's bar. Spice and Monique did not drink. We exited the restaurant and judging from the valet's expressions, I would succeed in my effort to cause a commotion. I noticed one young man still under the spell of his frenzied teenage hormones, point to us as his co-worker hurried from parking a vehicle to see us, or them, I should say. I quelled my sense of embarrassment and decided to gloat over the presence of the two ladies who rested under my arms as I had requested along the ride. Sugar staggered from the vehicle but gained her composure when she observed the aghast look of shock cross the faces of an older couple as we entered behind them.

The improvident maitre'd raised his eyebrows when I informed him I was Mr. Goulet and my party of four was complete and ready to be seated. Though he assessed our lives indiscreetly, he professionally escorted us to our seats, choosing a circuitous route which I supposed would make my group seen by the least number of people. I did not care. Of those that had seen us, I had received the response I had sought.

We enjoyed an expensive bottle of Merlot, then finished another. I was content to see Monique and Spice were drinking and felt they were more comfortable with the situation. Actually toward the end of the meal, I began to enjoy their company and I think we forgot, albeit briefly, our meeting had been solely a business arrangement. Sugar, on the other hand, had begun to suffer the effects of her chemical intake. She was drunk and the results of the coke had made her boisterous and unsettled. She openly complained about having no more "candy for Sugar" and periodically requested I provide some. Repeatedly, I informed her that I did not have any.

"Then, I'll need the money I'm supposed to be paid, Mr. GOOOlet." She demanded in a sarcasm soaked reply. The remark sparked Spice to intervene.

"Shut up. Let's go the ladies room."

"I'll need some money first, Maria." Unwittingly, she disclosed Spice's name. The revelation had no effect on Spice's intention to convoy Sugar to the ladies' room. She offered, "I'm sorry. She should not have drank that much."

"Do you need any…"

"No, no. We won't settle that here. That is not necessary." Spice convincingly raised Sugar from her chair. "I'll straighten things out. We will be right back."

The two walked away from the table. I could see Spice who, I liked better as Maria, assumed a role of responsibility for Sugar. The absence of Maria and Sugar left just Monique and me at the table.

"Did you enjoy the meal, Monique?"

"Yea it was good. I heard about this place but I never been here. I want to let you know though, time is running out."

"Monique. I am well aware of the time. Do you think that I am concerned about your hourly wage. If you think money is an issue, stop worrying. Now if you have to be somewhere then, let me know and my driver will make sure you get there."

"If your not worried about it, honey, then there is only one place I need to be." With that she slid under the table and rubbed my penis. Expertly, she had my zipper opened and my organ exposed within seconds. She engulfed me in her mouth and before I could protest she had me completely aroused. I sheepishly, looked for other diners who might notice. Given the circumstances, I was delighted the maitre'd had elected to hide us in an obscure southeast corner table with a dim view of dark and murky Lake Michigan. I felt for Monique and touched the silky-soft raven hair which crowned her head. I slid my right hand along her cheek and attempted to pull her face up from under the table. She resisted and continued her rhythmic blow job. Again, I tugged gently on her head but, with each adept encounter with her velvet tongue, I felt less inclined to stop her.

Suddenly, our waiter was upon me.

"Is everything satisfactory, Mr. Goulet?"

I looked up and saw him only a few less feet away from me than Monique. "Yea, Yea, its fine." I acknowledged with a flustered tone.

"Are the ladies planning to return. I noticed that two went to the rest-room. Is there a complaint with the food or services?"

I should say not. Monique was not deterred by the intrusion and seemed to increase the pace of her efforts.

"No, no its great. Really we are very pleased." My timbre was even higher-pitched than the previous response and it drew a suspicious expression from the waiter. Still, I was not sure if he hadn't noticed the activity of my precocious guest or he had disguised his displeasure and quietly remained at the table to enhance my embarrassment. I concluded I would never be back at the restaurant and I would undoubtedly never see him again, so I boldly raised the tablecloth and exposed my wanton date.

"Everything's fine here…"as I added the stereotypical, "Garzon."

He turned and left without leaving a clue to his opinion but, I decided his professionalism and practicality merited an excellent tip.

Monique rose from her station. Momentarily, she looked like a woman who had just given a blow job. Her lipstick was slightly smeared and saliva glowed along her chin. She classically wiped herself with the napkin as I began to try to place my swollen penis in my pants. It was not easy and the effort could not be completed inconspicuously. I thought I would be better served to pull the table closer to me and then allow the tablecloth to cover me until the thing retreated to its flaccid state. After I resigned myself to the situation, I noticed Monique pressing two patties of butter in her hands. Before I could protest, she had her right hand firmly around my penis. She pulled swiftly allowing her slippery hand to go completely from the base of the shaft all the way over the swollen head. The tension she utilized in squeezing my rock hard dick kept me from moving from her grasp. I looked at her body and despite her enthusiastic yanking observed that it all remained steadily in place producing no indication to others what she was doing. Only her hand and arm moved, jerking me furiously and quickly. I surrendered and allowed her to continue. I saw Sugar and Spice exit, heading toward the table but, there was to be no stopping Monique. As Sugar and Spice approached the table to sit down, I was ejaculating into the table cloth.

This, they noticed.

"What the fuck you doing?" Sugar retorted.

"Takin' care of business, Bitch."

"You fucking whore," Sugar swung at Monique but, fortunately, the table was far wider than Sugar's wingspan and she failed to connect.

I intervened. "Whoa, that's it, let's get out of here." I partially stood and quickly realized that my enlarged penis dangled from my pants. The look drew a giggle from Maria. I quickly sat down, pulled up my pants and summoned the waiter before I would become the referee of a three-whore battle-royale.

Two minutes later, we were out. I held my coat in front of my waste in case any errant sperm fell on my pants over the front of me. Dave was waiting in the car and seemed like he was pleasantly surprised we had not spent the entire evening in the restaurant. As we approached the car, Sugar and Spice still seemed to be in disagreement. I tried to resolve the conflict by intervening.

"What's going on here ?"

"We are having an argument. Mind you're own, Dude." Sugar said.

"Well, I didn't pay your service to send out two girls to yell at each other."

Sugar defiantly looked at me with drunk and dilated pupils. The make-up had shown signs of failing and her inebriated condition left her sloppy and unappealing. "Fuck you." She countered.

"Fuck me?"

"Sugar, shut up again, you stupid…"

"Fuck you too, Spicey. This guy ain't paid us nothing yet. Probably robbed some poor old lady of her life savings." She sneered at me, "Fuck him."

"I said be quiet Sugar." Spice retorted.

"Actually, it was a rich old man." I added, unable to resist.

By this time we had gotten close enough to the car to enter it. Dave opened the passenger door and Sugar, who was still muttering obscenities, was the first to enter. This time Dave did not examine her. Monique entered behind Sugar and acted as if her work had been completed. She was unfazed by Sugar's conduct and actually seemed like it was routine behavior she had experienced on other occasions. Maria approached me and gently squeezed my wrist.

"I'm sorry about her, Mr. Goulet."

"I didn't expect this, I paid for two classy ladies, Spice."

"I know you did. She gets this way when she gets messed up. I tried to slow her down."

"Listen, Spice. If you want to end the thing I will. I'm not going to pay you $1,800 for this. I'll give you, say…"

"No. I'm going to work this out. I can see you're going to pay us. I have to apologize for her. I have to tell you no matter what happens, we are responsible to the agency for some money."

I certainly assumed she was liable for some monies, probably the majority but, still not sure how much. I did like Maria and fully intended to compensate her for the evening but, Sugar's conduct had me wondering whether I had spent $3,000 to get a hand job.

"Mr. Goulet. I intend to fulfill the evening, if you want." Spice added.

That was precisely what I had hoped to hear. And I intended to fill Spice as well but, I had grown aggravated by Sugar's conduct. I asked Spice what price I should pay to get rid of her.

"She should get $600 for two hours."

"No, I don't think so. Your agency seemed reputable. In fact, I sent $500 over there to secure what I wanted. I don't think they are going to be happy when I call them and tell them that the only thing I got was a fucked-up bottle blonde and a bad headache."

Spice contemplated a solution while I asked her what she thought was reasonable. I considered Spice an equitable person and I sensed she was prepared to be fair.

"She is going to have to give them $500."

I entered the limo. I noticed that Dave had taken the liberty of lowering the divider glass between himself and the rear seats. Obviously, he hoped to hear and observe what was going to happen.

I addressed the drunk blonde. "Sugar, you don't want to be here do you?"

She sardonically replied, "Nope."

"And your attitude is ruining my night. I'll tell you what, why don't you leave. Here is fifty bucks, get yourself a cab."

"Fuck you. I want the rest, the eight hundred coming to me."

"Let's not kid each other, Sugar. You haven't done anything for me and your manager is not going to be thrilled when I tell her what kind of condition you showed up in."

"You fucking bastard. Give me the money. You want something, whip it out. I'll do a hell of a better job than your black bitch does."

I expected Monique to seize Sugar by her neck and strangle her. Instead, Monique sat there, staring out the window, unfazed and unperturbed.

I noticed Dave's supervising eyes through the rear view mirror. He had not started the limousine and now realized he had been caught blatantly eavesdropping on our conversation. Embarrassed, he moved to start the car.

"I got a choice for you, Sugar. You can take the fifty bucks and go home or you can do something else."

"Let's go, Spice. This guy is fucking with us. He's the one who is going to have the problem."

"I believe Spice is satisfied with the arrangement. You are the only problem. Now take this fifty bucks and get out of here or get yourself up in that front seat and you blow my good friend Dave and I'll see you get the rest of the money. And if he wants to fuck you, then you fuck him."

There was no retort. There was no reply other than the extension of her left hand for the money. I removed a bankroll from my pocket making sure Monique and especially Spice saw it. I peeled off eighteen $50 bills which had little impact on the copious wad. I threw it toward her, scattering the notes on her lap and the floor of the limousine. She eagerly collected the paper and stuffed the money into a small purse she carried. She exited the rear compartment as Dave sat quietly, feigning ignorance. She walked to the front and opened the door.

"Enjoy Dave."

Dave smiled like a starved Cheshire cat who had been dropped into a cage of mice.

"Now Dave, let's find a quite place and let me enjoy my evening."

Dave raised the smoked glass between the driver's compartment and the rear seats. We drove to an area I recognized to be near the planetarium, on Solidarity Drive, a road which extends out onto Lake Michigan. With the beautiful incandescent skyline of Chicago as the backdrop, I used a trifling portion of Jesus Santilles money to fulfill a long standing fantasy in the back of a black stretch limousine.

27

My frolic with the escorts had likely been a total waste of money but, when I had money to burn, as I now did, I decided to bake a bit of it. It was the only extravagant expenditure I allowed myself and there was no way I could be discovered unless I had been seen at the restaurant. Despite the flamboyant hookers and my dinner table interlude, I was convinced I was not. I maintained the opinion none of my co-workers frequented the restaurant. Of course, there existed a possibility that another agent had been employing the same techniques to enhance his income and clung to a similar fantasy. However, I dismissed the remote possibility he had embarked on an adventure similar to mine on the very same evening. I returned to work after the weekend quietly gloating about my night and completely confident myself, my chauffeur and my three call girls would be the only ones who ever knew.

The days that followed were routine. It seemed Sharkey and McKey continued to remain content to let the Waukegan case lie dormant for a while. Walker continued to remain almost exclusively in Waukegan, reporting bits and pieces of his activity to Hayes, less to me and none to Sharkey or McKey. As far as I was concerned, I would be happy to never work on the case again. In fact, my plans were to initiate a separate case that would require my efforts be solely directed toward its own development. I planned to inform Walker I could no longer provide assistance for his Waukegan investigation. I would have no choice but to regretfully relinquish my status as a case agent. Divesting myself from the Waukegan case would assure me of significantly limiting the possibility I would encounter Santilles and consequently, as long as I kept my expenditures conservative, I would never be detected. As the weeks passed, I became exceedingly proud of my theft. I also resolved it would be my last. I would be comfortable with what I had stolen.

Of course, divorcing myself from Walker's investigations did not preclude me from work altogether. There were other investigations to pursue and other agents to assist as winter surrendered to spring. By the end of spring, I had participated in several more arrests and surveillances but none more disturbing than a deal Phil Vreeswyck had set up involving a member of the Vice Lords Street Gang.

The deal was planned for an abandoned Kentucky Fried Chicken Restaurant parking lot at Kostner and Harrison Streets, a lively intersection in the heart of Chicago's dilapidated West Side. The neighborhood was dotted with a few well-maintained homes but was in reality, sparsely inhabited with most of its terra-cotta bricked residences deserted, vandalized and left to deteriorate. The few homes which were occupied housed residents who were struggling but proud people who attempted to sustain the appearance of their homes despite the urban blight gradually enveloping the neighborhood. Though the community was in its twilight and its demise was fast approaching, the decay did not stop many people from congregating in its streets, alleyways and forsaken buildings. Several closely grouped exits off the east-west Eisenhower Expressway offered unconstrained access to the area making the neighborhood an ideal place to engage in brief meetings. Those who chose to depart the Eisenhower to travel north on Kostner Avenue were people who meant to be in the neighborhood and were there for a specific reason. Due to the absence of viable businesses or livable residences most were not proceeding through the area legitimately. They were there to prowl the streets looking to purchase dope, most notably, cocaine.

The neighborhood residents were predominately African-American but, most of the customers were Caucasians. The deals were consummated quickly with both the patron and the seller willing to of provide what the other sought. A white guy sitting in a car for more than three or four minutes was the police. Anything less and he was a buyer and there were many more customers than there were cops.

The Eisenhower traversed the city, extending from the downtown Loop and heading due west to the far reaches of the western suburbs where the highway became I-88 taking its travelers past flat prairies and corn fields, one hundred and sixty-five miles to Iowa. Most of the people utilizing the "Ike" as it was called within the boundaries of Chicago, were commuting in and out of the city. They were employees of profitable corporations headquartered in Chicago's Loop. They were well paid people who maintained homes in the suburbs and for some, Kostner Avenue was an accommodating locale to purchase drugs to facilitate their bored heads through sleepless nights or a wild weekend. Typically automobiles, operated by white people in business or casual attire, lined Kostner Avenue while youthful blacks eagerly serviced the occupants, running from alleys, vacant stores and parked cars back and forth with handfuls of contraband. The drug dealing was blatant. Occasionally the Chicago Police would intervene, curtailing the sales, seizing customers' automobiles and arresting suppliers who had not been quick enough to run away. For the dealers and the customers, the irritating disruptions only served to suspend the operations, sometimes for days but, mostly only hours. The insatiable demand and financial opportunities presented by the product enticed those willing to risk jail, robbery and murder to acquire or disperse it.

Phil Vreeswyck, as he was inclined to do, abruptly scheduled an undercover deal for the delivery of two kilos of coke. The meeting was set for 3 o'clock on a Friday afternoon, in a lot just off Kostner. With the rush hour traffic heading west out of the Loop at that time of day it would be a significant nuisance just to make it to the deal location.

No one wanted to contest the herd of agitated motorists crawling to their suburban homes with grass plots and white fences. At three o'clock on Friday, most of the agents wanted to be heading home themselves, working out in the gym or planning where they were going to converge for a few happy hour cocktails. Vreeswyck had never recognized the appetite for relaxation, having been married to a woman who completely governed his life. With no craving to get home, he frequently attempted deals on evenings and weekends. Usually he found a few volunteers to assist him but, since his deals rarely went, few agents were ever needed. However, on this occasion, Vreeswyck had requested Hayes recruit agents since it had been an unseasonably warm day and he had received no volunteers. As a remedy, Hayes had directed several agents to assist in the deal. He had specifically chosen myself, Sandy Foster and Chad Jennings to be placed inside the special purpose surveillance van to act as the arrest team. Our job was to get as close as possible to the bad guy without being observed. We were required to covertly hide in the area. To do so we would have to leave well before the deal, park close to the meet site, draw the curtains and shut down the engine and the air conditioning. We would be required to sit, motionlessly monitoring the neighborhood. It was duty often reserved for unseasoned agents who were not wise enough to elude the obligation. I was surprised Hayes had chosen me and especially Jennings, who had voiced his protest at the assignment. Hayes rejected our pleas so we had no choice but to accept it.

It was a very warm day and we sweated profusely. The sealed up van functioned as an oven which left me feeling like I was melting. To aggravate the situation I had worn a shirt and tie to work. Though the tie had immediately been discharged, I didn't feel comfortable removing my shirt, a condition which allowed it to become saturated with perspiration.

Disgustedly, I sat in the rear of the van on an uncomfortable milk crate. As planned, we had arrived and hour and forty-five minutes before the undercover operative, in this case Vreeswyck himself, arrived. I had already become nauseous from the stifling humidity which readily developed in the vehicle. I had the foresight to pick up a gallon of mineral water and had already begun to drink most of it. I had been sharing it with my fellow agents and now most of it was gone and the U/C had not even yet arrived.

We parked in front of a storefront whose latest incarnation was that of a Missionary Baptist Church whose Pastor, Reverend Leroy Hightower, proclaimed from a painted caricature on the window "Give to God what is his or Go to Hell !" I watched the activity of the neighborhood hoping we had not been noticed pulling into the area but, I was certain someone surely recognized the vehicle as one that shouldn't be parked too long. I peered through a rear window at the various faces of loitering pedestrians in a community where only the mailman seemed to walk with purpose. Adjacent to the church was Miss Rosie's Inn where mugs of malt liquor were advertised to be half-priced on Tuesday's. Beyond the paint chipped inn was a barren, gravel lot where a man wielded a pick axe amongst puddles, broken bottles and a discarded and rusting baby carriage. He apparently dug without purpose in the impotent lot, raising the pointed instrument and repeatedly slamming it into the earth simply because it was something to do.

There had been two curious teenagers who had approached the van twenty minutes after we had arrived. They both wore the adopted colors of the Vice Lords, silver and black. One chunky youth sported a Los Angeles Kings cap, turned stylishly to the left with the visor bent upward while the second, lean and athletic-looking, wore a LA Raiders T-shirt, ripped and tattered on one side from excessive wear. He caressed a faded basketball, torn near the middle where it exposed its black innertube. They both walked up to the van and attempted to look through its windows. The darkly tinted glass and velcroed curtains prevented them from seeing us.

"Hey five-o." The shorter of the two said as he knocked on the window. He was no more than fifteen and didn't feel the least intimidated attempting to identify us with slang jargon used to describe law enforcement.

"Mudda-Fuckas come out," spewed the second, his urban street lingo thick with disdain and malcontent. Boldly, he smacked the passenger side view mirror with his left hand, bending it awkwardly toward the ground. Instinctively, as if expecting a foot chase, he leaped backward, waiting for the side doors to spring open. When they did not, he grew more contemptuous, and grabbed the silver handle, pulling hard in an effort to open the door. We had already locked all the doors anticipating from past experience the effort was a tactic employed by instinctively inquisitive and suspicious people. He yanked on the door which did not yield. He muttered something inaudible to his friend and the remark prompted derogatory laughter from both. They appeared satisfied, at least temporarily, that no one was inside. From the pitch of their voices, I could tell they were moving further away from the van. I thought about my pal, Brian Sullivan. I wondered if he had even seen it coming. I doubted he had but wanted to make certain if it was coming, I would at least have a chance to defend myself. I pulled back, ever so slightly, one of the Velcro strips and peeked out from behind the curtain. I watched to make sure they were not considering firing a round into its side. I saw the smaller one looking in the direction from which I peered. He squinted as if he had noticed the movement. It would have been difficult for him to see me behind the smoked windows but, possible. He moved casually back toward the van and I slowly eased the curtain back into place. I was confident he did not distinguish me but, he had obviously thought he noticed something. He struck the side of the van near where I was sitting apparently with a swing or an indiscriminate kick while shouting a stream of vulgarities, "What the fuck. Yo fuckin fat mudda five-o. Open up, you dick sucking bitches."

I looked at Chad who was perspiring heavily. His face was red with aggravation and I thought he might be contemplating opening the door and telling the punks what he thought of them. Sandy Foster, I noticed, simply looked worried. I was amused by the teenager's comments and sensed his threats were empty. I thought he was simply testing the waters again. At least, I hoped he was. I raised my index finger to my mouth, gesturing to remain quiet and patient. Chad sanctioned me with a nod but, without his knowledge, I unbuckled the safety strap on my holster. I waited until the harangue subsided and then I slid toward the window again. I cautiously peeled back a small piece of the velcroed curtain. I slowly raised up on my haunches to the window where I immediately saw a large splotch of disgusting phlegm-filled spittle dripping from the window in front of me. The saliva was speckled with green mucous and another yellowish texture that did not give the impression it was ejected from healthy lungs. The sight made me wretch but, the mounting dehydration prohibited me from expelling anything from my vacant stomach.

"This is the undercover, I'm in the lot," crackled a nervous voice from the radio. It was a good thing the U/C told us too, because no one noticed. We had already lost the ability to concentrate, having now been in the van almost two hours. We seemed only to have the energy to curse Vreeswyck, which we all took turns doing.

"I paged the dude and he will call me back." He advised.

He said "dude" inappropriately, the way a person says a word they are not comfortable speaking. Vreeswyck continued to transmit on the radio further relaying information many of us deemed impertinent. He habitually talked on the radio too much and if he ever conveyed information that was important, it was long lost on the fact that he had already been subconsciously tuned out during his long-winded transmissions. While Vreeswyck chatted away, we heard his cell phone ring. We wondered if it was the bad guy and hoped he was going to tell Vreeswyck he couldn't do the deal, releasing us for the weekend.

"That was the guy," Vreeswyck related, "he said he'll be here in five minutes. He's in a white Nissan."

Deals rarely went on time, particularly when Vreeswyck was coordinating them. We all thought something must be wrong, especially if the guy revealed the model of the car he would be arriving in. Sensing this, Hayes asked Vreeswyck specifically where he obtained the vehicle information pertaining to the white Nissan.

"He told me so, boss." Vreeswyck replied.

Hayes countered, "Be on the lookout for anything." Hayes experience and advice was heeded by all of us. He rarely pronounced suspicions but, when he did, his premonitions were usually correct. I thought about Vreeswyck, a peculiarly panicky individual anyway, who also heard Hayes foreboding prediction which probably caused him considerably more apprehension than he needed.

I examined the neighborhood through the small space where the window was not covered by the curtain. Tattered, plastic curtains hung lazily from several open windows and occasionally fluttered in a tantalizing breeze we could not share. Older model cars continued to amble by, most in various stages of disrepair. Occasionally an expensive luxury car pranced along the avenue, sparkling proudly after a fresh detailing at one of the hand car washes which consummated business in the area.

"O-one." Vreeswyck called using Hayes' radio number, "I've talked to this guy several times on the phone." Vreeswyck then went on to describe most of the details of their phone conversations, taking a full two minutes to do so on the air. Standard procedure requires transmissions be kept to a minimum with only pertinent details supposed to be related. Vreeswyck violated this policy frequently. Vreeswyck continued with some more remarks and had not finished when Foster observed a white Nissan pull into the parking lot and pull behind Vreeswyck's U/C vehicle. The guy's arrival had Vreeswyck scrambling to hide his portable radio, which he always carried with him, including home over most holidays. I figured he placed it right next to the turkey so the in-laws could begrudge it. We all peered out of the van and watched as Vreeswyck tried to beat the bad guy out of his car. The bad guy was out first however, and moved quickly toward the U/C. He was a tall, slender black male, about 22 years of age wearing a powder blue sweatshirt emblazoned with the logo of the University of North Carolina. From our vantage point we could see he wore expensive basketball sneakers and appeared well-groomed. Vreeswyck met him as he exited the UCV, the undercover vehicle. The bad guy offered his hand and Phil Vreeswyck took it, shaking it awkwardly. By the second and third gesture Vreeswyck was left bumbling and scrambling. They stood together for several minutes while we remained across the street monitoring their activity from a distance of about fifty yards. We watched closely, scrutinizing their gestures for behavior which might indicate confrontation. In the undercover capacity, the primary asset protecting Vreeswyck was his own instincts and us, parked half a football field away. Bullets traveled much faster. The bad guy assessed Vreeswyck while Vreeswyck evaluated him. I was nauseous and growing tired but, I had to concentrate. We all had stood where Vreeswyck was and he relied on us as much as we him when we had been undercover. It was something most agents were able to do, leave personal differences and opinions behind to protect each other. It appeared the conversation was cordial but, we all watched for the distress signal, the crossing of the arms across the chest in this case. It was the "help" signal and by doing it, the message was sent he sensed trouble and needed assistance. We watched the bad guy turn and walk toward his car. He entered and reached underneath the seat as if to retrieve something. Vreeswyck moved toward the bad guy's car and then ducked into the driver's window. This was an excellent chance for Vreeswyck to see the kilos if the bad guy had brought them. A clever dealer wouldn't have but since we had no way to judge the bad guy's capacity, we prepared for a bust or distress signal. The bust gesture had been agreed upon to be the raising of the UCV's trunk. Since Vreeswyck wasn't near his car, the bust signal would be the distress sign, the arms across the chest. A half minute passed with no indication then, Vreeswyck ducked out of the car and moved toward the U/C vehicle. The Nissan engaged and drove toward the mouth of the lot. The suspect's cautious activity indicated he was an experienced dealer. He signaled for a right turn which he could have made unabatedly however, he did not proceed. Instead he elected to remain in the lot. Despite the lack of traffic and relative ease which he could have made the turn, he chose to sit there.

"This is the U/C." Vreeswyck's voice sounded broken and fidgety as if he needed the relief of a drink of water. I hoped he wasn't holding the radio too high, where the bad guy could easily see it. "He says he's got it. That it will be delivered to me."

Hayes interrupted. "O-one to O-three. Follow the bad guy….loosely."

The Nissan had not yet pulled out and Chad Jennings whispered that fact into the radio.

Hayes retorted, "When it does, give me a direction."

"Ten-four." Chad responded, quietly.

"Break. Break. This is the U/C." It was a clumsy and unnecessary interruption but, Vreeswyck relished the opportunity to refer to himself as the U/C. "One, he wants to see the money, what should I do ?"

There was a brief pause, then the supervisor said, "Bluff him." That was not often the best advice but, Hayes had no choice. The support staff of the fiscal department had left after half a day and there had been no others authorized at the office to distribute flash money. It was another glaring example of the agency's over-reliance on supplemental staff to get anything accomplished. And given the fact Vreeswyck was not blessed with a good poker face, it was not the best strategy to mislead a seasoned dope dealer whose intentions were equally unknown. The bad guy was expecting $46,000 for the two kilos. Vreeswyck was expected to view the dope and give the bust signal. His rap would have to be very polished to see the dope without showing the money and without the money, Vreeswyck was in a precarious situation.

The Nissan had finally pulled out, north on Kostner Avenue but, instead of continuing north, made a sharp U-turn and pulled up directly next to us. We all squatted and tried to remain motionless. The Nissan's horn sounded twice. I considered looking out the window but, my movement could rock the van, motion which might be noticed so instead, I remained still. I hoped another agent, perhaps Hayes, would be in position to monitor the activity.

Loudly and unexpectedly the radio cracked. "This is the U/C." Jennings grabbed for the radio and groped at the volume nipple trying to turn it off. The transmission was cut off and we hoped it had not been heard outside the van. It remained off as we hoped the Nissan would drive away. A few moments of silence ensued.

"I'm gonna look up." Jennings said without confidence as if mentioning it out loud was a solicitation to Foster and me to confirm it was a good idea.

Unsure myself, I nodded in agreement.

Chad Jennings was six foot four and about 235 pounds. He was in decent shape but, still with his size, he was bulky. In addition, he too had been squatting awkwardly and uncomfortably like Foster and I had been. As he rose from his haunches toward the window, his knees cracked. He teetered and lost his balance. He tumbled clumsily but the descent was slow as if he was falling in slow motion all the while trying unsuccessfully to gain his balance. He desperately groped with his right hand seizing one of the velcroed curtains. The flimsy drape was no match for his ungainly descent and it tore easily away from its mount, exposing the whole window in the process. Jennings fell sideways to his left with his shoulder striking a small fire extinguisher secured at the base of the passenger seat. His huge frame made an audible thud against the metal cylinder which had been emptied a long time ago, probably during a lighthearted prank.

"God-damn it!" he shouted.

I looked at him then rose up to see if the Nissan's driver had heard us. The Nissan had fortunately moved and the immediate area around us was vacated.

Foster moved toward Jennings to get him righted. He flailed again, more humiliated than hurt. He quickly sat back up and assumed a spot on the crate. I leaned toward him and patted his shoulder which was soaked with perspiration.

"Are you alright?"

He brought his left hand to his left ear and pulled it away quickly, revealing a small smudge of blood.

"Fuck this fucking nowhere fucking deal. It ain't going to fuckin go. Fuck it." He announced furiously. "Vreeswyck is such an asshole."

I knew by Jennings familiar demeanor he was alright. His ego was more bruised than his body. I sat back onto my own crate and could no longer conceal a laugh. Foster began laughing as well. Jennings responded by balling the curtain he still held in his right hand and launching it at the wall of the van.

"Jesus Christ!" He said and began laughing too.

The levity of the moment temporarily diverted our attention from the deal. For a few seconds all of us forgot about the undercover, our discomfort and our purpose for being in the cramped van. It was mentally impossible for us to concentrate on what might appear to be insignificant details for two or three uninterrupted hours and the frivolity had been a welcome diversion.

"Where did the Nissan go?" Jennings asked, reiterating the purpose of our assignment. I pivoted up from the milk crate, which was too low for me to see out the windows.

"I don't see it." I extended my hand, "Give me that curtain you clumsy oaf."

"Fuck you." He responded, half serious, half embarrassed. He collected it from the floor and tossed it toward my direction. I straightened it out and aligned it properly against the Velcro strip.

Foster asked, "Is the radio on?"

Without answering, Jennings checked and we all realized it had been deactivated, tactically placed into that status when the Nissan had pulled up next to us. Jennings flipped it on and we heard a transmission in mid-sentence.

"…don't know what they're doing but, the number two just walked up. He looks like a kid."

We listened, trying to catch up to what had been transpiring, hoping we had not missed anything important during the minute and a half we were out of radio contact.

"There's the Nissan, behind us." Foster relayed, as she glanced out one of the side windows. Sitting in the car was the driver whom Vreeswyck had been negotiating with, as well as one of the two teenaged males that had harassed us while we sat in the van. It was the second boy, the taller one with the tattered T-shirt and the one who had been most verbally abusive.

"They're just talking. Can't see anything" chirped Brenda Xavier from an unknown position. The radio, now turned to an audible level, gave us clues to information we had missed.

Jennings described our experience with the second suspect. "Six to one. That number two had been checking us out big time. He may have made us." Chad whispered.

"Ten four."

We sat quietly, waiting for instructions that did not come. One thing any deal required was patience. I tried to put my soaked clothing out of my mind, though the feeling of damp underwear to me is one of life's most irritating sensations. Six delivered another radio message.

"Number two is walking away from the white car. It looks like he might be carrying a small bag."

Indeed he did. The suspect, number two as we now referred to him, walked right past our van without giving it any further consideration. He carried in his hand a small, white plastic bag, about the size one may get at a college bookstore. It had been wrapped around its contents and judging by its proportions certainly could have contained two kilos of coke. The teenager grasped it tightly as he proceeded along an abandoned brick-faced building. It was freckled with sloppy splotches of paint as if even the vandals were too bored to brand the space with their elaborate, urban tags and chose instead to simply throw what was left of their cans against its wall.

"He's waking toward the U/C now. It could be the package." Jennings reported

We watched as number two proceeded across Kostner Avenue, dodging a beat-up rusted Impala with distinguishably heavy bass influenced music thumping from its voluminous stereo. He continued toward Vreeswyck.

"Where's the Nissan?"

"Its moving," came a response.

"Where?" Hayes inquired.

"Phil is out of the car," said six and as he released the transmitter. We heard the buzz of static indicating two radios were transmitting at the same time. The interference lasted several critical seconds.

"…around the car to the trunk." Continued the disrupted message from someone else.

"Where's the Nissan at?" Jennings asked me as the same question was posed by one of the surveillance agents over the radio.

"Break! Break! This is three, where's the Nissan going?"

I listened but, concentrated on the U/C, our main responsibility. The driver of the Nissan was the source and his movement and subsequent arrest was critical. However, I watched the U/C as he stood at the rear of his automobile and near the trunk. He raised the trunk, presumably to show the bad guy his money but, to us, it was the bust signal.

"Its a bust!" I said and someone else shouted it over the air.

The sliding door flung open, crashing hard against its hinge. It was always thrown open like that no matter who opened it when the bust signal came. Adrenaline always fueled the energetic propulsion.

The three of us poured from the van and moved toward the U/C's vehicle, running. We advanced across Kostner. We could only see Vreeswyck and number two partially, because they stood behind the raised trunk which contained a spare tire, a couple greasy rags and jumper cables but, no money. As we ran toward the U/C, a magazine cartridge dropped from Jennings' pouch and his right heel kicked it high into the air. I heard the screech of tires, a vehicle accelerating abruptly from a stationery position, probably one of the other surveillance agents or maybe the Nissan seeking to escape. My focus remained on Vreeswyck as I traversed the gap between our van, him and the bad guy. I saw Bad Guy Number Two peer around the side of the opened trunk. We were no more than twenty yards away and I could clearly see the look of horror spread across his face. His brain was compelled to calculate in micro-seconds his course of action, fight or flee. Our minds were racing with the same challenges further burdened with the added anxieties caused by physical exhaustion. Our motivation was to protect the undercover and ourselves but, also to capture the suspect. Its a melodrama which plays out every day between the hunter and the hunted. In the safaris and wilderness, its the stalker and its prey. In civilized societies, its the cop and the felon. Number two chose to flee. He screamed and pivoted, running literally for his life. As he took his inaugural steps, he instinctively extracted something from his waistband which I recognized as a possible gun. His right arm extended capriciously toward us and the discharge confirmed my belief. I slowed looking for cover in an open parking lot where none existed while momentum propelled me toward him and his weapon. I wondered if I had been hit but, I felt no pain. I felt the power of my legs churning and my heart pumping. This all occurring in time marked in flashes, not seconds. The terrified suspect waved the gun behind him as he ran, pulling the trigger again, sending another shot randomly into the neighborhood but, by the grace of God, not through me. I dove to the ground for asylum and raised my weapon to shoot at him.

I brought the gun from the ground as I crashed into the asphalt paved lot, skidding on my chest along the scabrous surface, which at the time, made no impression on my elbows. I heard popping sounds. I moved to take aim and the boy instantly tumbled oddly, sprawling like a plane crashing to the earth. His head and upper body slammed against the ground and he rolled, the feet and knees tumbling forward over the torso with the shoulders and head following in a complete and crude revolution. His upper body flopped over and he landed on his face and chest. The sight of my gun followed the acrobatic body and continued to target him as he finally came to rest. I squeezed the trigger softly, a millimeter from sending my own sortie into him. I hesitated and on this occasion, the split-second decision did not cost me or my fellow agents.

I remained on the ground. Slowly, the sound of the chaos became recognizable. I heard screaming and yelling. A few moments later, I heard torturous wailing though it would be several minutes before I found out the reason. I rose slowly, covering the boy with my gun and peeking around behind me. I saw Jennings, on one knee in perfect marksman pose, still aiming at the prone boy. I crept toward the body and as I came closer, my instincts told me the boy was lifeless. Still, I covered him with my weapon, my heart pounding. I approached the figure and saw the blood already streaming from the right rear of his skull. There was a small wound but, I could clearly see the amber brain matter oozing from the opening. It looked like yellow cottage cheese floating in a deep, purple-red river. As I got closer, the river bubbled and spurted occasionally. I reached toward the youth, compassionately, to help the fallen human being. Just before touching him, I withdrew my hand recognizing the adolescent, the boy, was now reduced to inanimate evidence and, as such, I should not disturb it.

He lay in a swelling pond of his own life juices no more alive than the rubbish and the trash which littered the parking lot around him. I knelt beside the body as others formed a vague circle. I noticed Jennings among them standing authoritatively over the corpse with his hands on his hips. I caught a glimpse of a slight smirk of loathing cross his lips. He knelt down beside me and said defiantly, "Is the piece of shit dead?"

His brief life was over. His perforated skull made that obvious. Whether he was a piece of shit or not was a judgment his God would make. Society might view him with a contemptible eye. He was poor, he was a drug dealer, he was black. He was not an actor, an entertainer or an athlete. He was not even yet a man. His life would only be notorious in death. The news would cover it just because it was a shoot-out on a public street with federal agents. The fact it involved a white DEA Agent shooting a black teenager would curiously appeal to the news producers who would seize every possibility and pursue every angle in an attempt to lay blame at someone for the events which transpired in the desolate fast food lot.

I believed I retained the right to detest him. His actions could have killed one of us and it could have easily been me, laying in the street with a gorge in my chest spewing the contents of my organs out onto Kostner Avenue. I didn't feel that way, however.

I looked around and verified all my co-workers were safe. The wailing came from a woman who had been hit and dragged by the Nissan when the driver observed us converging on his accomplice. An ambulance siren wailed and we would direct it toward the woman, whose legs had been mangled under the rear wheels of the Nissan. She was still trapped in the wheel well when the paramedics arrived. The driver had only been stopped when he crashed his car into a dumpster after having lost control of it. He sustained only a broken nose.

I returned to the boy. The Chicago Police had arrived and a second emergency unit had as well. Hayes had removed Jennings and suggested we all vacate the area as quickly as possible. The inflamed neighborhood could become restless and Hayes did not want anyone giving statements until we all had a chance to talk about the incident. The DEA would investigate the matter as they did all shootings and there was no question Chad Jennings' actions were appropriate in shooting the teenager. The bag had contained two kilos of coke and the delivery boy's attempt to shoot us meant the use of deadly force would unquestionably be justified. I would attest to that fact. However, I didn't feel any better about his death because my partner would not be considered culpable. I approached the body again. By this time, the police started cordoning off the entire parking lot preventing curious onlookers from inspecting the fallen boy. I neared the police and identified myself. The officer allowed me to proceed close to the inner circle of paramedics and officers. They had turned the boy onto his back where I observed the surface of his face to be covered with blood. A grotesque tennis ball sized bulge had swelled above his left eye, caused by the streaking bullet pushing the brain matter and skull fragments through his head. They placed a modest grey blanket over him which failed to cover his legs. A rivulet of blood had emerged underneath him with two thick red tributaries heading toward the doors of the closed restaurant. Pictures and measurements were taken while the stream selected its path through tiny hills of litter and patches of uneven and broken concrete.

Night had fallen when his body was finally removed. Members of the coroner's office had placed him in a black body bag and loaded him like a bag of mulch into the rear of their van. Inexplicably, I ignored Hayes' advice to immediately leave and remained to see the deceased removed to be transported to the morgue. When they had lifted the body, several items had fallen from the pants pocket. They turned out to be baseball cards, local players on the Chicago White Sox. The cards were left behind and were eventually squirted to the gutter when a fire truck's crew sprayed water to disperse the coagulated blood.

I walked over to the curb and looked at the cards. They were the familiar ones from my own youth but with a greater emphasis on artwork and presentation. They had already darkened with the boy's blood. I thought about their owner, a mere boy given the sinisterly incumbent task of delivering $46,000 worth of cocaine, yet still innocent enough to maintain an assortment of a few nominally valued cardboard pictures.

In a moment of self reflection which was finally devoid of the rationalizations I had adopted for my own despicable thieving behavior, I analyzed what had become of my own values and ethics. I recognized my morality, once genuine and virtuous, had been turned upside down. What terrified me about this revelation was the fact I used my position as a federal agent to convince myself I was right side up within the discombobulated realm. Avoiding the collecting pool of blood and the fire hydrant which was left leaking, almost as if it was a city appendage urinating on the tragic scene around it, I recognized for me, for my survival and my sanity, the business of the powder and the paper had come to an end.

28

Hours after the appalling incident, after everyone who had been on surveillance had gathered to contemplate our actions and review the statements, I ventured home. On the way, I received several pages from individuals who I believed were only curious about the specifics of what had transpired. Most were co-workers, including a page from Walker as well as a call from a frantic female acquaintance who, in reality, seemed more fascinated about a city-street shootout than she was concerned about my welfare. I disregarded most of the others, uninterested in conjuring the sanguinary details involving the death of the boy. Walker paged me a second, then a third time, which surprised me but, did not overly disturb me despite the fact he included the code "911," a common tactic indicating his page was an emergency.

When I finally telephoned him, I realized Walker had been unaware of the shooting involving our group. I advised him what had happened and after expressing relief none of us had been injured, he relayed the reason behind his tenacious effort to contact me. Walker had spent the last several hours comforting Jorge Carrasco's wife. Her husband had been found in a cheap hotel room in nearby Wheeling with his neck slit open. Apparently he had been missing for several days and his wife had no idea where he had been. She said Carrasco had telephoned his wife a few days ago and said if he did not return, tell Walker. Earlier that day, the Wheeling Police Department found Carrasco not only murdered but, hog-tied and disemboweled. The police telephoned Carrasco's wife when they found her phone number among Carrasco's effects. Walker was outraged and upset and emphatically insisted Carrasco's death was irrefutably linked in some way to Jesus Santilles. Walker was right. Carrasco was the informant who knew the most information about Santilles. He had attempted to persuade Walker to believe Santilles was intending to return to Chicago. There was no way to convince myself my actions had nothing to do with Carrasco and I knew my robbery contributed, if not was directly responsible, for his murder.

Walker had attempted to console Carrasco's wife but, there was no way to successfully do so. After all, she believed it was her husband's association with Walker and the DEA which led to his murder. Walker chastised himself over the phone for his failure to protect his inform-ant. I had to feign sympathy and I told Walker it was not his fault. I knew earnestly it was not. Santilles had survived my assault and upon his return home to Florida he suspected Carrasco, and perhaps others, had been responsible for the robbery. The undeniable prospect existed there might be additional corpses scattered around in Northern Illinois, depending upon Santilles' degree of vengefulness and scale of suspicion.

Though I was exhausted, I offered to meet Walker immediately in order to ascertain the circumstances of Carrasco's death. Walker rebuffed me, acknowledging the murder scene had already been cleaned up and no evi-dence existed which couldn't be uncovered in the morning. I requested and eventually insisted Walker meet me in Lake County so that we both could piece together the possible reason for Carrasco's homicide. Walker finally agreed and recommended we should do everything within our power to ascertain why Carrasco was murdered. My intention, on the other hand, was to impede anyone from ever knowing the reason.

*

We met in the Waukegan Police Department's detectives offices, basement rooms in a smaller building which sat adjacent to the main police station. The thin, cerulean carpeted floors and hazy florescent lights always made me feel like I was in a dream and I felt lethargic in the office if I ever sat in there too long. The modern equipment and the money spent refurbishing the offices certainly made the building more comfortable than most antiquated and grimy police stations but, the office always seemed to leave me unsettled. I know we weren't welcome and the ill-will was justified. Walker's refusal to share the information we developed was deeply resented by most of the detectives, especially the members of the narcotics unit. The sole reason we were permitted to use the facility and some of the department's equipment was Walker had promised the Waukegan Police Chief his unit would share in some of the anticipated lucrative seizures from the case. That knowledge gave me a very ominous sensation especially knowing I had not only stolen close to three quarters of a million dollars from a crook but, in doing so, had essentially swindled requisite funding from the Waukegan Police Department. The officers were perpetually complaining about the stingy budget and aged equipment, a common criticism among most police, and even a modest percentage of Santilles' money would have greatly contributed to the department's hopes to upgrade. Though I was confident I had managed to succeed in the theft, I still maintained a paranoid fear I would be exposed. I considered showing up in Waukegan to be a risk but, I decided I would be much better prepared if I assumed an active interest in Carrasco's death. My participation would permit me to examine evidence of my involvement or culpable behavior and provide me a position to hinder or deter its discovery.

I entered the offices and proceeded to the basement where Walker operated from a makeshift desk seated next to the only detective who still spoke to him. Both were in another, adjacent interview room. I could hear Walker's distinct, abrasive voice as well as that of a woman's. Despite Walker's façade, his voice still sounded inconsiderate and uncompassionate to me. The woman replied in broken English. Her excitable accent was Hispanic and I surmised it probably was Jorge's wife. I listened and her intermittent sobs confirmed it. I sat with my back to the room's door, ashamed. I had no interest in being introduced to the woman whose husband I had a hand in killing.

I heard her say, "There's nothing left. I must go home. Hector doesn't know yet. I can't bear to tell him."

I immediately assumed Hector was Jorge Carrasco's son. A boy without a father.

"Mrs. Carrasco, I'm going to try to get approval for some money for you from my office."

The proud woman shot back a retort, "Hasn't your government done enough? Money? Money won't replace my husband. Money won't take my son swimming or throw him a ball. Money…Money is what put him into the mess. I don't want money. I don't want your help, James Walker. I want…" her voice quivered and she wept uncontrollably.

I heard chairs scramble and the door open. I bowed my head in compunction and with the hope I wouldn't have to see her. I was disgraced. Walker attempted to follow her out.

"I never want to see your devil face again, Jim!" She shouted as Walked ambled behind her.

"That's the drug business, senorita." said the Waukegan Detective sarcastically but, wisely outside of her grievous earshot.

I sat there and faded into self-consumed thoughts. I had been an equitable person. My family was decent, middle class, good morals. I was an honest young man when I started my job. What had I become now? A thief. A liar. Could I consider myself an accomplice to murder? Jorge Carrasco was murdered because I robbed a man who Carrasco was providing intelligence against. I thought about the word betrayal and couldn't think of a more suitable poster boy than me.

Walker returned. He carried a manila envelope under the crux of his arm. "Look at these." He tossed the envelope toward me and as it landed across the desk where I was sitting, one 4" by 6" photograph slid out. It was a naked Jorge Carrasco, discolored and bloated from the onslaught of decay. He was face down in a bathtub engulfed in a dried crimson lagoon of his own blood.

"Oh shit, man." I gagged and desperately attempted to arrest the nausea which climbed my esophagus.

"Are you kidding me ?" The amused Waukegan Detective announced. "You have never seen anything like that. Christ, you Feds are ridiculous. You should see some of the others. Man, we couldn't even show his wife them. Jimmy, show him the one with Jorge's sliced off dick in his mouth."

"Fuck you, douche bag." I said.

"Fuck me?" The astounded detective asked, "You're saying fuck me in my office, you faggot. No sir, Fuck you." As his rage built, he ordered, "Get the fuck out of here." The detective approached me to do the job himself before Walker intervened, stepping in front of the charging, affronted man.

"I'll be outside, Jim." I rose and left. I suppose I did look like a coward but, it wasn't the pictures that sickened me. It was me that sickened me.

"That's right, yellow-belly. I knew you were yellow. Get out, yellow fed backed-belly."

The detective managed to barrage me with several other nouns with the adjective yellow preceding it before I crossed the threshold of the office exit. I walked outside and down Sabonjian Place, the small road outside the Waukegan Police Station named in honor of the city's former mayor. I continued walking on the tree-lined street to a twelve-foot replica of the Statue of Liberty, dedicated by the Boy Scouts of America. There, I had a cigarette and contemplated the ramifications of my greed.

"You alright?"

The voice startled me. It belonged to Walker who was right behind me. I had been so consumed in thought I had lost sense of time and place.

"Yea. This stuff is just getting to me, that's all."

"I know." He replied.

I didn't want to be a coward. I didn't want Walker to understand or wonder why I had acted so strangely but, there was nothing I could think to say. I couldn't defend myself.

"This is a cold world. Drugs are a cold business. Dog eat Dog. Eat or you will get eaten, man."

Walker's demeanor had changed since I had spoken to him on the phone. He seemed less upset, less concerned with Mrs. Carrasco and the case. His attitude was glacial and matter-of-fact.

"I'm going to give Mrs. Carrasco a ride home. Why don't you take off, I'll talk to you tomorrow." He gave me a thumbs-up sign and walked away.

I sat on the steps for awhile, thinking about what I had become. Thinking about where I was going. I decided I should gather myself and leave. I didn't want to confront the detective again.

I started the car and drove out of the conglomeration of municipal buildings onto that familiar road, Grand Avenue. I thought a milk shake might calm my nerves so I pulled into a fast food place and waited in the drive-through. I sat in a line of about three cars, passing the time playing with the "good-time" radio hoping a familiar song would assuage thoughts of my own guilt. While I waited, the thought of a treat like ice cream consumed me with liability. I wasn't worthy of an innocent pleasure like ice cream. I pulled out of the line and drove west. After several blocks, I noticed the familiar black antennae of Walker's Regal. It was a half block in front of me. Walker was escorting Mrs. Carrasco home. Despite his social shortcomings, I surmised he probably was a decent man. Obtaining money for the family was a nice gesture but, Walker wasn't obligated to do so. Jorge Carrasco knew the dangers associated with being an informant, he signed a document outlining them. Walker would be required to submit a ton of paperwork to get approval from headquarters to pay Mrs. Carrasco compensation for her lost husband. Walker could have turned his back on her. Maybe, I thought, he was mellowing.

As we drove along, I noticed the Regal's right blinker flicker. The flashing light seemed to rouse me from my daydreaming trance. I realized we were nearing the intersection of Elmwood and Grand. Walker was making the turn. He was driving up to the house where Jesus Santilles spent his nights. I realized the woman in Walker's car was not only the widow of DEA Informant Jorge Carrasco, apparently, she was also the mistress of Jesus Santilles.

*

I was greatly concerned with this development, Walker's association with Mrs. Carrasco. There was no legitimate investigative purpose for him to maintain a relationship with her however, to protect himself, he should have made it known. For some reason, Walker did not. Mrs. Carrasco would have been a terrific source of information regarding Santilles. Being Santilles' lover in Chicagoland, she surely would have known when he intended to visit. She most certainly would be a very trusted member of the organization if Santilles was safeguarding his money under the roof where she lived. I had witnessed payments made to Jorge Carrasco for information he supplied but, I had never known his wife to be around when any compensation was delivered. I searched my memory regarding the first surveillances we had done, especially pertaining to Elmwood Street. I couldn't recall any details about the home or if Walker had ever really identified who lived there. I know Walker had never mentioned the address to me as Carrasco's home and though it was an incidental thing at the time, it was an incredulous error for me to have neglected to research who actually lived on Elmwood.

I read my notes and examined the case files in the following days looking for any clues pertaining to Carrasco's wife and her connection with Santilles. I reviewed CI Payments and found no information about Mrs. Carrasco. All of the informants in the case were males and notations and reports were accurately filed pertaining to the specific information they supplied and the recompense they were given. I had hoped there would be some reference to Mrs. Carrasco which would explain an association between herself and Walker. I knew Walker was a meticulous agent and would detail any related information about her to cover himself if any sordid accusation was ever made. The fact that Walker elected to leave her out of the case file worried me. He had to know about her when we saw Santilles depart the house and instead of informing us about her relevance, he elected to keep it to himself.

Walker was a married man with two kids, a steady, well-paying job and a bright future. He was respected and admired. He had wed his high school sweetheart, a registered nurse, and by all accounts, he was happy. His daughter had just started elementary school and when she returned home, it was to a three bedroom colonial on a small parcel of land in exclusive Winthrop Harbor. Walker should have been content to live the remainder of his life in comfort and contentment.

Jorge Carrasco's wife wasn't enough of a looker to risk that success. She was the wife of a petty drug dealer and the mistress of an insidious courier. Jim Walker was not, could not, be interested in Mrs. Carrasco sexually or socially. His clandestine association with her could only benefit him one way.

29

Solemn agents from the Office of Inspection flew from Washington to investigate Chad Jennings' shooting and interview all the participants. The inspectors were all former street agents themselves but, because they served to examine and scrutinize their own and their findings sometimes resulted in termination and occasionally prosecution, they were never welcome. I felt a particular fear at the prospect of being interviewed. One never was certain exactly what information the investigators had access to and occasionally, they were known to engage in witch-hunts and sting operations. Their reviews were based on investigations which resulted in dismissals and prosecutions and by virtue of their positions, their power and their goals, I had every reason to be worried.

The liberal Chicago media had pounced on the shooting incident the evening it occurred. Camera crews filmed their news station's reporters standing in the lot where the homicide transpired. In response, Our SAC, Kenneth Starr, issued a press release which included a concise and impartial statement in which the Drug Enforcement Administration refused to acknowledge wrongdoing for the boy's death. However, the honey-tongued communication also failed to provide conclusive and resolute support for my partner.

Admirably, Bobby Hayes had stepped forward and told Jennings not to worry. Hayes was "a stand-up guy" who always seemed willing to endorse his subordinate's actions. It was a quality I greatly admired but, disturbingly, found lacking time and time again in many of the DEA Supervisors, especially the younger ones who had been hastily promoted via patronage fueled by nepotism or beauracratic processes which had nothing to do with skill or ability to manage.

In the days following the shooting, protestors converged on the US Postal Plaza across from our offices in the Dirksen Federal Building to demonstrate what they termed "abuse of power" and "police brutality." They accused the DEA and its Agents of having no regards for human rights or life. During the demonstration, no mention was made of Rupert Wilson, the 22 year-old twice convicted felon who dragged an unfortunate woman under his Nissan's wheels attempting to flee. In my opinion, the time, effort and expense organizing and deploying the protestors would have been far beneficial if its impetus had been directed at helping the woman who Wilson had run over. She had been told she could expect to lose one of her legs. She was a cashier at a supermarket and the single mother of three.

I told the Inspectors during my interview that Chad Jennings, quite possibly, had saved my life. I did not feel it was an exaggeration. I added I not only felt Jennings had acted correctly but, my actions in not shooting at the suspect could have been judged negligent. I was asked to elaborate and I told the Inspectors I should have fired my weapon. I almost told them I had because frankly, I should have but, I decided against claiming I had fired in case someone else actually did and had hit something or someone which had yet to be discovered. I went through the remainder of the interview without consequence and was greatly relieved the inspectors did not pursue any additional avenues of investigation. I attributed it to their schedule and the collective public interest in Jennings' case. Thanks to the media coverage, their decision had to be rendered promptly and the fact "shit was hitting the fan all over the place" as one inspector put it, gave me relief they had no clue about my indiscretions. I learned several inspectors had recently been deployed throughout the DEA to investigate cases like the agent in Kalamazoo, Michigan who had discharged his DEA issued sub-machine gun off a cruise ship in an incredulous but successful attempt to shoot down several feeding seagulls. With agents like him and another, who had sprayed pepper gas under the door of a rambunctious newlyweds' suite, I knew the inspectors had very little time conducting substantially more challenging investigations like those required to catch someone like me, an anonymous and indistinguishable man robbing otherwise loathed drug dealers with the assistance and authority of a federal badge.

The internal investigation vindicated Jennings' actions completely and determined he followed guidelines as they pertained to the use of deadly force. Jennings, who had been understandably nervous throughout the investigative proceeding and the media focus, was eventually cleared. Apparently a few witnesses at the scene, who had no interest or motive to support the police, had volunteered their accounts of the incident. Their recollections supported most of the details we had related, especially the most important of which was the boy had a weapon and had discharged it. Though I was satisfied Jennings was cleared, I did not advocate his decision to have a small party at Cavanaugh's celebrating the judgment. Jim Walker, who by his own accounts dreamed of the opportunity to "cap" someone, organized the party and stated during it his only regret was not having been given the opportunity to "double tap" the boy himself.

The activities and revelations of those last few days had a profound effect on me. I couldn't get the thought of the teenager out of my mind. I knew in my heart that dead boy could have been me. He himself could have shot me or someone else might have, that day or some other. His prone body could have been Jesus Santilles up in Waukegan, crumpled and seemingly lifeless from my actions or Jorge

Carrasco for that matter. Carrasco was certainly as dead as the boy and admittedly, my actions directly led to his homicide.

When I had started my career I was filled with pride, honor, integrity and moral character. Then I chose to embark on a life whose behavior facilitated my descent into a filthy world of conniving, thievery and murder.

*

I decided on a weekend ride across the state of Illinois to clear my head and assess my life. I headed south on I-55 toward St. Louis leaving directly from work on a Friday afternoon. The additional stress of the heavy traffic simply departing Chicagoland contributed to my decision but, by Springfield, the Illinois State Capitol and about as heartland America as one could get, I had made up my mind. The concept of cocaine and its sales, its interdiction, its profits and losses, its existence on the streets, on the news, in our sisters and mothers and brothers, in our minds, in our souls, on our televisions and mirrors and disgustingly in my very lungs by virtue of my own hands had led me to the only conclusion I could possibly reach. I had to resign my position. I had to escape the world of drugs and leave the administration I had so dishonored. I had to quit to preserve myself and save my own life. On Monday, I planned to walk into Bobby Hayes' office and announce my resignation.

I knew people didn't walk away from federal employment, especially a secure job like I was fortunate enough to possess. More importantly, I realized my decision would arouse considerable suspicion particularly since I had made no overtures regarding disenchantment with my employment. I hadn't mentioned offers pertaining to other job prospects, either. I decided I simply would tell Hayes and the rest of the group it was a combination of stress, burnout and a need to depart the high cost of living and general strain of Chicago and big city living.

It had been a long time since the reserve of cash I had accumulated had been sub-planted from my main thoughts. I conceded by leaving the DEA I would be making a decision which would alter and probably derail my career goals. I hadn't expected to remain an agent for thirty years but, I did believe I would continue working until I was offered something in the private sector. I had hoped I would establish connections which would enhance my professional growth. I believed my experience with the DEA combined with the ever present concern about drugs in the work place would create a need for people with my background. I believed my abilities could someday land me a position at some large corporation as the Director of Security. I pictured myself travelling with executives to exotic locales such as Europe and the Far East. Accomplishing what objectives, I wasn't quite sure. I don't know why a company would require their Director of Security to travel with anyone internationally but, it had been an ambition to acquire such a position. By leaving the DEA abruptly, I acknowledged to myself those goals would probably never be realized. Though my career would be extinguished, I must confess, the longer I drove along those corn row highways of Southern Illinois, the less worried I became.

I knew that my thieving activities had serious repercussions for people. I could not rationalize their problems against my success. I was well aware the honorable thing might have been to donate the ill-gotten loot to well deserving charities. I was sure that doing so might someday, possibly, secure a space in heaven for my soul if there even was such a transcendent place. I believed there was. I knew contributing the money was an act which might cleanse my conscience. To disperse the money to goodwill would indeed, be the decision of a champion.

On my way back to Chicago that Sunday morning, having stayed in a budget hotel in rural Litchfield, Illinois, I resolved I was not a hero. I watched the farmers breaking their backs to sustain themselves and their families. I saw the middle-aged fast food manager retrieving plastic lids and sweeping the parking lot to pay the bills and I heard my front desk clerk tell her friend she worked three jobs to put her daughter through college at the University of Illinois. I knew I didn't have the courage or the fortitude to live such an admirable life. I realized I was a coward and conceded I would not be a champion. I considered all the options and concluded I would keep the money, all of it, and start a new life for myself. I would discreetly trickle some of it to my family but, that would have to be accomplished after I had established a business or some bogus entity I claimed generated income. I intended to donate some of it to worthy causes but, most would stay with me. Though it was harvested from robbery and murder, I intended to live the American Dream.

3 0

The following Monday, I determinedly walked into Hayes office and closed the wooden door behind me. Hayes, observant as always, sensed the seriousness of my entry. He removed his glasses and attempted to deflect the gravity with levity, "Connors, you're not going to tell me you're gay are you?"

"No Bobby but, this is important." I did not waver and told him about my intentions to resign. We talked for over two hours behind his closed office door during which time Hayes explored every topic and circumstance which had brought me to my decision with the exception of the particular issue which had contributed the most to my conclusion, my reprehensible thefts. He inquired about my personal life, my finances, my health and my sanity. I was satisfied that most of my life was in order, it was my conscience that was in disarray and a sustained association with the DEA would continue to wreak havoc with my life. Hayes spent most of the discussion attempting to talk me out of my decision and judiciously suggested I take time off before announcing it. He offered me several weeks and recommended I even consider a leave of absence before officially announcing a drastic action like a resignation.

His suggestions were all valid and his advice should have been heeded by an individual facing a critical career choice. However, I did not have a choice. I knew the recent history of my activities and the disastrous personal consequences I would face if I continued on the reckless course on which I had charted. I resolved that I had to leave the DEA and the recollections of what I had done behind me. It was impossible to convince Hayes without telling him my precise reason for quitting. I believed if I could tell one person, it would have been Hayes but, I respected him enough to keep my behavior to myself and not tarnish his reputation by admitting the actions I had undertaken while I was one of his subordinates. Hayes insisted I at least wait one more week before taking my decision to the ASACS. I agreed, though I was determined to submit my resignation. Hayes suggested I utilize vacation time to take the week and decide away from the distractions and influence of the office.

I utilized that week prudently and transported my fortune to Philadelphia. I rented a van from a local moving company and transferred the old recliner with its precious bank note stuffing. I also packaged the remaining funds from the closet wall into an old duffel bag filled with clothes. I loaded the van with other personal items that included my bedroom furniture and a few living room pieces. I drove the 775 miles across I-80 through Indiana, Ohio and Pennsylvania dutifully complying with all road signs and posted speed limits. My thoughts were occasionally pervaded by the clean living residents of the homes I passed along the way but, most of my attention was directed toward obedient driving. I proceeded as methodically and cautiously as Jesus Santilles had been when we had followed him. I arrived in Philly unannounced. I did not wish to disturb my parents with the news I was leaving the Drug Enforcement Administration. I feared their keen parental perception would see through my transparent facade and they would somehow recognize me for what I had become.

I safeguarded the money by obtaining storage facilities with fictitious identification. I had acquired the bogus credentials initially utilizing baptismal certificates which I had purchased in a religious shop. I had filled out the documents with legitimate information of real people which I had gleaned from our micro-fiche information regarding driver's licenses, addresses, social security numbers and credit checks. Assuming someone else's identity is ridiculously easy especially when one exudes confidence in his own fraudulent story. I claimed my apartment had been burned out and the only item of identification I had salvaged was an old baptismal certificate. Whereas social security cards or employment identification was not trusted, people readily accepted a baptismal certificate as legitimate proof as to who I was. I supposed it was their faith in people not to abuse religion and something as sacred as the Christian sacraments for sinister gains. Either way, I had obtained a plethora of identification which I used in Southeastern Pennsylvania to procure the storage facilities. After I returned to Philadelphia for good, I planned to move about a third of my cash inside my mother's home, secreting it in old childhood belongings where I reasoned if anything was to happen to me at least, some of that money might someday be found. Until then, it would have to remain hidden in cinderblock lockers. None of it was deposited into any account where it could be traced by inquisitive investigators.

Before I left for Pennsylvania, I had disposed of the various pieces of jewelry I had obtained. My provident nature prevented me from throwing the costly items into the trash but, I didn't want to risk being caught with them. I opted to drive into Downers Grove where I had a beer at one of my favorite sports bars situated on the perimeter of one of DuPage County's largest malls. Through one of the large plate glass windows, I observed people walking through the parking lot toward the shopping mall entrance. I waited until I saw a person that looked as if they could benefit from an unexpected blessing of discovered treasure. I intended to bestow the items on a person who I hoped wouldn't be ethical and attempt to return the items to their owners. I saw a thirtyish woman arrive in an exhausted and rusted vehicle with a cracked front windshield. She solicitously corralled her adolescent children and escorted them into the entrance of the mall's cinema. I finished my second beer and retrieved the jewelry from my car which included several watches and two gold chains. Among the collection was a Patek Phillipe 18K gold watch which I had determined to be worth more than nine grand. Three years prior I would have never imagined possessing such an extravagant item let alone having the wherewithal to give it away. I wiped the items clean of fingerprints, as a precautionary and excessively paranoid measure and utilizing the cover of nightfall, tucked the items under the front portion of her hood where the windshield and wipers were situated. I hoped no one would see them there while she was in the theater and that when she returned she would be pleasantly surprised by her discovery. I thought she might be perplexed but, hopefully would not be too alarmed. I went home, slept and set out for Philadelphia.

*

I returned from Philadelphia completely satisfied with my decision to leave the DEA. The week away from the office gave me an opportunity to think about my future and with $800,000 safely scattered about Philadelphia's Delaware Valley, I felt much better about my prospects. During the week and throughout my ride back to Chicago, I distanced myself from the severity of my behavior and rationalized I wasn't really evil, just, an opportunist. I began thinking about all the cash at my disposal and the fortuity it presented. I would spend it wisely and my plan was to start a small business, launder the money through it and invest my "income." My thoughts again turned to bliss with the realization I had gotten away with all my thefts. The last hurdle was to officially divorce myself from the DEA.

My announcement was met with suspicion, disappointment and jealousy. Upper management, including my ASAC, Joe Caravan, encouraged me to change my mind but, their efforts fell short. All of them suggested I consider a leave of absence before finalizing my plans but, I rebuked them all. I gave them two weeks notice which was probably the most honorable thing I had done for the DEA in my final year.

Towards the end of my second week, I detected slight degrees of jealousy by my counterparts who were very surprised to see one of their own leave on his own volition. I sensed envy that they witnessed someone who seemingly exhibited the courage to leave. No agent had left the Chicago office by way of anything other than retirement although Wendell Mack had most recently come the closest. The federal government offered secure, stable positions with good benefits and a dependable retirement plan and I was abandoning it all for the unknown and frankly, no one could comprehend it. It was for "peace of mind" as I called it, an abstract concept none of them could fathom. Of course, none of them would ever know how far from noble my intentions actually were. After all, I was leaving with more cumulative cash than any of them would possess over the course of the next fifteen years.

The most difficult task was returning my badge. The gold button and its accompanying identification was something I had been very proud to receive. When I walked across the stage and accepted my credentials from then Administrator John Lawn, I felt a sense of accomplishment that I had never known before. Many more days followed when I was proud to be associated with and a member of the Drug Enforcement Administration. Through the initial stages and certainly over the course of most of my career, I had given the Administration a sincere and honest effort. In return, the agency had extended me security, power and prestige. I knew ultimately though, I had sullied its reputation and was no longer deserving of the title of Special Agent. Recognizing that fact made returning it slightly less painful.

My weapon had never been something with which I was enamored and relinquishing it without hesitation was relatively simple. It was a terrific weapon, one of the finest .9mm on the market, the Sig Sauer P226. It had been issued to me with titanium night-sights installed on its barrel, rendering it more strategically useful in the dark. I had never fired it during the course of my career and that certainly provided me some respite. I knew that I had used it to smash Santilles with and the thought crossed my mind as I placed it into the box from which I first extracted it six years prior. Re-packing and returning it furnished me with a sense of purging and I hoped yielding it would allow me to think a lot less about Jesus Santilles.

I packed up my personal belongings which included many 3 by 5" photographs of me, with fellow agents standing in front of or behind large seizures of drugs, posing and mincing for the lens. One, in which I am standing alone in front of several cartons of cocaine, featured me smiling proudly. I remembered the day the photograph had been taken. We had seized 1,100 kilograms from a furniture shipment destined for Detroit, Michigan. It was a case I had assisted on but, unfortunately, I was not the case agent. I peered at the photo of myself, musing about the then, innocent face looking back at me.

There were other photographs, of friends and agents drinking beer and embracing. There was a few photos of some celebrities and athletes I had met during the course of the job. I had a collection of personal effects from some of the people I had arrested. Nunzio Maldonado's driver's license among them. I threw them in the trash. Worthless remnants of people I no longer wished to remember. As I went through the desk, I came across items I had long since forgotten about. A pin from a raucous St. Patrick's Day party during my first year in Chicago. Ticket stubs from a Black Hawks hockey game I had attended with Brian Sullivan and our dates. Creased business cards from police officers and agents from a variety of federal and state agencies. There were patches and stickers from a medley of law enforcement agencies and a t-shirt from the Chicago P.D. Homicide Unit which read "Our day begins when your day ends." I probed the depths of the last drawer and found a retractable baton and scattered bullets. Among the forgotten items was the 5 ½" serrated knife and scabbard Jim Walker had given me one

Christmas seemingly long ago. I chuckled at the notion of it and recalled the day Walker handed it to me, lovingly referring to it as a special weapon, "a stealth knife." At least, I reflected, it wasn't one of his blow guns. I knew that I would be without my gun by the end of the day, so I removed the knife and examined it. I thought it might be a good idea to have something so I wouldn't feel completely naked, so I affixed the scabbard to my ankle. It was the first time I had worn it since the day I received it as a gift. I slid the long, jagged blade into its sheath and rolled my pantleg over it and continued filtering through things I would never need or have use for like commemorative pens, administrative memorandums and typical office junk.

Agents and others I had developed friendships filtered by my desk offering me well wishes and luck. I extended the same entreaties to them. It was a fraudulently sentimental experience but, nevertheless welcome. Though I liked most of my fellow workers and respected a good portion of them, I was happy to leave with the knowledge I wouldn't have to rely on them again. As my final week came to a close, I truly relished the fact I was going to be free.

3 1

It was Thursday, the day before my final official work day. I had spent
part of the afternoon wandering along the avenues of the Loop, examining faces and assessing their accomplishments and desires. I found
myself appraising the people I observed, attempting to determine their
values and their successes. I concluded most were regular folks, hard-
working and decent. Their bodies were average and their looks
appeared to be ordinary. They went from place to place carrying the
tools of their endeavors, books, files, lunches and papers with some of
the more fortuitous relying on leather designer attaché cases to control
their belongings. Occasionally, I passed a man or woman who seemed
to walk with a certain swagger, as if they new whatever enterprises they
were involved in were more important than most others. It seemed
apparent these were the people society deemed we all should strive to
be, successful, wealthy, respected and admired. Of those, I wondered
how many had achieved their success through deceit and trickery like
me. I considered the face of a man who looked to be in his mid-thirties.
His suit stylish, his hair, even in the Chicago breeze, impeccably in
place. He moved quickly from one large office building to the corporate
headquarters of a bank across Adams Street. I watched him and cynically speculated whether he was a lawyer who had just filed another
fraudulent and overstated lawsuit. I considered the possibility he was a

stock broker who built his fortune on commissions by pressuring misinformed elderly clients into needless sales and purchases of stock. I thought maybe he was a doctor who stuffed his pockets by overcharging health insurers or perhaps the insurer himself who profited from ridiculous premiums designed to protect his firm's international investments, in the process enriching him and his fellow board members. Maybe he was an accountant who juggled figures and directed his affluent clients to manipulate our tax system so they could hide their income and assets to dodge the responsibilities of our fortuitous country's tax system. I wondered if he was the son of a politician who accepted kickbacks to vote for and promote needless programs and studies that siphoned tax dollars which could have been better used to educate our young and rehabilitate our poor. Or maybe his thefts were not sophisticated at all. He could have been a bookmaker or a drug dealer. Maybe he held up chain drug stores and Ma and Pa corner groceries. Maybe the woman in the designer suit who followed him in was the mistress of his father, the politician and she made her money through blackmail. Or perhaps she was a high priced call girl who pulled tricks to support her improvident lifestyle. Or maybe she was the broker, the accountant, the lawyer or the doctor.

They were people in solitary motion moving in all directions, east, west and north and south. Throngs of people with little interest in the others around them who were sharing their sidewalk and their journey for twenty feet, a block or maybe several. They all had their goals and their methods to achieve them. I wondered how many would stoop so low to reach their lofty plateaus, resorting to what I had done to achieve my own. I considered their ultimate fates which all the money in the world couldn't change. Cancer, heart problems, Aids, car wrecks, strokes, old age. I caught my reflection in one of the smoked glass tiles of one of the high rises on Michigan Avenue. I stopped and focused on myself as anonymous people hustled and passed me by. I was cognizant of the people who moved in front and behind me crossing each other in parallel blurs but, I concentrated on my own image. Physically I was among them but, fiscally I was beyond most of them. I was now among the rich. Investing wisely, I could live comfortably the rest of my life, doing the things I always wanted but, in accomplishing the lofty goal, I had lost track of the important things life had to offer. My depraved motivation for money had resulted in behavior which I considered reprehensible and never would have imagined myself engaging in only a few short years ago. I made a promise to redeem myself. I vowed when I returned home I would get involved in the community and I would work towards enriching lives rather than demoralizing them. I decided my goal would be to make others happy and hopefully, in so doing, I would regain sight of the gifts life can present.

I returned to the office prepared for my two last days. As I rounded the corner of Monroe and Dearborn, I came across the deformed man I had been accustomed to passing on my way to or from lunch. He still maintained the impeccable U.S. flag mounted to his wheelchair. Without provocation, he smiled at me. I reached into my wallet and gave him all the bills I had, maybe $60 or $70. I wished him well, entered the building and went back to my desk.

Walker approached me.

"So you are really going through with this. I can't believe it."

"I am, Jimmy. You know something, I can't wait to leave here either."

He patted me on the shoulder and said, "Well, I know you didn't want a going away party but, some of the agents want to say goodbye. You know, they want to wish you well."

I considered the offer and sarcastically offered my assessment for the real motivation, "You mean they need an excuse to come home late. An excuse to get drunk."

"Whatever, don't be so cynical. C'mon Mark, we planned to meet after work."

"Where?" I asked.

Walker laughed and waved his index finger sideways, gesturing that it wouldn't be prudent to say. He offered, "With all these Inspectors around lately we wanted it to be low-key. Just some of the people in the group."

I thought it might be nice to say goodbye to my closest associates and friends a little more informally than I had done. I thought the offer was a good idea and I accepted. Walker agreed to give me a ride, volunteering to be responsible for my well-being should I become intoxicated.

*

We headed north on I-90/94 in Walker's Regal. It had been one of the newest models and its distinctive features had made it easy for me to identify it when I had pulled my shenanigans in Waukegan. I never had any occasion to be in it, especially in my final week of service. The following day was my last and I doubted I would even report to the office. There wasn't any need since all the administrative requirements of my resignation had been completed. My belongings, the difficult things to move like furniture, electronics, books, and clothes were all safely back in Philadelphia. I had terminated my lease agreement and the only obligation left for me to fulfill was pay off a few outstanding local bills and say goodbye to a couple casual girlfriends.

Walker and I talked about a variety of things which included my plans for the future, as well as his.

"Are you going to try to get into security work?" He inquired.

"I don't know Jimmy. I'm just going to take time off. Get to know some of my family members again. Relax." That was what I had planned to do but, I sensed my nonchalance aggravated him. He asked me how could I afford to do it, financially.

"I've been single and living pretty economically. Other than my rent, I haven't had much in the way of expenses, I put some money away for a rainy day."

"I bet." He indignantly responded, in a provocative tone. He paused then brought up the Waukegan case. "You think I'll ever make any headway on that one."

I considered it suspicious he would make a sarcastic comment relating to my savings and segway into a question about Waukegan. Then I dismissed it as paranoia. "I don't know but, you definitely have something there. Quality dealers." I paused myself and added, "I have to tell you, I won't miss that drive up there."

He shrugged.

"Where we going, anyway? I figured we would get out of the Loop but, how far?" I asked.

"Well, Hayes and I discussed it and we figured the best thing, with all those inspectors poking in and out of the building, was to just have it at someone's house so, I volunteered." Walker checked his rear view mirror and ran a hand through his thick, coal black hair. "People are going to meet at my house."

It was a revelation I did not expect. I felt a sense of trepidation. Walker lived very close to Waukegan and it was the last place I had hoped to be on my final day. "OK." I reluctantly conceded.

"Have you turned in all your equipment?" Walker asked.

"Yes," I responded. "Everything, including my badge and credentials."

"That is why you don't need to be pulled over leaving this party drunk." He laughed.

I had been to Walker's secluded house in Winthrop Harbor only once, on a Saturday probably more than two years ago. I remembered it as being at the end of a cul-de-sac, on a remote circle with only two other houses nearby. There was a large undeveloped field behind his home and a moderate track of wooded land beyond that. We had a barbecue and watched college football. I remembered the day because I had taken quite a ribbing from some of my fellow workers and friends. I had bragged all week my alma mater, Temple, would upset their omnipresent state rival, Penn State. State ended up whipping my favorites into submission, beating them by more than forty points. The occasional posting of the score on the screen brought rich laughter from my friends, especially as the afternoon wore on and the span between PSU's score and Temple's expanded. Anyway, it had been a fun day. We were boisterous but no one had complained due to the distance between us and the other neighbors.

"You still have that fantastic stereo system and all those CDs?"

He smiled broadly. "Oh yea. That's why I asked to have it at my house. Its centrally located, I've got the room and its no big deal. Its the least I could do to show you some appreciation for your help in Waukegan."

I considered his statement about the location of his home. It was not "centrally located." Virtually no one lived north of Chicago. Most of my fellow agents lived in the western suburbs and another twinge of apprehension surfaced.

We were only a few minutes away and I asked Walker, "Who knew about this thing because no one mentioned or let on about it."

"It was hush-hush. In fact it was only put together earlier this week. You know you didn't give anyone but Hayes much notice."

That was true, I hadn't.

"Actually its a little early. We figured on 7 o'clock or so."

It was only 5:30 and another pang of skeptical discomfort rippled through me. I didn't speak for the last mile or two to Walker's house. I was partially comforted we didn't have to drive through Waukegan to get to Walker's house but, I still felt uneasy thinking about the secrecy of the impromptu celebration. It was somewhat strange we were having a "going-away" party at someone's residence. Customarily, they had been held at Cavanaugh's however, it was certainly plausible to have held the party at a discreet location given recent developments. Still, I was surprised my partner, Chad, hadn't mentioned it to me. He had been maintaining a low profile since the shooting incident and I hadn't even seen him for most of my final week. As we approached Walker's isolated home, I was sedated by the familiar sight of Hayes' vehicle parked in front.

I exited the car followed by Walker. We advanced toward the house but, Walker walked slowly and inappropriately behind me. I stopped at the door and turned to him.

"Go in, its open." He offered.

I wondered why his door was open. Of course, Hayes had been there but, it seemed to pre-planned. Too staged.

"Go ahead." Walker suggested again.

I had a bad feeling but, I entered. Hayes was sitting on a couch drinking a beer. He saw me and did not smile, something he had usually done, at least outside the office.

Hey, Bobby." I proposed "How are you?"

"Connors." He acknowledged but, without affection.

It was wrong. I noticed Walker locked the door behind me and I knew their motivations were ominous. I trusted Hayes enough to ask him, "What's up here, Bobby?"

"We are here to handle our little problem." Walker said, behind me.

I looked at Walker and then turned back to Hayes, "What problem, Bobby?"

Walker offered again, "Our little misunderstanding."

I was not about to answer to Walker. Walker had been a co-worker and Hayes had been and, at that moment remained, my supervisor. I turned back to Hayes, "What is this about?"

Walker again answered, "This is about our money, Connors."

"You aren't my supervisor, Walker. I don't answer to you." I defiantly countered.

"This isn't about rank, Connors. This is about…"

Hayes interrupted, "Walker…, "

Walker shot back, "No Bobby. We settled this thing. He" as he pointed to me, "has to make good."

"I'm out of here." I walked toward the door. Walker responded by brushing his shirt aside and withdrawing his sidearm.

"Walker, god-damn it." Hayes yelled.

Walker didn't point the barrel at me but, kept the gun pointed at the ground.

"Connors, it doesn't have to be this way. Sit down, let's talk." Hayes said.

"Do I have a choice, Bobby?"

Walker interjected again, "No, fucker."

He worried me. I was scared. It was apparent this meeting had been planned though it seemed their strategy was being dictated by Walker. Hayes had always been a strong, cogent supervisor. Here, it seemed Walker was giving direction and making decisions and he seemed full of venom. I was nervous and didn't trust his judgment.

"Sit down, Connors." Hayes offered, again.

I continued to watch Walker, he was the one with the gun. He approached me, gun still at his side. "I'm going to see if he's armed."

My gun had been turned over but, I had the stainless steel knife fastened to my shin. The same knife Walker had once given me. If I was going to make a move for Walker's weapon this would be my opportunity. Walker calculated my thoughts and did not come within arms reach. He stopped. He raised his gun and pointed the weapon at my chest. It was only the second time in my life I had a gun pointed directly at me and both times had been by federal agents. Like the last time, I was terrified.

"Lift up you shirt, show me you don't have anything."

"Calm down, Walker. I told you I returned my gun and creds at the office." Assuringly, I raised my shirt to affirm my defenseless state.

"For Christ sake, Walker, don't shoot him." Hayes responded. The offhand manner in which he said it frightened me as if it had already been casually discussed.

"I don't have anything, Jimmy."

"Let's go downstairs then." He demanded.

"Why don't we talk first?" Hayes requested.

"No!" Walker screamed and I knew then he was in charge of the operation. It had been Walker's idea to bring me here and it would be Walker's decision how it would end. Under these circumstances, Hayes was Walker's subordinate. "Downstairs, Connors!"

"No, Walker." I resisted. I wasn't about to be beaten or slaughtered in Walker's basement. I began searching for avenues of escape. Other doors, a large enough window to leap through. The door behind Walker.

"Then I'll kill you right here." Walker raised the gun again and I thought he was unbridled enough to do it.

Hayes demanded Walker holster the weapon. Walker ignored him. I cowardly conceded I would go to the basement but offered pathetically, "I still don't know what you want."

"Go down stairs and you can tell us what you did with Santilles money."

I knew for sure I hadn't gotten away with it. I agreed to go down the steps hoping it would buy me time to solicit Hayes' wisdom. I deliberated what my course of action would be as I proceeded toward the basement. I would share the money if that's what they wanted but, I had to consider the possibility this was some elaborate scheme initiated by the inspectors. I decided my strategy would be to continue to deny. I walked down the steps following Hayes and saw, sitting in two chairs, two people tethered to chairs with duct tape and rope. It was Santilles and Carrasco's wife. They were disheveled and their shirts stained with perspiration. Santilles had been blindfolded. I recognized by their haggard appearance the two had been there for several hours if not more. There was a third chair, empty and presumably for me. At that point, I was sure this was not a scheme devised by internal affairs investigators. I saw a roll of grey tape and a handkerchief that could be used as a blindfold or a gag. I determined right then I would not be placed in their charge, confined to a chair. I was about to rush Walker when Hayes offered.

"We are not going to tie him up, Jimmy. He isn't one of those."

"That will depend on Connors. If he wants to play ball, we'll play ball."

I descended the remainder of the steps with a small glint of hope that Hayes would assume charge and restrain Walker. I reached the bottom of the stairwell and examined the two captives. Mrs. Carrasco did not raise her head. Her eyes remained toward the floor. Santilles, blindfolded, was oblivious. I did not want to see him. I looked at Walker who had in his possession his DEA issued Colt Machine Gun as well as his holstered handgun. He had his finger on the trigger.

"Jesus Christ, Walker." Hayes said when he turned and saw Walker with the additional firepower. Evidently the gun had been placed somewhere along our route from the living room to the basement for easy retrieval. There was no doubt everything had been arranged but, I knew by Hayes shocked reaction, I realized it was not the plan he envisioned. Panic began to seize control of me.

Walker approached Santilles, cautiously stalking around me. He stood over him, menacingly but, still glaring at me. He pulled down the blindfold unexpectedly "Hombre! Estola la bolsa!" He paused then yelled again, "Estola du dinero ?"

I didn't understand what Walker had asked and judging from Santilles pained expression, neither did he. Santilles' face move toward me and he examined me with his vanquished eyes. He looked tired and confused, much too old to be tied up and blindfolded.

"Is this the man who stole your money?" Walker demanded.

Santilles did not respond. I could not assess whether he was afraid or simply uncooperative, I could not determine. Walker extracted his own knife from his holster in a quick and skillful display. He sliced at the tape while keeping the colt machine gun trained on me. He freed Santilles from the constrictive tape as I considered running. Hayes blocked my path up the stairs and Walker was so full of fury I thought the delay in getting past Hayes would allow him ample time to gun me down. I was sure Walker was serious but, I still wasn't convinced he was prepared to kill me. I knew he really wanted the money and as long as I was alive, he maintained a chance to get it. He placed the knife into his waistband and yanked Santilles from his chair in much the same manner I had extracted him from his automobile. Seeing the virile Walker dominate and brutalize the old man disturbed me knowing I had once done the same abject thing.

"Is this the mother-fucker who stole my money?" He asked again, more emphatically.

"Please James." Mrs. Carrasco cried, "don't hurt him."

"Shut the fuck up." He responded. "This is the last time I ask old man, this hombre estola du dinero?"

Exhausted, Santilles pitifully offered "See, Senor."

Walker heaved him toward the wall and fired a burst of three rounds between his shoulder blades. The force of the bullets entering his fragile torso propelled him into the wall from which he rebounded forcefully and fell back toward us. His head slammed onto the concrete floor close to Carrasco's feet. She screamed in horror as Hayes yelled at Walker. Walker fired another round into his forehead to quell the purl of air percolating through his lungs. Immediately Santilles mouth hung open and his eyes gaped at nothingness.

I was frozen.

"What the hell did you do that for?" Hayes demanded.

Walker offered no answer. He moved toward Carrasco who was screaming, vacillating with fright and misery. Walker expertly removed his knife and sliced her across the face while still maintaining the machine gun's barrel aimed at me. "I want my money, Connors!"

"Calm down. Walker. God-damn it, calm down." Hayes pleaded.

Walker again ignored Hayes. By not even looking at Hayes, I knew he had no regards for his opinion. I knew if Walker had killed Santilles he probably would have no qualms, maybe even no choice but, to kill me. If he killed Carrasco I was next and I hoped even Hayes would realize he would be a target as well.

"You see, Connors. That was our suitcase you got. That was set up for me and Bobby in that house on Elmwood. I worked quite a while putting that thing together and you don't think I spent all that time fucking and snuggling with this bitch to see you run off with the money do you. Now, where is it?"

"How do you know I took the money?" I stalled, frantically searching for an opportunity.

"Connors, this bitch knew everything that bastard did." He gestured toward Santilles, "She knew when he was coming. She knew when he was going. I was waiting with her that night. Me and Bobby saw the whole thing. I'll admit it was a daring move but, you went about it all wrong. You could have just been sitting there waiting like we were. I never knew you were inclined but, I had my suspicions." He smirked defiantly and added, "That shit don't matter anymore. I'm not going to repeat myself again. Where is our fucking money?"

"Its not here, Walker. I moved it."

"That's the same bullshit Sullivan said."

"Shut your fucking mouth, Walker!" Hayes screamed.

Sullivan.

"He didn't know when to keep his nose out of people's business either. That fucking piece of shit deserved…"

I heard the report of two rounds. Walker's head jerked twice while one of his eyeballs exploded. He fell clumsily toward Santilles and dropped across the old man. Hayes had shot him. I turned toward Bobby who already had his weapon against his temple.

"God forgive me."

"No !" I howled as the weapon discharged sending a clod of Hayes skull over his shoulder. He fell backwards across the small wooden banister which collapsed under his weight. He struck the steps and half-rolled down the final two.

I rushed toward Hayes. Carrasco was screaming and wailing, hysterically. My first notion was to flee and I ran up the steps, leaping over my fallen supervisor. I pushed open the door and went through the kitchen, my heart pounding more that it ever had. I went for the phone and grabbed the receiver. I dialed two digits, 9 and 1, then stopped. I stood there looking at that white button with the black one printed on it. A little square piece of plastic that I knew if I touched again, would plunge my life into the control of others. Lawyers, judges, police, arraignments, interviews, confessions, pleas, incarceration. I paused, fast forwarding through my options in my mind's eye. I hung up the phone. Carrasco continued howling as a witness to the whole episode. I stood there motionless, the past, present and future fusing together into an inconceivable quandary which demanded an immediate solution. I approached one of the kitchen windows and looked at Walker's closest neighbor's house, some fifty yards away. The home was dark and deserted. The other residence was even further away and looked equally desolate. I walked back toward the basement door and closed it, attempting to muffle the screaming women so I could think. I noticed when the door was closed it effectively silenced Carrasco's hysteria. I waited for a moment imploring my thumping heart to abate. I assessed my options then I walked halfway down the basement stairs and gestured for Carrasco to be quiet. She did not. I examined the scene. Hayes was dead. There was no breathing. I walked gingerly down the remaining steps and jumped over the last three so I would not track his blood. I moved around Santilles' tipped chair and examined Walker. His left eye had bursted, ravaged by one of Hayes .45 rounds. His right eye was wide open with the same glazed death stare as Santilles. I verified as best I could they were both dead without touching them. I moved to Carrasco, careful not to walk in the swelling puddles of three men's blood. I moved behind her as her shoulders heaved in desperate sobbing. Blood snaked down her face from the wound inflicted by Walker. She expected me to free her from the constricting tape. I extracted my knife from under my pant leg. I avoided her eyes then brought the blade down and sliced across her throat with a half-hearted effort. The attempt only slightly lacerated it. Recognizing I was trying to kill her, she flailed violently, knocking herself off balance and tumbling, still tied to the chair, onto her left side. I grabbed her head forcefully now and sliced at her throat with such impetus I sank the sharp instrument deep into her larynx. She gasped and gurgled and I swiped at her throat a third time, exacerbating the gorge in her neck. She contorted for several seconds, perhaps thirty. I refused to look at her face, instead watching the legs until they no longer kicked. When their frantic movement had subsided I walked back upstairs and retrieved a dishtowel. I wiped the handle clean and returned to the basement. I kicked Walker's knife with his fingerprints on them into the bubbling tarn of her blood. I placed my own knife back into its scabbard. I wiped the chair in which I had been sitting. I returned to the first floor and meticulously considered everything I might have touched. The only thing I remembered was the door knob which I delicately swabbed. I closed the door, relieved darkness had fallen. I walked across the field and into the woods. I found a road which I followed briefly back to the interstate. I found my way out of Winthrop Harbor, past Waukegan and ultimately away from the powder, the paper and all the vice with which it came, to begin my life again, another successful citizen living in America.